FOUND STORIES OF THE
OLD DUCK HUNTERS
AND OTHER
MACQUARRIE
ADVENTURES

Previous Gordon MacQuarrie
books published by
Barnes Area Historical Association

Right Off The Reel (2018)
Dogs, Drink and Other Drivel (2019)

Work in Progress

MacQuarrie on Muskies

FOUND STORIES OF THE
OLD DUCK HUNTERS
AND OTHER
MACQUARRIE ADVENTURES

by
Gordon MacQuarrie

Compiled and edited by Dave Evenson

Published by the Barnes Area Historical Association
BAHAMUSEUM.ORG

Cover design by Creative Identity, Cumberland WI, cre8id.com

Editor photograph by Keith Crowley

Printed by Kindle Direct Publishing

ISBN 9798847905541

For my friend Keith Crowley.
Without his persistent research,
These stories would have been lost.

Contents
Part I
The Old Duck Hunter Stories

The Wind-Blown Flight 11
High Up, an' Coming Fast 21
The Convert 29
Rainy Day Ducks 39
"Gentlemen! We Give You Pa'tridge!" 49
Less Haste—More Ducks 59

Part II
Further Adventures of Gordon MacQuarrie

Rainbows of the Brule 67
Night Casting on the Brule 77
You Take Your Worms...85
Ol' Greeny 95
Back in There..105
Rascals of the Rice..113
K-a-t Spells FISH...125
Fishermen with Women 137
Rascals of the Riprap 145
Everybody's River 157
Stand the Logs on End 166
Get Out of That Rut! 177
Sportsman's Journey 189
The Prodigal's Return 201
Pheasant Capital of the World 211
The Cottontail Annual...221
Sourdough Geese 227
The Life of an Outdoor Writer..237
Nothing to Write Home About 249
Old Indian Chief Dead, But His Lesson Lives 256
Somewhere in Ptarmigan Valley 258
My Favorite Spot - The Jack-Pine Barrens of Northwest Wisconsin......265
Here Come the Biologists 275

Introduction

In his introduction to *MacQuarrie Miscellany,* Zack Taylor chuckles over the earnest but irate reader who told him he didn't have the right to deprive readers of the Old Duck Hunters stories that had not yet been put into a book. He writes, *"What started out as a pleasure has now become a duty. Nice duty, though."* This present book continues in that same vein of pleasant duty.

It happened like this. In 2018, at the first Barnes Area Historical Association (BAHA) Old Duck Hunters Association Pilgrimage, I was on the podium for a question and answer session. I can easily remember an earnest and distressed, in both voice and demeanor, Lance Achterberg (ODHA Circle Member number 11) asking, "So, are we never going to get to read those stories that didn't get into the books?" I didn't have a good answer at the time, but it did plant the seed that maybe someday BAHA could put the missing ODHA stories into a book. So it's been good duty for this current group of publishers too.

The appendix to Keith Crowley's *Biography of an Old Duck Hunter* lists 144 MacQuarrie magazine stories. A few have been found more recently, and perhaps there are still some to be found. If you have read all the books, *The Trilogy, MacQuarrie Miscellany* and *MacQuarrie Treasury*, you know 73 stories, including all but six of the 62 Old Duck Hunters stories. This book sets out to bring you the last six ODHA stories as well as the best of the rest.

Especially early in his career, before he realized what a great foil Al Peck and the Old Duck Hunters were, Mac wrote quite a few adventures featuring other characters who were almost as much fun as Mr. President (almost!) Mac wrote quite a few "how-to" stories-how to set decoys, how to care for woolen clothing, how to take photographs. I passed on those stories and included mostly MacQuarrie adventures where Mac was out fishing or hunting.

Acknowledgements

Thank you once again to the volunteers who make the MacQuarrie Museum at the Barnes Area Historical Association (BAHA) the best collection and display of MacQuarrie items in the world. They administer the Old Duck Hunters Association Circle (you should be a member), lead the Annual ODHA Pilgrimages in late summer and publish *The Other Drivel*, a magazine full of facts and tidbits relating to MacQuarrie and friends.

The collectors, Dale Arenz, John Case, Chris Risbudt, Gary Smith and others found most of the MacQuarrie magazine stories, and Zack Taylor put many of them into print. But it was not until Keith Crowley made a concerted effort to find all things MacQuarrie that some of these stories came to light. This is especially true for stories not found in the Big Three of outdoor magazines. And some of those stories from magazines with lesser circulation are among the very best. Thank you, Keith Crowley.

Mike Cole has been my co-conspirator in getting hold of the musty magazines, watching online auctions along with me, not bidding against each other and buying some each. Other stories come from the museum's collection.

I'm a two-fingered typist, so I was amazed and awed and thankful when Jeri McGinley, BAHA treasurer, offered to use some magic software to transpose the magazines into electronic stories. In like vein, once I had the book basically compiled, I turned to my friend Leah Hullinger to do the magic that made it acceptable to Kindle Direct Publishing.

I especially need to thank Peter Rycraft and his daughter Bee Jasko, for permitting us to reprint these stories. Living in York, England, they never knew Gordon MacQuarrie, only Ellen MacQuarrie Wilson and her second husband Harry Wilson. Gordon MacQuarrie's copyright ownership passed down through time to heir Peter Rycraft. All MacQuarrie readers owe these two people a great deal of gratitude for making these stories available

To the woman who loves me In-Spite-Of-Everything I give my thanks for putting up with musty magazines, hours of hogging the computer and a constant mess of paper. Shirley Anne, I love you.

You're going to like this story. MacQuarrie had been writing for the Superior Telegram *for about eight years, but this is his second free lance article for a national audience, and the first about the Old Duck Hunters Association. Already that fraternity is well defined, although he and Al Peck had been duck hunting for fewer than three seasons. MacQuarrie included a great amount of detail in his writing, right down to their underwear. That detail would lessen as his writing grew tauter in future articles. The great part of this story is the love of the hunt, but also the love of family, as he includes grandmother, mother and young Sally back at the cabin. Mac seldom included his family in magazine articles, but we read about them more often in his Milwaukee Journal columns. There are a few in the Barnes Area Historical Association book,* Right Off The Reel, *in which cases Mrs. Peck and Mrs. MacQuarrie are right out there gunning with the men.*

When you get a chance, go read "The Bluebills Died at Dawn," a story considered one of MacQuarrie's best. It's about this same hunt! Mac wrote it for a different magazine and stripped it down to the essentials, and, in so doing, he perhaps made a more appealing story for the manly readers. The date of this hunt can be identified quite precisely. Sally MacQuarrie, 14 months old in this telling, was born in the summer of 1929, and the weather for both stories is identical. Weather reports from the Saskatoon Star Phoenix *and the* Milwaukee Journal *confirm that this hunt took place on Saturday or Sunday, October 18 or 19, 1930.*

The original story was illustrated with line drawings. The photographs here were found in "The Bluebills Died at Dawn."

The Wind-Blown Flight

Sports Afield, December 1931

There was no dawn that morning on Lake Nancy. The roaring gale from the West, which had blown for three days, rushed into the east with enough fierceness to beat back the struggling sun. Out of the black spaces came the frigid wind, swooping and twisting over the lake as though it would never stop. I could hear the waves crashing on the beach and was glad that most of our journey to the blind would be in comparatively sheltered water, close to the shore along the edge of a mile-long peninsula, upon which our cabin was situated.

"We'd better hustle if we want to get into that blind ahead of some other hunter," I shouted to the President of the Old Duck Hunters' Association as we stumbled down the sand trail to the boat. My voice drifted off somewhere among the jack pines and other second growth. The trees, crowding close about the trail, made the blackness even blacker. Overhead the gale crooned through the boughs.

1: *Mr. President at a Shallow Bay sunrise*

"Lots of time," the President shouted back, and as he turned his head to make himself heard a gust lifted truant sparks from his crooked little pipe. "Lots of time," he cried. "Only a pair of saps like ourselves would get out on this kind of a morning!"

I snuggled down into the blessed comfort of a blanket coat, with hood to match, and pondered upon the matchless virtues of a wife who would buy a husband such a Christmas present when she really wanted to buy him a new occasional chair for the front bedroom—or maybe a pair of dancing slippers.

We stood on the shore of our little bay and loaded the green steel boat. Sacked decoys first, into the bow—35 of them and if one drifted away the President would take another one in because he believed ducks would not decoy to an even number. Then shell cases, heavy with number sixes, then guns and, lastly, upon the top of the heap, a thread-bare auto robe and a barn lantern with which the President made shift to thaw out congealed toes and fingers. He always held that a horse blanket was warmer, especially if it were one that had been used on sleigh rides, but I filed this along with the odd-numbered-decoy superstition. The President of the association had prerogatives and it was up to me, as the membership, to submit to them, which I did right gladly.

The wind seized the light boat as we pushed off. It was a fight from the start, with both at the oars. Ordinarily the President occupies a seat of dignity and honor on the poop deck from where he is entitled and empowered to regale the crew with all manner of tales but under extreme conditions such as we met that morning he acted—but only, let it be known, in emergencies. The coldness of the wind was unbelievable, even beneath our layers of clothing. I wore heavy woolen underwear of soft, gracious texture, a flannel shirt, an Indian-tanned buckskin jacket of proven warmth and over that the woolly blanket coat that, my wife assured me, kept even the Indians of northern Canada from freezing. The coat also served as a kitty for Sally, 14 months, and there have been times when I have braved the outdoors because that person would not relinquish it.

The President was equally heavily clad. Among other things I know he wore a flannel shirt, leather jacket, huge mackinaw coat and both wore plenty of socks inside of rubber-bottomed leather boots. But we were cold in spite of our clothing and our exercise. It was only mid-October. Later, when a native told us his thermometer dropped to two above that morning we believed him. That kind of cold, pressed home by a merciless wind, is far worse than 20 below with little or no wind. It finds openings.

Up the long peninsula, keeping in its shelter as well as we could, through the deep wall-eye hole, past the short point that projected at right angles almost to the long one, and so into Shallow bay we rowed. The bay got its name from Joe Hollis, duck hunter extraordinary and fisherman without par. No sign of the sun yet, but away down the shore we made out a moving light—another hunter. That cheered up the President considerably. He said he thought we might not be as crazy as we looked. Then the boat stopped, with a sharp, high-pitched cr-r-runch! My heart fell. We were frozen out of our splendid blind and point on the far shore of Shallow bay and would now have to make shift to hunt somewhere on the shore of the long peninsula or on the tip of the short point.

"Let's try and break through!" cried out the President. I made deference to the valiant timbre of his voice by remarking that if anyone could do it he could and laid on the rowboat seat, beside him, a piece of the ice that we had smashed into. It was an inch and a half thick, and would be thicker the farther we got into it as we were on the edge of the ice. All I could see ahead of me, into the dearly-beloved Shallow bay, where the divers came for their breakfast, was a gray void, with no movement of waves. It seemed frozen solid and in the daylight we found this to be the case.

The point we chose for our set had shallow water on each side and extremely deep water directly off its end. Further, it was a scant 75 yards from the opposite shore, but with plenty of water on all sides except in front and in back. It was bad, but not hopeless. I maneuvered the boat as well as I could while the President, not without some well-timed grunts and mild objurgations threw out the decoys. It was an evil-made set but it had to do under the circumstances. Some of them broke their stout strings in the heavy water and drifted away but we let them drift, beached the boat, and concealed ourselves behind the jack pines that lined both sides of the narrow point.

We danced about to get warm and achieved some comfort as the pines made a dense windbreak against the blast. They proved fine for a blind, concealing the hunter from the ducks and the ducks from the hunter. That is a sporting proposition! It was growing lighter in the east. Banked clouds, running wildly before the half-gale, caught and reflected, dully, the first rays of the sun. Feeble, sickly rays they were, but man loves the light and our spirits rose.

I was still dancing an earnest war dance when the President seized my arm and pointed out toward the crazily-riding decoys. Through the dull light I saw ducks, scores of them, swimming about. We crouched in the pines until it became lighter, then stood up and kicked a shell box. That brought results. The ducks hustled, bluebill fashion, along the surface for a few feet before taking the air. I shot twice, like the amateur I am, at the spot in the air where ducks were thickest. The President shot twice, too, although he was using an automatic. Those two shots of his sounded calculating and fatal to me and later I did not argue when he said he must have downed his two for we found only three birds on the water.

It grew lighter and the ducks began moving. For minutes at a time there was always a flock—sometimes four or five to try and watch from the very effective screen of trees. There were so many ducks, and they were traveling in such numbers that we could hear them despite the noisy confusion of the wind and waves. A large flock flew over the blind, in back of us. Too high for a shot, I estimated, but the President shot upward and one bird fell to the beach. I decided then and there to shoot at everything that came along and was gratified, at the next opportunity, to see a bluebill do a thrilling tailspin to the water. They flew everywhere and from other spots about the big lake we heard shooting.

I always looked for birds at Lake Nancy, especially from the west, but the birds were here in number beyond my fondest hopes. A summer of disappointing duck news, with the game commissioners of Alberta and Saskatchewan reporting a tremendous falling off in breeding, owing to the drought, was being climaxed by one of the finest duck flights Upper Wisconsin has had in recent years.

We were starting the first day of an annual week's vacation and had selected this week on the spur, making the great last-minute preparations attendant to the transfer of two wives and one 14-month's old potential duck hunter to the duck camp. For a week I had watched weather reports and our pleasure at the thought that we had struck the height of the flight dispelled our disappointment at not being able to reach our favorite blind. From Winnipeg, Calgary, Port Arthur, Helena, Fargo, weather observers had gathered the data that had sent us on our pleasant quest. The birds had apparently been frozen out up north and were heading southward. It was a most unseasonable blow and that first morning, after the sun arose, it began to snow, lightly. But we forgot discomfort at the thought of our good luck.

The ducks were here—in such numbers as one does not always see in this Upper Wisconsin pine tree country. Douglas county and adjacent counties seem, usually, on the edge of the flight following the Mississippi Valley and it took a major weather disturbance such as we were experiencing to blow them our way. That, at any rate, was the way we adjudged it. Once before in recent years exactly the same thing happened. In 1919 a flood of ducks poured into northwestern Wisconsin after a prolonged blow from the west, accompanied by a lot of snow. The President alleges that, during that fall, he stuffed four feather mattresses for his grandmother!

A flock of a dozen or more mallards, lazy in flight when compared with bluebills and butterballs we had been seeing, came sailing majestically from the east. They wheeled and climbed at 50 yards and one uttered a warning "quarnk." Our pellets found them and two fell with such a thump as only rice-fed mallards can make.

A phalanx of butterballs, led by a gallant knight in white made a picture as they sizzled along, to wheel and swing toward the decoys. They were so close on the first trip by that the white cheek markings of the females were plainly discernible. How they flew, for all the world like a squad of scurrying motorcycles ushering some potentate along Michigan boulevard. I fired both barrels and a barrage sounded from the automatic. Four remained behind.

A magnificent recollection I have of that morning is a flock of bluebills sighting the decoys and maneuvering, carefully so as to light properly. To do so they had to fly across our point, for our decoys had been set in the shallow water where their strings would hold. Later we put 40-foot strings on several birds and placed them in the deeper water. Try winding them in on a cold day!

Like well-drilled cavalrymen the bluebills obediently turned and faced about, swinging only low enough to top the little jack pines. A few more wing strokes and they planed into the decoys. As their wings stiffened we fired. Not a feather fell and I knew we had shot over them. Shots at going-away ducks have always bothered me, perhaps because of the haste with which I shoot, thinking that the ducks are soon to be out of range. Though we killed none of them I shall never forget the picture of their deliberate parade into the decoys. It is easy to close my eyes and see them now, coming directly toward me, now 15 feet above the water, 20 or more of them, eagerly looking to the company of the sanctimonious blocks they took for friends.

Other ducks came and more were killed, some in easy fashion, others falling from heights sensational enough to please any duck hunter. By 9 o'clock we had a goodly bunch of ducks behind the jack pines and while we could have gone on to reach easy limits of 15 each, we felt the need of warmth and shelter. Too, we looked forward to bragging expansively before the red brick fireplace in the cabin, for the edification of two wives and the urchin. The last-named was getting a magnificent start as a duck huntress. The autumn previous she had vacationed for a week, when only 10 weeks old, at a duck camp—and gained more weight than any other week since—and I considered her education well enough advanced to show her pictures of ducks in books and magazines.

2: Mr. President with the day's bag at the big red cabin on the hill

We inspected our bag of ducks. Aside from the two mallards and five or six butterballs, one an elegant drake, tailored in the height of Arctic fashion, all were bluebills. Most of them were greater bluebills, with a green sheen to their jet black hoods. A few were lesser bluebills, their heads shot with purple flashes when one held them to the sunlight just so. Some had both green and purple flashings in their head feathers and these we decided must be hybrids. Later on in the week we were to kill more of these birds. All were large, however, which led us to the conclusion that the greater bluebill strain predominated. Incidentally, we noticed that some of the bluebills had markings, especially on their breasts, like ringnecks or ringbills. The breast and neck feathers were darker than bluebills and the line of demarcation between the dark of the breast and the white belly feathers was very sharp and drawn straight across, such as is found, typically, in ringbills. Perhaps I am treading upon unsteady ground as an amateur scientist but our experiences led us to believe there must be inter-breeding among the two bluebill species and the ringnecks.

The President wanted to know how long he had to stay out in the cold to qualify for another term in office. He had been in the chair for some seven or eight years and, inasmuch as his accumulated wisdom had never been matched by any other aspiring members, there was little possibility of his being turned down this year by the electorate. I pondered upon his virility and stamina as he stood over the dead birds.

A man well beyond the prime, but who had followed the open all his life, on trout stream, chicken field and in duck blinds, he would test the staying qualities of many a man half his age—and usually wind up at the end of the day with more ducks or more trout, and more funny stories than anyone else in the party. I wondered if I would be as hardy and vigorous and youthful at that age. Every fall he seemed more eager for the week's duck shooting and it was a source of amazement to me how he could remain, for hours in a cold duck blind, so intent upon the sport that he forgot the cold, while I was out walking around a lake to restore circulation. I shall always respect his calculating carefulness as a hunter, in the face of obstacles and discomforts that hamper the outdoor craftsmanship of others; nor have I seen anyone who watched for ducks with more assiduous intensity. One would think his eyes would tire from incessant searching but he always forgot to remember that he might be tired—until it was all over.

That morning, of course, was incomplete without some sort of a walk. I have always failed to understand the philosophy of the point-hunter who remains in his blind all the time, too lazy to take a stroll in the woods back of him or indifferent to the fact that he may, by walking about the shore, locate and put out of misery some of the ducks he has wounded. There has been too much said about the impossibility of killing wounded ducks, especially wounded diving ducks, once they get away. I believe it is largely poppycock and that most of the hunters who never try to track down and kill their wounded swimmers are just too lazy to go out and get them. Any number of articles and books on duck shooting will tell you "a wounded bluebill, diving, is almost sure to get away." I disagree. A little patience and a little effort and you can put that gentleman—or lady, in your game bag and go home with a clear conscience, knowing that you have left no birds to die a miserable, lingering death on the water or in the brush.

As the day advanced the cold did not abate. Even in the face of the bitter wind ice formed readily in the few shallow spots still left open along the shore. The snow blew into our faces with stinging impact. It was all such a tremendous change from the same day of the week previous when I had sat in my shirt sleeves in a blind on the same lake without seeing a single duck. The sudden advance of the Arctic front had, indeed, made our day's sport possible and we imagined, rightly, that many lakes in Minnesota and farther north had frozen in the last three days.

A Canadian jay frisked about our blind, very confidential and unafraid and a flock of 20 or more russet blackbirds dared enter the shallow shore water in search of food. Even the trim chickadees were present and we spied occasional flocks of wild geese. Truly, we had found the birds at the peak of their migration and we looked forward eagerly to the week of sport. After a decent bag had been obtained our interest would lie largely in securing different kinds of birds.

At 10 o'clock we picked up. It was at this pick-up that I discovered a little trick that will help many a duck hunter. I had been walking on the lake shore and had become well warmed up when we set out in the boat. I found that my hands withstood the cold so much better than if I had begun this task directly after an hour or so of concealment in the blind. Duck hunters! Take a walk and then pick up the decoys! Do it with your bare hands and you will be surprised how they can ward off the cold. As we were picking up, several small flocks scudded by, of course, and Mr. President, ever the duck hunter, expressed the customary regrets. But we had more than enough ducks and the red cabin beckoned.

"I wonder," I said as we rowed back gaily with the wind astern, "if Sally will know a duck when she sees one. I've showed her pictures of them. Sometimes she calls them bow wows but a little urging produces the right name."

"If she does she can join the association without even an entrance fee," said the President. I considered that splendid of him inasmuch as the usual entrance fee, for even a week-end membership, was often exorbitant to say the least.

Equipment beached, ducks over shoulders, we mounted the sandy hill. Our entrance was to be dramatic. That is understood by all successful hunters. We were to be hunters home from the kill—and with meat! A large percentage of the pleasure comes from this final phase of the hunt. It is an art to attain the right degree of modesty and indifference. Really, this is the most effective form of bragging. Through the door we came and shut it quickly lest the draft blow in, and there we stood before the assembled ladies. We beamed.

From the other room came the scraping of little shoes on the floor and the squeak of a patent vehicle of triangular dimension by which Sally made her way here, there and yon. The baby, face beaming at the anticipation of play with a couple of fools, pink hair made more pink by a ridiculous blue ribbon, appraised the ducks. She raised an eager hand, with crooked, pointing finger, and said:

"Guck!"

Right there she was sworn in as a member in good standing in the Old Duck Hunters' Association

This hunt took place on Shallow Bay, with the evening frivolities at the big red cabin on the hill, owned by Joe Hollis. MacQuarrie didn't give us clues to tell when it took place, although the 1932 publication date would indicate 1931, or possibly earlier.

I would like to visualize Gordon excitedly telling his father, William, about this great place and sport, and William MacQuarrie being the "Mac" of this story. Alas, Bill Stewart, quoted in Keith Crowley's biography, states that the elder MacQuarrie had no sense of humor whatever. So this playful "Mac" doesn't fit. We'll probably never learn who he was.

MacQuarrie used the story about the lawyer bringing home the gift ducks in the Milwaukee Journal *which was reprinted in* Dogs, Drink and Other Drivel.

High Up, an' Coming Fast

Hunting and Fishing, October 1932

The rising sun just topped the pines across the lake, forming a glorious background for the five ducks, high up and coming fast. In front, and on both sides of us, were waves of sun-touched water. Behind stretched a forested point of land on the end of which our blind was located. And nearly overhead—those five ducks. Too high, I knew. But beside me in the blind was Mac, my inexperienced guest. And I was painfully aware that he expected much of me.

Mac crouched and watched, tense as I, even though he had no gun. And I couldn't run out on him. "I want to see how it's done," he had said, and had arisen at 2:30 a.m., driven seventy miles to see. I owed him a just debt for his enthusiastic expectation. Hadn't I boasted to him of this very point where we now sat, calling it the breakfast table of all the ducks in Wisconsin? Hadn't he listened credulously to my tales of spectacular crossing shots, and "tall ones" tumbled from this very point? There was nothing for me to do but deliver the goods.

We sat on the edge of the pit, screened by a semi-natural growth in front and on the sides. As those five feathered rockets darted straight over me, the pit seemed awfully deep. It swallowed me up, hugged me into the earth. Every duck hunter knows that sense of paralysis, just as the birds dip down.

Then the fliers, still some distance out, flared high, but kept their course. I fired the first barrel when they were towering and I saw a bird sail down. The others swung on with incredible speed, but my second shot was easier, and, from a great height, the leader pitched downward.

I think Mac will never forget that shot—nor will I. The first bird had simply slanted into the sun-dappled water, but the second one was in good view, with the sun at our backs. Like the breathless descent of a carnival high diver he came, down, down, down. It was the luckiest shot I ever made and to this day I do not care to speculate upon how high those birds were.

I told him I would never make such a shot again. "Are you trying to make me think you're good?" he demanded. The man actually thought this was the regular thing!

3: "When ol' Betsy speaks she means business" -the President retrieving the bird

"I'll miss the next chance if it's anywhere near as hard as that," I protested. The next opportunity came when fifteen birds wheeled in from the right, and Mac, with supreme confidence and unnerving certainty, looked on, refusing the loan of my gun.

As the cautious strangers wheeled high over the outer edge of the decoys, I let go. Three bluebills tumbled from the flock and went bobbing with the waves toward shore.
Mac shouted his excitement. I said nothing. I think he thought I was trying to be bashful. If he only knew!

Another flock showed up—coming from the right. "Don't try to make me think it's hard," whispered Mac. These birds were careful—a big flock—and they just skirted the edge of our set-up, a long way out. The gun boomed twice, and, miracle of miracles, two fell out!

Then the Other Duck Hunter came back from his walk and I pulled out for *my* walk, mighty glad to be out of that place! The Other Duck Hunter is Al, famous President of the Old Duck Hunters Association, Inc.—the blessed person who first stuck me in a brush blind behind thirty-five bobbing wooden blocks and told me, later in the day, that the swishing sound I heard that morning was ducks! Mac had only been introduced into the association that morning, having passed all the degrees, under questioning of the President, with flying colors. Someday the President's oral oath of office must be published, so that all may know.

This year the Old Duck Hunters were concentrating their duck shooting on an arm of a large lake in northern Washburn county. The lake over which we shot was shallow and filled with wild celery, water lily roots, and other duck food. It was marvelous shooting all that fall.

I walked around the "breakfast table" as we called our little lake and by the time I returned the sun had disappeared and a steady, drizzly rain had set in. It lasted all day. But Mac was happy. I found him sitting in the blind, covered from head to foot in a raincoat. He greeted me with a grin! How that man did enjoy seeing someone else shoot ducks!

I haven't said much about the President himself. So many people around these parts know him that much needn't be said. I had no sooner reached the blind when the magic cry sounded:

"Mark!"

It came from Mac—how quickly even the uninitiated pick up that word! Six ducks were speeding straight at us.

"Keep down," hissed the President. The only sound was the dripping of raindrops on the leaves of the blind and the steadily growing sound of duck-wing beats.

"Now!" cried the President.

Mac crouched even lower, while we two stood up and fired. How different ducks look over the top of a blind, as compared with how they look when sighted *through* the blind! Our guns opened up and one bird fell—a whistler.

"That makes eight for me," said the President, calmly. "Poor shooting, boys, poor shooting."

"What!" I cried. "How do you know you dropped that duck?"

"Didn't I fire and didn't the duck drop?"

"How about me?"

"You got your ducks already today," he declared. "When ol' Betsy speaks she means business."

That should serve to introduce the President to everyone. There never was another like him, taking into account his merry eyes and all.

At noon we moved back into the woods, lit a roaring fire, and the President told his deathless story about Lawyer Smith and the ducks.

The facts in the case are these. Smith, we'll call him, came into the President's office one Saturday morning and whispered, "Let's go duck hunting. I gotta quart." Of course the President told him he would go, that he was emphatically not interested in mixing DuPont oval with 100 proof Old Smuggler, but he'd go, he'd go, let's not quibble about it!

They went into the Yellow lake country in Burnett county and, when someone rapped on the door to awaken Smith and the President next morning, the former was immovable. Everything was done to awaken him but the President was finally forced to sojourn to a mallard hole by himself. Let the honorable President pick up the narrative at this point.

4: *Mr. President scans the sky*

"I went out into the coldest November day I remember in a long time," said he. "And I came back without a single duck. When I returned Smith was going like a house afire. Now, Smith is a very cautious man, but he was contributing his own share to the general conviviality and the others were responding gallantly. If I recall rightly, Smith was interrogating in song, at the moment of my entrance, another fellow sportsman, thusly: 'Are You the O'Riley They Speak of So Highly?'

"After dinner we packed up to go and the aforementioned O'Riley, out of the kindness of his soul, stepped forward and offered Smith eight canvasbacks that had been killed earlier in the week. I got four and Smith got four; and I found out, before I took mine in the house, that they had been dead too long, without benefit of cold storage.

24

"Not so with Smith. I learned later he marched in the house with a conquering air. Mrs. Smith registered, first, surprise, and, later, appreciation. But her woman's eyes were not to be fooled as easily as those of her husband. She inspected the birds closely and found they were not all they seemed.

" 'Did you shoot these yourself, John?' she asked sweetly.

" 'Why, sure, sure—of course! Why do you ask?'

" 'Oh, no particular reason, except that these ducks are positively mouldy!'

"Did Smith give in at that? He did not. He picked up one of the ducks, inspected it quickly, and tossed it back on the kitchen table.

" 'Don't worry about a little thing like that, Mary,' he said. 'It's the moulding season for ducks, you know!' "

It was raining harder when we knocked off and sped back to Joe's cottage before an increasing wind. Mac was in high fettle. He is, I firmly believe, the only duck hunter in the world who ever went hunting, never fired a shot, and enjoyed every minute of it. His eyes were shining that night in front of Joe Hollis' big wood fire.

Mac winked at the President and began: "I think you ought to give a good deal of credit to the President of the Old Duck Hunters Association for those ducks. If he hadn't left the blind, you wouldn't have got the chances, you know."

"That's common sense talk," exclaimed the President, before I could get their minds off that kind of logic. I felt something was going to happen to those ducks of mine.

"I accept the new member's explanation of the phenomena," he went on, "and move that the seven lucky ducks be turned over to the Association, to be disposed of as the majority rules."

5: *The President strutting homeward with my birds which he voted to Mac*

25

"What do you mean, 'lucky ducks'?" I roared.

"All in favor of the motion say 'aye,' " ruled the President.

''Aye!" he and Mac both shouted in unison, and Joe came in from the kitchen with a tardy, "Me, too, whatever it is, Al," and a hearty laugh. Meeting stands adjourned," commanded the President.

It was on me! And as I tied seven webbed feet with a carrying cord, it occurred to me that I can no longer truthfully point to Mac as the only sportsman who goes duck hunting and never brings home any ducks. And Mac's weren't even "moulting."

Al Peck was identified as Mr. President of The Old Duck Hunters in the very first duck hunting story, but it took MacQuarrie a few years to identify him as such in trout stories. In "Down Went McGinty," published in 1932 but written in 1931 or earlier, he was called the Piscatorial Prevaricator and Ichthyological Ingrate. Here in this story from 1933 he is "my companion" and "the ingrate," In "Trout Town," published in June 1934, he is identified as The Fellow I Often Fish With. Perhaps "Trout Town" was written before "Upstream, Downstream," which was published in October 1933, because by the time of that story, MacQuarrie was comfortable calling Peck President of The Old Duck Hunters, Inc., even in a trout story. Perhaps his reading fans, or the editors of the magazines had learned of the magic and were clamoring for more ODHA stories.

Further in this present book you will find a retelling of this day fishing in "My Favorite Spot," in which MacQuarrie identifies his benefactor and dry fly expert as John Ziegler, of Superior.

The Convert

Field and Stream, February 1933

That first day I learned that even the Brule, where Presidents fish, may have rivals

I had not been in the stream five minutes when he struck. The Black Gnat, tied wet and fished very wet, had drifted about two feet with the current into faster and deeper water. It was my first cast to the spot—indeed, almost my first "business" cast on the river. Other attempts had been those tentative, elbow-loosening tosses that an angler employs to remind his arm of its duty.

The single somber Gnat on the end of a dry-fly leader, flung across the current from behind a bush-covered island not six feet square, moved lazily at first, then gathered speed suddenly, without any apparent line-drag. It almost shot into the deeper water, near the end of its unimpeded flight.

6: Good trout are often taken from water only six or eight inches deep

The brown trout took it confidently, as is his way when he does make up his mind. There was no preliminary feeling-out, only a heavy vicious wrench, and he hooked himself solidly. His first rush, as positive and instantaneous as his acceptance of the fly, took him only a few feet before he left the water in a desperate leap that I shall always remember. Then he fell back downstream ten yards or so. No more leaps. No more flashes of glorious spotted coloring, but fierce struggle against a merciless rod and a fisherman who controlled his first impatience well enough to realize the advantage of good tackle and not-too-fast water. In ten minutes he was netted, and I was completely sold on the Namakagon.

The 20-inch brown, from a stream I had hardly seen before, made a welcome weight in my fish pocket, and an hour later, when a dry-fly man proudly exhibited a 14-inch trout he took from the same spot, I had not the heart to display my fish, nor tell him the manner of its capture. I knew he pitied me, trudging along with my single wet fly, and he was great among those who woo the Namakagon. Why spoil his perfect pursuit with recital of my sudden success? The sun shone warmly. He was triumphantly happy, and I was glad he was, for so was I.

That is the way I came to know the Namakagon. It is an old log-drive stream of wide and shallow dimensions near its source, the crooked-shored Namakagon Lake, said to have more shore-line than any lake its size in Wisconsin. Coursing south and west, it finally merges with the far-famed St. Croix, and eventually its waters join those of the Mississippi. As might be expected, it produces, in various parts, pike, pickerel, bass and, I am told, even muskalonge. Its brown-trout water of greatest fame lies not far from Cable.

Up in northern Wisconsin, where the map is veined with rivers and spotted with lakes, one is supposed to speak only in reverent and hushed tones of the Brule, where Presidents fish. My first day on the Namakagon, however, taught me that even the Brule may have rivals, and I unhesitatingly name the Namakagon as one of its greatest. Lest I offend those ruling piscatorial red gods who roll the dice when one angles, let it be said that the Brule offers more varieties of trout, larger trout and, perhaps, even sweeter-tasting trout, for its water is always very cold.

But the Brule seizes one in a rough embrace. It snatches at one's waders with a pull that quickly tires. Its rock-strewn bottom demands incessant alertness. Progress along its bed requires constant attention, and there is always the danger of being flung, without warning, into one of its deep holes. After a tussle with the Brule one retreats gladly to the more hospitable Namakagon, where the browns lie in water not a foot deep and the wading is mere child's play.

My first introduction to the Namakagon came in the middle of the afternoon in late summer. While the rest of that day brought nothing more than a few small trout as a result of my downstream wet-fly efforts, I was convinced that the river had much to offer. Out here in Wisconsin one hears much of such Eastern streams as the Neversink, the Beaverkill, the Willowemoc and other trouty-sounding names, and invariably reports of successful sport in those waters also include a discussion of dry-fly angling. The turbulent Brule discourages that form of fishing, except on its upper reaches, and there it must be done from a boat, floating downstream usually. It can be and is done very successfully, but not by everyone, and only when a sympathetic boatman is working in close harmony with an understanding fisherman.

Ignorant of the practical handling of the dry fly but with a smattering of its theory, I resolved to make conquest of the Namakagon the next time with a wet-fly upstream, in order to acquaint myself with upstream fishing preparatory to essaying the use of a dry fly.

For some time I had fished with a single fly, wet, but had followed the trail blazed by so many successful anglers who fish with such flies downstream. As most of my fishing had been on the Brule, upstream angling never got much of a trial. It would take a Sandow to work the Brule upstream in most places.

A winter of time for consideration and discussion intervened, and the next spring I was back there on the first opportune Sunday, prepared to fish with wet flies and, if conceit in my ability held out, with dry flies as well. My companion was a confirmed wet-fly fisherman, always working downstream and across, persistent to a superhuman degree. With him I had held important conferences during the winter anent my forthcoming debut as an upstream fisherman and, possibly, a dry-fly fisherman. He had given me comfort and spiritual sustenance, and indicated his willingness to forget the old method long enough to give the new a trial.

The morning was fine but chill. From the river's bank where we struggled into waders, there was no sign of fish feeding. I felt my carefully built theories of a single fly, wet or dry, upstream, being washed away like a castle of sand in a cloudburst. Every fisherman knows that sensation—the sudden departure of careful plans when the mocking river is actually at hand and the panicky impulse to return to old methods that have been tried and found good. My companion, who had listened approvingly and with nodding of head for several months—in fact, since the final day of duck shooting the previous autumn—deliberately and wantonly deserted the good ship Theory at the last minute and left me all alone.

I must admit that he showed traces of shame and remorse when he first began knotting up his cast of three wet flies. He seemed to be muttering to himself. Said he: "Have your fun. I'll go get some meat."

I have ever felt inward shame for such action on the part of a fellow man, one who, willing to listen and plot through the winter, suddenly deserts a fellow mortal in dire distress, stranded, as it were, on his own theories.

"So you'll have none of my dope, eh?" I said in the manner of one who has been shamefully betrayed.

"Go cast your fly. I must be about my fishing," he replied grimly, and he looked at his brand-new McGinty, Hare's Ear and Gray Hackle the way Babe Ruth looks at his favorite wagon tongue before poling one out of the lot.

"Curses on you, Montmorency," I managed with a trembling voice. "Go chase yourself," he retorted, "I know a lot of better words than that, only I like you too well to use them."

He departed up the trail, the ingrate, and left me alone. Alone with my single, insignificant little fly on the end of a hair-fine tapered leader and no confidence to speak of. The boy on the burning deck, compared to me, was in a throng of seething humanity.

I began in a quiet stretch. How hard it was to refrain from tying a certain simple little knot in the leader, attaching a dropper fly to the loop thus formed and setting off downstream as he had done, proud of my superiority over the fish and arrogant with the certainty that I should succeed. A cast of wet flies never appeared fishier to me than that morning on the Namakagon, and there I was, bound to a stake of my own making. I shuddered when I recalled that I had even been talking to him about dry flies on the way down.

For a half hour I worked the water carefully, and nothing happened. I saw no sign of a fish anywhere, and in spite of my painstaking efforts to drop the fly like a feather and let it float, à la dry fly, without motion except that imparted by the river, I achieved not even a single strike.

I submit my experience as descriptive of some of the throes through which an angler passes in changing his mode of fishing. It is quite agonizing, especially when one realizes that he may be up and playing the old game in the limited time at hand. I have thought since that it might be simpler for a beginner at dry-fly casting to plunge right into that method, without having to renounce his old, successful way of getting them with wet flies.

Try it once. If you have been wet-fly fishing, change to dry flies. Or if you have been worm-fishing, change to flies. Then you will learn how deeply you have worked yourself into the rut of your own pet routine, how inflexible your plan of attack really is. No wonder changes are coming so slowly in fishing methods. No wonder so few anglers quit their wet flies for dry flies. It is written that such revolutionary transmogrifications must come slowly, after much travail and misery, and I experienced my share that morning.

Then, in a little rapid, I felt a strike. Just at the edge of the rapid it came, but the fish was on only a moment. The speed of the fly in the faster water may have prevented the trout from taking hold, I thought, and that guess stands, for I have found those Namakagon browns deliberate risers. Another period of inactivity and disappointment ensued, when it seemed to me there was not a fish on the river. And I had not yet scaled the worst peak—the dry fly. I was still wet-flying it, merely having acquired the dry-fly man's mode of traveling upstream! A wet-fly angler passed me, headed downstream. He told me he had three, and the trout were hitting a March Brown like fury. But I kept on, buoyed up by a faith the very dregs of which were drained that morning.

At the foot of another rapid, in very deep water, I hooked my first fish. The fly was sent up fifteen feet into the fast water and allowed to come down, willy-nilly. It came that way until the slow water was reached and the brown took hold. He headed into the rapid, but I dared the newness of the slight leader and worked him into a quiet pool.

My left hand felt for the landing net. It was gone. I could not believe I had lost it, and almost scratched a hole through my canvas jacket trying to locate it. A very kind providence held everything while I worked the brown into shore and swept him on to the bank. He weighed a good pound.

With renewed faith I worked into condition the Hare's Ear which had deceived him and set forth once more. A second trout, smaller, was taken in a rapid, and I began to feel better. Where before I had felt the demure Hare's Ear skulking along the bottom with its light under a bushel, I now pictured it as dancing with every whim of the current and all the wiles of a fishy Cleopatra. And that kind of faith, I am convinced, is what makes the difference between anglers who catch fish and those who don't. The trick is to feel that every cast is going to catch a fish. Witness the boundless optimism of your true angler. Some achieve it. I never have and never will.

"What luck?"

The hail came from a fisherman of unusual ability, a dry-fly man of great repute, who thinks enough of his fishing to buy $35 rods for two young sons. That's faith in its purest sense. I told him, and he confided to me the great secret of the Namakagon. "It's dry flies," he declared. "And on this stream, one particular dry fly seems best, regardless of conditions."

He gave me two of them, very plain affairs with brown hackles, no wings, Cow Dung bodies and three black-spotted brown wisps for tails.

"It may be," he explained, "that this water produces consistently a fly of which that is the best imitation, or perhaps it is simply a good-floating, good-looking something that appears edible to brown trout. It is a fact that it is the business fly of the Namakagon."

He revealed that it had been developed by an angling acquaintance of his whose reputation is quite well founded in upper Wisconsin, one of those unassuming fellows who never says much himself but can fish like the old Harry.

"Another peculiarity of the Namakagon is the effectiveness of midday fishing," he went on. "I have fished it dozens of times, and usually midday brings the best rise. It may be due to the sun bringing about the necessary effect on the eggs in the stream-bottom about that hour, to cause a good hatch. At any rate, don't stop to eat lunch if they begin to work along about noon."

I thanked him and proceeded. In my fly box was the choicest collection of bivisibles, fan-wings, flat-wings and just plain dry flies that one could wish for, but I chose to cross my dry-fly Rubicon with one of the nameless brown creations. While I had employed dry flies before, it had been only in haphazard fashion and with indifferent success. Now I was about to storm the citadel with what should have been a firm resolution built up by a winter of fasting and prayer.

True to my friend's prediction, trout began poking their noses above the surface during the noon hour. I tied on one of his flies, oiled it and shot it out over a turbid stretch of water that only a beginner would have tested with a dry fly. The fly bobbed and tossed, but a fish touched it. He was gone before I could act.

In quieter water I worked for several minutes, and another fish struck. I do not know whether my nervous reflex hooked him or he hooked himself, but he was played and landed, without a net, at that. Two more came my way, and I began to get cocky. I found it hard, as I had when using the wet fly upstream, to hold the rod motionless for a second or two after the fly touched the water, but the habit is acquired with a little practice. I began to feel that I had successfully laid the first bridge between the old wet-fly method and the new and more promising game of dry-fly fishing. With the dry fly, of course, the slightest motion of rod tip after the fly alights will impart motion to the lure and destroy the illusion of a natural insect, unattached to anything.

For twenty minutes or slightly more the browns were rising freely, and I registered a dozen

7: A handful of Namakagon browns

35

strikes which an experienced dry-fly man would likely have counted as creeled fish. But I did not care. I was jubilant and happy with the thought that my day of pioneering had not been fruitless. The fish were through feeding in a short time. Then I resorted to everything in my fly box that would sink or float, but they would not respond.

"It's no use," called the friend of the private fly, passing me on the way back to his camping place. "They were rising splendidly for about a half hour, but it's all off now. Better let them alone and save your strength. There may be another rise along in the evening."

I continued fishing within eye-range of the morning starting-point and with fond hopes that the companion of my angling and hunting moments would hurry up. I knew that if he planned on getting back for lunch by twelve he would likely show up along about two o'clock, dog-tired, bolt a sandwich or two and return to the river with a desperate fervor I have never before witnessed in either man or beast. It is not that his life is dedicated to my complete effacement as a catcher of fish or a shooter of ducks. He just doesn't know when to stop.

He reminds me of the blind horse the fellow sold. The horse promptly bumped his head against a telephone pole. The buyer returned with the horse.

"This horse is blind," he stormed. "He just split his head open on a telephone pole."

"Oh, no, that horse isn't blind," came back the former owner. "He's not blind at all. He just doesn't give a d—!"

I saw my friend coming around the bend. He weighs 160 pounds in his wet waders, and his wading brogues came from England, where they have lackeys (or is it gillies?) to transport them to and from the river. I had the lunch ready when he hove to.

"Been fishin', I see," I began.

"Say, this is a big river," he replied. "Been down to the mouth. Gonna make another trip this afternoon."

"Got any fish?" I couldn't hold it back.

"I doubt if Hoover can be elected," he answered.

"You won't be cross-examined?"

"These hard times can't keep on forever. The automobile business is getting better already. I did $15,000 more business the first month than last year."

"Wait a minute. Did you catch any fish? No answer, no lunch."

"Who—me? Oh, sure. Just fill my cup half full with coffee. I'll fill the rest with cream. I take a little cream in my coffee. Ha! ha! Good joke."

I peeked into his creel. Two browns that could have taken part in a piscatorial version of Singer's midgets were therein. I showed him my catch and told him how it had happened, and that act alone is proof of my kindliness to all mankind, for he has never since found much trouble in catching more fish than I, when both employ the same methods.

You can't fool these Namakagon browns with wet flies jerked across the current," I concluded my rehearsed discourse. "They're too wise. An occasional trout takes 'em, of course, but it's not consistent and it's not half as much fun. And if you persist in fishing with wet flies, take off the gaudy ones and put on a shy sister and treat it like a dry fly. It might produce."

And it did for him that afternoon, too. He borrowed my other nameless Brown Hackle, stole my bottle of oil out of my coat pocket, and worked out his own destiny late that afternoon during a hatch that sent every trout in the stream on the feed.

On the way home he said, "Don't forget to remind me to give the Salvation Army those old snelled wet flies of mine."

Here we learn more about Fred, who together with Mr. President froze out the young MacQuarrie in Norm Dunn's thin-walled cabin, prior to the hunt in "Ducks? You Bat You!" Fred Weade was Edith Weade MacQuarrie's brother, thus Mr. President's brother-in-law. Fred and Grace Weade and their son Warren lived at 703 E. 7th Street, a block or so away from the Pecks and MacQuarries. Fred was employed at a coal company earlier in his time in Superior and in his later years was employed in sales at the Philadelphia and Reading Company. You may remember that young Gordon worked a summer in his teens at a coal company- we don't know the name of either coal company, but it's fun to speculate. Young Warren lived at home and worked as a proof reader for a daily newspaper, according to the 1930 census. Again, speculate away, but it's likely it would have been MacQuarrie's Superior Evening Telegram.

Both father and son served, Fred in the Spanish American War and Warren in WWII. The Weades belonged to the Hammond Avenue Presbyterian Church, and Fred was a member of the Masonic Lodge, like Al Peck and Gordon MacQuarrie.

Fred Weade died at age 54 on February 23, 1930. While MacQuarrie stated in this story that this hunt took place in 1930, he must have missed the year- it would have been in 1929. Weather records would point at the rainy weekend of November 9-10, 1929 for this hunt.

Josiah Bond, one of the founders of nearby Minong, Wisconsin had a daughter, Nancy Bond, who at the time of this writing lived with her aunt, Edna Kimball, about six blocks from MacQuarrie. Both women were part of the same church as MacQuarrie and Peck. There are also lakes in the area named Bond and Kimball.

Rainy Day Ducks

Outdoor Life, October 1933

It rained that day—but there were lots of ducks. It was so black when we set forth at 4:30 a.m. that there was no way to distinguish between the thick darkness of the atmosphere and the mysterious substance through which our boat moved, unless one stopped rowing long enough to listen to the whispering of the needle-fine rain on the lake's surface.

Our boat, laden with four hunters, was part of the black, wet void into which we progressed toward a distant blind.

"Any duck fool enough to be out in this kind of weather will certainly get himself killed," grumbled Fred.

"I always did hate duck hunting," sympathized Al, president of that grand old organization—the Old Duck Hunters' Association, Inc. Al sneaks away from his office so often during the duck season that his practical-minded stenographer has urged him to establish a branch office on a certain lake not far from Superior, Wisconsin.

The third member of the party was Fred's son, a husky lad of twenty-five who yearned to know more about the uncomfortable but fascinating sport of duck shooting. I was the fourth pilgrim.

The plan was to skim down a long stretch of shore, pass a narrow opening where a lengthy point reached almost across the lake, and then shoot across another part of the lake to a familiar headland that was somewhere out in the inky blackness. Upper Wisconsin duck hunters know the place well—Lake Nancy, in Washburn County, famed alike for its small-mouth bass fishing and duck hunting. Incidentally, the lumberman who named it, gave it the name of his daughter, who is, today, a neighbor of mine. But we lost the opening in the dark and wasted so much time finding it that the neophyte and I volunteered to get out, when we came to the narrows, and try our luck from behind the jack pines, allowing the other two to proceed at a faster rate, as much of the rest of the course was over shallows through which a heavily-weighted boat must proceed very slowly.

So they let us out, tossed a bag of decoys toward us and

vanished in the drizzling bourne which by that time was turning from black to a heavy damp gray. I can see them pulling away from our point now, Fred rowing and Al sitting in the back seat "picking the course." How that man can pick courses for someone else to row!

Warren—that was the neophyte's name—and I set out a dozen decoys in the shallows off our point and located ourselves behind the stubby jack pines that stood like sentries along both edges of the point some distance back from the water's edge. From across the shallow little lake came the creaking of the oars as Fred threw his 225 pounds into his job of rowing. We heard them land, heard them toss the blocks out, with much splashing and some cussing and then all was silence from the other point, which, by the way, is not a bad place from which to shoot ducks.

In the east, what Warren humorously referred to as the sunrise finally provided enough light to permit us to see through the woolly darkness. As it grew lighter I thought I descried bunches of water growth on the surface, about 200 yards away, between our point and the other one. The frugal illumination of the alleged sunrise picked out other new patches of weeds and my incipient doubts were suddenly brushed aside when, in the stingy dawn, I saw one of the weeds rise and flap its wings!

Fred and Al must have decided the weeds were ducks about the same time, for Al dug out his quacker and sent forth a few tentative welcomes to the breaking day. I knew it was Al calling because he won't let anyone else call when he's present. As president of the association, we respect his whims, but it is a fact, known generally by the majority of the association's membership, that his calling isn't unusually productive of ducks. The sounds he makes aren't so bad in themselves. The only trouble is he can't get them right on the first try and always "takes overs," so that the procedure is more or less a constant rehearsal instead of a finished symphony.   Once at Yellow Lake, in Burnett County, Al called, with his duck quacker, two hoot owls and a liver and white pointer dog that had been missing from the neighborhood for a week. That's some calling, it must be admitted, but I depose that when a man is calling ducks he ought to lay off of hoot owls and pointer dogs. With Al it's all the same. If ducks come at his behest, that's good work. If something else comes, that's genius.

A family of mallards far down the lake (they were a very long way off and must have been hard of hearing) answered Al's call, strange to say, and it wasn't long before a family of bluebills found their voices and were matching their guttural pur-r-rts with Al's quacks. But a bluebill is dumb, anyway, so they say.

Not a duck took to the air. The heavy weather made them disinclined to move. They swam about in patches here and there, suspicious of both points where the shooters were, but curious, too, for the first flock I had sighted kept edging closer toward us. And it kept getting lighter, which helped some. Flocks of feeding ducks began to show up on the leaden water. On one side of our point, at our backs, was a bay of extremely deep water on which there was not a single duck but in the shallow bay, on the other side of which Fred and Al were located, there were plenty.

Warren, crouched beside me behind a bunch of jack pines, leaned over toward me and whispered: "Gosh, are those all ducks?" I explained as best I could that they were, but that our chances of getting even a very few of them were not particularly good as our decoys were not set right, our point came too close to the further shore and I doubted, in view of my ripe experience as a hunter of five years standing, whether ducks would come into decoys with that other shore so close. It didn't appear to offer them enough space for wheeling and maneuvering.

"The most ducks I ever saw before was in the garage after the October storm in 1919," whispered Warren. (Everyone who goes duck hunting in Upper Wisconsin learns about October, 1919, on his first trip. It is fully as important a date to local nimrods as Nov. 11, 1918, is to war veterans. Ducks fell like manna from the skies!)

The closest flock kept swimming closer to our set-up. It looked like they might come in when: Bangity! Bang! Bang! Bang! The silence was split wide open arid the misty air rent with streaks of spurting flame as Fred and Al went into action. We heard the spent shot dropping on the water in front of us. Two automatic 12s can throw a lot of shot. After that, like the perfect witness in a murder trial, "I forget."

As I look back now, I wonder if it is my imagination or my memory which is on the job as I attempt to recall what happened. Where we had thought there were scores of ducks there were thousands. From places on the little lake where we had thought there was nothing but four feet or less of mud-bottomed lake, masses of birds arose on beating pinions, and lit out for other parts. The upper air seemed suddenly alive with wheeling, climbing squadrons of startled birds, and, as is always the case, they began to cross our point from entirely unexpected angles.

When we would mark down a flock of moving birds which we thought might head our way, we would suddenly become aware of pulsing wing-beats much closer, from a different location, and we tried to make a Roman holiday of it. The results were disastrous. I think we both used up half a box of shells before we settled down and began to think about killing a duck instead of some ducks.

The first casualty was recorded in the death of a dashing white male butterball, which shot straight over us from behind. Warren stood up, with his dad's old Parker 12 with thirty-inch barrels, and the gentleman butterball did the first and last duck loop-the-loop that I have ever seen. It was a queer reaction to a shot and I thought for a moment the duck was uninjured, as it resumed its flight, in an instant, flew nearly a hundred yards with undiminished vigor and then suddenly dropped like a stone into the jack pines across the narrows. We found it later, very dead and very small, shot through the head.

It developed that our natural blinds of jack pines were not as good as they might have been. If you have ever tried to play Santa Claus and got involved with a Christmas tree, you know how evergreen needles get in your face. And the trees were pretty much in a line, so that ducks flying in toward us, circling over in back, had plenty of chance to see us. Our decoys didn't attract many to close range. The wooden decoys were too close to the shore and too far from us, but we soon discovered that many of the birds driven out of the lake were coming over for a look at our ducks and then shooting right over them. So we abandoned the wooden fellows and decided to take our chances with the high fliers as they came over. The birds, mostly bluebills, ringbills and a few butterballs and some redheads and whistlers, were loathe to leave the little lake, with its succulent water plants, and would return, after being scared out, within fifteen or twenty minutes. They were crossing over to a large deep part of the lake but, finding no food there, were always tempted to return to the easy feeding in the shallow water.

Warren and I had downed four or five, out of three times that many good chances when Warren, an amateur but a good natural shot, decided it was time to kill something in due form.

"Let's get two apiece out of the next bunch," he suggested.

We were both on our mettle, by that time, both a little bit ashamed, both annoyed a whole lot and inclined to wonder why the other fellow was missing so many.

A flock of seven came over from somewhere down the shallow lake, fairly low and close together. They wheeled over the decoys, too far out for a shot from where we were located in our new position, but, after renouncing the decoys, they beat straight across our point. Here was the big test. Warren's Parker and my Lefever let go about the same time and birds began to drop. Two of them lit on the point and we could see three more a short distance offshore. Warren rushed forward to pick up one of the birds.

"Say, we've got some dandies this time!" he yelled to me.

"Good!" I replied. "Let's see one."

Warren, his eyes shining, brought the two closest birds to me.

"What do you think of those for ducks?" he asked, weighing them in one hand and casting admiring glances at their resplendent plumage.

They were both mergansers—the big kind, with red bills. They seemed three feet long as he dangled them before me. I hated to disillusion Warren, but his mother is a fine woman and I couldn't impose on her to the extent of letting her smell up her kitchen cooking the mergansers. So I told him.

"But, they're beautiful birds," protested Warren. "They don't smell a bit fishy now."

"Never mind about how they smell now. If you want to keep a drake and have it mounted that might be all right but they just ain't edible. No fish-eating duck is."

Warren was skeptical. He would not believe me. I was constrained to spend some little time telling him just how bad the best merganser tastes and smells, even after soaked for two days in water with soda and vinegar in it and finally won him over. I even told him that one about the sage who advised a friend not to fight a skunk with the latter's own weapons, if he intended to fight the skunk at all, and after that he was convinced. So, the five mergansers, the fruit of our best shooting that morning, were food for the minks on the shore that night.

About nine o'clock we picked up our decoys and rowed across to the other blind. How I love that blind. I built the first one on that particular point, and killed my first duck from it "on my own." I had killed ducks before but discovered this place, fixed up the blind and was vain as the deuce about it when my veteran hunter friends, learning of it, began to abandon favorite blinds at other spots and began coming with me. Now I wish so many didn't know where it is, but maybe that works out all right, too. It forces me to go and find a better place and I have been lucky enough to do just that, with the result that I have found several other places, as good or better.

Rowing over, through the rain, we put up flock after flock of ducks that kept coming back into the shallow lake in spite of the heavy bombardment. Most of them were bluebills, but there were some redheads and a few sly canvasbacks. On the way over we ran down and killed a huge brick-topped redhead that the shooters in the other blind, or perhaps we ourselves, had wounded.

The day was one of the most unusual I have ever experienced. It rained just steadily enough to fill the air with a fine mist. Parts of my gun barrel would become wet, dry partially when held under cover for a while, and show rust, which I wiped off quickly. All of us were shooting No. 6s, heavy loads, in spite of the president's predilection for No. 4s. The reason was that they were my shells, so the president tolerated the inconvenience, with only a few passing remarks about people who wound ducks with fine shot. Great guy, the president. He says he's going to buy a box of shells next fall!

It seemed to make no difference how much we fired; the ducks always came back for more. It is possible they were new arrivals from the North, hungry after a long trip, but I must report, also, that every one of them were fat and seemed in unusually good condition. Joe Hollis, patron saint of the Old Duck Hunters, had phoned us two days before and the flight had increased since then. Those ducks were not to be driven away from the little lakeful of food. They held on, that year (1930) until the last week in November, waited out one freezeup of about six days, and piled into the little lake again on the first morning the ice was broken up by a strong southerly wind.

At the other point Al and Fred were waiting with broad smiles. A trickle of water dripped off Fred's shooter's cap, and Al was pretty wet too, but a happier pair of duck hunters I have never seen. As we two were getting fixed in the blind—it was a big blind—a flock of redheads coasted in from the left, gyroed over the decoys and departed, without a shot being fired.

"What's the use of being hoggish?" queried Fred, with a glance at the neat bag of retrieved birds lying concealed beneath the scrub oak thatch-work of the blind.

It rained and it rained and it rained some more! And don't believe it didn't rain ducks, too! I doubt if there were ten minutes at a time, all during the morning, when we did not have some action, and there were scores of birds in the air almost constantly.

At noon my three companions went back into the woods to build a roaring fire and grab a bite to eat,

8: Fred gets a line on one

while I held down the first watch during their absence. It was pleasant to be in the blind alone, to be dependent on my own eyes and ears to tell me when birds were coming. With four, or even two, in a blind, there is always some indecision as to when to shoot. One does not like to shoot too soon for the other fellow may not be ready and regardless of carefully laid plans as to who will give the signal, it usually develops that you just stand up and let go when you think the birds are in range.

I had not long to wait when a large band of bluebills, flying high, appeared from the left, from the deep lake, and headed for my decoys. Fred had told me they had been in the habit of passing over the decoys just once on entering the lake, so, when they swept by, in good range, I dropped two, one for each barrel. One struggled on the water, some distance out and I made for the shore to kill him before he swam away. As I reached the shore and was hastily jamming a shell into the breach, the air was suddenly torn by a roar as a flock of fifty or more swept over, saw me and sped onward. I was so flabbergasted I pulled the wrong trigger to explode the single shell

45

and when I did finally fire, at the scudding birds going away, not one was harmed.

Then I looked for my friend, the wounded bluebill. He was nowhere to be seen, and never was found. Moral: a duck dead on the water is better than fifty in the air!

But we all had other opportunities. It took those ducks until about two o'clock in the afternoon to realize that the only safe place for them was on the opposite shore. They would not leave the little lake but they did discover that they could get out of range by hugging the other shore and all that afternoon we could see them, five or six hundred yards in front of us, a faint dark line on the water, which grew longer and longer as the afternoon waned.

9: Mr. President holds the bag

We might have returned to the point on the opposite shore but we had plenty of ducks and we found community duck shooting pleasant. Also—that big fire back in the woods was pleasant, about every hour.

As the short afternoon waned (it was the second week in November) the birds became restless and incomers from the deep lake began to show up. Shooting became more interesting for a while and Fred treated us to some grand snap shooting on a couple of singles. Everyone had ducks and no one even blinked when a fellow missed a shot. It wasn't meat we were hunting for that afternoon. Lazy shooting it was, and different, for this country, where one usually must hunt hard for his ducks. But we enjoyed it. A half dozen days like that in the memory of a duck hunter serve to keep the home fires burning with more than accustomed spirit.

There was still a lot of daylight left when we waded out and picked up the decoys. Overhead, as we wrapped the cords about the wooden ducks, we could hear the ducks coming into our lake for the night. The air was sibilant with their whispering wings. Long, slow pla-a-a-ashes sounded over the lake as large flocks planed into the water.

It need hardly be recorded that Warren and I rowed back. Fred offered to take a turn at the oars but Al, who had not been president of the Old Duck Hunters for nothing, said he broke a pair of Joe 's oars the autumn before and Joe had forbidden him to lay a hand on an oar. Also, there was some talk of lumbago and his recurrent dandruff.

The happiest, chucklingest man of the four was Fred. He sat in the middle of the boat like the hale old patriarch he was, hunched over in his well-worn canvas jacket, which was pretty well soaked, but Fred didn't mind. The best shot in the bunch, and one of the best fellows who ever lived, I have since been awfully glad that he had such a good day. It was the last time he went duck hunting. After more than forty years of shooting ducks all the way from Southern Minnesota to Northern Wisconsin, during which time he actually killed ducks, in his boyhood, for feathers to stuff mattresses, he had his final shoot—and it was a good one.

There he sat, his gun resting against his shoulder, a happy gleam in his eyes, a bedraggled cigaret in his lips, fighting to stay lighted in the rain. I don't remember what he said. He never used to say much about duck hunting. He was too busy enjoying it. I think I can find, in Fred's demeanor, one of the reasons why I like the sport so well myself.

When Fred passed on, four months later, it was a heavy blow to the Old Duck Hunters' association, but let it be recorded that none of the members ever catch the whispering whistle of a duck's wings as he drifts over, early in the dawn, but what he thinks of Fred, who always shot them on the wing, never took more than his share, and loved the sport for its own sake.

The years 1932 and 1933 were peak years in the ruffed grouse cycle. In 1932, as told in "Weary Weekend," found in MacQuarrie Miscellany, The Old Duck Hunters *hunted the simultaneous opening weekend for grouse and waterfowl on Saturday, October 1 and 2, 1932. The last cover they hunted was the scene of this story as well, Repke's farm near Crotte Creek, Douglas County. In the present story Mac returns to those familiar haunts on the second day of the season, thus the early start,on October 1, 1933.*

By today's standards, the seasons were very short, five days in 1932, and 13 in 1933. In years before and after this, during lows of the cycle seasons were closed.

Again, here we get a glimpse of Helen the outdoors-woman, who picks up a partridge while hunting with her dad, Mr. President.

"Gentlemen! We Give You Pa'tridge!"

Sports Afield, January 1938

You'll know the place well. A meandering old Wisconsin tote road. Starting nowhere. Going nowhere. Fighting to beat back the forest that is narrowing it more each year. A twisting, lazy trail where one momentarily expects to see a husky team of woods horses. Harness jingling, runners creaking, a tobacco-chewing teamster riding the toe of the front bob.

A hallway of departed echoes that once rang with the cry of "Tim- ber-r-r!" as a tall tree fell. An avenue of wealth that led mackinawed axemen into the forest's heart to claim the white pine, as rich a treasure as any wilderness ever gave.

No ruffed grouse hunter could possibly mistake it. Among the sweet fern and ground pine, from the motley bottom-tangle where the ash and maple boles start for the sky—there you will find the pa'tridge, as we call him in Wisconsin. Dub him ruffed grouse if you will. But pa'tridge or ruffed grouse he's still a regal rocket of brown, lovely as a poet's dream, alert as an Arab sentinel.

I came to this road to hunt the pa'tridge and to hunt again the nameless charm that hovers over these old trails like an ancient truth.

I came in the still, dewy dawn of an October morning and stood on the old dam embankment where, years before, the creek had been swelled to a pompous river so that it could carry the 16-foot pine sticks into the surging St. Croix.

It was dark and damp in that forest aisle where I stood. But not in the tree tops. There the golden morning sunlight played on October's painted leaves. It was still as the grave excepting for my footfalls in the leafy forest floor. From afar came the muffled rumble of a drumming grouse to make one wonder if they drummed in autumn from sheer exuberance, as well as in the spring to boast a lover's conquest.

There were many roads I might have taken. All were the same. No—not quite. The one straight north that cut the county for 25 miles to Bear lake—should I try its shadowed length? The very crooked one that poked about among the humble little hills—should I sample its vagrant charm? The dank, dark trail that led along the creek bottom—would it produce more grouse in this dry weather? Or should I take the old, old favorite that bent into the rising sun, beckoning onward to the majestic St. Croix itself?

My mind was made up almost before I had decided against the first three roads. Old friends are best friends. I wanted to see again the little openings where the carpet of grass is always clipped like a lawn. (No one seems to know why.) I wanted to search through the yellow thickets along the hillsides where I knew birds were always found. I wanted to test once more the armchair comfort of a certain round dead bole just off the trail.

I was alone. I accused myself of selfishness as I locked the car and poked two number sevens into my double gun. It was a place to be shared with others but those who should have come had begged off on the plea too many early risings still lay ahead, with the duck season in the offing.

I lit my pipe and drifted down the dam embankment to the creek, leaped across and climbed the gentle slope of the other side. No need to hurry. No other hunters were ahead of me. The tote road was mine alone. The very trees about me, somber, patient, counseled deliberateness.

How easy it is to fall into the spell of the pa'tridge woods. How completely the cares of a hectic workaday world vanish in the witching windings of the tote roads.

Up the little slope and into the first grassy opening in the old road—almost before the road had begun to be a road. On the lawn-like grass the robins were bouncing about at breakfast. They scattered into low bushes as I passed and their sudden flight aroused me from my reverie.

What if one of those robins had been a grouse? Should I have snapped into it soon enough to stop him before he gained the thicket? Perhaps not. . . .No! Certainly not. Don't kid yourself, mister. You know you would have missed and your heart would have beat like a trip-hammer for five minutes afterward! Better wake up! Come alive! These pa'tridge get off their marks long before the starter's gun and they do the hundred in better than 10 flat!

Come, come! This early morning mooning is all very well and good. But pa'tridge are here! I shook off the contemplative mood. I knocked the dead ashes from my pipe. I unbuttoned my shirt at the throat and removed my gloves. The chill struck in and helped enliven me.

I stooped and tied a loosened shoe lace. There! I was a hunter again. No dreaming laggard could hope to cope with pa'tridge and come away unbeaten by brother pa'tridge. Thus re-born I tramped along.

There is a place on this road where the trees have fallen and the sunlight streams in. The grass is deep there. It has always served to whet my keenness, probably because the first time I walked this tote road I killed a bird there.

As I approached I grasped the forepiece of the gun with my left hand—prepared. I was not too soon. In the grass plot, off the road to my right a skulking pa'tridge catapulted into headlong flight. I swung in its direction. A thicket of dew-laden brush stood between my muzzles and the pa'tridge. As I fired through the brush a momentary rainbow of many colors sprayed out of the thicket and through its brief gleam I saw the pa'tridge go down.

I found the bird, a lusty hen. Now there was time for a pipe, a look around. I tucked the season's first grouse in my jacket and sought a handy log. It was great to get 'em—great to nail 'em through the brush. H-m-m-m. . . .This grouse shooting isn't so difficult after all. All a fellow has to do is—
B-r-r-r-r-whoosh!

The rocketing flight of a second grouse from the same little patch literally knocked me off my lazy man's log. And knocked the conceit out of me, as well. I fumbled to my feet and pulled a rubber trigger. I had forgotten to re-load the discharged right barrel. No use to try with the other. That grouse was over the hill and far away before my finger crept back to the other trigger.

H-m-m-m-m. . . . I picked up my pipe from where it had fallen among the leaves. I was a chastened, a wiser man. Oh, well, a fellow can't expect to keep himself in hair-trigger expectancy all day.

What was it the psychologists claimed? That no one can concentrate on one thing longer than—doggone, how long was it? Ten seconds or 10 minutes? Who cares? Psychologists don't hunt grouse as a rule. If they did they'd find the No. 1 pa'tridge hunters concentrate for hours at a time.

That second pa'tridge had whipped me neatly. But it did seem to hang a little longer in that open spot above the trees as it flew away. An easier shot than the first one. Maybe it knew I was sitting on a log smoking a pipe bragging to myself.

Maybe. . . .Maybe hell! You know doggone well it always happens!

It was growing lighter in the tote road. The early light had provided a mere gray gleam along the aisle. Now it was swelling to full daylight. The crackling leaves of October were beginning to

10: Down at the old dam

tremble in the growing breeze. Squirrels were gossiping. The promise of a warm, full Indian summer day was carried up and down the trail in little puffs of wind and reminded me to unbutton my jacket.

Day was here. Dawn was gone. What to do? Breakfast, of course. I had pried into the secrets of the hardwood in the magic of the sunup hour. Now it was time to appease an appetite sharpened by such early rising.

I found one of my friendly logs with a projecting stub for a backrest—can any man claim a finer throne? I fished out my sandwiches. And looked back over the morning.

The day had begun well. What a start I had thought to have on other hunters and how surprised I had been at 4 a.m., driving through the city streets, to find half the town awake, breakfasting or darting away from curbs in cars that had that unmistakable haste imparted by an anxious hunter at the wheel.

I wish you could have driven out of that North Wisconsin town with me that morning—the first day of the upland bird season. The shooting had begun legally at noon of the day before but the real business of going hunting commenced that morning. A hunter starts his day with the sunrise. Lighted windows, behind which one caught a glimpse of sleepy wives pouring coffee, speeding autos, hustling with an important air, a staring cop on the corner—all these gave evidence of the great impulse that animates man in the time of the hunter's moon.

I had thought the road would be my own on the 60-mile drive. I should have known better. The highway from the town limits was like a boulevard with traffic. Sparkling tail-lights jerked up and down the hills before me. Once I stopped my car on an eminence and looked back. I counted 11 cars within a mile. Then felt I must be getting on. After all, I had a rendezvous with pa'tridge.

At the turnoff I had abandoned the parade and driven into the woods of my own delight. Down past the tidy log farm house, around .in back beside the place where the new well was being drilled, thence into the tunneled road where the maples crossed. And so to the old dam where I had joined the issue with the sparkplug of the flaming uplands.

Sandwiches consumed, I marched again along the tote road. The bulging bird in my pocket was consoling. The sun was gathering power, trying its

11: On the Wisconsin tote road

best to seep down even into the shadowed aisles of the tote road. The stillness and morning charm had vanished but the sun was bringing the woods to life.

I had no watch but knew it was still very early. After all, time didn't matter. Far better for the gunner in such places to leave his timepiece home and chart his actions by the natural necessities of the moment—hunger, thirst, weariness. People should abandon watches when they go to have it out with brother pa'tridge.

I was scheduled to be back on the dam embankment at noon or before to meet my wife and her hunting dad, who is, of course, none other than the President of the Old Duck Hunter's Association, Inc. As I went along I felt sorry for them. They should have come with me and tasted North Wisconsin in an October dawn.

The aroused spirit that the sun always brings made it easier to preserve that constant vigilance so necessary in pa'tridge hunting. And I felt more confident with a bird in my pocket, despite the one that had brought me up short-reined. So I was prepared for the next one.

Out of a place where the sun struck in full force against a carpet of mottled gold I heard a throaty cluck. There was a scratching among the leaves, more clucking. Silence. I tried to make out the bird against the perfect camouflage of the leafy floor. It was impossible. I froze in my tracks, tense as a fiddle string. I had not long to wait.

A sudden roar and he was off, heading straight toward the tote road from my left. If I could halt that headlong dive as the bird crossed the road he would be mine. If not there was only the slim chance of a going-away shot as the pa'tridge sped through the brush on my right.

I saw him coming, a marvel of twisting, planing flight. I shot before I realized it. I was lucky. The number sevens caught him cleanly as he spanned the brief space above the tote road and he fell into the brush at my right. I could see exactly where he had fallen. No need to retrieve him now.

Wait! There may be another.

There was another. The second one sprang from the same spot, headed toward the road, but then careened to the left, as though it sensed my presence. The second barrel sent a harmless shower of sevens through the thicket.

The dead bird was a cock. His old fashioned shawl of black and green was a perfect ruff for his royal neck. It is part of the rite of all pa'tridge hunters to admire their birds, to ponder their weight, to stroke their wondrous colors. And whoever yet heard of a hunter of the upland woods taking a grouse without spreading its fan-like tail to guess its breadth and mark the exact stenciling on each feather?

Now I had two birds. The limit was four. I must not "use up" my limit too quickly. No need to hurry now. The tote road beckoned and I followed. The country changed as I went on. I had never before been so far along this road. It became more interesting. The hardwood gradually thinned and soon I was swinging along through popple. I crossed a dry creek on a shaky log, then climbed a slight incline. At its top the backward view over the creek's modest little valley held me for a moment. But I must get on. The sun was doing its best. I opened the jacket wide. And wished I'd brought a cooler garment.

In the popple patches one seldom finds pa'tridge but one little hardwood patch provided the day's supreme thrill.

Did you ever get close to a bear in the woods? I hadn't. I had always felt that if I did encounter one it would not alarm me. I knew bears were harmless. At least the black bears of Wisconsin. I honor the state of Wisconsin for protecting them. But I had never seen one in the woods. . . .

In the hardwood off the tote road to the left, down a slight declivity my ears caught a scratching sound.   It might be a pa'tridge. I moved quietly into position so that I could see over the top of some short brush at the roadside. There was my first bear— wild—not 35 feet away, grubbing at the foot of a rotten stump. He was not a big bear. But he was a bear. And he was big enough.

As I watched him all those armchair ideas about bears faded. A bear is a bear. Though I knew I would laugh at myself later I quietly slipped a couple goose loads into the double gun—those two hopeful husks that duck hunters always carry.

There! I felt better about things. The bear was deeply engrossed in his search for food—most likely ants for there was an ant-hill butting up against the foot of the stump. He must have winded me for suddenly he raised his head. The motion gave me a start. I gripped the gun more tightly. I saw his black nose covered with particles of earth and brown, rotten wood. Then he turned tail and lumbered off. My! How he ran. And if he had only known how he could have made ME run. His sudden dash flushed. a grouse that flew into a tree 75 yards back from the road. But I decided against stalking it.   The bear, you may recall, is said to run only a short distance at a stretch. . . .

The third grouse of the day was standing in the middle of my tote road as I gained the top of a little rise. He took off in a long gliding plane, straight down the center of the road. I saw him veering into the safer cover at the right but the number sevens halted him. It was the easiest shot of the day. He fell almost in the middle of the road.

It occurred to me as I picked him up—he was another cock—that pa'tridge hunters do not actually put their guns to their shoulders at all times. Years before I had wondered how it was possible to get the gun up where it belonged for such snap shooting. That morning I realized the problem had automatically solved itself. I did not get the gun up. But merely let fly. The shot must be taken as it is offered without any thought whatsoever as to position of gun, stance or swing. It is the only way. There is no other in the pa'tridge woods.

I was tiring. What was the distance supposed to be to the St. Croix? Eight miles? Or was it only six? No matter, a long hike—and the same hike back to the old dam and my car. A drink of cold water—what would that be worth at that moment? One of my pa'tridge? No, not that much! A box of shells though.

I rounded a bend and a jolting car was coming up that narrow tote road. I knew in a flash who it was. None other than the President of the Old Duck Hunter's Association who'd suspected I would be down that way and had driven into the road from its navigable end to see if he could find me. No walking back now. I drank about a gallon of water from his thermos jug.

Mister President got out to stretch his legs. He felt my bulging pocket and counted as he groped:

"One—two—three!"

"Not bad, eh?" I said.

"Not bad for a young gaffer, but going through that tote road you should have taken your four in the first half hour."

"And let the whole afternoon go by without firing a shot because I've filled my limit? Not much."

"Climb in there," he ordered.

I am, of course, a mere subject of the President of this remarkable organization. His wish is my action. It has always been so. As I broke my gun and laid it on the rear seat my eye caught brown feathers on the floor. Four shawled pa'tridge, beauties reposed there.

"Where? When? I—I thought you didn't want to get up so early?"

He grinned in his sly way. And said: "Let it never be said the President of the Old Duck Hunters let any whipper-snapper steal a march on him."

"But I wanted to hunt during the afternoon. I wanted to get that last one with you."

"Get in and shut up. Your wife who is my daughter, heaven help her, got the other one for you. Now she wants to go fishing. I know a lake ---."

"But there are some beautiful tote roads I want to see yet today."

"Get in! We're going fishing. Too much of a good thing is bad for a growing boy."

And now as I look back I guess maybe he was right.

Weather records and Wisconsin's deer seasons give us the likely day for this hunt, Saturday December 1, 1928. At that time Wisconsin had deer seasons only in even numbered years (hard to imagine now!) November 1928 was the warmest November since 1923. That day, December 1, 1928, had a high of 32 and a low of 26 degrees with 0.3 inches of snow in nearby Spooner. Shallow Bay would also have been full, as the drought of the 1930s was not yet upon them.

That would have been pretty early in Mac's duck hunting career for Mr. President to be testing the neophyte. You'll remember that Mac had only been introduced to duck hunting near the end of the season in 1927, the year of his marriage to Hizzoner's daughter, as written in "Ducks? You Bat You!" so Mac would have had only the 1928 season under his belt.

Less Haste—More Ducks

National Sportsman, October 1940

Mr. President gives a demonstration of duck hunting technique—and proves his point with ducks

Nothing that I have learned from the president of the Old Duck Hunters Association has been so aptly taught as one unforgettable lesson in considered action. This he imparted to me one day while hunting ducks in northern Washburn county, Wisconsin.

Before leaping full-toothed into this object lesson, I might say that I have for some years been exposed to the benefits to be derived from deliberate slowness of thought and action. I have long been aware that some plodding people seem to have a great deal more accomplished at the end of the day than their flashier, hastier brethren.

I think it was somewhere in Stewart Edward White's *The Forest* that I gleaned a bit of that writer's philosophy in this regard. He was building a log cabin. It required hand-sawing many logs. Though Mr. White was in the best of physical condition, a trail-worn neighbor woodsman could out-saw him any day of the week.

This annoyed Mr. White until one day he asked the veteran why it was. The woodsman pointed out that when White put his comparatively inexperienced hand to the saw his mind raced ahead of the job. So that he kept pressing on, faster and faster, getting more and more tired. The woodsman advised White to imitate his own deliberate sawing. White did. And got more work done. Whereat was disclosed the common sense secret that the chap who sees the end of the job too soon is often weary before he finishes.

In the physics classroom this phenomenon goes by another name—the law of diminishing returns. You notice it paddling a canoe. With a given amount of effort you go five miles an hour. By doubling the effort you will not double the speed. It can be worked out with slide rules and things if you are one to play with such affairs.

Personally, I am content to accept the object lesson as worked out for me by Mister President himself.

I mention this as a prelude to my day's experience, for I know that so many others, especially city folks, make the same mistakes in the woods, whether fishing or hunting. They simply go too fast. They think they are getting over ground when they are merely working themselves into a lather.

The especial lesson to which I refer came about thus-wise:
It was late in November and early in the morning. So early that a typical Lake Superior autumn fog had rolled far inland from the south shore of that lake. It compelled me to drive slowly, with straining eyes the whole 70 miles to a place where I knew there would be ducks.

The fog was bad enough. To make matters worse, a tire punctured when I was within 15 miles of my destination. There in the bleak darkness, with the eerie fog eddying around me, without a flashlight, I changed the darned tire.

I remember how I cussed the President of the Old Duck Hunters as the auto jack, on the first lift, keeled over in the soft sand of the road's shoulder. Then I had to start all over again and it was a good half hour before the tire was changed.

By that time it was growing light. But that meant little in

12: "Ducks are smart. The fellow who gets 'em should know more than they do."

the all-enveloping fog. The stuff hung like a fuzzy robe over the jack pine and scrub oaks. Only long intimacy with those twisting sand roads of the North Wisconsin barrens saved me from becoming lost.

Driving fifteen miles an hour, I recounted to myself the current delinquency of the President of the Old Duck Hunters. My thoughts were interpolated with objurgation that at times approached profanity.

The President had deserted me. On this, what would likely prove the last day of that duck season, he had brazenly told me the night before he was going deer hunting. I recalled the scene only too well.

It had never entered my mind that this peerless knight of the gun and rod would not go with me. But he had come to my house and said he was "going out and get me a deer." So I was alone when I wheeled away from my curb at 3 a.m. It would have been easy to get another to go in his place but it is not apropos among the Old Duck Hunters, Inc. to close the season with other than bona fide members in good standing.

All the way down old highway No. 53 I cussed him—the ingrate. I recalled the brief scene in my own living room when he had said "You ought to see if you can kill a duck without me."

Well, I'd show him. I'd take a limit of ducks that day or bust.

Later I had pleaded with him in his home. But his mind was made up. I even inferred that he wasn't going hunting at all, that maybe his wife had put her foot down on all hunting for a while. He responded bravely:

Ain't I the boss in my own home?"

From the other room came the challenge: "What's that?"

Equal to any occasion he responded: "I said I took a loss on that loan."

He also said to me: "What you need is the acid test. You are at the stage where you are letting people think you're some peanuts as a duck hunter. Here's your chance to show if you're the real goods or just a camp follower."

These, then, were the events which led to my lonely departure for the duck holes of Washburn county late in November and early in the morning.

By the time I slid the car into second and eased it down the last hump in the trail, past Joe's cabin where he slept the sleep of the just, the sun was up. I couldn't see it. It lay behind a billowing, rolling wool comforter of fog.

But daylight was at hand. It gave me reason for hurrying. Ordinarily, cruising to that place, I would have been in my blind at that hour. It had taken me three hours to negotiate 70 miles of driving. It was late and nothing can make a duck hunter madder than being idle.

Coupled with my ire was a pretty fair sort of guess that most of the lake would be frozen. It was. So tightly, that I could not budge one of Joe's steel rowboats that lay half in water, half on shore. In moments of great stress like that the duck hunting mind works rapidly—too rapidly. At least mine does. Occupying my own blind meant a three mile walk around the lake loaded with decoys, gun and shell case. By tramping only one mile along another shore I could come to a point 200 yards across the water and opposite my blind.

Fifty pounds of decoys, an eight pound double gun and a 30-pound shell case went along with me on the shore through the fog. Ere that mile was over I was perspiring. The decoy bag straps cut into my shoulder. The heavy shell case numbed my arm.

Opposite my old blind, which I could not see through the fog, I strung my jet black decoys, hiding the strings as best I might. The ice would not bear me and I slid the decoys out on it, like a Scotch curler heaving his stane. I knew out there a ways would be open water in the hole in front of my blind.

Wiping sweat from my brow I looked around. The visible forest about me was covered with hoar frost. As I watched the top layers of the fog rolling as the warm sun bit into it, I could see now and then vagrant rays strike into the silvery top of a high pine tree to reveal a diamond-set fairyland. So thick was the fog at first I could stand on the bare bench and feel concealed. Slashing wings overhead chased me behind the jack pines from time to time but I got only glimpses of them as they showed for seconds through the fog.

Almost an hour passed during which I thought I heard someone cough in my blind across the way. A sudden burst of gunfire confirmed my suspicions that someone smarter than I had hiked around that three-mile shore and occupied the blind. There was more shooting, but I did not get a shot.

When the fog finally lifted I made out the figure of a man sitting in my blind. Out from me a hundred yards was ice but beyond that and up to the shore near my old blind was open water. And while I watched, a pair of bluebills came in perfectly to his bobbing stool. He collected them both without troubling to rise from his sitting position.

The rising wind was at his back. Ducks were coming to him beautifully. The conviction grew on me I would have to pull out of my inadequate spot behind the jack pines and go around to that blind. No thought of trespassing in another's blind occurred to me for all the natives and others who shoot there are friends of mine.

I set out for the opposite blind. Even the gun and shell case alone were burdens. I have lugged that shell case to the ends of the earth for ducks and will never be without plenty of shells since one day I encountered one of the biggest bluebill flights I have ever seen—and me with 21 shells in my jacket and 20 miles to the nearest source of supply. That sturdy metal box has dragged my arms down for many a mile, but in the long run it has paid me well.

When I got to the blind it was empty. Whoever had set the decoys knew well how to string them in true north Wisconsin style with one line of teasers stretching out into the wind from the main group. I sat down to wait. In a few minutes the crackle of brush in back of me announced the return of my mysterious hunter.

Instead of some native of the barrens there stepped into the open the President of the Old Duck Hunters himself!

There he was, in well worn gray woolen trousers, boots and the familiar threadbare brown mackinaw with its one lone button-up near the collar. He came in and sat down beside me, deliberately opened a thermos of coffee and broke out sandwiches. He wrapped the old horse blanket around his knees, settled himself comfortably and said:

"I knew it. I knew you couldn't meet a duck emergency without me."

"I thought you were going deer hunting."

"Never mind that," he said. "I told you yesterday you had arrived at a point in life where you ought to be anyway half as smart as a duck. What the hell were you doing over on that frozen side of this hole?"

"I couldn't make it around here in time."

"How did I get around here—in time? If you can count you will perceive, by peering through the blind, that there are some eight or nine ducks lying up ag'in the ice out yonder."

"You upset my plans by not coming. I couldn't lug all the junk around to this side."

The President jammed his crooked little pipe with "burning tobacco" and made clicking sounds with his tongue. Then he delivered himself of what is a rather lengthy speech for him:

"Why don't you have your duck stuff in shape to meet any emergency? You could have reduced the number of decoys, taken a couple of shell boxes and your gun. I did it. Trouble with you is you hunt ducks by habit. You've always sat on that blessed shellbox so you thought you'd have to lug it over here. The derned thing must weigh 30 pounds filled.

13: "It's your chance to show if you're the real goods or just a camp follower."

"Another thing—when you came in this morning the fog was heavy. You know these fogs around here. They hang on for at least an hour. You can't shoot in 'em. You had plenty of time to hike around the lake twice if necessary. But you were in too darned much of a hurry.

"I heard you come in. You came busting down that far shore all in a sweat and took the second best way out. I heard your car when it hit the top of Joe's high hill. I just waited—knew you'd be along. I knew that if you were smart you'd come around. But you didn't. You stayed over there—and the fog was so thick you didn't even know how far out the ice extended from that side.

"No duck with an atom of sense is going to wheel into that 40-foot wall of pine you had your back up against. No, there wasn't any wind when you got there, but there was a breath of it shortly after. That alone should have driven you out of that spot. The wind was right in your face.

"You're over-trained. You've lots of steam but lack a governor. I've seen lots of duck hunters exactly like you. You go out and hunt ducks season after season just the way you did the year before. Ducks are smart. Every day in a duck hunter's life is different from the one before. The fellow who gets the fun—and the ducks—adjusts himself to changing conditions. He's gotta know more than the ducks do."

He warmed up my coffee. Just then his sharp brown eyes caught moving feathers to the right. "Take 'em," he said, and the coffee was spilled in the sand as I seized my gun. Two of the five that came in joined their cousins on the water.

That made the President grin. I studied him. He puttered with his side of the blind, adjusting a peep-hole here, building up an open spot there. I decided it pays to putter in this outdoor game. Watching him made me realize that deliberation is the mother of accomplishment.

The President is a past master at puttering. He never wades into any job. He stands off and sizes it up and then sort of sidles up to it on its blind side. He'll walk around a dead-fall rather than climb over it. If he must lift a heavy object he'll first locate the place where it can be hoisted easiest. When he goes fishing he takes every imaginable piece of equipment with him in his car. He is never without the one indispensable article you want to borrow—from a piece of string to a jackknife.

I settled down with him that day for one of the finest bluebill shoots I ever had. It was along toward the tail end of the day when I was emboldened to ask him why, after all, he hadn't gone deer hunting.

"Well, sir, if you must know," he confessed, "my wife found out and decided it was too dangerous for a young feller like me."

As best as anyone knows, this is the first story MacQuarrie sold to a national magazine.

In the 1950's, Mel Ellis, MacQuarrie's successor as the Milwaukee Journal *outdoor writer, wrote a column about escaping the same red clay hills in a downpour, this time in a station wagon. He and his wife had just about resigned themselves to a cold night's sleep and little to eat, when Mel decided- why not try, and dried the mud as he went, spinning his tires mercilessly.*

I have driven those two hogbacks on the way to McNeil's landing multiple times, and I departed one morning after an all night rain that left the Brule chocolate brown and unfishable. It never even entered my mind at the time that I might not be able to escape. The hills have been tamed with gravel up to good town road standards, and of course, we're not driving rear wheel drive cars with slick tires anymore!

Rainbows of the Brule

Outdoor Life, September 1931

The Brule River of Wisconsin is born anew each moment, its single pulsing vein of life issuing with virgin freshness from nature's womb, formed of inaccessible, saturated swamp lands in southern Douglas County. It is such a stream as anglers dream of, giving shelter and life to four or five kinds of trout and even a few occasional grayling.

The rainbows, steelheads and browns were put there by the U. S. Fish Commission about 1895 and they have thrived mightily. The west-coast rainbows and steelheads make an annual conquest of the Brule in the spring, to spawn, that is one of the wonders of the region. Thousands visit the river in March to stand on bridge or bank and watch these monsters. A hundred or more may occupy a large spawning bed, made of sand nosed up with some semblance of arrangement, to which the eggs fall. They are then covered slightly, with sand and gravel, to germinate. The spring spawners lie in serried, pugnacious ranks. Fish here and there continually turn sideways and quiver suddenly, as though to release the burden of spawn. Then the long dark forms are transformed instantly into splendid, animate life, the sharp ribbons of purple or red on their sides in startling contrast with the rest of their

14: Fast water on the Brule

silvery bodies. In another instant the picture vanishes, as the fish resume a natural position, and once more they are somber-colored trout giants. This instantaneous revelation of their glorious coloring is one of the glimpses of intimate wild beauty that attracts, year after year, hundreds of persons, many of whom never wet a line in the Brule.

Always an indifferent but persistent angler, the writer found himself, toward the end of 1930's dry season, more anxious than ever to test himself against the whimsies of the stream. Early-season fishing has brought fair catches upstream but luring them to the fly in the hot days had become steadily more difficult as the sun grew stronger. Two days before the season closed, I set out alone to try again, while there still was time.

It had come to such a pass that I feared the wrath to come, from fellow fishermen, if the day should prove to be empty of fish, and while I have never felt sorry for myself when leaving the Brule with a small catch—which has been often—I have that familiar habit of many anglers of making off on my own once in a while. After all, the prudent fisherman essays few widely-heralded trips, but is a sulking, solitary figure, full of secrets. I aimed for the lower Brule, a spot not more than 8 or 10 miles by river from Gitche Gumee itself. The soil here is a red-clay debris left by receding glaciers. The clay when wet is very slippery and always thirsty for rain. It loves to clasp itself lovingly to the wheels of automobiles. Perhaps half of the river from the lake shore north runs through this type of soil, but the river itself, mindful of the needs of angling men, has brought down from the sandy area upstream, millions of tons of sand and rock, to give footing to all who would wade.

To reach the river at this point it was necessary to negotiate two very steep hills. They are abrupt, pitiless hogbacks formed by ravines which lie all along the south shore, becoming steeper and more sharply defined as one approaches the lake. These same gullies are one of the reasons that the State of Wisconsin, several years ago, abandoned the project to lay a road along the very shore, and there are many fishermen who never regretted that, although I believe it a woeful mistake. Only a brave motorist, or one ignorant of the suddenness with which a Lake Superior clay road can change from a firm highway into a slippery, dangerous hazard, would penetrate into the Brule's mouth in wet or even threatening weather. Many a fisherman, who has learned from bitter experience, keeps one eye on the sky while fishing the lower Brule, if he has come in by motor car, and the usual thing to do is to cut and run when it looks threatening. Thus, even the humble under-wheel clay stands guard for the lower Brule and there are many who forego the river's pleasures at this point for surer sport elsewhere.

The sky was heavily banked with clouds but I did not worry particularly for it had been threatening for days. I felt quite composed about invading the lower river. Over the steep hogbacks, down

15: A rustic bridge over the Brule on the Pierce Estate

the last grade, across the wooden bridge and into the meadow to the lone white pine I drove. Lazy fishermen like myself are pleased to lean their rod against a tree while rigging up.

I am always too eager when I go to fish the Brule. I can stand with perfect composure on the bank of many another stream and lay cold-blooded plans of conquest, but the Brule strikes too hard at one's fancy. The possibility of catching big fish—as big as 10 or 15 pounds in early season—is unnerving, and because my first juvenile efforts to catch trout were undertaken on the Brule, I seem never to have been able to shake off that trembly, small boy feeling. I catch myself missing one of the rod guides when stringing up, or forgetting to put socks over waders before pulling on boots. Sometimes I think this is the best part of the whole business.

A Hare's Ear with a red tail was my first offering. I recall the confidence I felt in it for it is a fly a very successful doctor-fisherman of the Brule has developed. It is better to work it upstream but few stick with that game because of the strength of the current.

Were it narrower one would be compelled to do this regardless of its current. But downstream fishing on a wide river can be made to simulate upstream fishing, in that the fly can be directed across and even upward to a considerable extent. The Hare's Ear brought nothing and I changed to a Royal Coachman, resisting the

69

temptation to fasten on a pair of flies. It is a fact that many competent Brule devotees always use one fly, wet as well as dry: George Babb, who taught President Coolidge the intricacies of the dry fly, and who is the best-known guide on the stream, has no patience with the fellow who dredges along with two flies. The three-fly man he castigates with an unmerciful verbal torrent that will make an army mule listen with new interest.

The bright Coachman brought nothing. I placed it, as carefully as I could above sunken rocks, behind such rocks, let it drift, innocently, into foam-covered holes near the bank, and jerked it brazenly across the current. It began to appear as though the day would be fishless, and I was almost congratulating myself for telling no one of my venture. I had arrived at the stream late in the afternoon, near 6 o'clock. It is so close to Superior one may easily obtain an evening's fishing after a 30 or 40-mile run. Clouds in the west were becoming blacker and I found myself paying more attention to them than the casting of the fly. I have been stuck so fast in Lake Superior mud that only the perseverance of three men pushing, with socks wrapped around the tires in lieu of chains, has brought me safely to graveled roads. One lesson like that lasts a long time. And on that summer day I was alone and my car had disc wheels!

I had worked downstream about 400 yards when the first drops fell. They were large, straight-falling water-globes that hurtled earthward in an exact vertical line, contemptuous of anything but a stiff breeze. They shattered with sibilant splashing on the leaves and produced jaunty little waterspouts on the river as it danced to meet them. Their piercing music added a new note to the Brule's monotone. They spat on canvas jacket and flannel shirt, on old felt hat and bare forearms with a friendly warning. They said to me: "We are here now, the good wet raindrops that have been away so long, and if you are wise in our ways, you will go."

A little rainbow struck the Royal Coachman. Whether it was the protection from sight of me that the dappled river surface afforded, my own persistence, or some explainable phenomenon in the fish at the arrival of the rain, I shall never know. The rainbow was 10 inches long and I welcomed him happily. Another cast, with the same fly, without moving my position and another rainbow, about the same size, took hold. I was sure then that the rain had brought the change; how that change was effected was not material. The fish were biting and I was there, in the middle of the Brule River, marooned on an island of red clay, as it were. I netted the second one in a quandary, sparing no time in taking him, although even 10-inch rainbows, on a 5-ounce rod, in fast water are not to be yanked in as perch from a mill pond. Three more, all rainbows, came my way quickly. And with them came more raindrops, pelting into the river with reiterated warning for me to flee.

The decision to abandon the sport came with the fifth fish. I stumbled hurriedly back over the rocks and wondered, as I progressed, if it were, even then too late to negotiate those stupendous hills. The slap of the raindrops grew constantly—no needle-like hum such as fine rain produces on water—but a vigorous, steady roar. I was drenched but that was nothing. If I could only get over those two hills before they became too slippery I would be safe. I had visions ascending one hill part way and then sliding backward, willy-nilly, to come to a devastating stop in the brief ditch. If I must slide I would prefer a forward movement. I even saw, in my mind's eye, my wife, who loves me, even though I am an angler, sitting at the window waiting for my car lights, fully convinced, as all fishermen's wives

16: This rainbow proves the size of trout the angler might get on the Brule

are sooner or later, that I had come to some grief in the river. That was the impulse that hastened my steps. I tried to make a little more speed by clinging to the shore where the water was shallower. I turned over many a stone that late afternoon breasting the current.

A big pool, hard by some one's 10 x 10 fishing cabin of logs was my undoing. The pool nestled beneath an outstretched pine. The stream nuzzled softly into it, hesitated a while and reluctantly departed. Little water corkscrews floated over its pool's surface and vanished. It was comparatively undisturbed beneath the branching pine. It tempted me greatly though the urge to move homeward was also strong. With hardly a halt in my stride upstream I sent the Royal Coachman on a careless mission of investigation. It alighted above the arched pine and joined the river's ceaseless flow amid the raindrops. It was, by this time, a mere spot of mangled red and white.

The fly sank from sight. I lowered the rod tip to permit the line to clear the pine branches and then raised it, once clear, rather sharply. That movement, which was done merely to make easier the retrieving of fly and line, hooked solidly for me the largest trout I have ever taken on a fly. The fish struck and fought instantly. There was no interim for me to wonder if he had been hooked well. It seemed that he felt the point in his first eager rush upward and, feeling it, kept right on going to the surface where he writhed powerfully, to sink in another instant out of sight. I guessed him to be a steelhead, by his terrific pugnacity and whiteness as he came into view on that first jump, and explained such a large fish on a fly at that season only by the fact that I was close to Lake Superior. Perhaps he was some buccaneering vagrant from the lake, in quest of smaller fish—even spawning browns which were then on the move to spawn.

The electric quickness of the steelhead is greater, I believe, than even the rainbow. The browns and natives occupy a lesser place for doggedness and power. My steelhead plunged upstream 40 feet or so, and made another leap into the air. No Olympic pole vaulter scaled the heights with more grace than my trout in his try to break away. The rain was now streaming downward in long pencils of water that permitted me but a blurred glimpse of subsequent leaps and surges. The moisture of many weeks was released in that inundation. It streamed from me in rivulets, even penetrating the ventilation eyelets of my hat. I was part of the river, part of the rainstorm itself and between my nervousness over the big trout and my apprehension about ascending those hills, I was well occupied. For a time I even considered letting the big fellow go, but came to a saner and sportier conclusion that the road, by that time, was about as bad as it could be anyway. So I remained to fight it out.

I tried to hasten the end but the steelhead would have none of that. Once he buried his nose in the bottom of his pool and remained motionless for, perhaps, two full minutes. Do what I might, I could not stir him and I was almost convinced that he had succeeded in fastening the fly into a rock or deadhead. It was incredible that a trout—even a big trout—could be so insensitive to pressure. The line, when I exerted a pull on it, became as taut as a well-secured fiddle string but the bulldog fish on the end held only tighter. I marveled at the muscular mechanism that enabled him to make such a stand.

When he got tired of that he made another rush, this time downstream and I followed him blindly for 50 feet or more. Back upstream he went to the pool and back I went with him, and this time I was able to steer him away from the deepest part and work him somewhat closer to me. He never returned to the pool after that, but sheer luck and strong tackle were all that prevented it for I exerted more pressure on his mouth than I had any right to. Even his dead weight, as he tired, was load for the rod. Closer he came and rolled, showing a white side with a faint purple wash down the center. Had he been a rainbow the stripe would have been a rich purplish red. My net was too small and I actually horsed him through the last few feet of water to a miniature sand beach, then knelt down, all a-tremble, between the fish and the stream, to prevent him from flopping back. When I put him in my game pocket a head and tail protruded from opposite sides so that his royal length half surrounded my waist. Never have I been more regally guerdoned.

If it had rained before it was now pouring. I crashed through trees and brush on the shore, not halting to disassemble rod, but only hoping that I had one last chance of scaling those red ramparts of clay. At the car I plunged into the seat, waders, boots and all, like an excited spaniel after a plunge. The 9-foot bamboo protruded through a window. Out of the little meadow, over the plank bridge and with motor shrieking in second I drove madly into the first hill. Under a tree stood a man in a long yellow slicker. I must have given him the real thrill of that day.

"You'll never make it!" he shouted encouragingly as I passed him, and I have never taken more pleasure in a human's disappointment than when the car surged grandly to the top. The rain had run off to a considerable extent, and the wheels found enough traction to pull me through. Had another car followed my tracks I doubt if it could have pulled through for the clay ruts would, then, have been smoothed down and made slippery by my wheels. A dizzy slide down the other side, another dash at full speed ahead and I barely scaled the second hill. The next 4 miles of driving to the main road was mere ordinarily treacherous navigating in clay. As long as the clay remains fairly horizontal it is not so difficult for one used to it.

Reaction and weariness when I hit the good, safe graveled highway caused me to stop, strip off my waders, take down my rod and inspect the steelhead. It had ceased raining and I found a dry cigarette in the car. The steelhead reposed on the running board for inspection. He was as long as my arm, but had he been half so large I should have esteemed him as dearly, for had I not fought him and taken him from the haunt of Winnebojou, spirit of land, when even the rain gods conspired to protect him?

I blew a billowing smoke offering skyward to Winnebojou, and hoped that he saw and accepted my token for his medicine is mighty and good.

You've met George Babb in "Babb of the Brule" in More Stories of the Old Duck Hunters *and read another* Milwaukee Journal *story about him in* Right Off the Reel. *Those were stories about Babb written by MacQuarrie; this one is actually fishing with him.*

Night Casting on the Brule

Hunting and Fishing, March 1932

It gets pitch dark in the Brule river valley shortly after sunset. On nearby lakes the departing sun leaves an afterglow—the typical long, northern twilight, but on the Brule the sun lurches behind the cedars with down-hill haste, and the angler of the night line pulls on his jacket sooner than he had expected. Down in the deep, damp valley the night wraiths of mist are rising while there is still lots of daylight on higher ground. Only the lips of the rapids, where the water curls, and in the fast water where the surface is white and broken, does the river's surface have any power to catch and reflect the little light reflected by the sky. On cloudy nights even these tell-tale white spots are absent and the river becomes a colorless, creeping rope of water, twisting down its lonesome course to Lake Superior.

Feather-light dry fly tackle was carefully taken down and packed away in the sturdy cedar river canoe and a single, heavier, more practical rod rigged for the night's fishing. The gentle little rods that had served during the daylight hours were no match for the task ahead—that of holding brown and rainbow trout in fast water and inky blackness. My companion and host, George, dry fly instructor to President Coolidge when he came to the Brule, and one of the most deadly performers with the dry fly that I have ever seen, grinned in the circle of light cast by the flashlight as he rigged up the heavy rod. From beneath the hat whose brim is always pulled down on all sides, I saw that grin and it spelled confidence. He broke off a piece of the leader with a quick jerk. Too rotten. He chose another, and it did not give beneath the stress.

"You've got to test 'em for this kind of a job," said George. "Those big fellows in this water are bad enough in the daytime. At night, in the dark, they're just plain murder. Make up your mind to lose a lot of them, if they're working tonight."

The whippoorwills had started their night music when we set forth from the luncheon ground where we had dined belatedly. Where, an hour before had been a friendly river, sparkling with life and color, was now an expanse of coursing water; almost invisible but much more talkative. If the river disappears at night its voice grows stronger. One follows the channel almost by sound. I was in the rear, handling pole and paddle, with net and flashlight at my feet. George occupied the front with a Callmac bug on the end of a rig-up he kept as short as possible.

I worked the boat out into the current, through a small run into quieter water at the foot of what I sensed to be another stretch of rapid water, by the river's sound as it plunged down the rocks. Out in the pool at the foot of the run, where the current was fairly strong, in spite of greater water depth, George tossed the big bug, so different from the dry flies we had used that afternoon. It handled awkwardly in the air on the first cast and came to the water with a light spat. The cast brought a rise and strike but the fish was on only a moment. About the sixth cast brought another. There was a ka-chung somewhere out in the dark, a spattering of water as the trout tried to thrash off and then I maneuvered the boat into quiet water and turned on the flash light.

17: Getting dark on the Brule

The light illumined the foam-flecked pool, the line cutting the water and the vibrant rod, held high and straight overhead. I heard the reel squeal out about a half dozen yards of line and then heard George mutter: "That won't do. He'll be in the rocks if I give him another inch." Slowly he let the trout tire itself out. In five minutes he had regained enough line for me to begin thinking of the net. The brown was maneuvered close to the boat's edge and when the light was thrown on it, it promptly ran beneath the boat. I saw him flash by and realized, as he ducked under us, why George was not risking his four-ounce rod. It was a wonder the tip of the five or six-ounce rod held out under that sudden submarining. Another wait of a few minutes while the brown wore himself out and he was brought to position once more. This time he lunged into the net as he swept by and I scooped him inboard.

"Don't throw him up in the trees," laughed George as the net soared upward with its writhing freight. I unhooked him and placed him in the built-in live-box, 20 inches of mad, spotted beauty, to keep company with a two-pound rainbow that had risen ravenously to my dry spent wing that afternoon on the still water of Big Lake, an enlargement of the river.

"Do they always hit as quick as that?" I asked.

"Not always," replied George, "but they're far more willing to feed at night under most conditions. Many days that won't bring a rise will bring action at night. In a way it's unsportsmanlike, and I presume a law will be passed against it in the future, but the number of fish taken at night is very small because so few anglers care to fish in the dark. I'd rather fish in the daytime but like a night trip occasionally. The river is so different and I keep so few fish, anyway."

"It's certainly different," I agreed as the boat was caught in the current and saved from being carried sideways downstream by strenuous exertion of the pole.

"Most fishermen simply don't do it at night because they're afraid of the dark, I think," went on the veteran of 35 seasons on the Brule. "They're not cowards, but mighty few fishermen will meet the river at night on its own terms, when they could be smoking a cigar on the front porch of their cabins. Then, too, the confusion of getting tangled in branches and the utter impossibility of getting untangled in some cases, without cutting things to pieces, discourages a good many. I took a friend—a very good fisherman, too—out one night and he got hung in a cedar. After he fell in the river trying to free himself and finally stepped on the tip of his brand new rod, he announced he had enough. It's no game for anyone without a lot of patience. We'll be hung up a-plenty tonight so be prepared to smoke your pipe and bear it."

And I was to learn, in the next few hours, that not everyone can fish successfully on the Brule at night, even though they have the patience of a Job, for a thorough knowledge of the river, its holes and fast water, is imperative. George seemed to sense where the channel was and directed my propulsive efforts with well-placed "rights" or "lefts." For all I knew we might have been chasing up the river Styx, the place seemed so unfamiliar, although I know the stream well enough by daylight.

We proceeded upstream and I held the boat in a rip of fast water while George worked the spots just above where the water curled over the rocks. It was hard work holding the boat in the current and my arms ached but I would not admit to George that I could not do it, for such a task is an everyday trick with him. My patience was rewarded when another fish lunged at the bug about the twelfth cast. I was relieved to let the canoe drift backward down the rapids while he played the fish. It tired more quickly than the first one and was netted, a good fish about 16 inches long.

"Now you try it," said George, and I was not slow in accepting his invitation. It would be a pleasure to let someone else hold that craft in the rapids.

We proceeded upstream for about a mile without getting a strike, and after carefully fishing some of the choice spots along the way. George was mystified. He had usually taken trout at his favorite places. It was not until we neared a pool a hundred yards below the famous Cedar Island where Coolidge summered, that I had my first strike. The fish was on and off before I could set the hook.

"They'll spit that bug out quicker than a fly," advised George. "Maybe it's because it's bigger and they sense more quickly that it is not the real thing."

I struck quick and hard on the next one, out of the same pool, and he took to the air on the first try to escape. I held the rod straight and depended on it to do its work without much help from me, for it was black as the inside of a dirty coffee pot. I hardly knew whether we were in the center of the stream, or at one of the sides. One loses all sense of location in such darkness, so I simply let the trout take the line until I guessed he had enough, which worked well enough, for he responded to a little tightening at the end of the run.

If you anglers would envision what happens in such circumstances, close your eyes, and keep them closed, the next time you hook a good trout. Let the fish match his strength and courage against your self-imposed blindness and see what happens! Even then you will not be so badly off, for you will have had the advantage of knowing your ground from the sight obtained before you shut your eyes. No, I guess the only way to experience the night fishing thrill is to go and do it, on a nice black night in fast water.

I'm making rather difficult work of trying to tell how confusing and fumbling it is to fish at night, but, pray, let me offer one more suggestion to those who want a comparison. Go into your basement some night after the neighborhood handy man has straightened it up, moved things hither and thither, and, without a light, try to sprint from one end of it to the other. The final results may be somewhat different than fishing the Brule at night, but you will have grasped the general idea, what I mean to say.

The boat is apt to swing into the cedars on the shore when your boatman lays down the pole for the net and flash light, and if there's a rapids anywhere within 10 yards you are bound to shoot them sideways, and may even ship a couple pailsful of water. The fish will never pass up a chance to shoot beneath the boat the minute you put a light on him. He seems to welcome the darkness of the boat's bottom, which is natural enough. Friendly branches swipe you in the face as you drift downstream and the same branches have a habit of scraping everything out of the boat that is not held firmly in place. Wherefore, before you start on your night fishing expedition, see that all coats, hats, tackle boxes, spare paddles, poles and rods are placed securely in the bottom where they cannot be brushed overboard.

I had almost forgotten my trout. He finally yielded to persuasion and was dipped into the boat and live-box to join the others. One more large trout a short way upstream, right in the middle of a rapids and we found no more on night sentry duty until Cedar Island, the former Coolidge summer home was reached. The big pool just below the cedar-barked main lodge brought nothing and we moved onto the point where water from the Pierce hatchery was coursing into the river. A long cast, in the comparatively clear stretch of the river brought a lunge and a jerk but the fish was gone before he was hooked. Persistent casting for, perhaps ten minutes, resulted in a second strike and that one was hooked. When he was netted a few minutes later, we found the hook holding loosely in his lower jaw, in such a way as not to interfere with his gill action. No wonder he fought so hard. Five good fish, besides several smaller ones we had taken in the afternoon were in the live-box by this time so we decided to call it a day—or a night.

As we rounded the island where the lodge stands the waning moon became visible over the treetops. It had worked up through low-hanging clouds and was gradually flooding the valley with its light. The river took on an entirely different aspect. It became, once more, friendly and familiar and I felt it to be more the river I was so well acquainted with. Familiar little features stood out faintly in the moonlight and while the sense of the river's mystery was not completely dissipated by the moonlight, I nevertheless felt myself once more on familiar ground.

With the fishing over and the downstream run begun, George found time to reminisce. He pointed to a large pine near the president's former summer home.

"I was out on the river one night with Colonel Starling, head of the secret service detachment guarding the president," he recalled. "Starling hooked a heavy trout just in front of that tree. He played him for a few moments but the fish broke free. It was quite late— after midnight and I presume the colonel thought the situation and the circumstances called for a few cusswords, in subdued tones. I was offering oral sympathy. Neither of us dreamed anyone on the whole estate was awake, when the president stepped out from behind the tree and said: 'Didn't get him, did you?' I forgot what we said but I know he didn't say any more but walked back to the lodge. We heard him chuckling to himself."

Coolidge, his former instructor revealed, became a devotee of night fishing. He plied the river early and late, seldom retaining any of the fish he took, and sometimes remaining out in the roughest kind of weather. The night before he left the Brule for Washington he remained on the river until long past midnight. It thundered, and rained but the imperturbable Vermonter fished on, clad in a heavy slicker. "I'll never forget that night," commented George. "I wanted to go home and go to bed, because I like rain about as well as a cat does. But I would have stayed until noon the next day if the president wanted to. I sure felt sorry for him leaving such a place for Washington, and you know, I think he felt kind of sorry for himself."

The trip downstream was far easier. The moon lighted our path most of the way and at places where the river narrowed and was overhung with trees we made use of the flashlight. We stopped in one rapids for a few casts and a tremendous trout smashed at the bug but did not touch it. George was in hopes of hooking a real Brule mastodon but his wish was not granted that night. His record brown, taken about ten years ago, weighed 12 pounds.

We brought 13 deer into the circle of our light at close range that night and heard twice as many more snorting and whistling in the woods on both sides of us. The night had grown more chill and we had just pulled on our coats when George hissed for silence and pointed ahead. Out from a little point, in shallow water, five deer were drinking, all not more than a few feet from each other. Our boat was aimed directly at them. Slowly I put the light on them, for a fast, flashing light frightens them. Their movements were indescribably quick as they craned and twisted trying to discern better the single-eyed object coming toward them. As we came closer they grew restless and milled about nervously, but before they snorted and dashed into the woods they were so close I could have reached them with the eight-foot pole we carried in the boat.

I snapped off the light and as I did a big buck which we had not seen, on our other side, plunged forward in the water, apparently frightened by the sudden disappearance of the light, and splashed noisily across the river.

It was after two o'clock when we climbed into the car and started on the back trail.

This is the only magazine story to feature Mart. Readers of Right Off the Reel *will know that Mac wrote his* Milwaukee Journal *column "Mart the Liar" on January 18, 1937. That story begins: "The most engaging deceiver I know in the fishing-hunting game is a friend of long standing with whom I have fished, hunted, starved and lied for many, many years." It is obvious that MacQuarrie thoroughly enjoys this rascal. In that story the number Mart consistently used was 15.*

Mart also played a major part in a cisco seining story also found in Right Off The Reel *from* The Milwaukee Journal, *October 1, 1936, "Ever Go for Ciscoes?" Mac wrote, " Here's the way we used to do it. On the first really frosty November afternoon Oscar would come in and ask me if I were going. Going where? Ciscoes! Sure! Then Oscar would go away and get Mart and Hilding and Gus, who used to always be at the Eagles club and off we'd go. You can't go cisco fishing, by rights, without Gus. Not only does Gus have the proper gear but he knows the best technic (sic) required in getting 'em. In fact, Gus knows everything." On that adventure Mart took a slight bath.*

Mart is Martin Flesvig, a stereotyper at the Superior Telegram. *He was seven years older than MacQuarrie and he lived at 644 22nd Street with his wife Josephine, their three children and his father-in-law John Spera.*

You Take Your Worms

Field and Stream, January 1933

The Brule makes its choice between flies and worms

I like Mart Fleswig, even if he does chew snuff. There probably are people who don't know what snuff is, but there aren't any in Superior or Upper Wisconsin who don't, and, similarly, there aren't many who don't know Mart Fleswig. Mart bosses the stereotyping department of the Upper State's biggest and best newspaper. That is to say, in the city directory there is some such designation after his name describing his vocation. As a matter of fact, that's a blind. His real purpose in life is to fish for trout with angleworms—and chew more snuff. He does both perfectly.

Mart's snuff comes in a box about the size of a hockey puck, and I have accused him of feeding his special angleworms on it to make them fighting mad. I even hinted once that maybe he kept the worms in the box when he was out fishing, and he practically admitted it. He alleged one big night-crawler, after a pinch of snuff, grabbed a six-pound northern pike and broke its back with one shake, but I didn't believe it until, in a moment of weakness, I tried a chew myself. While not immediately fatal, it must be recorded that its effect is most virulent. There are no rattlesnakes in this country; so I am at a loss for a good local comparison as to its potency. Now I know that night-crawler was in its death throes when it grabbed the pike.

Fishing stories begin in the strangest places. This episode began in Mart's grand cubicle, amidst the clank of rolling things and the gush of hot type metal. I sauntered in one afternoon, and Mart whipped out the snuff box on me—drew from the hip, as it were. He snaked out a chew arid laid it reverently in his lower lip.

"Have a chew?"

"You'll excuse me, Mart. I just had a shot of cyanide in the engraving department. It's milder."

Mart rolled his quid unctuously. "I've got a notion to take you fishing," he said finally. "You've been whipping the stream a good many weekends. How'd you like to go fishing with Mart and his anglebugs?"

"Martin," I replied, "you are a most deplorable character. I would not go fishing with you for all the snuff in Copenhagen. You dunk angleworms in the Brule when you could be having some real sport with flies. In addition, you permit your wife to desecrate the inside of a trout with tomato stuffing; and furthermore, you drive your car at reckless speeds over all roads in Douglas County at all hours of the night during the fishing season, endangering life and limb of honest farm folks."

"Yep," interpolated Mart, "and I sleep with my boots on when I go fishing, and whose business is it besides mine?"

18: If you will put your flies in the impossible places, you will take fish that the other fellow passed

He got it off without losing a grain of snuff.

"And to make matters worse," I resumed, "you sneak away by yourself with your worms and snuff two days out of every week before we get the home edition down and then come around in the morning to tell me you got fourteen trout."

"You've eaten 'em, too, lots of times."

"If you had any ingenuity, you'd change your figures. It's always fourteen. I'm suspicious of your statistics."

"Today's Saturday," came back Mart laconically. "Tomorrow must be Sunday. You take your flies, and I'll take my worms. Any under fourteen I catch cost me a cigar for every fish. Make it the Brule. I'll honk you up at five in the morning. Bring a sandwich. I'll take an extra box of snuff myself."

Mart was tapping the cover on his box of Copenhagen when I appeared the next morning. Our departure for the field of honor was unmarred by untoward incidents other than the untimely crowing of a neighbor lady who thus expressed her displeasure at our obviously piscatorial quest on the Sabbath. She arises with the sun because she likes to watch the birds in the morning, she says. I'm convinced she gets up early on Sundays only to crow me out of the neighborhood and announce to all my respectable neighbors that Gordon MacQuarrie is going fishing again.

"Cock-a-doodle-doo," she mocks.

It's getting so I have to sneak away like one disgraced, and the earlier I get up the louder she crows. She sings out most derisively, and all I can do in return is laugh harshly when she goes out with her husband to play golf.

"Have a chew?" offered the amiable Mart, thrusting forward the lethal box.

Incidentally, in this connection, it might be well to set forth that there are people who chew snuff. They do not "take it" through the nostril, like George Washington did, but plant the damp variety in the lower lip for several minutes or an hour, depending on the hardihood of the individual.

Within an hour we were parked and marching through the brush. We hit the stream at what is known as Big Lake, which is merely an enlargement of the river, perhaps two hundred yards across in the widest place. The variety of rapids and pools above Big Lake was my destination. It's no place for the automobile angler who looks for his fish twenty feet from the running-board. A dense growth of cedars and pines, with tangled roots, makes the going very difficult. Few go there except by boat, and it takes too long to get there in that fashion.

At the head of Big Lake the river comes roaring into it down a narrow rapids. The chute of water is almost covered with a natural tree archway, and the strength of the fast water carries the flow at quite a pace far out into the still waters of the "lake." The pools on each side of this spearhead of fast water in the "lake" are those foam and bubble-covered places where fish lie in wait for food. When they aren't right in the current, fighting for the river's gifts, they'll be back in the pools or just at the edge.

It had been quite a walk to get to that spot and it looked good to Mart. He sat down on a rock and took out his snuff box.

"Here's where I fish," he announced.

"But you ought to try the water up above as well," I suggested.

"Too hot," said the perspiring piscator, and he commenced the business of setting up his rod.

"If there are any fish in this part of the river, they're right around here. I've got a hundred yards of good fishing. That's enough for any common old wormer like me."

I looked at my watch. It was a little after seven. "I'll be back here at eleven for those cigars," I boasted.

At the top of the rapids dashing into Big Lake I hooked two small rainbows and let them worry off. They were about six inches long, and every time I hook one like that I marvel anew at their pugnacity. In fast water they can make a five-ounce rod feel as though it were really going to work.

How those bantam-weight rainbows rare and tear, and what fierce energy they exhibit in their lightning leaps! There is something ridiculously heroic in those desperate baby trout, giving promise of what they will do a few years later.

I worked the river carefully, but in spite of my deliberate and careful efforts there was nothing doing; so I disassembled rod and rig for a plunge into the jungle on the right bank of the stream. I knew a place—several, in fact. The difficulty lay in the fact there is no path along the river at this point—and perhaps that is in the river's favor.

The day was stifling hot, and by the time I began the trek through the woods the sun beat down unmercifully. With heavy waders and wading brogues and a flannel shirt which I had donned, coward that I am, in the cool of the morning, I messed my way through the tangle. You who have been there know what it is like. Not three feet of level ground for a single normal step forward. Deadfalls ten feet high. Slithery damp bark of fallen trees and everywhere the gnarled knees of cedar roots. The labor is terribly exhausting.

To anyone who has never understood where the water from a spring-fed river comes from, such a walk is educational. The bank teems with springs, and I should not like to fall into some of the soggier spots. A treacherous, quaking growth of moss and greenstuff covers many of these places, and the job of pulling one's foot out of the soft spots is not an easy one.

I had not gone one hundred yards before perspiration was getting into my eyes and my waders were as wet inside as out. Of course, one might discard waders on such a trip, but the discomfort of fishing the Brule, even after prolonged heat spells, without waders is not to be tolerated. I know anglers who do it, and they can have their rheumatism. On most streams it is feasible. On the Brule it's foolish.

I worked upstream for about a mile. Most of the time I was on the bank, but occasionally returned to the river to cool off and renew my courage. My goal was a certain place where the river widened, then narrowed farther upstream a bit. The narrows emptied into a long, deep pool; and when I finally got there, I was farther away from Mart and his snuff-box than I cared to contemplate, knowing that I had to go back the same way. But I had staked all on that pool.

19: The chute of water is almost covered with a tree archway

A Hare's Ear, the fuzzy modesty of which has always appealed to me as a good all-

89

round buggy-looking fly, graced the end of a dry-fly leader, but the fly was without oil to make it float. My first casts were for the purpose of giving myself a rest and getting the feel of the rod, but a 10-inch brown seized the Hare's Ear on about the fourth toss.

A 10-inch brown! I can see the contemptuous grin of some of my angling contemporaries. But don't confuse those Brule browns with their tamer brethren who manage to thrive so well in much warmer water. These boys don't live with the rainbows for nothing. They've got to fight to live. As one angler remarked to me after landing a medium-sized brown, "The fish in this water have to keep moving, or they'll freeze to death!" Which is a bit exaggerated but covers the point.

The little brown fought under water with the dogged determination of a rainbow. He shoved his nose toward the bottom of the deep pool and explored it for a convenient rock to hide beneath. He tried to run between my legs on a downstream dash and nearly did, but I finally netted him and was glad when I scooped his spotted honor out of the water. And I might go farther in talking about "10-inch browns from the Brule." If anyone is interested in the other side of it and has first-hand knowledge of these Brule Europeans, let him issue complaint papers and I'll file a brief with testimonials from every angler on the Brule. They are champions in their class.

The delicate leader was getting well-soaked and the Hare's Ear was drifting deeper and deeper as I advanced slowly into the pool, reaching every inch of it with the fly. Not twelve feet from where the first brown had been taken, a second one hit, and the submarine battle was re-enacted. The fish was perhaps an inch longer than the first. How good his round, solid body felt as I removed the fly and tapped him with the knife handle before creeling him! Still another brown, about the same size, took a fancy to the Hare's Ear. The pool was certainly delivering. In fifteen minutes' fishing I had landed three good fish, and I was beginning to feel sorry for Mart.

Every fisherman's day has its Big Disappointment—the one moment we try to forget but can't, for days after. Mine came after I placed the Hare's Ear almost beneath an overhanging cedar. As I made the cast I looked down through the water to make sure of my footing and felt, rather than saw, a huge trout lunge at my fly.

Unnerved and unprepared, I jerked the fly away, and so established one more regret among my angling memories. There was simply a swirl and a sound of water suddenly broken as the big fish curved for the fly, then nothing more than slow drift of river and the dark green line bellying emptily downstream toward me. That kind of fish would not rise again, I knew, for a long time, although I tried him with everything available. Maybe he only weighed a pound, but his approach sounded like two, and I'm willing to remember him at three. That kind is in there. My! If I could have brought back that trout and laid it at Mart's feet!

A moment after, casting to forget, I hooked a good rainbow. Later he measured fifteen inches, but there's no use in reducing a rainbow's gallantry to mere mathematics. He took the fly and made two aerial take-offs before I joined the battle by taking in the slack line. Then he scampered out of the pool as fast as he could go, downstream, which pleased me, for I had designs on his cousins and uncles therein and hoped his disturbance would not frighten them to cover.

The straight-up leap of a rainbow, leaving his natural element for thin air, is one of the noblest acrobatics any fisherman ever sees. The pointed head and the carmine-striped side of this rainbow were as sharp as a knife against the dark water. How animated and beautiful a pool becomes when a fighting fish surges to its surface to do or die! The energy of the rainbow's leaps carried him a foot above the surface each time, and so powerful were they that there seemed to come a moment when, at the height of the ascent, he was immovable in the air.

Once I thought I had him ready to net and brought him to the surface, close to me. The sight of the net set off another charge of dynamite, and he shot downstream for thirty feet, then sulked, broadside to me. I could see him holding there, slowly weaving. The sun was bright on his red-ribboned side, and he found courage and strength to resist the pressure of the line for many more minutes before I brought him in.

I felt there must be one more hungry trout in that deep pool, and sure enough, two more, not so large as the rainbow but large enough to necessitate caution, fell victim to a Royal Coachman. The sun was getting stronger, and I was thinking of turning back, but I did not until I had worked another pool above, without result. They had apparently stopped feeding, and even a nameless brown fly, fished dry, that a dozen or more anglers hereabout are using with phenomenal results was ignored.

The trip back was lightened by my selfish hope that the redoubtable stereotyper had fared poorly at Big Lake. Those six fish in my creel did not weigh much, nor did I feel like a fish hog, but something told me they were sufficient to win. I felt that worms on such a day, with plenty of food of similar kind in the water, would not be unduly attractive.

I knew Mart was a most efficient worm fisherman, that he practiced his art with all the careful attention to detail that it deserves, and even bribed his small son to keep an angleworm ranch for him in his back yard, where he placed captured wild worms and tamed them for the hook. He put them all through a rigorous training before taking them out, and I have heard him discussing, with furrowed brow, the relative merits of coffee grounds, and corn meal soaked in sour milk, as angleworm training fodder! I almost forgot the heat and the windfalls on that return trip, in evil anticipation of the forthcoming denouement.

As I rounded the bend there was Mart, sitting on the same rock. He turned a sun-burnt face toward me and grinned. It was Mart's give-away grin, after I've caught him telling whoppers.

"I know the worst," said Mart. "How many?"

"Just six, but I fought for 'em and I'd get six more if we could hang around for the rest of the day. You must have got something, Mart."

"Honest, I haven't the heart to lie. You know how it would ordinarily be."

"Sure, I know."

"I threw salmon eggs and angleworms and every combination of both with spinners and never got a nibble."

"Not a strike?"

"Not one."

"Not a single peewee fish?"

"That's right; rub it in—rub it in good all over. Here I take you fishing and get skunked and holler 'nough, and you pour it on."

"I love to pour it on, Mart."

That might be the end of the story, and it might have been a darned sight more dramatic if Mart had caught those fourteen trout.

But it just didn't happen. There he was, troutless, licked, skinned, and I don't know but that Mart got a bigger kick out of it all than I did. He's usually happy because he's alive and able to go fishing, and he has shared my joys and disappointments on trips before. He is, I would say, the most efficient and estimable liar I know, and I wouldn't trade him for a dozen good fly-fishermen.

Homeward bound, Mart turned to me. "What kind of cigars do you smoke?"

"Forget about the cigars," I replied. "Buy yourself a couple of good flies and say—pass the snuff box. I feel like I could stand a chew today."

Roy McMinn was an important person both in Superior and in the lakes community of Barnes, Wisconsin. In Superior he began with burlesque theater, and got in on the ground floor when silent movies were introduced. As manager and president of Capitol Amusement Company, he built the spectacular Capitol Theater, the first to show talking Hollywood movies. Later in life he spent a lot of time at his cabin on Upper Eau Claire Lake in Barnes and in the 1970s he was the Chairmen of the Board of Supervisors and town constable. This is Mac's only magazine story about McMinn (perhaps the only time he was brave enough to accompany him!) MacQuarrie did feature the McMinns in a Milwaukee Journal *column on June 6, 1948, "Progress Seems To Be Here To Stay." This column can be found in* Dogs, Drink *and other* Drivel. *An excerpt from that story relates back to this trip.*

Out on the porch, Roy got reminiscent:

"Y' remember that night out of Red Cliff in the old canoe when we ran into the pound net. . . and the fog so thick we couldn't catch the lighthouses. . . and we slep' on the beach across from Oak island and the mosquitoes got to work and you swelled up like a poisoned pup. . . and next day over the 'hump' off Devil's island we got into those lakers with a McMahon spoon. . . and a line squall come up and we beat it back to mainland with all the seagulls in the Apostle islands following us?:

I remembered."

Ol' Greeny

Field and Stream, June 1933

Fishing for big lake trout in Lake Superior

One of the privileges of living in Superior, Wisconsin, is that one can throw open bedroom windows and drift to sleep with the distant music of Lake Superior in his ears. The melancholy music of Ol' Greeny on Wisconsin and Minnesota points, rising and falling with the whim of the wind, has become so much a part of the city that hundreds of its oldest citizens think no more of it than they do of the distant rattling of a street car. Indeed, many of them, if asked about the persistent overtone that fills the night air, might answer that they did not know what it was. It's part of them, and like healthy humans they throw open their windows, gulp in the cleansed ozone swept to them over six hundred miles of the world's purest water, and let it go at that.

Superiorites have a healthy respect for Ol' Greeny. They know the lake well. They have seen it suddenly change from millpond placidity to an angry maelstrom of waves within a few minutes. They know it can lift 600-foot steel lake freighters like chips and batter them to pieces. They saw it, in November, 1905, smash the steamer *Matafa* and its crew to death within sight and sound of the main street of Duluth, and every autumn they read with horror of the disappearance of such ships as the *Kamloops*, the *North Star* and scores of others.

This brings me to the subject of Roy McMinn and the Apostle Islands, where we went in a 17-foot canoe to troll for lake trout. I was scared, that night at Red Cliff Bay, when the intrepid Roy backed his car into a corner of a field, launched the canoe and declared in a loud, unafraid voice that we were going to make Oak Island that night. I counseled a camp on the shore until morning, but Roy would not have it. He was all for getting to Oak Island so that we could start fishing the first thing in the morning. The lake was smooth as glass, but it was unbelievably dark and to me there was something sinister in the phosphorescent glow as the kicker shot us out into Raspberry Bay.

Trips that start badly sometimes end well, I consoled myself. It was about midnight, and we had made the 75-mile trip from Superior over a road made treacherous by the heaviest rainfall of the season. We should have arrived before dark, but the road cut our speed greatly. The keeper of the Red Cliff Bay Club shouted to us from his porch to avoid the pound nets, pick up the gas buoy on our left and then run for Raspberry Light. Within twenty minutes we were out in the bay, and the stabbing light of the buoy came into view. It seemed to take us hours to reach the buoy light, and after we passed it there was nothing ahead but—well, just nothing.

The water streaked away from the prow in hissing little waves. Conversation was awkward with the roar of the twin motor in our ears. We did catch one or two glimmers in the distance, where Raspberry Light should have been, and confidence rose within me. Roy pronounced it Raspberry Light, and we sped on.

But Raspberry Light failed to materialize. What had been a pin of light had been swallowed in the lake. Did that bother Roy? It did not! When the shore—the good old shore—on our left began to fade, I seized the big flashlight and turned it on. I just had to have light.

20: Here's proof that we got two big ones

Then we both got the biggest surprise of the trip! A fog so thick as to be almost impenetrable had descended without our realizing it. The shaft cast by our torch was only a milky ray of fog.

It was easier to see the dim shore-line without the light; so I snapped it off. Roy persisted in his hunt for Raspberry Light; but when the fog became so heavy that it felt like rain on our faces, he turned landward and was surprised when its prow touched shore so soon.

"I didn't think the fog was so thick," he said, once on land.

"You didn't even know there was a fog until I turned on the light," I accused my brave navigator.

"Neither did you," he retaliated, and laughed long and loud.

"And if you had kept on for a couple hours, as you intended, we'd be somewhere out on Lake Superior."

"That's all right," answered my seafaring friend. "We've got fifteen gallons of gas and two motors."

We made a hasty camp.

"This must be Frog Bay we've landed in," said Roy drowsily as we drifted off to sleep.

I reached over and patted the ground-cloth of the tent and murmured, "Good old Frog Bay."

I've got to be careful in this narrative, which is supposed to be a fishing story, and not tell too much about Roy. Not that he would mind. He minds nothing—absolutely nothing. He's the hardest-boiled fisherman I know, and I know quite a few. Nothing of the braggart about him—just a nerveless tough guy who'll try anything to get at some good fishing. When one goes fishing with Roy, one goes fishing in a big way. It has always been my idea to smooth it when I go a-fishing, but Roy just looks around for trouble. If things come too easy, he sees to it that there's an adventure. Strenuous companion for a fellow like me.

Four years ago a friend told him he ought to have a hobby, and he picked fishing. He bought everything he needed right off. Perhaps he is the best accoutered lake fisherman in Wisconsin. But he wanted something more in fishing than just catching a lot of fish. He found he could get a thrill or two out of it by toying with Lake Superior up around Isle Royale and on some of the bigger inland lakes along the Minnesota-Canadian border.

Roy ducks off for the north every so often, sometimes alone when he can't get Al Yeager to go with him. Al is really a brave man, but he won't try some of the stunts Roy suggests. Last spring Roy spent two solid weeks cruising the border lakes and going in with two guides away off the beaten track. According to Al, Roy was showing the guides the way around before he got through. I extend hearty sympathy to the guides.

We turned out at 5:00 A.M., cooked breakfast as the fog kept rolling landward in yellow, billowing clouds, and were off for somewhere at six o'clock. Roy had a chart of the islands in an aluminum rod case, and he would take this out and look at it about every twenty minutes, smile wisely and give the outboard motor a little more gas.

It had been calm in Frog Bay, but out in the channel, between the mainland and Oak Island, it began to roughen. Roy's canoe is a 17-footer with sponsons and square stern. I still marvel at its ability to travel in the trough of the waves. We had about two hundred pounds of duffle, including the extra kicker for trolling at a slower speed. The weight seemed to make little difference to the boat. Islands loomed up out of the fog on all sides as we sped along. I hadn't the remotest idea where we were going, but Roy had his compass and chart and was just having loads of fun.

After passing the lee of an island, which we had only glimpsed as the fog lifted for a moment, we found the waves higher. They were coming at us ten feet high, I estimated. Roy himself grudgingly admitted seven and a half feet that night. We were taking them almost sideways, heading for an island. Half the time the motor was out of water, but in the presence of Roy's phlegmatic demeanor I couldn't very well protest. Anyway, it was too late for that. We had to make the island. And we did, but Roy confessed, as we hauled into a little dock, that he didn't know what island it was.

When Captain Christiansen, the light keeper at the other end of the island, told us that we had landed on Devil's Island, the outermost of the Apostle group, Roy let go another peal of laughter. "I didn't think we had come this far," he roared. "Boy, what do you think of that for navigating in a fog?"

I was beginning to have my doubts about Roy's sanity, but found later that was just his idea of a good time. We visited awhile with the genial captain and proceeded to our fishing.

The breeze died about 10:00 A.M., and we fastened on the little kicker, rigged up trolling equipment and proceeded to make a circuit of the island. The natives on the mainland had told us to try for lake trout in about forty feet of water, and two little trout of about four pounds each were taken that way.

I was using an ordinary bass rig, with a Pacific trolling spoon. The spoon was down no more than ten feet when I caught my first fish. Roy's outfit was down much deeper, as he was using a braided copper line.

After a lunch at noon we set forth again, heading for Outer Island. From Devil's Island it looks to be about two miles away. I suppose it really is about seven, and when we were halfway across it began to blow again. Suddenly, without warning, there was a wind and we were running with it. I made a few choice complaints to Roy. Finally the wind got so bad that he put on the big motor and turned back, so as to get under the lee of Devil's Island. I think I told him, among other things, that the rocky soil of Devil's Island was very firm, very solid, very immovable—an excellent place to be when the wind blew. He just laughed his hearty laugh and told about the time he took the same little canoe across the lake from the mainland at Grand Marais to Isle Royale.

"And the old Scotch fisherman said, 'Show me the canoe,'" laughed Roy, "and I showed it to him and he said, 'Not for $10,000 would I do that!'"

Now I knew he was plumb crazy, but I resolved to make the best of it. That afternoon we trolled about the island, going down not too deeply, but caught nary a fish. Toward evening we made supper on a huge ledge of rock, cooked one of our trout and watched the big lake steamers passing, far out. It was a beautiful evening of reds and purples and green lake stretching everywhere. Too bad the Government did not act favorably upon the move to make the Apostle group a national park. These islands are beautiful beyond compare.

That night we were stretched out on Captain Christiansen's dock, under blankets, with the cool night wind blowing over our faces. We talked until the stars winked us to sleep.

"We've got to go down for 'em today," said Roy as we rolled out the next morning. "No more fooling in the shallow water. I think the natives are wrong. The big ones are leaving the shallow water."

"And that means Outer Island?"

"Sure."

And so we went. I had the jitters, of course, after the rough crossing to Devil's Island that morning, but the lake was flat. There were boats everywhere—but bigger ones than ours—trolling for the ubiquitous lake trout. I was always looking for a smaller boat than ours, or one just as small. It would have made me feel better. Misery loves company. Everything was packed into the canoe. Roy always did that, he said, so that if we were cast ashore some of the duffle might float in and we could maybe salvage enough to live on until help came. It was getting along toward noon, when we were scheduled to start back, before we reached the magic spot.

When we were about four miles off Devil's Island, I exchanged the bass outfit with heavy sinkers for an unbraided copper line. Our trolling speed was about three miles per hour. I must have had about two hundred yards of line out, and we estimated it was getting down about a hundred feet.

Suddenly the rod was nearly jerked from my hand. The Pacific spoon had found something down there. And that something was making a great commotion. Roy stopped the motor as I pumped the fish in. It was slow work. The fish did not seem heavy, but was very active for a lake trout.

We caught our first glimpse of my fish when it was directly below the boat—a greenish, twisting form in the clear water. About twenty-five feet down it was, shaking and bulldogging the spoon. As it came nearer the surface we saw that it was wrapped in the copper line. We gaffed it—a 10-pounder, the first good one of the trip. I was jubilant. It had been years since I had caught a lake trout.

Roy swung into action next. His fish was a good one, and a much harder battle ensued. It made several long runs and looked like a whopper as Roy slowly worked it upward through that green stairway of water.

Lake trout are not the fighters that other members of the trout family are. Everyone knows that. But they do battle, in their own way. They're sulky and whimsical. Sometimes a 10-pounder will outfight a 20-pounder. They are capable of long, fast runs, and pound for pound I would put them just about on a par with a northern pike. I have the impression that both the pike and the trout have one thing in common—they don't know their own strength, which is evidenced by the way they give up completely and then return to the fight with terrific energy just when one is beginning to think it is all over. What they lack is brains, not strength. If they used the tactics of a rainbow, they would be terrific fighters.

As to eating qualities, no fish that swims inland waters is sweeter or more tasty than a Lake Superior trout. All of them taste the same, not fishy, though they are sometimes very fat. Their flesh is firm. Slices of lake trout, fried properly in deep fat, not just scorched in a frying pan, will rival any fish on the table.

The third big fish was mine. He hit the same old Pacific spoon with a solid wrench and took out line immediately. I had a real tussle with him and had to resort to ocean fishing tactics to bring him in, alternately pumping and reeling until he was alongside. It was near noon. We had found the .right spot and felt we could have caught an unlimited number if we wished, but we had about as much meat as though we had gone out and killed a deer; so we pulled out for home.

But Ol' Greeny was not through with us yet. While we were intent on our fishing it had grown cloudy. A gentle rain on the water drew our attention to the weather. In the excitement of fishing we had been quite unmindful of it. Roy had some idea about continuing on to Outer Island, even while we exchanged motors for the trip back, but I changed his mind for him. The fact is, he would have gone home right then and there even if I had been forced to bean him with an oar. Yes, Roy carries oars, too. He has in mind a trip across Lake Superior in his canoe and is fitted out with everything.

It did not rain heavily, just a little tapping rain that made the water even smoother, and we had put a couple miles behind us before anything happened. Devil's Island was getting pretty small, but we were still miles from Oak Island when a sudden gust of wind, like a blast from a furnace, ripped across the water and whipped Roy's hat off.

The hot wind, from a perfect calm, smelled funny, even to Roy. It raised a little chop—nothing serious—but it was spooky, if you get what I mean. True, it was a land wind, and that explained its heat, but it wasn't a nice thing to encounter all of a sudden. The clouds were heavier in the west, from which direction the wind had come; so Roy hauled in to Oak Island, where we had the last meal of the trip. After feeding the gulls and otherwise appreciating the solid comforts of land underfoot, we set out again. It wasn't bad until we rounded Oak Island and got into the channel between the island and the mainland—Raspberry Bay.

The wind blowing down the bay was piling up heavy waves, and we were taking them nose on. Everything was covered with a tarpaulin, and we both wore heavy coats. The thing is thrilling, I suppose, in something more substantial than a 17-foot canoe, and heavily loaded at that. I like spray in my face as well as anyone, but it feels better from the deck of a big, husky tug that knows how to stick its chest out and let Ol' Greeny do her worst.

The actual dangers did not worry me. I knew what the boat could do. It was a remarkable performer. Away out of its own element, on a big, rough body of water, it had performed with uncanny stability. But there is something else about Lake Superior. It's fickle, and anything is liable to happen anytime. The thing that bothered me was not the rough weather we were encountering, but the rougher weather we might run into any minute. That's the difference between Roy and me. He doesn't worry much about the next minute as I do.

Running up Raspberry Bay, Roy informed me that he had taken out an extra insurance policy. "I always get one just before leaving on a trip," he said. "One of those short-term affairs."

I protested that he might at least have tipped me off so that I could offer a little more to the folks if anything happened. We hauled in safely at Red Cliff Bay, however, packed up, loaded the canoe on the trailer and made the trip back to Superior in two hours flat. While roaring along state highway No. 13 (it's the crookedest road in Wisconsin) at sixty-five miles per hour, Roy turned to me and remarked, "We could make some real time if that trailer weren't hooked on behind."

I just hung on and said nothing. Home was getting closer.

We drew up in front of my house, and I grabbed my duffle to depart.

"Say," said Roy, "I'm going to Houghton, Michigan, next Friday and ride an airplane from there to Isle Royale. Fish around the island and then fly back to Houghton. Friend of mine up there has an old plane he thinks can make it."

"Roy," said I, "I'm going to church next Sunday and can't go with you."

If you have read "Man Friday Folds Up" in MacQuarrie Miscellany, *you know of the long drive home from Red Lake, Minnesota in 14 inches of snow, that resulted in Mac's weariness. The* Saskatoon Star Phoenix *and the* Milwaukee Journal *ran stories on October 24 and 25, 1933 about 12 to 14 inches of snow from scores of Canadian cities down to Duluth.*

Big Ben Klugherz was a six- footer and 220 pounds. He was born in 1892, eight years before MacQuarrie. His profession was a buyer for a dry goods store. This is the only magazine article to feature him, but he and that long drive home showed up a few times in the Milwaukee Journal *columns.*

Back in There

Outdoor Life, August 1934

Pothole Shooting in Upper Minnesota

I fish but to float flies. Without going too deeply into what might be a painful subject, I will admit there is some truth in that. People who don't like it will have to put up with it. Likewise, I confess one of the impelling things that drives me out after ducks on cold mornings is the fun of seeing the sun rise. All this I freely concede despite the fact that this world holds no sweeter joy to me than a warm bed at the uncouth hour of 4 a.m.

So you will know why I went with Ben and Max. I am no He-Hunter but the call of the flesh was too, too strong. I catch few limit creels of fish and fewer limit bags of ducks, but I went. It is good for the soul to go and sate the hunter's appetite in some faraway Valhalla where the ducks are as the sands on the seashore. Ben knew about it. He and Max both told me about it, with a faraway look in their eyes. A 240-mile drive over treacherous roads through a storm that left an even foot of snow behind brought us to the place—Red Lake, Minnesota, which you can find on a map and which will surprise you by its size.

Ben, who is so big he looms wherever he goes, got out of the car at Red Lake and shook himself like a tired airedale. It had been a long, hard ride but Archie Gwinn, confederate to a hundred duck hunters, warmed us all with a meal and off we went, with an Indian guide.

"Just wait till you see these ducks," chuckled Ben. "Will we give 'em the old mountain music this morning! Well, I should say. Boys, this is where all the ducks in the world come in October."

It was pothole shooting. We walked or drove into potholes back in from the big lake. They are all small, all filled with celery, water lily roots, pickerel weed and whatnot. The first pothole bore not a duck. Ben was mildly surprised. The second showed a lone bluebill on its surface. Ben scratched his chin. The third pothole was bare. Ben said "What the heck?" to the Indian guide. The Indian guide said nothing. To make a long story short, there was hardly a duck in any one of ten potholes we visited. Ben, who had promised us ducks in any number, shrank visibly from sight. He was on the verge of tears. The upshot of it was we picked out one pothole, set decoys in it, and slew a bare half dozen ducks in the course of a day's shooting.

Mark, now, the true spirit of the duck hunter. Ben, the most completely disappointed and demoralized duck hunter I ever saw, went to bed that night in Archie Gwinn's cabin muttering to himself and there was none there who did not lend him a word of cheer. His "mountain music" had failed to materialize but, as Gwinn said, "If it blows off the lake in the morning, you'll see a flight."

21: We had no boat and it was a job getting decoys out- as well as in

It blew. It blew ducks—so many the thought of enumerating them bewilders me. Potholes which, the day before, were glassy under October's gray clouds, kicked up their heels in little wavelets in welcome to the myriads of ducks that poured in. Ben's first glance at a feather-covered hole brought him back to a divine state of animation in which his beaming smile seemed a very wreath of joy. He plumped down his shell box, all oblivious to Max and me, gazed thankfully into the blue, where darting thousands of ducks were pouting at being chased from their breakfast.

Ah, Ben! Ah, rare Ben Klugherz, to paraphrase someone or other: I think that as you stood there that morning you represented the grand apotheosis of all that is praiseworthy in a duck hunter. Some day, when the medals are being stricken off and all the fellows are standing in line waiting for theirs, I hope the Maker of Medals strikes off one of gold for you. On one side a hurtling duck and on the other simply "The Old Mountain Music."

Ben remained there. Max and I, guided by the Indian, were headed in farther back, and as we topped a rise we looked back to see Ben knock down two with one shot. He was 200 yards away but his great voice boomed across the snow-covered jack pine country like a foghorn: "It's the old mountain music, boys."

It's queer duck hunting up there. It lacks some of the savor and wishful expectancy of tamer hunting, and there is an absence of dearly beloved duck hunting trappings that grieves me, but it is sensational, withal. If the ducks are coming right, as they were that day, with the wind chasing them in off the big lake, there is no need for decoys. You simply stand on a point of vantage, behind a blind of a bush or two, and wait your chances as the ducks come by you, over you, back of you, straight at you. You pass up many— thousands. You get hundreds and hundreds of shots, at every possible angle. Later you learn to drop them coming over the land so they may be retrieved, as we were without a dog or boat.

You see how it is? Just out duck hunting, that's all. I had heard of the place for years but had never believed it could be true until I saw it. Nor do I want it for a steady diet, but as a place to make a dream come true, to satisfy a whetted hunter's appetite, I challenge anyone in these United States to find a better place outside of some baited clubs.

Back in there among those potholes, mallards land in your decoys. Bluebills cannot be driven from those succulent bottomed ponds. Teal, shovelers, redheads and canvasback show no more caution, plunging by you as you stand quietly on the shore, in full view, if you have no time to get behind your little blind. It is explained by the fact that most of the ducks there are perhaps fresh from the north, or are bred right there. The Indians of the region do not kill them. Shells are too expensive for ducks as a shell costing the same will bring down a deer.

The country is a typical barren land in many places, covered with jack pine and scrub oak. The potholes, those calling cards of the last glacier, support an abundance of plant life. The Indian guides—a necessity according to law as we hunted on Red Lake reservation— are the finest you can find. They are big and strong, clean-limbed fellows with none of the taciturnity generally accredited to the Indian. I wish you could have seen our guide grab an 80-pound sack of decoys in one hand, an axe and shell box in the other, and stride off through the brush for a lake a mile in. I am good at guessing weights, usually. I ventured he weighed 165 pounds. He smiled. "No, 195." Fellows like that explain Jim Thorpe.

I cannot pass an opportunity to praise these people. They are genuine folks, living in the tidy little town of Red Lake or on their farms and while I did not get a chance to meet the superintendent of the reservation, it must be recorded he has done a noble work and lives among a people who appreciate him. There is nothing fancy about Red Lake. Little effort is made to attract hunters or fishermen. Still a good many know about Red Lake. Few talk much about it. They want Red Lake for themselves. One can hardly blame them. I asked Archie Gwinn, our host, if there was any trout fishing in the vicinity. "Golly, I suppose so," said Archie, with none of the press agentry of the resort owner. "I never bother about 'em, but the Indian kids go down to the river and catch them with their hands!" I believe that.

There is a school of hunters and fishermen who refrain from mentioning, specifically, the places where they hunt or fish, with the idea that too many will be attracted to their favorite spots. That may be all right, within limits, but I have not very much time for the average, run-of-the-mill bird who keeps such secrets. The truth is his secrets aren't much anyway and I feel that such conniving is not at all in keeping with the true spirit of hunting or fishing. I may be wrong about this. But I don't like the secretive method and I like my stories about hunting and fishing to tell where and who and how to get there, else I'm likely to brand brother angler as a selfish fraud.

With Ben back on Pothole No. 457½, from whence we heard a constant concert of "mountain music," played on the slide trombone Mr. Winchester makes, Max and I located behind an utterly inadequate blind, but later learned a blind was not necessary. Bluebills, redheads, canvasbacks made up the motley congress that swarmed into the pothole. They rose from the place in long streaking masses. A couple of thousand ducks milled away from us as we were sticking up our joke blind. They did not leave the pothole.

It was hard to believe. Yesterday these same potholes were as barren as the Sahara. Today they teemed with waterfowl. The leaden sky in every direction was constantly covered with a tracery of flying ducks—whirling, dashing flocks flitting restlessly from one pothole to another.

My first choice was a husky drake bluebill. They call them "Northern bluebills" up here but I think they are all lesser scaup. (Incidentally, will someone step forward and explain what kind of a bluebill is the drake with both purple and green sheen in his head feathers? The greater scaup is supposed to flaunt the green overcast while the lesser scaup is supposed to have a purplish cast in his head. In all truth, I have never seen a drake bluebill in this region that did not possess both these colors in his head feathers. Hybrids, maybe, but it doesn't stand to reason there are so many hybrids.)

My first bluebill was downed but another, ten feet behind him took a dive into the snow. The No. 6s were spreading—or maybe those ducks were just spreading themselves. We retrieved them both instantly as it would have been hard to locate them in the foot-deep snow later. Such ducks. Heavy-bodied, fat as domestic fowl with their lush diet in the potholes, they represented the typical leaden-weighted bluebill of the North, as heavy for their inches as any bird that flies. Max could hardly believe it. He had found only five shy birds on that same hole the previous day. Today it was impossible to drive them out of the coontails, celery and water lily roots they were feasting on.

Shooting such as this does not happen often. A good shot could have killed any number. These ducks seemed to have little fear of man. How different they were from the ducks hunted 200 or 300 miles south, after they have run the gauntlet of 12 gauges.

To those who have shot over decoys in heavily-hunted country, where most of the shooting has been at twenty-five to thirty-five yards, there is a distinct thrill in taking a chance on ducks that climb up to fifty or even sixty yards in the air. You can afford to take chances under such conditions. If you miss, another bunch is coming along right behind them. For the first time in my life I had a thorough appreciation of the terrific efficiency of modern shotgun loads. Decoy shooting, where ducks are not many, serves to develop over-cautiousness. A half hour on the shore of this pothole and that was all forgotten. Let 'em come and lead 'em twice as much. That was the order of the day and while we missed many, there were also many that dove into the snow where kicking feet betrayed their presence.

It was luxurious shooting. A drake mallard, alone, wheeled with mallard dignity down the middle of the pothole, saw our decoys sitting timidly on the edge of the boggy hole and came over high, almost out of range. He was almost directly over us when Max stood up. Before Max had fired the gun he almost fell over backwards but the carry-through was perfect and at the shot the greenhead collapsed and came hissing earthward. He dropped not twenty feet from the blind with a dead "plump." Stretched out in the blind, we wondered if he would weigh four pounds. He was huge but we had little chance for speculation.

The parade of ducks continued. There seemed no end to it. We sat immovable on the shore and would come to the alert only when we heard the searing rush of speeding wings signaling the passage of a flock. Then it was time enough to locate the birds and get up for a shot when they came over behind us.

There is a thrill in stopping a hurtling duck that decoy shooting cannot match. Your bird is picked out when the flock is perhaps 200 yards away. You trail the chosen victim carefully and at the proper moment rise as smoothly as you can, without taking your eye from the duck. At the moment you stand the ducks are likely to break the order of their flight and flare sharply to one side. Then it is one feels the impotence of his position—standing there with a gun whose shot knows no swerving drive such as the ducks. How insignificant, how trivial one feels as they roar over at sixty miles an hour, their wings slashing the wind, their white breasts defiant before wavering tubes of steel.

Your bird has shoved his helm hard over and is cutting swiftly to the left, presenting you with a pretty problem in quick geometry. You raise the tubes a mite more, sweep them across the fanning wings of the scudding bird, pull ahead—oh, a long ways— keep the pull in line with the duck, and touch off the trigger. If your sweeping drag across the flight of the duck was smooth, sure, if you were relaxed and your gun still moving when you squeezed off the trigger, you have likely killed your bird. If not, if you jerked the trigger and knew when you jerked it, if you varied the lead from the plane of flight, then you failed, and you knew, almost the minute you shot, that you had failed. That kind of shooting makes you realize how unimportant is the trigger finger. The trigger finger becomes merely a little valve down at the end of your arm that the mind opens after the shoulder and arms, coordinated with the eye, have carried the barrels up to the right spot.

Head-on ducks, birds that have baffled me consistently, offered opportunity for putting it on them, carrying through overhead, sometimes shooting at a duck that was completely blotted out by the rising barrels. Those are the most satisfactory shots. At least they are to me, and while I am a mediocre shooter, with incomers toughest the plenitude of birds that day seemed to rend a confidence that I never before possessed. The taut nerves so customary in more limited shooting areas were entirely absent.

The "piece of the flight" we saw that day gave evidence of the tremendous breeding ground for ducks that is northern Minnesota. Pessimistic reports from the governments of both the United States and Canada, coupled with tales of ducks dying by the thousands because of the drought, were hard to believe. It is possible we saw only a concentration of ducks, but opinions from others in the Northwest that are coming in bear out the belief that the North has once more found a place for its wild ones to breed.

Until you have seen the upper part of Minnesota you can have no conception of the hundreds of square miles of swampy, rivery, breeding territory the state offers to the ducks. And a week after our trip to Red Lake we were informed the flight there was even greater than when we were there. The same story came from all along the line, starting at Winnipeg, where ducks in unlooked for numbers converge upon hunters fully prepared for a meager flight.

After we had taken our limit, picked up our wooden blocks and dragged them back to the car we went off to find how Ben was doing. He certainly was doing "awful good" in Max's own words. He was on the shore of pothole No. 457½. The once disconsolate sheepskin coat he now wore like a cavalier. There was an extra dent in his hat and he just grinned when he saw us.

"How you doing, Ben?" I asked.

For answer Ben bent his features over the back-stage end of his pump gun, coolly picked out a greenhead from a flock of passers-by and turned to us, his face lit up like an angel's.

"The old mountain music, boys, the old mountain music!" he chuckled.

The members of the Old Duck Hunters Association, Inc. fished for small-mouths in "I'm After Bass Again" published in Field and Stream, *June 1935, and a year later, Mac published this account about fishing the exact same waters, but this time without Mr. President.*

I shared the photo of the St. Croix with my friend, local historian extraordinaire, Brian Finstad, assuming it had been taken from the Gordon fire tower. Here is his excited response:

"It's not the Fire Tower, but it's even better actually. It was taken from the spot that is now the "Chief Kabemabe Overlook." It's a scenic overlook above the spot that was Chief Kabemabe's village. It is between the Lookout Tavern and the Gordon Dam. Chief Kabemabe (spelled many ways- also Kabemappa) was the most significant chief of the Upper St. Croix and signed all of the major treaties except in 1854, as he died that year of smallpox. What makes this photo even better is that the area where his village site was, which was a large permanent village with gardens, a cemetery, and even a scalp pole (yikes), was flooded in the mid nineteenth century (very early) by the first logging dam at that site, and remained flooded until well into the 1900's. Then it would have only been drawn down for roughly a 20-year period before again being flooded by the modern Gordon Dam. This is the ONLY photo from that draw-down period. So, for 167 years, this is the one and only photo that one can see the village site in its natural state and understand where the river and creek channels were, how the shoreline boundaries contoured, etc. I would think if any archaeologists ever did work at this site, this photo would be an invaluable resource. Even without actual digging, it is extremely interesting to study just to understand the site. I was transfixed when I first saw this."

Rascals of the Rice

Sports Afield, May 1936

Old Sam, the Chippewa from Odanah, wrinkled his mahogany face in a smile as he accepted a cigar. He pointed a paddle-gnarled hand out over the tawny wild rice of the St. Croix river flowage and said:

"You go catch all the bass you want. Leave bullheads for me."

"Are they better than bass, Sam?"

"Goo'ness yes," replied the Indian. "Catch 'em at night in deep holes—big ones. Skin um, fry um. Better'n bass. Better'n trout. Better'n venison!"

My companion and I loaded our boat before pushing through the rice into the river and Sam called over the water as we poled out:

"You catch some bullheads mebbe you don't want?"

"You can have 'em if we do, Sam," I assured.

"You bring in four, five, I see you get some good wild rice."

"It's a deal."

He waved farewell, a wonderful figure of an Indian over 70, with strength undiminished and eyes snappy. With him camped on the flowage bank were his smiling wife and "Little Sam" who is really bigger than his father. All the way from the Odanah reservation they had come to harvest the bountiful rice of the St. Croix flowage. Thousands of acres of rice stretched away on three sides of his camp, at a place called Stuckey's landing. Here he planned to garner from 600 to 1,000 pounds of the stuff, parch it and retail it at 35 cents a pound. One year, to Sam's great delight, it went up to 90 cents a pound.

Dennis and I pushed through the rice. That is, Dennis did the pushing while I set up a bass fly rod and a bait casting outfit. I was going to two-gun 'em that day and after trying it once have since wondered why I had never thought of it before as a settled method for small-mouths.

Through a tortuous channel in the bending rice we went. Small flocks of blue-winged teal permitted us to get within 25 yards at times. Thousands of red-winged blackbirds, packed so closely together their red spots gleamed strongly, wheeled and funneled in the early-September air. Occasional squads of black ducks and mallards jumped up before us from the rice and one lonesome wood duck, his questioning neck twisting from side to side, wheeled over the boat.

The lovely flowage, an eight-mile long by one-mile wide field of rice, one of the greatest stands of this grain in Wisconsin, beckoned us. What is there about such a swamp that attracts men? I had been trout fishing only a few days before and actually had the jitters from my trip during which I had cursed the nervousness of trout. These bass—they were pugnacious. They were audacious. They had guts. They were airedales. Trout are spaniels. I longed to hunt a scrapper that would let me throw hardware at him more than once. I did.

Down through the center of the flowage runs the St. Croix, a hundred feet wide in places with here and there side channels. The current averages about two miles an hour. The water is clear and cold, just out of amazing Lake St. Croix six miles away, a lake so surrounded by springs the town there has been named for them— Solon Springs.

It was one of those days. Not just a day but a blue September event with just a hint of crispness and autumn haze. A day when one may wear a flannel shirt and boots and stout pants and there's wool next the skin and boy, doesn't it feel good after a summer of sodden heat and sunbaked water!

All was right with the world that day. Back on the sand barrens Doc Smith, whose boat I was using, worked his pointers for the coming field trials. A dozen Indian families gathered their wild rice crops. More local mallards and black ducks than had been seen here in years wheeled over the sunny flowage. It was good to be alive—good, especially, to be going fishing for a fish that stood up to hardware and didn't get hysterics when a No. 12 instead of a No. 14 fly was floated over him.

I save the St. Croix flowage bass for the end of the season—for that interim between the end of trout fishing and the beginning of duck shooting. We passed a couple bait fishermen coming in through the rice. Nothing doing, they said—at least on bait. How about flies? "Gee, try 'em. The bass are boiling up all along the river."

As I .finished the job of fastening on a bass bug I thought of another follower of the flowage—Hale Byers, formerly solo saxophonist with Paul Whiteman, who had come to me with staring eyes only a few days previous to beseech, urge and command me to "get down there right now. The first frost has hit and the small-mouths are hitting flies like murder." Up from Detroit where he is program director of a radio station had come Hale to hold his annual rendezvous with the small-mouths. A finished artist with the bass rod, as he is with almost any musical instrument you can blow into, he and his partner had reveled in five days of unparalleled sport.

"Get down there," he had admonished, "before it gets too cold. They're just right now. Over their summer lethargy. The water is about 10 degrees colder and if you want to see ducks—say, I shot a hundred with my rod case!"

So you see why I had hustled down to the flowage.

Upstream from what is known as Stuckey's Point (almost an island) we went. Dennis, an ardent boatman with rare attainments as befits an Irishman, bent nobly to the oars. The barred-gray bass bug searched the edge of the rice beds—just where the tangled rice straw stops in its conquest of the deeper channel. I permitted the bug to float dead, as a dry fly. One small bass burbled it but spit it out and I was not sorry. I had seen him.

Another cast was a flop and the zooming bug fell in the middle of the river in front of the boat, with slack line draped between my feet. That bug was far from its goal near the rice. It slid backwards toward me about 10 feet while I retrieved line. Suddenly Dennis was frightened out of his wits as a fish plunged along the surface for a full six feet before smashing the bug, then made a twisting turn into deeper water. He untangled that slack line in a hurry!

"Damn it!" I said.

"Cripes!" shouted Dennis. "It's a shark!"

He let go the oars to extend his arms descriptively.

"No, just a nosey northern pike of about six pounds," I explained as calmly as I could with the rod vibrating in my hands. In about 10 seconds he'll saw off that leader and –oop! There goes 50 cents worth of bass bug!"

The trailing gut was stripped in while Dennis moaned. I was not disappointed. I know any northern over two pounds will knock the hell out of a gut leader before you can horse him.

"Do they always scare a fellow like that?" asked Dennis. "Heavens, that was a vicious-looking baby."

"Wait until I get hold of one with this bait rod and a wire leader. Then you'll see what they carry in their face for biting off leaders."

"My pulse is 'way up," he said.

We worked upstream to a place where one of the many channels runs into the main current with a somewhat faster flow than usual in the flowage. We circumvented the hole carefully and went above it, letting the boat drift against two dead snags while the current pressed against its upstream side and kept it in position. I know the place well. Hale Byers has sat there in a boat and taken many a limit without moving. A 10-foot deep hole, 20 yards in diameter, moving water coming in, dead snags in the bottom. A bass hole if I ever saw one.

Out went another bug. The first cast put it up into the current coming out of the side channel and it drifted down naturally into quieter water and then lay there dead. A mere dimple on the water— Dennis didn't see it—two seconds of waiting to let him have it and then strike! This one fought deep, ranging the pool in circles. I kept him as close to the surface as I dared, mindful of the underwater snags. In a few minutes he was in the net, a gasping, living thing of bronze and black, spines erect, red-rimmed eyes burning back at me through the net mesh as I held him up.

We waited to let things quiet down. Perhaps 15 minutes passed and I saw another underwater swirl. They were on the move again. I tried everything. Dead floating bug, twitching bug, jerked bug, wet flies that went deep, wet flies with a spinner. They'd look the stuff over, I could see by the bulgings, but wanted none of my feathers that time. I had one more darned good shot in my locker and used it forthwith. A pikie minnow on the short rod landed with a terrific splash in the center of the pool and was jerked suddenly backward toward me—not reeled—jerked, as though it had hit the water, seen the bass and wanted to get right out of there. It hadn't gone three feet when there was a bass on it.

What's the use of telling how they scrap after that first frost? What's the use of comparing them with trout? What's the use of going into the old "pound for pound and inch for inch" argument again? I simply say bass are bass and this baby was hooked just through the lip by a single spear and what he did to my nerves can never be equaled by anything they have at Coney Island. It was five minutes before he was between my feet in the boat, a black demon of a bullet, getting that plug as thoroughly wrapped in the meshes as he could before receiving the coup de grace.

Would Hale's hole produce another? Let's see. Feather minnow on a fly rod this time. No good. Put a little sinker a foot above the minnow and sink it. Twitch it in. There, he touched it! He's got it! He's on! Keep him out of those snags. Out of those snags! He's big. Oh, he's off—set the hook too soon. My old weakness after fishing for trout all summer.

"Might have been another northern," I said, to console Dennis. "He had that twisty jerk."

On the flowage you get so you can tell the difference. The long body of the northern gives him the power to exert a powerful, spring-like pressure on a rod. The small-mouth is likely to rush and then tug like a bulldog, with straight jerks. I worked the hole carefully, resting it, but no more came our way.

Upstream again, through a heavy weed growth and 50 yards ahead a bass rose on the edge of the rice. Dennis said he must have been scratching his back in the rice and blessed the Duke of Argyle for the bass's sake. But if he was doing that, it was nothing to the scratch he imparted to my feather minnow. I didn't want to move the boat too close to him. It was a long and difficult cast, calling for more skill than I could muster. I had to put the feather minnow over a mess of grass that had stuck to the deep log under which the bass might be hiding. I just couldn't do it. Four feet from the spot was the best I could do.

That bass solved my casting problem for me—ever hear of a trout doing that? He decided the chap throwing that tempting morsel was an unhandy person and made one tremendous surface rush of four feet. Out of water he was, for the whole distance, with spray flying two feet upward. I set the hook too fast—as who wouldn't when such a creature emerges from the water and comes toward one. He was on for maybe two seconds. Then I felt the single hook slide loose in two little jerks. Goodbye to him until next time. Anyway, I'll bet he had to see his dentist.

"Holy smokes!" said Dennis. That was all. I don't say that bass was big. I'll settle at two pounds. And that's plenty for those armored destroyers of the St. Croix. No fat in their carcasses. They get thin fighting it out with the current. I saw one last fall caught in the flowage that would have weighed seven pounds if taken in a lake. As it was he went only a little over five.

Downstream after that, with the bugs floating ahead of the boat—an excellent way. Just let it float at the same speed the boat is going. It'll cover a lot of territory. The boat became hung on an underwater snag and I reached for an oar to help push it off. From my right came a woosh! and a smash! He took it just where the water from Hale's deep hole began to shoal. Whoosh and smash! That's just the way they crack it. He wasn't so very big. Not two pounds but the 5½-ounce bamboo was bent like a rainbow as he did barrel rolls and jack knifes with it. No use. When they whoosh it and smash it they fasten onto something. He was mine and the little trout creel was getting heavier.

A period of drifting downstream with nothing but little northern pike—pounders, caught and returned to water. Snake 'em in quickly, those little fellows, before they get their saws working on the gut and you'll save your bugs. I changed to a small white bucktail, thinking to manipulate it just to see what they'd do. Nothing. Time passed. The sun mounted and we covered a mile of river. At the head of another hole on the left bank a small-mouth—the littlest of the day—had the bucktail, then floating dead, halfway into his stomach before I knew he was on.

It must have hurt him for he provided the supreme battle of the day. He deserted the familiar underwater haunts and took to topwater like a dog with a running fit. His compact little body smashed up and out and down with a slap on the surface entirely out of proportion to his size. When an angered *micropterus* hits the water coming down—writhing—it's like dropping a two-inch plank flatwise into the water. I couldn't see anything of the bucktail so knew he had it deep. He scrapped to the last ditch. When the net enfolded him he was practically dead. So die the gladiators of the St. Croix—with their boots on, so to speak.

And maybe I am to be shot at sunrise, and I have never found it possible to admit this before, but here goes: a bass has more courage in five minutes than a trout has in his whole lifetime. Give him a bow. He's got what it takes. Oh, I know I'll be tying No. 14's to 4X gut all next June and July but Brother Bass, in the Moxey department, is the champion.

Flowage fever held me fast in its grip all that day. It grew warmer and I unbuttoned my shirt to cool off a bit. Between 11 and about 4 p.m. the bass rested in their holes. Occasionally one would burble a bug but their hearts were not in it. Dennis and I pushed into the rice and let the September sun beat down as we lunched. Boatloads of Indians with rice straw ready for winnowing and parching passed us. Cheerful folks, those Indians. Some of them use a short little flat-bottomed boat of about 60 pounds weight, of light pine material that seems to possess all the qualities of a canvas canoe with even added ruggedness. They spread clean canvas in the bottom into which they beat the rice heads. Their boats for this job must be dry, otherwise the rice will be dampened.

Shortly after 4 we took to the river again, moving down through a series of holes. For variety in the feel of bait casting I changed from heavy to light plugs, then dug into the bottom of my kit for a strip of pork rind which was fastened to an Oriental wriggler. Incidentally, that bottle of pork rind, still half full of preservative and pigskin, has been with me since 1924—11 years. The manufacturers of that stuff are making it too good. Some of

119

those strips—all still as white as ever—have been attached to lures by me as many as a dozen times.

I sent one out into a left bank hole studded, beneath, I knew, with old dead stuff. The thing had wriggled its way almost back to the boat before a northern of about five pounds took it. Dennis saw him get it and said he never before had seen such a malignant apparition. Truly, the barracuda-like northern, trailing a lure underwater, then grabbing it and twisting his facile body as he goes back, is a fearsome and thrilling sight. All of the treachery and cunning of the underwater world seems embodied in these great marauders of the North.

I've seen 'em dash up out of a weed bed and grab a plug a few feet from the boat. At such times those cold, staring eyes seem to look right into mine. And once one did that, saw me, and didn't turn about but kept right on going, underneath the boat. Show yourself to a northern after he's hooked and the fun is doubled.

I returned him to the water and we moved into another hole—or to the edge of one. While working the hole a bass from almost beneath the boat smashed the pork rind twice. He failed to connect both times, but such action is added proof that our friend of the stickleback is not afraid of hardware or boats alike.

We worked slowly back upstream to the little channel that runs back into our landing place. The sun was reddening in the west and the ducks were beginning their evening prowl. Two owls began their mournful song somewhere out beyond the rice and the muskrats began slithering into the river from the rice, leaving silver wakes in their paths.

There we were, in the midst of one of the greatest limberlosts in the Northwest, a sun-drenched bottomland of fish and swamp life unequaled anywhere in Wisconsin—not even by the famous Horicon marsh. In a few months, five miles below where we sat in our boat, a 12-foot dam will be closed and the water will slowly back up to form eight-mile-long Lake Douglas. Off to our north a little more than a mile is the southern boundary of the field trial grounds of the Northern States Amateur Field Trial association, 22,000 acres of rolling upland closed to hunting for all time and producing hundreds of sharptails and pheasants upon which dogs may work. In the center of the tract in the only exclusively field-dog-trial clubhouse in the United States, built at a cost of $6,000 this summer as a rendezvous for years to, come of the hunting dog men and people of this North who have come to follow the dogs as they do amateur baseball.

Truly a wonderful country, with fascinating possibilities.

Eight miles from our boat, as the crow flies, was the head waters of the Brule, just north a half mile from Lake St. Croix, the source of the river St. Croix. Interspersed over this northwest corner of Wisconsin are scores of other lakes and rivers, and woods abounding with deer and other game. It was good to sit there and speculate upon the natural resources of my own home country. Good to reach over and heft a willow creel of such treasure as are black bass. Good to know that soon the frosts would fall and that, as the trees shimmered with silver in the morning I would be out somewhere in a duck blind. Good to know, too, the country was "going to bed wet" for the second successive year, after a four-year drought, with a total rainfall in the last 13 months of 46 inches!

All these things have little to do with bass fishing but they inevitably come into the mind of one like myself who feels an abiding love for the place where he was born. I hadn't meant to make this a sales talk for North Wisconsin. I'm afraid the editor will frown but these things well up inside and out they must come. To all men there is that sacred corner of the globe where the blazed trail of memory shines particularly bright. It may be in the Ozarks. For some the eastern shore of Maryland. To others the canebrakes of the south. For mine I'll take the sandy barrens of North Wisconsin, forever closed to extensive agriculture, tailor-made for recreation.

Back at the boat landing old Sam came down to meet us. In his teeth he still clenched the remains of my early morning cigar. On the ground near his tent lay a huge pile of rice straw, the fruit of the day's labor. Young Sam nodded from behind the parching fire he was tending and Mrs. Sam smiled a welcome in the dusk.

I had forgotten about the bullheads! Sam's face fell when I told him but he lighted up when I showed him my creelful of bass.

"Catch 'em on fly?" he asked.

"Fly and plug."

"Nice fish, pretty fish," said Sam. "Bullhead best, though." Then suddenly: "I get some tonight. I catch 'em all right."

I prepared to go, after loading the car. Sam emerged from the firelight with a lard pail in his hand.

"Got something for you," he said briefly.

The pail was filled to the brim with newly-made wild rice, the most delectable grain that grows. That four or five pounds of rice represented a lot of toil and effort. I handed him a dollar bill which he took, but seemed surprised.

"You come again before ricing is over and I'll show you how to catch bullhead."

"I'll do it, Sam," said I.

And I will—but if we catch any he can have 'em. Make mine bass, please, Sam.

The working title for the second book out of Barnes Area Historical Association was Dogs and Drink, David and Drivel. *Those of you who have read it already know a lot about David V. Nason. There's an entire chapter there on his exploits, including a Sunday feature article of this trip. I changed the title when I realized nobody would know who David was until they read the book, and some might think it referred to me.*

K-a-t Spells FISH

Field and Stream, November 1937

When it's lake trout and walleyes you're after

If you can't spell or pronounce Katimiagimak, don't worry about it; hereafter we'll refer to it as plain old Kat. It's a lake. But hold on! It isn't just another lake. It's a certain kind of lake—one of those geologic wonders that the last glacier had a big hand in making up in Canada when it scraped away the surface debris and got right down to igneous or fire-formed rock.

Well, let's get down to cases on old Kat. It's about sixteen miles east of famous Lake of the Woods. I don't know exactly how big it is, except that in Wisconsin it would be "figgered as a good-sized piece o'water," whereas in Canada it just makes a pin-prick on a big map.

Anyway, it's big and it's clear and you can look down into it for twenty feet and see the picture of royalty on a Canadian nickel. And it's studded with little islands that look like steamboats when the spruce trees stick out of 'em just so. And it's off the beaten trail and it's altogether lovely and worthwhile. Five of us had such a good time there that we hated to leave, even though a forest fire was threatening the trail leading out and it was high time we were moving along.

When a fellow has a yarn to spin, he always disposes of the essential background first. Not that the essential background in this case is anything to be sneezed at. It's just that stories about old Kat ought to bust right out like sky-rockets on Fourth of July night. Or they ought to pour out gently and serenely while one cozens a pipe in an ingle-nook and the winds of January swirl the snow over the roof-top.

We were five: Kenneth MacCleod and George (Big Jarge) Perkins, Canadian woodsmen; Irvin V. Maier, advertising manager of the *Milwaukee Journal*; David V. Nason, also of Milwaukee, who once stood off the Portuguese navy with a crate of overripe oranges, and the writer. Up through Wisconsin from Milwaukee we had come to Canada, like this: Wausau the first night; Superior at noon of the second day; Virginia, Minnesota, by 4 P.M.; then a certain camp on Sebascong Bay, Lake of the Woods, Canada, by 7 P.M., and right glad too, for we were hungry, especially Dave, who will eat anything that won't bite back at him.

Sebascong Bay at present holds the world's record for a muskie taken on hook and line—58¼ pounds. It is big water with 14,000 islands, miles of little-known shoreline and plenty of walleyes. Northern pike, or jackfish, as the Canadians call them, are just a nuisance there. We fished the bay the first day, which happened to be a Sunday, and came in with walleyes and northerns and the memory of one muskie that smashed at my plug. That night in our cabin, with Kenny and Jarge leaning over a map, we laid our plans for conquest of old Kat.

Oh sure, they'd take us to Kat. There were some cabins there, also boats. Even some cached gasoline. There was the little matter of a two-mile portage, but tosh, tosh! Whoever stopped at a little thing like that? Your correspondent studied the floor and spoke not when portages were mentioned, recollecting the torture his city-softened muscles had endured on certain trails in Superior National Forest many and many a time. Portages? Well now, fellows, that sounds like the real stuff, and there was in the voices of those two city guys the vicious pride of youth. As for Dave—"Say, didn't I lick the whole Portuguese navy with a crate of oranges in East Africa in 1916? Sniff! Sniff! Lead me to that portage!"

He was led. The next morning the two Canadian heathens we had chosen as guides, both abysmal men of the forest, met us on the dock, and we began our journey. A nice ride it was down Wigwam Creek, with the mallards and black ducks dodging into the rice as our outboard sputtered by; then two short jumps in which boats were carried. Finally the two-mile trek began.

It was hot. It was still. It was sultry with wood smoke from forest fires here and there over the Canadian lake country. We had gear. We had two motors and plenty of food and plenty of fishing tackle and plenty of clothing. We were laden. We tramped. The sweat stood out on our bellies like 10-cent-store beads, and Dave said he was going to die and could he have state-of-Maine men for polar bears at his funeral. He meant pall-bearers, but he wasn't particular at the moment. Irv chewed his pipe-stem and buckled in harder and took it on the lug, because Irv is made that way. I wilted.

But then I am an expert wilter. I've wilted on portages all the way from the Brule-St. Croix portage in northwest Wisconsin to that honey which stretches between Slim Lake, beyond Burntside Lake, out of Ely, leading into Big Lake.

At the half-way mark, Kenny and Jarge called a halt. They had been whistling while they toted twice as much as the rest of us. Whistling and chuckling, I'd noted, through the welter of sweat and dizziness and little dancing green balls that engulfed me. So we all keeled over on a big rock and lay there panting. Dave was too tired to take off his coat, and Irv and I considered shooting him where he was, inasmuch as it appeared he couldn't make it any farther.

"Shoot me!" Dave gasped. "Didn't I stand off the Portuguese navy?"

So help me, he rose from the dead and staggered

22: Not bad, not bad. Kenny with some Lake Katimiagmak trout

forward with his pack and his two hands full of gasoline tins and fish rods and things. To the honor and glory of all the Nasons between Milwaukee and Boston, be it reported he faltered not at all, though he didn't know what he was doing that last mile.

Katimiagimak—one of thousands of such lakes. I write the name reverently—as reverently as one may write anything with so many "aks" and "ims" in it. There it was.

The Nason corpse was strewn into one of the boats, the gear packed in, and we were off. At once there was a change. Here was no blooming green water of the Lake of the Woods. Here was pure green water and eternal quiet except for the eerie cry of loons. Here was something good and unspoiled, and it left its impress on all of us. Even on Dave. Within ten minutes he was sitting up lighting a cigar and screeching to high heaven that he was going to jerk the wisdom teeth out of a 25-pound lake trout ere nightfall.

Such places come upon men as a benediction. I hadn't intended to barge into the sublime from the ridiculous with such suddenness. I only know that old Kat took hold of me and made me feel again as I did when, as a kid ten years old, my dad showed me my first real wilderness lake. It was lonesome and faraway, and there was a brooding stillness. In my heart something said: "This is the real thing. Don't ever forget it."

We fished. But first we unloaded at the cabin on the island and stored our gear and dunked our sticky selves in the good cold green of old Kat until we were alive and new. Then we fished. Irv and Kenny and I in one boat, Jarge and Dave in another. Deep trolling, for it was mid-August. Deep trolling with copper lines and even an added weight or two to bring them down.

Let Kenny row. He wants to row. He wouldn't be happy unless he was rowing. Anyway, he weighs 190 pounds; and despite the silver plate in his thigh that he got fighting for Byng at Vimy Ridge, he's a better man than you or I, Irv. You're right, McGillicuddy, let him row!

Oop! I've got one. Hold 'er, Kenny! Maybe it's a rock. Ever see a rock move? Easy! Easy, Irv! Where's that gaff? Oh, let me catch that fish! Not too big, but I'll bet he'll go seven pounds. Look at the iron gray of him. You say these are land-locked salmon, Kenny? Naw! Lake trout! Land-locked salmon is just a local name. Real land-locked salmon didn't thrive when they were planted here. This is good old *Cristivomer namaycush*—lake trout, togue, Mackinaw trout, gray trout. Call him what you will, he's a great guy. Hold 'er, Kenny! I've got one.

Things went on like that until somewhere around 7 p.m., when the craft carrying the mortal remains of Mr. Nason was seen to head toward the island camp, and we followed him in. We had a half dozen or more lake trout. We had, too, the warmth of the August sun in our souls and on our bare backs. We had the memory of a family of loons, split by our fishing, and the mama loon, fool woman, caterwauling her advice from the safe side of a little rock island while her babies drifted at the mercy of this new monster.

Into camp. Dave beat us in. He had five. And while big, husky Jarge had iced his fish in the emergency ice-house thrown up on the isle the previous winter, Dave had stood on the little log dock and in three casts had snaked in a muskie. The muskie went into the pan. Jarge had to cook. Only because he knew how. Kenny said he never cooked when Jarge was around. Jarge is very young. He will learn. Trouble is, the longer he cooks the better he gets. But his cooking doesn't hamper his appetite: He and Kenny between them wolfed down pounds and pounds of victuals while we three city guys, who thought we had appetites, sat there staring at our plates, ashamed.

Dishes done, beds made up, we sat in front of the cabin and looked out over old Kat. The island was high enough to afford a good view. Forest fires, scattered but worrisome, filled the air with smoke. Distant islands swam half in smoke, half in water. The sun was a round crimson blister against the plumbeous sky. We smoked pipes and talked. It was peaceful talk, about winter in this place. Winter and summer and spring and autumn, and the wind and the rain arid the snow. Such peaceful things do men hunt in the woods on the pretext of going fishing. Such things as fill their city-warped brains with calm thankfulness. Such things that cost so little and, being cheap, find not many takers.

Then it happened. I can see now the pipe come from Irv's open mouth, see Dave's wondering eyes pop, hear Kenny whisper "Sh-s-s-s-s!"

It is the song of the wolf pack. Suddenly, dramatically, as though waiting for this beautiful, sinister moment as the day is ending, there comes from the depth of the spruce forest the weird, age-old cry. The sound is an abysmal dirge, rising and falling. An untamed prelude to night. It is not a howl. More beautiful than a howl, it is a baleful barcarole. One strong throat carries the burden of the music. It starts low in the scale and climbs majestically, hollowly, increasing in volume until its primeval throb fairly fills the cool air, stabs through the smoke pall, spreads over the lake, echoes from cliff to cliff.

We listen in mute wonderment. Sharp and far-carrying with the undertone come the cries of others in the pack. "Pups," the guides whisper. They seem to be imitating the older ones, and at times their yapping assumes the full color of a howl that blends artfully with the predominant note.

The sound seems to come not a hundred yards from us, but the guides estimate the wolves are two miles back in the woods. The water carries the sound admirably. There is something about it like an organ. We remark that it might be the hymnal of the wild and the steepled spruce the spires of churches. We wonder what a great composer would do with such music. Then the music dies away, fades to a lonely cadence, grows duller, stops abruptly.

We have listened to the call of the pack and it has been tremendous. But there is not space to go on. It will be remembered. No coyote yapping this, but the full-throat-ed cry of timber wolves. Yes, it will be remembered. As well remembered as the amazing snores that came from the lips of David V. Nason, one hour later. Soon after the body was deposited between blankets he paid tribute- to the labor of the portage by unloosening his tonsils.

My ears are sharper than my eyes. I hunt ducks by ear on windless days. I often look with my ears. I have never, in all my wanderings in city and woods, heard such a performance as Mr. Nason gave. There was in it at times the skirl of bagpipes, and I saw the Highlanders coming to the relief of Lucknow. Then an epiglottis or something opened, and Jess Crawford was musing over an organ. A tightening of the larynx, and the organ music died to a constricted squeak that broke in a jumbled, hacking explosion.

Irv says: "Run for your lives! The dam has broken!"

We lay there and chuckled. We shouted. We threatened. But finally we gave up and laughed, and the snores of Dave rose triumphantly into the cool Canadian night.

Well now, about this fishing business. I have been fishing for fish for twenty-six years by the calendars and the family Bible and I have fished for every kind of fish that dwells in the Middle West, and the more I fish for fish the more I catch people. There have been times when I have caught many fish and times when I have killed many ducks, but I am momentarily, at least, weary of writing about them. I think people have fish beat all hollow. There must be some fishing to make a trip a success, because most people think it is that way, but there are so many other things which we outdoor writers have a tendency to ignore in favor of the fish.

I am completely out of patience with fishing yarns that put two fellows in a boat and proceed to enlighten the reader as to how they wrapped their angleworms around the hook, or how they substituted a Yellow Sally for a Black Gnat and began to take trout immediately. Understand, I am not opposed at all to this technical literature. It is a necessary part of the game. But it strikes me that when two fellows get in a boat anywhere at any time they do a lot more than talk about wrapping angleworms around hooks. I'm all for sticking around until they loosen up and talk politics, philosophy, literature, love, crap-shooting or other sporting ventures. Which is to say, summarily, that fish are fine but people are better.

We went fishing again. We quit old Kat and lugged our two boats over a hog-back portage into a small, deep lake that few get in to because of that hogback drag. It was supposed to be a sure-fire, but spoons down 150 feet in its clear water turned up only a few small trout. Kenny told Irv and me it was a natural for muskalonge a month later, and we said, "Why not now?"

"All right, if you want to waste your time," said Kenny.

"Well," said we, "if the muskies are here, why won't they hit now?"

Kenny said he didn't know, which was an honest and unusual answer from any guide and goes to show what sort of man Kenny is. The upshot was, we insisted on being ushered toward the muskies. Kenny resigned himself to the whims of a couple of tenderfeet and rowed us over into a corner. For an hour we threw hardware into that corner, and on almost every cast muskies from six to twenty pounds followed our lures. But they would not take. We tried everything we had, which was plenty. Every trick and knack, but no muskie took hold.

"What's the matter with 'em, Kenny?"

Chary of words, Kenny had already spoken. But he was patient. He said again he didn't know.

"Well, why don't you know, Kenny?"

Kenny filled his pipe and smiled.

It was apparent that Kenny wasn't going to bother with the subject again. He knew the muskies were off in mid-August, had tried to find out why in thirty years of living there, had laughed at folks who spoke of muskies getting sore teeth when he couldn't find any sore teeth, had failed to find the reason, and that was that.

As we rowed back to deep water and lake-trout fishing, Kenny said, "I knew you'd get nothing but follows. I've had lots of experts tell me they knew how to get 'em when they were like that. But they never do. I guess I'm not an expert."

So if you believe wilderness muskies aren't as temperamental as those nearer the populated resort centers, think that one over. And this happened on a lake where Kenny, in one day, caught thirty-three muskies, replacing all but the limit of two.

On the fourth day Kenny, who had been studying a forest fire south of us, decided it was time to get out. He said he'd never seen the fires so bad since the year he and his cousin Angus cruised for three months up north of Sioux Lookout seeking out fur country. He was sure the fire had already consumed a brand new canoe he had hidden on a lake south of us and that it was time to haul stakes before the fire got into the portage trail. The rest of us felt that a little fire on that portage couldn't possibly make it any hotter than it was the day we came in, but we heeded his word and, as Kenny himself put it, "took out for home."

You may believe it or not, but on that back trek over the portage Irv and I discovered a good-sized lake, the shore of which we had skirted on the inward journey, but so tired had we been that our eyes, glued to the ground, had failed to note it. Going out, we were lighter, and the trip was made in jig time, about fifty minutes, which is good humping for city softies over a rugged two-mile trail.

Irv sort of put the pressure on. Laden with fifty pounds of stuff, he stretched his long legs to such advantage that he led the pack over the trail. Dave brought up the rear with a cigar and a story about the time he went to Iceland and slept in a feather bed.

Back at headquarters camp, a day was spent fishing Pine Lake for walleyes. Blooming though it was, we had pretty fair luck on both walleyes and northerns. All of these last-named were put back—even the 10-pounders. It is no trick to take fish here, and there is no excuse for heroics in telling about it. They just hit a spinner with a pork rind on it and you have fun and that's all there is to it.

But hark now to the events which l transpired after Mr. Nason of Iceland, South Africa, Europe and Cumberland Boulevard, Milwaukee, made up his mind to relieve the tedium of fishing. Irv and Kenny and I were minding our own business fishing off an island in Pine Lake. Dave's boat, manned by Jarge, came speeding toward us. As his boat neared ours I noticed that Dave was fumbling with something in the bottom, but thought nothing of it.

The Nason craft swept in toward us in a grand parabola, and the nemesis of the Portuguese navy suddenly stood up. In his hands was a stick with a wire on its end. At the end of the wire was a porcupine, dangling by one leg.

Dave swung the porky gracefully from his boat into Irv's lap. Reflex action is fast. A split second after that thrashing porky landed in Irv's lap, it was kicked into the middle of the boat, and Kenny lurched to his feet and yelled: "Man the lifeboats, men! Women and children first!"

I armed Kenny with a paddle, and eventually the porky was shoveled overboard. About the time the porky was waddling up the gray stone shore and Irv was wielding his fishing pliers, removing quills from boots and boat seat, we looked over to where Dave and Jarge had anchored nearby, both in a state of collapse.

Miraculously, none of the quills had entered Irv's hide, which makes him about the only guy that ever held an angry porky in his lap and came through unscathed. Admiral Nason's victory in East Africa, when the Portuguese midshipmen picked orange seeds out of their hair, was as nothing to the porcupine triumph. After that, I believed he had beaten the Portuguese navy. Anyone with the ingenuity to toss a porky into a boat would be a problem for even the British navy.

It developed that Jarge had lassoed the porky out of a tree after Dave had sighted it from the boat. Dave explained that he had tried to get it into my lap, but Jarge swung the boat in wrong. Kenny, with a resourcefulness born of long life in the woods, said he knew where there was a can of glue which is good for pouring in shoes, but Dave overheard him and slept with his shoes under his pillow.

23: George prepares a walleye for lunch on Lake of the Woods

That was the last night. Also, the night we got Kenny really talking by sticking a map under his nose. He grabbed a pencil. His eyes burned. He rocked back and forth on his feet, pointing, tracing, speculating. He outlined canoe and hunting and fishing trips until we were dizzy. He told of the thousand-dollar beaver catch he'd made a few winters before, of the caribou he'd killed "up narth a bit—not very fer" and of his winter trap line. And how he once tried to work in the paper plant at Fort Frances but "give it up—it wasn't good for me."

Great people, Kenny and Jarge. Reeking with health, powerful, with great endurance, we knew how Byng must have felt when those Canadians marched into the front-line trenches.

In conclusion, it should be mentioned that Canada has opened up a new road between Fort Frances and Kenora. The story is this. On July 1, 1935, Canada opened, with great ceremony, the trans-Canada highway between Port Arthur on Lake Superior and Winnipeg—some 450 miles of brand new east-west highway. As a feeder to this road from the south, on July 1, 1936, the Peter Heenan highway was opened. This takes you all the way through from the Minnesota line north to Kenora, on the trans-Canada. Parts of this highway, blasted from solid rock, cost $100,000 per mile. It penetrates a region of little-known lakes. Smart trippers from the states immediately leaked in over this splendid rock road into new country like mice through a granary crack.

We came home that way, heading first north, then east at Kenora to Port Arthur, then down the north shore of Lake Superior to Duluth and so home to Milwaukee. Seventeen hundred miles, in all, our log read, but I have long since forgotten that. And I've long since forgotten the trout and the walleyes and the northerns. But I haven't forgotten Irv. And I haven't forgotten Dave.

As long as I live they will be remembered as the best fish I caught all year.

We learn more about Helen Peck MacQuarrie, Mr. President's daughter, in this story than in all the rest of MacQuarrie's writings combined, and we learn more about their sporting life together. In the first story in this book, "The Windblown Flight," the Pecks and the MacQuarries, with little Sally, went duck hunting at Shallow Bay for a week in 1930. Here, in this story, we find that they had been in duck camp 10 weeks after Sally's birth on August 12, 1929. In the Milwaukee Journal *column of October 29, 1936, "Women and Ducks," reprinted in* Right Off the Reel, *he wrote about spending a week in 1935 with Mr. and Mrs. President and his wife Helen duck hunting, and in that case both women were in the blind, not just in camp. Helen out-shoots the Old Duck Hunters in "Shallow Bay Comes Back," also in 1935. One has to wonder whether that third week of October wasn't a regular vacation date for the two couples in the years not mentioned as well, at least while the MacQuarries lived in Superior.*

For the most part, Gordon wrote the women out of the stories for his mostly male audience, except when it served as the focus of the story, as in "Shallow Bay Comes Back."

Fishermen with Women

Field and Stream, August 1937

Unless you want her around every time, don't teach her to fish

So she went fishing.

Her husband, a trout-stream addict, helped her string up his second rod, gave her a handful of flies and plopped her into a pair of rubber boots. She looked pretty good, but there was no telling whether the experiment would take.

She stumbled only once on the long, steep path leading to the Brule above the old Stone Dam. At the river, the husband, in hobbed brogues, plunged into the current. She hesitated, and he extended an arm. They made the center of the current, where she found an island of sand for her sliding feet.

Then came instructions. The husband knew an awful lot about fishing. Every piece of his equipment bespoke the expert, from the three-ounce rod to the wide-mouthed net, secured by a button under the back of his coat collar. She didn't say a word. In fact, she couldn't, as she had just lost her voice the day before from a minor throat infection.

The doctor had been asked about the fishing trip. "Nothing to worry about," he had said. "The sore throat is gone. Her voice will be back in a couple of days."

So the husband talked a lot. It was an opportunity that no husband could pass up, although the wife did what she could with head shakings and arm wavings. He was surprised at the expressiveness of even a temporarily-speechless woman. He showed her how to swing the rod, tie on the flies, keep them out of the trees and maintain her balance against the deceptive current. She made a little headway and indicated she wanted to go somewhere else; so he escorted her downstream to a long stretch of quieter water.

His own rod was under his arm. He whipped it suggestively once or twice. She was getting her bearings, and liked it. "Go 'way," she spoke with her lips and her hands. He was willing to be a martyr and stay a while to see how she made out, but she was insistent. She indicated again he should go away. It looked O. K. He said, while she ignored him:

"Stay out of fast water. Always have one foot planted solidly before you move the other. Keep out of soft bottom. Look behind before you cast. If you get a strike, strip in the line. Forget about the reel. Take it easy. Don't lose those leaders. They cost six bits apiece."

She made words with her lips that might have been either "get to hell out of here" or "will you please go away and let me fish."

He was an expert. She was a realist.

He left her dropping bird's nests on the majestic Brule and departed downstream to the end of a long, slow stretch. It was a leisurely day. He rigged up methodically, as befits the scientific man of the river. He daubed his Quill Gordon thoughtfully with oil and lowered his dignified expertness into the flow. There is a royal aloofness about such fishermen. None of your hasty, jump-into-the-creek stuff for them. He was of the dry-fly elect with a broad background of La Branche, Hewitt, Connett, et al., stretching respectably into the past.

Trout fishing had been a whim on her part. Maybe it would click. He wasn't sure. She had been a duck hunter for some years, but fishing was watery. He hadn't pressed the issue. It had been of her own volition. The strongest hope lay in her natural heritage. Her father was known more or less favorably as President of the Old Duck Hunters' Association, Inc. which titular honor infers also a close acquaintance with whirring reel and straining bamboo.

The husband lit his pipe and forgot her in the quest of a choosy brown in front of a difficult rock. The fish refused his best. He moved upstream and tried another sure-fire spot. It was barren. Into the stronger current at the head of the flow he tried again for first blood, but emerged defeated.

A brother of the trade came along. Greetings. Condolences. Hopes. Alibis.

"They just ain't hittin'," said the friendly newcomer to the husband. "Only fish I've seen today was caught by a woman a couple of hundred yards upstream."

So! She had a fish! She was the only fisherwoman anywhere near Rainbow Bend that day. It must be his wife. He scrambled back into the stream. Gone was the professional equanimity of the dry-fly expert. He was a fisherman taking a licking now.

"How big was that fish?" he called from the river.

" 'Bout 20 inches," shouted the other over the roar of the current.

The husband frowned. He'd try the fast water. Big No. 8 Badger Bivisible. Lots of oil to float it. Shorter and stouter leader. They couldn't see the bigger leader in that water, and if one of 'em hit it—

Blop!

Damn! He missed the rise, thinking about the fish his wife had caught. And that was the best spot in the immediate vicinity. He should have known. That rainbow would never rise again today— picked his teeth.

A cold horror slowly engulfed the dry-fly man. What if he couldn't deliver in the face of that 20-incher? What if—God forbid!—she actually caught more and bigger than he with that old wet Dark Montreal? Incredible. Impossible. Unfair! And when she got her voice back—

His professional calm was badly ruffled when the next fisherman hove into sight from upstream. The husband waded ashore for tidings.

Greetings. Condolences. Hopes. Alibis.

The newcomer was chuckling.

"Funniest thing I ever saw," he related with streamside camaraderie. "There's a woman fishing upstream. I was standing below her. She wanted to get around me and, like a good sport, got out of the river. Had on the biggest pair of boots you ever saw. I said 'Good afternoon' and raised my hat, but she only smiled at me. She had a great big trout flopping from her belt.

"Ha-ha-ha! I'll never forget it as long as I live. You know that spring hole where the black muck is always pushed up in the spring—deep as the pit with the log across it? She started to cross the log, and the rubber boots lost their grip. Both legs went straight down about two feet. She was in no danger with that log handy, but it was a nice fix. She couldn't budge either of her legs, and finally solved it by hoisting out onto the log and pulling her feet out of the boots.

"Ho-ho-ho! Then she reached in and pulled out both boots, lying on her stomach on the log. I headed for shore to offer help, but she waved me away. She even shook her fist at me, but she was laughing. I said, 'Fishing's hard work, eh?' That's when she shook her fist at me. That gal's a fisherman. I asked her if she ever fished trout before. She shook her head, got a fresh hold on that trout and moved along to try another hole. Ha-ha-ha-ha-ho! Is that lady making us boys look silly!"

Was she safe and sound?

"Mister, that lady would take care of herself in a raging flood—and come out of it with her boots full of fish!" concluded the fisherman.

Like all days, this one ended, and the husband and wife convened at the car on the hill as the sun went down. The lady's boots had leaked. The mosquitoes had bitten. The sun had burned. The husband was toting a dry creel, but Poor Mom, who had no creel, boasted the 20-incher and two smaller ones, all victims of a wet fly. She couldn't talk, but she could whisper.

To the husband, the woods fairly rang with whispers. And that, gentlemen, was the beginning of chapter two in the conversion of my better half to the game of outdoors.

Up to that day, come trout season, she was just Poor Mom. Some years before, the ripping of silk in the dawn—ducks passing by—had won her over, but on summer week-ends she either stayed at home or wheedled the husband somewhere far from the babbling brooks. A fairly good working arrangement had been established whereby said husband used up every other week-end in his own way, leaving friend wife to make her choice on the alternate week-ends. From that first trout day on, however, the lady's holidays were spent along the stream.

There is abroad in the land a feeling that woman's place in the outdoors stops at the edge of screened porches of swank resorts, that the good wife and true hath no place in the boat on the lake or in the frigid duck blind. This is a false notion. It is passing out, but in the remoter settlements there are husbands who fare forth strictly without women. These go to duck shacks and fishing cabins and let their whiskers grow and get indigestion, and play cards too late at night.

I know. I used to be one. The turn came when the aforementioned Mr. President, who has a fine capacity for making himself comfortable, suggested we take our wives to a certain red cabin in northern Washburn County, Wisconsin, for a week of duck hunting.

They came. They cooked. They conquered.

Each year since then they have come, and we are glad to have them. We sleep on clean sheets. We rest our flanneled elbows on white tablecloths. We dine like humans. The frying pan-poker era is definitely of the past. Up to that time we had been getting sandwiches and indigestion. Now we even wash behind the ears at 4 A.M., preparatory to getting into a blind, and the virtuous feeling derived from that alone is worth the effort.

Yep, it would seem that the day of the corduroyed wolf of the big timber, alias Mr. Milquetoast, is passing, and it can't go too fast. The old tradition of masculine messiness in camp is dying or dead. And I say that as one who has worshiped at the shrine of real campers like Nessmuk and Kephart all my life. They never stood for some of the things we have stood for. They always knew better. It was one of them who said that a fellow goes into the woods to smooth it, not to rough it. Truer words were never spoken.

Modern ladies in trim breeches and boots, who can sling a mean fly or lead a mallard just enough, are helping change things. Of course, it may cost a little more at first, but the ultimate result is thrift, for those previous concessions to what we thought was independence, in the form of new dresses and hats, are not so necessary.

Poor Mom is definitely a part of the outdoor picture, and who will say she doesn't look good there? I've known husbands to decide their wives weren't so bad after all when they saw them freshly clad in the gear of the outdoors.

I don't mean that these new wives are necessarily going in for the near-by sports either. They are going back in with their husbands, and carry packs and fight mosquitoes. Take a trip into Superior National Forest by canoe, and you'll find about as many women as men plying the lakes, portaging their stuff, making the best of it. Note the auto stream of tourists in upper Wisconsin and Minnesota. Those ladies in the cars are going places and doing things.

And lots of them are doing it better than the old man. I know one blond chit of twenty-five who, dragged into the backwoods on a honeymoon by an unsuspecting husband, broke down and bawled when their destination was reached. That was a few years back. The other day she told me she was going to show her husband how a roll cast really should be made, just as soon as she got a new $60 rod. And the rod meant the sacrifice of a spring outfit.

I know another of slightly maturer years who, on her first trip with her husband after prairie chickens, was ignominiously and accidentally shot in the trousers by the same husband. About a dozen shot landed there. She is still hunting with the old gent—and at least three of the shot are right where they landed, so I'm told on good authority.

The never-say-die devotees of solitary discomfort in the big woods have their arguments. For instance, those of the "escape school." They plead they have to get away from it all or they'll crack up. Bunk! They would hang together better on wifie's cooking. Look at the insurance company figures. You'll find the married variety lives longer.

Then there's the plain and fancy school of hard-drinkin', hard-shootin' lads who sleep in their socks and play poker all night. These fellows not only undermine their health but waste time and money going so far from home to get tight.

You will note I make no mention at all of the simple justice of the thing. It's a good argument, but not necessary because the women have won their spurs on their own merits as good sports, not because they are the frailer vessel and therefore require some such defense.

Think of having a wife who will brave the icy floor in November to start a fire and fry the bacon! Don't tell me the pioneer woman is gone. Try it and see if the good wife and true doesn't get the spirit of the thing, perhaps more fully than you do. You'll recover your sense of fairness to your family—if you ever lost it— and your wife will love you more than she does.

Kids in the family? It can be managed. I had one duck hunting for a week when she was ten weeks old, and she gained more weight that week than any other in her first year.

The thing to do is to make it a party. Get your pal to take his wife, and find out how nice it is to come in off a lake or a stream and wash your face and comb your hair.

You'll be surprised how quickly a woman falls into the routine of fishing and hunting. She will get to know little tricks that men never think of. My wife, for instance, can build a better duck blind than I can. She knows how to camouflage it without using too much material. Women have the touch.

If you are wise, you will get into the thing by easy stages. Take her for a ride into the country some day and find a boat, by accident, on a lake. Then—another accident—you discover your casting outfit in the car. Suggest a row. Well, you might as well take your outfit as long as you've got it.

Go. Fish. On the first strike thrust the rod in her hand and grab the oars. Then let nature take its course. If she kills that fish, half the job is done. There are instances of immediate conversions, but generally the process is slower. It may take years, but it's worth it—think of those home-cooked meals, my friends.

I well remember my wife's first duck. She was sitting in a blind with Mr. President and me. She had on a red hat and wouldn't take it off, which shows how much she knew about ducks then. A flock came along, and I pushed her down low and thrust a 16-gauge into her hand. It was early morning, and six mallards lit in the decoys. I decided to murder a sitting duck to make a duck hunter. I told her to pick out the one at the extreme right; then, standing back of her and to one side, I trained my own gun on a point in the air three feet above the unsuspecting susie.

I saw my wife's eye squint along the ribbing, saw her finger squeeze down on the front trigger. As she pulled I fired. The recoil thrust her back, and when she looked again there was a dead duck on the water. She does not know until now that I killed that duck, that our shots were almost simultaneous, that the duck actually dropped three feet to the water after she had shot.

Now she knows, but who cares? Then she was being inoculated. Now she's taking me places.

Other women by the hundreds are finding their way into the fishing country. Perhaps not so many of them are trout fisherwomen as lake fisherwomen. Some of the best muskies and bass caught in upper Wisconsin answered to the skill of women vacationers. And once bitten, the woman generally becomes more enthusiastic than the man, like the one in Van Dyke's story who didn't like trout fishing at first but finally wound up by wearing her husband to a frazzle each season.

It is my earnest conviction that if women ever go in for fly-casting for trout in a big way they will devise ways and means to make the old-timers sit up and blink. Trout of these days, especially browns, must be wheedled, as we all know. It's a delicate game. There's no place in it for the rough and ready fisherman. It requires finesse and endless attention to detail.

Women are equipped for it. By the way, women tie most of the flies used in the country. Just wait until they all begin throwing 'em around. They are in a partial state of subjugation as yet. But the day is coming—and fishing will be a better game, and there'll be better fishermen, better rods, better lines, better flies.

The answer to why women can tie flies is found in the twinkling hands of any woman who knits. What man can ever achieve that sensitiveness and accuracy in handwork? Oh, maybe there are exceptions, but you don't find many men knitting. Yes, trout fishing is a woman's game today. More women should be playing it. More of them will be playing it. They may not win any fly-casting contests for distance, but look out for those accuracy competitions!

Up in this neck of the woods one of the best trout fly casters is Mrs. George Babb, wife of the man who taught Coolidge how to fish with a dry fly. One day while watching her husband in an exhibition, a fisherman standing near me remarked, "He's good all right, but he never lets his wife get hold of a rod when there's a crowd."

I told George about it later. He winked at me and answered, "The guy who said that is no fool."

Rascals of the Riprap

Field and Stream, July 1938

Teaching the bass of the upper Mississippi some new tricks

A long, square-ended finger waggled a warning just above the bridge of my nose. Behind the pedagogical digit was a hawkish Scandinavian face, whose austerity was repudiated only by a pair of jolly eyes, partly hidden behind spectacles.

The owner of the finger and the eyes was Ed Anderson of Red Wing, Minnesota. He was standing with me on the limestone riprapping along the Mississippi, giving me final instructions on what he claimed was something new in the way of bass fishing. We had just unloaded a canoe from the top of a car, and while it floated at our feet Ed delivered himself of what you might call a speech:

"You do a lot of fishing. You've caught lots of black bass. But I doubt very much if you've ever caught largemouths like these. Mississippi tackle-busters or in the quantity that we'll catch them."

I smiled. Long, many years ago had I heard 'em tell it. The lake where you've got to stand behind a tree to bait up. The trout stream that nobody else knows about. Always these piscatorial paradises shrink in importance and size of fish the closer one's informant gets to them.

But here was a fellow who, standing on the very bank of his promised land, was more serious than ever. Here was a fish-crier whose hand was actually trembling a bit as he gesticulated.. Here, by the Lord Harry, was a man who either had the courage of his convictions or had actually underestimated what he was about to reveal.

So you still don't believe it?" asked Ed sadly.

The proof was in the pudding, I thought, as I watched the early morning river mist whirling about our heads. I didn't say it. But Ed must have read my thoughts, for his blue eyes gleamed. He grasped the canoe with a firm hand and said in a resolute voice: "Get in mister! I'm going to make you look bad in about ten minutes from now.

145

Oh, he's going to make me look bad, huh? So he's got bass out there in that yellow river that hit like trout? So he's got 'em by the thousand? So he's telling me to adjust my sights and shoot the minute I see the whites of their eyes? What does he think this is- the upper St. Croix, with it's smallmouths?

I said: "Work her along the bank about thirty-five feet out. I'll do the same for you later.

24: Ed Anderson with some Mississippi River tackle-busters

On my oldest and heaviest fly rod I had strung a new cream-colored, trick-tapered- one of those limp-torsoed lines that behaves like a well-trained nautch dancer. To that was affixed a short bass leader, and on the business end was a yellow feathered minnow.

It was on about the third cast when one of the submerged limestone rocks six inches from the shore-line, made a three-foot bee-line for the feathered minnow. Unprepared for such a sudden coming-to-life of a gray chunk of limestone, I missed the strike.

"Struck too fast," I said.

Ed's comment was, "Horsecollars!"

In the next ten minutes, four more bass came smashing at that yellow wad of feathers. I missed them all. Each time I gave the bass a little longer time in which to strike. Each time the snorts from the rear of the canoe became more significant and the silence between each missed strike much heavier.

On the sixth miss I turned to Ed. Helplessness and defeat must have been written on my face. I mumbled something about never seeing largemouths strike like that- not even in a river.

"So?" said Ed.

"So."

He had won an uphill fight to convince a stranger to the upper Mississippi bass that here was a fish which could sock like a trout. He made a speech. It was the same old speech he had been talking since I'd met him the previous day, but it had a new and confident ring to it now. Considering everything, he was very kind. He did rub it in a little bit but that was his privilege. I had discounted his fishing methods, and he had me dead to rights. He told me what to do.

"I have," he said, "fished for everything in Minnesota and parts of Canada. I know of no largemouths anywhere that smash tackle like these fellows. When you fish trout, you strike when you see a flash near the fly. You must do that with these bass, or you'll miss all of them."

He let it soak in. The long, square-ended finger went into action again as he continued:

"Not long ago I took a friend of yours out here from Chicago. In two hours we had fifty-four strikes and he landed three bass!" He let that sink in, too.

"These babies fight for their living with the current. They are not lake largemouths. You'll see when we catch one—if we ever do—how they're stream-lined. You never saw heavy largemouths from any lake as trim as these. Their bellies are slim. Their shoulders are like a snow-plow. When they hit, they hit. I never yet saw one just reach up and suck in a lure, the way a brown trout will."

Chastened, I started casting again. Gone now was a certain indifferent manner—at least indifferent compared with my lightning reflexes when trout fishing. This was sport of a high order. These bass were like torpedoes. I riveted attention on the yellow lure and stripped line with deliberate care on the retrieves to insure a tight line for hooking.

It wasn't long before I had another chance. *Ker-r-r-shwock!* I had one. The smash through the five-ounce rod was as solid as a punch on the jaw. I felt the jolt of that strike to my toes. The bass flung himself four feet along the surface from the riprapping. I saw plainly the place from which he started his dash.

He leaped three times, and I could have made him leap more, but I encouraged him to stay down. I wanted that bass. He was a fin-bristling brown-green devil in the eddying mists. I think it was on this first one that I weakened the rod at the ferrule below the tip joint. Anyway, it busted later in the day on a hard backcast. My only excuse is that I was not prepared for bass like those Mississippi murderers. I tried to horse the first one. We finally netted him, but the rod had acquired a slight set.

Let me halt a moment to unlimber one fisherman's feelings about bass. All my life I have fished for them. I have caught more than my share. I have never believed the late Dr. Henshall's historic remark concerning "inch for inch and pound for pound." It just isn't so; still we must give the good doctor a world of credit for coining the phrase and attracting the attention of millions to this splendid fish. My own private hunch is that the gamest thing with fins is a rainbow in the Brule River of Wisconsin.

But here were bass striking and fighting like trout. Gone was the sluggish come-in I've noticed in many a lake largemouth after a brief struggle. Gone was the deliberate strike of the slower cousins of slower water. Gone was the surface-floundering sprawl of some sluggish bass that people describe as leaps. These fish came out into the air as clean as a whistle—clean and high and vibrating.

It was with a new respect that I continued fishing. I was learning things about Mississippi largemouths. Mind you, these were not smallmouths, generally held in this country to be a shade above the largemouths in pugnacity. I agree with that. The smallmouth is a tougher customer, but under no circumstances let that fact (if it is a fact) permit you to discount brother largemouth that dwells on the riprapping. He'll fool you.

In the following three hours I became as completely engrossed in the business of bass fishing as I ever was with trout fishing. Trout are my dish. They enthrall me. I can develop long and rigid intensity while fishing for trout. Never in bass fishing before had I had this same "trout-stream feeling" as on that particular morning with Ed Anderson, except possibly with St. Croix River smallmouths.

Along the seemingly endless Mississippi a prodigal Government has indirectly helped the fishing while aiding navigation. Millions of dollars have been spent in rock riprapping and wing dams, intended to control the current in proper channels and force the banks to stay put. Bass love rocks. They loiter above them, awaiting their chance to pounce on a careless crawfish. Early morning and late evening the bass come in from deeper water to feast on the food about the riprapping and wing dams.

These wing dams near Red Wing, above 23-mile-long Lake Pepin, are from 25 to 150 yards in length. They are mere rubble heaps thrusting out from the banks, some of them not more than a foot above the river's surface. Bass prefer the upstream side, perhaps because here, facing the current, they are in better position to seize food. On the downstream sides of the dams one is more likely to take pike or white bass.

Wing-dam fishing on the Mississippi is not new by any means. But it has been in need of a rediscovery in recent years. Pollution from cities has injured fishing to the point where many ardent bassers have forgotten about it. Now it has come back, and a trip into this fishing region will indeed be a worthwhile journey for those old-timers who remember it before pollution spread its evil poison.

Between St. Paul, Minnesota, and Prairie du Chien, Wisconsin, there are only two cities still without sewage disposal plants. These are Red Wing and Hastings, both in Minnesota. For both of them sewage disposal plants are projected. The river is clearing. It is not the crystal green of Wisconsin and Minnesota inland lakes. It never will be; the Mississippi carries too much sediment for that. But it is cleaner, and Ed Anderson, who has fished it since 1907, says it is far clearer than it was a few years back.

On top of this improved condition there is one more vital change being made. To insure a nine-foot boat channel the Government is now completing the expenditure of $500,000,000 in dams. These are raising the water, so that bass formerly stranded in inland sloughs and pot-holes are no longer cut off from the main stream, but can come and go as they choose. Fish-rescue work on the Mississippi in the backwaters still continues, but the navigation dams are lessening the need for it.

So we have, in short, a changing river, a beautiful river, an accessible river. The old Mississip' has been neglected by angling men. Its tawny flow has not held for them the lure of clearer lakes. Always there has been a band of loyal devotees who have clung to the Mississip', but Wisconsin and Minnesota are lake-minded states, and the big river, as well as others, has not received the attention it deserves.

The fishing on the Upper Mississippi is extremely accessible from Chicago, for instance. A Chicagoan can climb aboard one of the fast, modern trains at about 1 P.M. and land in Red Wing in four hours. Accommodations in the towns thereabout are not those of the typical fishing camp. This has not encouraged the promotion of the river at this point.

The river has been a burden-bearer—not the typical intimate waters of the fisherman. It has never had cast over it the aura of publicity that the northwoods lakes have. It has gone about its business of breeding fish and carrying barges, and it has not been fastened in the mind's-eye of the Middle West fishing clan as one of those far-away places.

Still it is beautiful. The 300-foot-high bluffs along its bank are rather startling, viewed from a boat or from an auto. The highways on both sides of the river carry automobiles through scenery that is admittedly as striking as anything in either Wisconsin or Minnesota.

Accommodations can be had—plenty of them. Not, however, as simply as one can roll into almost any northwoods camp and tumble into a bunk. There are some resorts. There are boat liveries. All the little towns—Hager City, Diamond Bluff, Alma, Nelson, Lake City, Wabasha, Red Wing—have their hotels, their tourist cabins, their inveterate fishermen. But the thing is by no means on the same basis that certain well-known northern camps are. Perhaps this is the principal reason why fishermen have not used the river more. They simply haven't been invited to do so.

Fishing the Mississippi can be something of an adventure in friendship. The way to do it is to drive into any of the above mentioned towns. Look up the town fisherman. Every town has an outstanding fisherman. Maybe he is a barber, a gas station attendant, a carpenter. You'll find him a highly agreeable person. You will not have the slightest difficulty in finding your way around after you have met up with this fisherman. A fisherman just can't refuse a pal anything.

If you are one who must have guides, boats and motors waiting for you when you hop out of your automobile, the upper Mississippi is not for you. But if there is in you an average-sized spark of initiative, if you have a ready smile and know your way around, you can find fun aplenty around these pleasant little valley cities. An outboard motor is almost necessary. The river loafs along at only two miles an hour in most places, but it is a husky current and you can cover ground much better with a motor. Your boat should respond easily to rowing, for you will use oars when the fishing begins.

The fly rod is the supreme weapon. Bass bugs and flies of all shapes and kinds are used, but the favorite is a yellow feathered minnow. Yellow for bass. No one seems to know why, but the loyalty of a Mississippi bass for yellow is striking. Veteran anglers on three famous Wisconsin bass streams-the St. Croix, Totogatic and Namakagon- are partial to yellow in both flies and plugs for bass. A Yellow Sally fly is a standard lure on the Namakagon.

The three-day stay that I enjoyed in these fishing waters developed into something of an endurance contest. Between Ed Anderson's insistence on filling my every hour with fishing and my own eagerness to enjoy it to the full, I started each morning at three o'clock, sleeping in the middle of the day and going back in the evening for more. The river and Lake Pepin provided me with some of the most intensively interesting bass fishing I have ever had. We were strictly in search of bass. Walleyes, northerns, pan-fish-all the common lake varieties are here in numbers but being in such bass waters with a fly rod had only one answer for me—bass!

Restless Lake Pepin was marvelous on the cool, still morning when we launched Billy Walters' boat and started for the eastern or Wisconsin side. There was no hint of a breeze, yet the lake was in constant motion. Turbulent, short-troughed little waves were everywhere except under the towering bluffs of the eastern shore, where by four o'clock in the morning direct sunlight was still three hours away. Surrounded by these tremendous bluffs, one has the feeling of being in a deep-set horse trough. It is not the best place to be caught during a blow.

Here, again, the largemouths reacted as usual. Ed and I worked our fly rods until Billy Walters, wise and good citizen, made feeble mention of "a pretty good plug I've got there—I call it the kidnapper." We "shushed" him, but eventually, after repeated hints, Ed seized the short rod and began taking bass at the rate of one about every five minutes. Billy Walters' kidnapper was a battered red and white underwater wabbler.

During the course of that morning on Lake Pepin a five-pound sheepshead—of all things—hit the wabbler. We took bass limits for two and called it quits. A very delightful thing about men like Ed Anderson and Billy Walters is that they are satisfied to fish where there are plenty of fish without taking limit strings at every opportunity. We kept a few for the purpose of displaying to a skeptical world that the Mississippi was still good for something besides floods.

25: *The backwaters and sloughs along the Mississippi are filled with largemouths like these*

One other session—this one on the river—will be remembered for a long time. It was with Russell Kolb, one of the engineers on dam No. 3. The fortunate Mr. Kolb, who fishes the river daily, first came into my life early one morning as Ed and I passed him in a canoe. Kolb was standing, casting from an anchored rowboat into the riprapping. He shouted to us to paddle over, and held up a 4½-pound largemouth. Others he had put back. Last year he nailed one that went close to seven pounds. Pretty good for a trim-lined river bass. He catches bass every day on his fly rod, despite an old shoulder injury which prevents him from making a true steeple cast with a fly rod.

That evening we sped up the river from dam No. 3 for about three miles, until we were opposite the little town of Diamond Bluff, hugging the big cliffs. Russ Kolb called his shots. We had begun too early. The bass were not yet on the riprapping. But by 7:30, when the evening chill began ascending from the river and the sun was well down, those rascals had moved in to their favorite feeding grounds over the riprapping and about the wing dams.

We caught them and put them back. We changed from feathered minnows to bass bugs, to flies and back again. The feathered minnows—yellow ones—certainly seemed to work best. One inshore bass gave me the big thrill of the trip. It was then barely light enough to make out the shore-line. The yellow sneaker dropped inches from the shore and was worked out slowly.

A bass rushed after it, plunging for perhaps two feet, and then disappeared. He had not touched it. I jerked the lure ever so little, and the bass materialized on top of the water like magic. This time he took it hard and fair. It reminded me, for all the world, of a skilled pugilist demonstrating a one-two punch. You have seen it. A left goes out—misses. It is withdrawn in a flash. There are two fists back in striking position. Which one next? That's the question. In a split second the right lashes out and the blow lands.

Nothing in the swift science of the prize ring is more effective. It was just like that. The bass missed. He waited, ready; then he smashed out again.

This one, while not more than 2½ pounds, seemed very strong. He leaped five times. It was growing darker, and I had trouble in following all his maneuvers. He dived under the boat and forced me to stand and tease him out in the open.

And I had thought to offer lures to these bass with a 3-ounce trout rod! I'm glad now that I did not. While I might have saved the rod from a punishing set, the time required to land these bass would have been too long. It would have been stealing time from the better fun of seeing them smash the bait at the shore-line. The fight is grand but the strike is better.

I still look back at this fishing as a rediscovery of some fishing waters that needed rediscovery. I can see those bass now, shouldering out of the water after my yellow fraud. I can see the crawling mists of early morning hanging wraith-like over the Father of Waters. I can see the savage plunge of a wing-dam largemouth and the lashing strike of his cousin from the riprapping.

And I can see the happy gleam in the eye of honest Ed Anderson when I thanked him and went my way. That day I drove some 165 miles. Twisting and turning over the beckoning roads of Wisconsin, I found it hard to forget certain scenes. Everything that swam into my consciousness somehow seemed crowded out by memories of plunging bass. Events seemed to go in a circle.

That was it—a circle. Like the story Ed told about the farmer who built the round barn. The poor fellow, Ed declared, finally went crazy.

"Why?" I asked innocently.

"Trying to find a corner to lean a pitchfork in," Ed yawned.

I know just how that farmer felt. Because I doubt if there's a corner of the riprapping or wing dams where a fisherman has half a chance to lean a feathered minnow without it being gobbled.

By this time in his Milwaukee career, MacQuarrie was well versed in all of Wisconsin's geography. This story takes place in northeast Wisconsin, not his first love, the northwest. The two characters he is fishing with both are part of the Milwaukee Journal *family. Fred Peters was a frequent contributor to the outdoor page before Mac got the full-time job, and he also became one of Mac's sources. R.G.L is Russell G. Lynch and he's actually Mac's boss, although it seems Mac was secure enough to take jabs at RGL fairly often. Many of his columns told how "This Old Eskimo" was put upon by the editor.*

Lynch tended to write more about the ball sports than outdoor sports while MacQuarrie was alive. He did take over the Right Off the Reel *column a few times while Mac was up north during Helen and Sally's TB treatment and wrote both witty stories like Mac and hard-hitting conservation stories during one of the years of over-populated deer. After MacQuarrie's death, Mel Ellis took over the hunting and fishing stories, while Lynch took on the growing environmental protection scene.*

Lynch also was the first recipient of the Gordon MacQuarrie Foundation award "for outstanding achievement in telling the conservation story." This foundation was set up by Gordon's widow, Ellen, and Walter Scott (Harry Nohr was second president of the foundation). Lynch also is a member of the Wisconsin Conservation Hall of Fame. In his bio for the Hall of Fame, it states that Lynch is believed to have been the nation's first full-time natural resources reporter. This may be Wisconsin hubris, but, if true, it's another coup for the Milwaukee Journal.

Everybody's River

Outdoor Life, August 1939

Can you blame 'em for swarming all over the Wolf when it opens a month ahead of time?

There's a gallant old river that springs from the cut-over stump lands of Wisconsin's north, spends its lusty youth as a trout stream, and then sweeps on to brimful maturity, to the very edge of the most densely populated corner of the state.

That river is Old Man Geology's finest gesture to the city folks of central and southeastern Wisconsin. They greet the southward-bearing Wolf as a kindly old savage from the far places bearing the old, old tidings that the ice is out, the white-throats are singing, and the fishin' season's open.

Its very name connotes the wilderness from which it comes— the Wolf. Only the outlanders tack on "River." Wisconsin fishermen honor it with the terse, strong name—Wolf.

No river entirely within the state's borders has wooed, and held, so many fishermen and such a variety of fishermen. A trout stream up above, with bass and wall-eyes in its lower reaches, it holds the answer to the angling prayers of thousands.

The other day in a Milwaukee tackle shop I encountered one of its ardent worshipers, George Roux. He was making ready for an opening-day assault upon the trout in the Wolf's northern reaches. With him was another of the Faithful, Jack McBride. They were going over the wrappings on a $60 rod, to make sure that the tournament lance of the McBride was in prime condition for the quest.

Leaving there I met another of the Faithful. No $60 rod for him. No number 16 flies in his humble kit. He was a follower of the lower reaches, a cane-pole man if you please. He made his peace with spring and the music of the spheres via five bucks' worth of treasured gear like the kind you found in the attic after Grampa died.

Fishermen are all one and the same to the Wolf. Trout? Well, how'll you have 'em? On a big wet streamer in some of the smashing rips that stiff-arm the boulders down along by Billy Alft's historic fishin' hangout. Rainbows? Speckles? Browns? The Wolf entertains them all and smiles at you betimes. Bass? The Wolf can fix you up. Northern pike? Indeed. Wall-eyes? Bless your heart, one of the greatest fish migrations of the Middle West is the annual run of wall-eyes up the Wolf from Lake Winnebago. White bass? Now, mister, if you can wait until a month after the wall-eye run, the white bass will be along to spawn just like the wall-eyes.

Everybody's river indeed. Because it offers fishing for everybody.

You there, in the funny hat with the bottle of dry-fly oil and scissors hanging from your jacket, get in above Shawano. Just drive

up, turn to your right or left at Shawano, and follow your nose. Anyone will tell you where. And you, John Citizen? I see you have the missus and the four kids and a cane pole for everyone. Good! Take one of the bridges—Fremont or Winneconne or wherever you like the view best. Or you can rent a boat almost anywhere for six bits a day. No trouble at all, sir. Hope the kids can swim.

Some rivers you feel you can shake hands with and pound on the back. You get to feeling that way about the Wolf. There she is, coursing down from Up There, raising fish and merry old Cain in seasons of high water. And you can hardly blame a fellow for being prejudiced in her favor; for along in March, when a man is waiting for May 15 and the general fishing-season opening, he can begin polishing up spoons and spinners for the opening on the Wolf, which will be somewhere around April 20. It all depends on the conservation department's schedule.

You see, they aim to let those migrating wall-eyes get upstream, deposit their eggs, and start down again, spawned out, before the season is opened. It has worked out well these last few years, and the stream is open almost a month before the lid goes off in the rest of the state. So that the Wolf stands alone that first three or four weeks, offering quick relief to sufferers from acute impatience, galloping frustration, and four months of snow shoveling.

You've got to see it to believe it. Folks up that way begin to wear fishin' poles on the tops of their cars on opening day and put them off like straw hats about September 1. Traveling salesmen working the country invariably carry a bit of tackle so they can fish from bridges. School kids play hooky to hit the wall-eye run at its peak. Old women, young women, old men, and young men living up there close their eyes at night on a fixed image of a downward-dipping fish rod.

The wall-eye run into the Wolf begins, they say, even when ice still covers huge Lake Winnebago. Before the parade starts, maybe there's a convention—there's plenty of room for one beneath Winnebago's ice, for the lake measures 30 by 12 miles at its widest points. By the end of March the fish are well on their way, returning, salmon-like, to the places from whence they came—the wide, sun-beaten sloughs and back channels that stretch off on both sides of the lower Wolf.

The Impatient Brotherhood of the Wistful Eye wait and watch. They keep daily tab on things. Are the wall-eyes up yet? Are they spawning? Are they through spawning? Will they get back to Winnebago before the season opens? It's the same old story every spring. To Milwaukee, Chicago, and the teeming places to the south the grapevine carries the story of how things are going as the Great Day nears.

When it finally arrives, it brings the first real trip of the Faithful for the season. From Milwaukee it's a two-hour drive or better, some 100 miles. From Chicago it's 200 miles. The fugitives from winter stream along the highways in a long, happy parade, boats, atop or aft of their cars.
Come with me. We're going up to Fremont and take in an opening.

It's maybe 11: 30 p.m. of opening eve when we arrive there. We rumble across the bridge and survey the town. The place is as bright as day. Lights are on everywhere. There's a chill northwest wind beating downstream. The town is alive with fishermen—visitors as well as natives. Cane poles, steel poles, fly poles and just poles bristle on the big steel bridge. Gasoline lanterns light the fishermen at their vigils. The bridge has a hundred hopefuls strung along both sides. Mackinaws, sheepskins, even the arctic, felt-lined overshoes of the ice fisherman are in evidence.

Cold? Hell, yes; but the season opens at midnight, and they wouldn't miss it for anything. This chap is from La Crosse, on the other side of the state. His neighbor is from Eau Claire, almost 200 miles away. He wants to get into a flash-light picture so he can prove to his wife

he drove that far to go fishing for a single day—and night. (He got in.)

No, those little round pails aren't lunch buckets, stranger. They're bait pails. Every one of them contains its quota of mud minnows or Milwaukee shiners. Oh-oh! It must be near midnight. Some of the boys are baiting up. They're getting ready. There they go, overboard with an ounce of lead, a wriggling minnow, a length of line, and numerous murmured prayers.

In a minute you'll see something. There's the first one! That chap in the heavy overcoat has hooked one. Wonder if he can derrick his fish the 15 feet up to the bridge and over the rail? He's done it. The first firm, cold wall-eye is thumping on the bridge floor, and there's a hot time in the old town tonight!

And so it goes. Far, far into the night. Upstream and downstream lights gleam from the river where fishermen are anchored, testing the promise of the mighty Wolf. They do catch fish. Look at those yellowbellies filling the stringers on the bridge. And remember, this is going on from other bridges, and from banks and from other boats.

Everybody's river? You're darned right.

And do they love it! Your fisherman is a social animal in the extreme, and this is the one great chance of the season to do things en masse. Many a man will stick it out all night. It's a ceremony. Like a convention, only unofficial and more fun.

By morning you can stand on the bridge and count 200 or more boats in both directions along the stream. Bends in the river hide the rest. No area in Wisconsin includes so many boat liveries. Fred Peters, the hale and not too old sage of Gill's Landing, estimates that a good opening day will see between 1,000 and 1,500 boats along the 20 miles of river between Weyauwega and Fremont.

Well, that's one way to see the Wolf. Then there's another way—a way I usually reserve for about the fourth day after the opening. Comes a nice sunny morning, and at 5 a.m. I am driving through Milwaukee's widespread environs to the adjacent municipality of Wauwatosa. Therein dwells a man who will bet you anything you wish to name that he can spit farther than you can, either between the teeth or trench mortar style.

He will be R.G.L. There was a time when R.G.L. felt a deep affinity for the game of cards called bridge; but he has slipped some since he learned there is something mysteriously delightful about an unknown something on the business end of a fish pole.

Through the fresh Wisconsin morning we drive north 65 miles to Fond du Lac, 20 more miles to Oshkosh, and then another 30 miles or so to Weyauwega, where a brief telephone call confirms a previous agreement that one Fred Peters is "on the dock and waitin' fer yuh." Then we drive out by the fairgrounds, down through the long willow grove, and there's Fred with his ancient river vehicle.

The wall-eye run is still on and the river is already alive with fishermen: Hooky-playing school kids, thrifty housewives, overalled farmers, with here and there a fly-rod devotee. They sit, lie, perch, and stand on bank, in boats, and anywhere convenient to the river.

Fred gives the motor of his lengthy inboard a whirl, and we chug into mid-river. Just to be on the water again, slipping the ferrule into the grip of a certain 5-foot steel rod, is very grand. The Wolf is high. The fish are still coming down.

Passing anchored craft, we see fish stringers already taut where they hang overboard. Friendly yips from the dunkers on all sides brighten the day. We anchor at the place where the Waupaca

River gives up trying to amount to much and surrenders its burden to the Wolf. There is a deep hole here, of about 20 feet. A dozen other boats are spread over it. As we jockey the boat around to toss in the anchor there's a whoop near by, and one of our neighbors is standing up with his 16-foot cane pole, wrestling a wall-eye.

26: MacQuarrie of Fremont, Wis., with an opening day string of walleyes, half of them his

Poor fellow. He has a cane pole without a reel. This is going to be fun. The Wolf travels about 4 miles an hour at this place. The wall-eye is a good one, knows how to bend sidewise against the current. Brother Cane-Poler is having a difficult time. He can't shorten line.

He bends backward dangerously while his gallery yells "Oo-oo-oop!" He tries to work the rod back with one hand and reach for the line with the other. He can't make it. The gentleman is being hoist with his own petard. He has not caught the wall-eye; the wall-eye has caught him. The tower man from the near-by Soo Line bridge stands on the trestle and yells, "Get a net!"

The gallery has forgot all about its own fishing. Advice pours in, interspersed with laughter as the gent with the long pole makes ineffectual efforts to tame his fish. He is advised to climb the pole, slide down the line, and tap the fish on the head. He is like the Irishman who started a scrap with a wildcat, then cried:

162

"Now, sthop! Sthop! Can't ye see we're both makin' damn fools of oursilves?"

By this time R.G.L. has bet the gentleman with the long cane pole his extra cigar that he will not land the fish. But a neighborly fellow drifts over and nets the wall-eye, and amidst the general applause Fred Peters calls off all bets for interference or something. The laughter dies away, and within the Peters ark the serious business of returning to one's boyhood days begins.

You dip a hand into a bait bucket and try to get the biggest mud minnow. You will do well if you come up with the next to smallest. You insert a snelled pike hook through the accommodating mouth and out through the gills, give it a twist, and insert it in the martyr's back. With plenty of lead 5 feet up from the bait you drop it overboard and settle back.

The current takes out the bait. The phoebes sing in the trees. A kingfisher darts by on some silly, screaming errand, and R.G.L. bets his extra cigar he'll get the first fish—"not counting Fred Peters, though."

Fred always gets the first one. And the last one too, if he feels like it. Fred has lived in a house by the side of the Wolf for 20 years, a fugitive from Chicago and a friend to man.

We sit. We dunk. We like it. The amenities resound on all sides. The folks up that way are largely amphibious during the wall-eye run. They greet one another on the river of a morning as they would on the streets of the near-by little towns. I once made a date for a haircut with a Weyauwega barber as he put-putted by upstream, bent on obtaining a couple of wall-eyes for breakfast.

It's feast-and-famine fishing. You may collect your limit in a hurry, or you may have to wait. When one is hooked it is likely that several more will be taken. The theory is, the fishing is best at the warmest part of the day. Warmth, 'tis held, sends the wall-eyes off the spawning beds into the main channel and downstream.

We sit and soak it up. We are arranged on the soft sides of the thwarts, bait pails within each reach. The Wolf swirls by in little whirlpools and eddies, sucking at the anchor rope. We see how far the eye can keep in sight a bit of drifting foam. It bobs along—

Oomph!

That's a wall-eye, sure as guns. Just plain oomph! is the word. Nothing flashy. No lightning dash. No flashing leap. Oomph!

Then wiggle, wiggle, wiggle. You reel him in carefully, let him make a run or two, see that he's hooked nicely, and swoosh! Fred Peters has him in the net.

Kid Wall-eye is an obliging customer. He invariably wears a hurt expression when you escort him inboard and slide him onto a stringer. His sensitive nature has been wounded. He didn't dream anyone would do that to him. Not on such a nice day, anyhow.

How about that extra cigar, R.G.L.? Well, O.K., but it's on the block for the next one! R.G.L.'s extra cigar has been known to change hands as often as five or six times in as many minutes when a school of wall-eyes slides beneath searching the sandy bottom for feed.

Not very satisfying fishing? Well, sir, we're not going to argue that. But there are times when it is not a bad idea to adapt oneself to conditions.

Indeed we would prefer to fool a wall-eye with a deep-going artificial.

Indeed we would rather make a two pound brown think we'd just served him a club sandwich off a 4-ounce rod.

But also indeed, we love to dunk the minnow in the swirling Wolf and shuck off about 20 years of this too, too restive civilization.

Your thoughtful cane-poler of the Wolf has met his problem of simple equipment by taping on a reel and line guides. Casting rods do very well in a boat; not so well at the minnow game from a bank. Fly rods are used, but it takes a good one to stand the double strain of the current and the heavy lead required to keep that minnow from floating too close to the surface.

After a bit of probing in the Waupaca river hole, Fred ups anchor and we plow upstream through the festival of fishermen to another favorite spot, the Devil's Elbow, where Peters has plumbed 52 feet of water. The old river drivers of "Come and Get It" days named it the Devil's Elbow because of frequent log jams there.

At the Elbow you may have to wait your turn for a spot to anchor, but we are lucky. Fred coaxes the big boat inshore and keeps it out of the current with a prop of long, strong down-timber. That keeps us out where a man with a casting rod can see action.

R.G.L., released from his manifold labors, gives undivided attention to the tip of his rod. Fred saws wood with that constant jigging of the line. The stringer overside grows heavier. A careful count is kept to see that the limit is not exceeded. R.G.L.'s extra cigar is getting frayed from changing hands. Lunch is broken out. The game goes on. Necks and chops redden in the April sun.

One by one, neighboring boats drift into midstream, whirl their outboards and head for home. Finally Fred announces that the stringer is full. "Enough is as good as a feast, boys." R.G.L. Has been in possession of the extra cigar for half an hour.

But mine was the last wall-eye on the stringer. I claim the cigar.

There is no answer from back of me, where R.G.L. has sat still as a mouse these many minutes. But a telltale odor drifts toward my end of the boat. I turn to confirm a sudden suspicion.

R.G.L. Is almost asleep, the half-burned stogie wagging up and down with his nodding head, in time with the ceaseless pulse of the Wolf.

Stand the Logs on End

Field and Stream, January 1940

Here is the cabin that you have always wanted

Time was when a man could build a log cabin easily and cheaply. All he needed to do was get a couple of demijohns of hard cider and call in the neighbors for a log-raising bee. The logs were to be had for the cutting near by. The man power was on hand to raise them into the wall. And any man worth shucks had the skill to wield ax, adze and chisel.

Times have changed. Except in remote areas, logs are at a premium. The few that remain in the cut-over states bring more at the mill than they do when sold to summer-home builders. With rare exceptions, the log-cabin builder of today, employing the pioneer's method of using horizontal logs, is up against an expensive building proposition. The remaining ax men familiar with log work are likely to command fancy prices.

27: Put the pump in first and build the cabin around it

Some courageous spirits, determined to possess a dwelling the like of which Abraham Lincoln and all great men were born in, will accept no substitute for the real thing. I know one who started out to spend $5,000 and was glad to settle for $15,000. His dream expanded, as building dreams will. The cost was upped by such little items as imported Western cedar telephone poles for the walls, expensive wiring and plumbing jobs and $20 per day which two native ax men charged for their combined services—and earned.

For years I was one of those folks who wanted a cabin on a lake. It was my pleasure to insist upon a true horizontal-log building. There was to be no truck with modern methods. I wanted a log cabin that would stand forever, with a huge stone fireplace, plenty of windows and an old-fashioned wood-burning kitchen range hard at work over in the corner, by gravy.

Wanting such things can be a personal and urgent matter. It is not easy to sway the fixed ideas that people entertain about homes. Certainly these seasonal dwellings on lake and stream, being sentimental vacation places, are no exception. Circumstances, however, deflated my dream of a horizontal-log building. No matter how I figured, I was faced with the fact that such a building would be too costly for me.

But the matter was finally solved, and it has only been since I started to write this that I realize how bitter was my disappointment in giving up the idea of the old pioneer cabin. That disappointment has vanished. The cabin is complete. It has proved its utilitarian and artistic worth through two winters and two summers.

And it is not a horizontal-log cabin. It is a split-log cabin, and I am so sold on the method that my wife has said it may be necessary to pin my mouth over like an apple turnover to keep me from boring people. Everywhere I go I meet someone who is about to acquire "a place at the lake." People are fleeing the cities in droves. New leisure is making dreams come true.

When I meet someone who has been inoculated with the summer-cabin virus, I get him aside, clutch him by the lapel and compel him to listen to my exhortation on the split-log idea. No loquacious survivor of an appendectomy can outdo me in offhand filibustering. Once begun, I never pause. I take him right through from the concrete pouring to the installation of the woodpecker door-knocker.

In conducting these voluntary clinics, I am both windy and technical. I beat about the bush a good deal, but I mean well. There is no stopping me when I set out to do good. Some people never get the slightest inkling of what I am talking about, which comes from the fact that I am a post-graduate split-log builder, while they are undergraduates and cannot vision things like us upper classmen. The fact that I could never be taught in school to plane a board square is neither here nor there.

The split-log idea is not mine. It is merely mine by adoption—and improvement and glorification, by gad. I did not originate this boon to the common man; I only sound as though I did.

And I might as well intersperse here that this sermon is addressed not to those who want something ultra-ultra on the streamlined order. I speak for the full-booted, blizzard-panted, sunburned gent of the outdoors who appreciates red flannels, fireplaces, buckwheat cakes and Saturdays off for fishing.

To these and their tribe I say, without reservation or halting equivocation, the split-log cabin is tops. It is handsome. It is economical to build. And anyone with a primitive knowledge of tools can do most of the work himself.

The thing goes by several names. It is called the stockade cabin, the vertical-log cabin, and even the fence-post cabin (which is a dirty plot to discredit it). The name "split-log," so far as I have been able to discover, was officially applied to it by the Extension Division of the University of Wisconsin. This same division of the school where "the Wisconsin idea" came from gave the split-log building its biggest boost in the three lake states of Wisconsin, Michigan and Minnesota.

28: Stuffy McGuffy, the springer, was as happy as we were when the cabin was complete

No one can say how long split logs, in one form or another, have been used. The Scandinavians and Finns of north Wisconsin and Minnesota had a lot to do with developing the split-log idea. They are expert workers in wood, can do wonders with an ax, and their environment in the lake states gave them plenty of opportunity to keep in practice. They found the big logs getting scarce and expensive. They began using smaller stuff. I have seen split-log cabins—good ones—made of logs not more than three inches in diameter.

It was quite natural, as the big sticks dwindled, for the lake states settlers to use material that the sawmill operators would not buy. These back-country builders did learn they couldn't lay these little logs horizontally, as they had done with the old whoppers of cedar and pine. There wasn't enough supporting strength in them; and furthermore, they had got down to using popple and jack-pine in many places. Well, sir, when you lay that kind of flimsy material horizontal, you leave cracks where rain settles and rot develops.

So they stood their logs on end. In the development of the split-log idea, the moment that was first done may be compared in mechanical progress to the time someone discovered the principle of the wheel. The first structures built in this way consisted of merely these small logs, in the round, up-ended and toe-nailed at the bottom. Various chinking was used—moss , clay, plaster, even cement—and later, new chinking materials which expand and contract the same as wood. This method is still good. But there's a better one.

The next step was probably taken by some practical-minded, old timber thief back in the cutover who saw that he could get two pieces of material out of one log. Perhaps he had a portable sawmill out by the smoke house. He ripped his logs right down the center. The edges of these were uneven; trees grow crooked. A lot of chinking was required.

By and by some smart old savage with a circular power saw discovered he could "saw-edge" those logs, evening up the sides so that they butted together tightly in construction. Right there he was pretty close to what the lumber trade knows in its refined, jointed state as log siding. But hold on a minute, you lumber dealers. I don't want any interruptions, and, anyway, I've got a Plan for Lumber Dealers.

These backwoodsmen who buzzed up the first split-log stuff laid them into the sides of their buildings, round of the logs outside and inside, flat surface facing flat surface, joints overlapping. That was the beginning of it. People learned they could make fine, sound buildings out of material that the lumber-mill buyer wouldn't take for wagon stakes. The split-log cabin was on its way.

In 1933 the University of Wisconsin Extension Division gave the split-log method a hypodermic. The Federal Government had a project in mind that would put settlers on subsistence tracts in the cutover of Wisconsin. They called it Wisconsin Forest Homes, Inc. They went to the Extension Division and asked the farm and home experts to evolve the cheapest and best kind of structure possible for settlers' homes, preferably dwellings to be built from the material on the land.

The experts went to work and picked the bugs out of the split-log dwelling. They published Bulletin No. 158, which is the most complete thing of its kind I have seen, and I have written a dozen states and the Federal Government asking them what they, in the profundity of their knowledge, know about the split-log cabin. One and all reported they knew nothing about it officially. Wisconsin's Extension Division leads the pack and reprints the bulletin every so often to take care of the demand. If you are a Wisconsin resident, it's yours for the asking. If you are a non-resident, you pay 50 cents and bless the day you heard about it.

29: Our pride and joy, that natural-rock fireplace

Eventually the forest-homes project was abandoned for something else. But people had heard about the university's research along the line of improved, refined split-log cabins. Hundreds got the bulletin and started sawing and hammering. They have used this method for beach houses, garages, woodsheds, dog houses, summer cabins, winter cabins, ice-houses and what-not.

The bulletin tackles the job from the ground up. It presupposes its customers know a try-square from a jack-plane, but not much more. It tells what to do about concrete piers in varying latitudes, depending on the depth the frost goes into the ground. It tells what to do about preserving with creosote the underpinnings and any other parts that might need preserving. It discusses sash and door. It includes a dozen or more complete plans, floor and elevation. It treats of roofs, air spaces in walls, flooring, chimneys— and what more do you want to know?

The method can be adapted to almost any building plan. I know, because my cabin evolved from a plan that cost two bucks spot cash, including a cardboard model that gave a preview. The plan was drawn with regular frame construction in mind, but never you mind that when you get your floor plan. Old 158 will see you through and leave a comforting bulge in your billfold to boot.

I am not an architect. I am not an engineer. I am not good at fixing leaky taps, and electric-light sockets leave me helpless. All I knew when this cabin fever started was that I wanted something big and good-looking and comfortable, with two bedrooms, a bathroom, a kitchen and a living room—and a big red pump in the kitchen, with the handle projecting out in the right direction.

I started by drawing my own plans. These were inscribed on the backs of envelopes, restaurant tablecloths or anywhere. I finally got one that was just right. I showed it to an architect friend. He said it was admirable—"beautifully conceived. There is only one thing wrong with it. You can't put a roof that won't leak on that kind of a house."

I slunk out of his presence and was prepared to abandon all hope. But one evening my wife leaped up from her chair, waving a magazine, and said she had found the exact plan she wanted. Being no fool, I agreed she was absolutely right, and that's the plan we got. I mention this so that others will not fiddle around with their own plans unless they were the boys who got pretty high marks in second-semester architectural designing, 23B, Main Hall.

Bulletin 158 crept up on me insidiously. At first I was skeptical. I parted company with the dream of the horizontal-log cabin with reluctance. But I came to cherish good old 158. Especially after I found out I could get enough split cedar logs for the whole shebang at a cost of $142.

How people can sell cedar logs at that price is beyond me. Your split-log adventurer in the lake states has some surprises in store when he starts dickering with the portable mill owners and the farmers who keep busy winters with a bit of logging. My logs were seven to ten inches in diameter. The dealer, a farmer, cut them, peeled them and trucked them forty miles to the building site on the Middle Eau Claire Lake in Bayfield County, Wisconsin, for the aforementioned honorarium. And felt he was making a neat profit.

Prices will vary. You may as well know that now. The cost will depend on the material, accessibility and transportation. Jack-pine or popple is usually cheapest. Cedar, balsam or hemlock will come higher. There is no standard of prices in the regions where most of these cabins are built. Many a family living in the cutover subsists happily through a year on not much more than a few hundred dollars in cash. And incidentally, a lot of silly pity has been wasted on some of these folks who often get along better and lead healthier lives than the summer people who deplore their "lack of advantages."

30: We all studied and we all worked

Every split-log builder will adapt his plans to the conditions where he builds. He will look up the local man who has the logs. He will find the sawmill owner. Often they are one and the same backwoods merchant. He will, if he is wise, employ local help in the actual building, which is not only sensible from the economy view-point, but makes friends as well. It is a good idea to have some friends in a neighborhood where you may abandon a summer place for months at a time.

Our plan called for a certain number of concrete piers. We put in twice as many, just to be on the safe side. The size of our place is 20x40 feet, with a 16x16 foot wing, making it L-shaped. The piers, set in perfectly drained sand, are 12 inches high, 10 inches at the base and taper to six inches at the top. They are spaced 5½ feet apart throughout the building. The sills that ride these piers are six inches square, obtained at a portable sawmill eight miles distant. The joists on the sills are 2x8 inches, with 16-inch centers, which means they are that far apart, beneath the floor.

On the joists went a flooring of hemlock (portable sawmill again). Over that rough flooring went heavy tar paper, then eventually the finished floor on top, which is edge-grain Western four-inch fir. From here on, including that top-grade fir flooring, it will be noted that much of the material is of the best. That is because of the rock-bottom original cost of the split logs. With a more expensive outside wall material we would have trimmed all the way. As it turned out we sort of splurged. And we are not sorry. And the lumbermen we dealt with are not sorry. Which leads us to the conclusion that lumbermen, far from decrying the split-log method, should boost it all the way.

Around the edge of the floor was laid a "water-table" of 2x8 inch fir. That husky plank is what the split logs ride on. The water-table slants outward to shed water that drips off the logs. The outside logs went up first, with the round side out of course, the flat, sawed surface facing inside. Over that inside surface of the outer layer went heavy tar paper and (another luxury) a nationally advertised insulation board. One-inch strips were nailed over the insulating board for an air space, and the inside logs were put on.

We have a living room 18x27 feet. It may sound large, but it isn't. We left the logs off the inside of the two bedrooms, the kitchen and the bathroom, and used knotty Western cedar for an inside finish. All of which amounts to an additional benefaction made possible by our old pal No. 158 and the low first cost of split logs.

To hit some of the other high spots in the building, it might be reported that the rafters for the roof were 2x4's spaced 16 inches apart, covered with ship-lap. Then this was covered with a mineral-surfaced roofing. When you roll it out, it looks like shingles, only it goes on quicker. The valleys in the roof are 16-inch copperized iron, and a false ceiling of cedar boards (a gift from the split-log dealer!) was laid from plate to ridge. Big balsam logs were used for living-room beams, and false rafters running up from these are five-inch spruce logs. This gives the beam and rafter effect on the interior, and the four-inch space between the false cedar ceiling and the true roof above it provides insulation winter and summer.

But enough of these building details. Yours will be different. They are all different. You start out with something in mind and wind up with something else, depending upon local log markets, your current state of affluence and what you last saw over at Joe's place that seemed attractive. Smart folks undertaking this type of structure go around with cameras and notebooks recording things seen and heard. Some people like French windows. Some don't. Some like cobblestone fireplaces. Some like split-rock fireplaces.

We were fortunate in having the job directed by my father, who is a skilled builder. That expedited matters tremendously, but the thing can be done, and is done everywhere, by amateur builders. Wiring, if it is to be included, should be considered early in the game. We erred in this respect. We wired it a year after it was built. An electrician took one look at it and breathed, "An electrician's nightmare." Nevertheless he wired it in a day and a half by ingenious borings through walls, all the while remarking what a snap it would have been to put the wires in during actual building.

The cautious split-log fan will go slow in choosing a site. Where women are concerned, the remote wilderness site is often out of the question. Roads are often expensive to cut through forest cover. Wells can be cheap or expensive. An old deer-hunting companion of ours, named Hank, drove our well point in two hours and charged two bucks. But we knew before we started that the water was there, just under the sand. Another cabin builder I know built high on a rocky hill. It cost him $900 before he got water into his kitchen.

Are such places warm? Could one use them for a winter camp? I am often asked this question. Not long ago I was up there when the thermometer dropped to 13 below zero. A small wood-burning stove taking only 24-inch chunks was all that heated the place except when the kitchen range was lit, which was not always. That cold morning, upon getting up, the whole house was comfortable. With that trivial heater it has been lived in with the thermometer at 30 below. Insulated as it is, it will repel cold better than the well-built city home in which this is being written.

In summer it is airy and cool. It has more than its share of windows. The plan called for a front porch, but we built it on the back instead. It was handier. The plan called for a smaller kitchen. We stole some space from one bedroom and widened the kitchen a couple of feet. The plan called for dormer windows. We omitted them to save expense. I cite this as indicative of how a plan using split logs may be adjusted to needs and conditions.

I know a man in Door County, Wisconsin, who built three small summer guest cabins by this method at a total cost of $79. I know a neighbor on my lake who built a huge floorless woodshed, roughly but adequately, appropriate to its surroundings, at a total cost of $24. These costs are low. The material is at hand there. It is also at hand through the East: in Pennsylvania, New York, Maine and other states. It is at hand in any place where lumbering is a thing of the past, where there is cut-over country with small second-growth coming up and rip-saws to cut it.

Your log house can be unpretentious or lavish. Probably as much fun as you'll ever have will come with the actual building. But there is always something else to be done when the main job is completed. The split-log method is the method for the fellow who likes to putter, who plumes himself on his ingenuity and resourcefulness, who wants his summer place to be something of his own creation.

There was a time when I felt nothing would satisfy me but a horizontal-log structure of the good old rail-fence, early-American, backwoods school of architecture. I changed. I came to appreciate the soundness and goodness of this form of building. Its utilitarian value had its effect upon me. There is nothing artificial about it. The logs are real, standing there like the trees around them.

I see little reason why the man of average means cannot provide himself with this type of home in the woods. Remember, mine is a little on the deluxe side. Useful little one-and two-room affairs can often be had for the price that some families expend on a single summer vacation. The method is sound and economical. The results are more than adequate, and the possibilities for variation are fascinating.

This story is a compilation of several examples, most of which Mac shared first with his Milwaukee Journal *readers and which you can read in* Right Off the Reel *and* Dogs, Drink and Other Drivel. *The anecdote here about Hizzoner's secret trout stream was also related in "Backache Bass" in* Stories of The Old Duck Hunters. *A different telling of this story is found in a local tourist brochure that can be found at the Barnes Area Historical Association MacQuarrie Museum.*

Get Out of That Rut!

Field and Stream, July 1941

Maybe you are in a fishing rut. Maybe you are overlooking sport close to your home

I drove into Mercer, Wisconsin, one day last summer and immediately looked up my friend Frank—trapper, fisherman, first-class woodsman. "How are they hittin' in Long Lake? In Mercer Lake? In the flowage?" You fling those questions at a man like Frank almost before you have shaken his hand.

He studied me. "How good are you at lugging a canoe?"

"Just fair, but willing."

"Come on."

"The truth is," Frank explained as we drove off with a canoe riding the car top, "the lakes that everyone is fishing are not turning up much right now. But I know some pot-holes. . . ."

That one-day expedition into those pot-holes—unnamed, unsung, largely unknown—turned out to be one of the best fishing trips I had that season. It also turned out that Frank was kidding about the canoe. He carried it.

The canoe was dropped into a pretty good-sized pot-hole lake. "No name for it," said Frank. And it was a half mile long and half that wide! On about the tenth cast a five-pound northern pike slashed out from beneath a brushy spruce which had fallen into the water. He was released. It was bass we were after. And, as the feller says, did we get them!

While scores of vacationing fishermen on more accessible near-by lakes were bewailing indifferent luck Frank and I literally knocked the spots off large-mouth bass in a series of five pot-holes. It was simply the difference between following the beaten path and getting out on your own to some place where the other fellow wasn't.

These particular pot-holes, north of Mercer, are no especial secret. Aerial survey maps of north Wisconsin show them up plainly. The reason why they remain pretty much virgin is because you have to tote a canoe a half mile over a rugged, brushy trail before you can wet the bottom of it. The fact that so few seem willing to do that sort of thing nowadays does not speak well for the pioneering instinct of present-day fishermen.

Only the handful take the harder road. A lot of others complain about the poor fishing. You would think fishermen looking for "a better 'ole" would get out there and frog around. Darned few of them do it. They return again and again to the handy spots. This reporter hates to preach or be preached to; yet he can do his brethren of the cult no greater service than to shout: "Get out of that rut and get back in there!"

That day with Frank was one of many such days. The temptation to jump into a boat at the nearest dock, or put into a stream which you can drive to by car, is a great one indeed. But wiser fishermen are striking out on their own, some of them actually exploring new places and, of course, taking that long chance of finding nothing. Mostly, however, unexpected fishing dividends are turned up by the curious ones.

31: A pothole lake largemouth that will test the scales

Before Frank and I finished that day in the unnamed pot-holes—and Wisconsin has hundreds of them—we had each taken a limit of largemouths, some close to three pounds. We had seen virgin timber—hemlocks two feet through by the thousand, white pines not much smaller. We had jumped deer from their feeding places at the water's edge. And we stirred out of one pot-hole weed bed a veritable leviathan of a muskie, which we did not land. After which Frank, sizing up the bass, allowed "enough is as good as a feast."

It was indeed a day to remember, and this push into back country was made in a day. No camping impedimenta. Just the canoe, tackle and lunch. On one of those pot-hole gems reached by a short portage over a steep hill Frank showed me his pet beaver dam, a description of which is apt to make a liar of any man.

The dam splits this particular little body of water plumb in two. It is about one hundred yards long, perhaps twenty-five feet in width and ten to twelve feet from top to bottom. This sort of wilderness treasure, guarded by its inaccessibility, is just the extra dividend that the questing fisherman finds.

Pine trees fourteen inches in diameter grow from this great dike of mud, stones and sticks. How old? Frank couldn't say. He guessed several hundred years. There it lay, a monument to the industry of the beaver, not five miles from a heavily traveled highway. Over the great rubble heap you saw where fresh cuts had been laid. Frank, who keeps an eye on this sort of thing, estimated that only fourteen beaver remained there now, as a result of recent trapping seasons, but that they would quickly build back through closed seasons, now in effect.

On one side of this dam the water was six feet lower than on the other side. Both the bodies were deep little spots. I took a largemouth from the lower pond. He insisted on grabbing a lure after it was dragged over a log. The fish followed it to the log. The lure was hustled over it, a foot out of water, dropped in—and Mister Largemouth nailed it. I remember that was fun, but the big beaver dam is the thing I shall remember longest.

That night was one for the bass fisherman's book. Thunder-heads frowned down in the north, and out of them came a cold wind. But the west remained alight with a dramatic sunset, and Frank said, "We'll stick with it and let it rain. They're goin' to start smashing things."

Out of one fair-sized mass of spatter-dock we took bass after bass. They would lie there in the tangle and slide five feet along the top after a double-spinner affair, with a red bucktail between the spinners. As Frank put it, grinning, "Those babies really come out and bark at you!"

I could write a small book about that one set of pot-holes off the beaten track, but there are too many other precedents to mention which help prove the case.

Up in the Superior National Forest of Minnesota several years ago I had a similar experience. Barney Thomas, Duluth photographer, and I left Slim Lake, which is not far from Burntside Lake, out of the city of Ely, and portaged two miles over hardly more than a deer trail to a bass fisherman's Nirvana. Completely worn out from the portage, we made camp, heated the quickest meal in our pack—a can of dried soup—and then looked around.

I walked down to the lake. To this day I do not know its name, or if it ever had a name. A tangle of logs reached out from shore. Eager to fish, I walked out over these, intending to cast into deeper water beyond. Before I got to the end of the tangle a bass grabbed a pork-rind lure which I had trailed in the water. We camped there five days. We caught bass at will. Only the few we ate were killed.

And here's another precedent, pertinent if not legal. About ten miles out of Portage, Wisconsin, near the little hamlet of Briggsville, runs an unassuming little river, the Neenah. It empties into the historic Fox River about fourteen miles as the river flows from Briggsville.

One nice autumn day, while hunting pheasants with Otto Byer of Briggsville, I dropped a bird on the opposite bank of this stream. Byer's German shorthair pointer swam the stream for the retrieve.

Until that moment I had regarded this modest stream as just another watercourse. But the husky dog had a bit of trouble with the current. The Neenah was deeper and stronger than it seemed. So I asked Otto about it.

"It's plenty of river," he said, "but few pay much attention to it."

The following summer Otto and I drifted down the beckoning Neenah River, and what we did to the bluegills was a caution. At times it is supposed to produce good bass fishing. Byer estimates that not more than four or five parties float down it annually—"they can't be bothered hauling in a boat!"

That little river went through a lush green northern jungle of hardwoods. Wildlife was on every hand. I have never been so close to the great white American egrets as going down that stream. A few deer were seen. More would have been sighted if the day had been warmer, for then they would have come to drink. The point is, here is a red-hot pan-fish stream, slightly more than one hundred miles from a city of 600,000 (Milwaukee), and "they can't be bothered hauling in a boat!"

In that same country, in the fall of 1936, to the accompaniment of laughter and much joking, a crew of archers, including Larry Whiffen of Milwaukee and myself, went up there during Wisconsin's first archery season for deer. It fell to Whiffen and me to drive out a 180-pound buck which was killed by Chet Sroka, Portage fire chief. And perfectly good citizens in Portage had told Chet there wasn't a deer left in the Baraboo hills! You should have seen Mr. Sroka take that big buck into Portage on his car.

Isn't it strange that people should get so far away from their own back yards that they do not know what is in them? What have you missed in yours?

I used to know a fishing-hunting chap who lived in the heart of great sporting country. Muskies, deer, ducks. People came for hundreds of miles to prod around in his back yard, but he always went a-fishing or a-hunting to the same old places. Oh, he had a hundred places where he wanted to go look-see. But he never got to it. He forgot to pick himself up by his bootstraps and do it.

Here's still another case in point. I own a little place on a lake in northwestern Wisconsin. It happens to be the Middle Eau Claire Lake, but what is said of it will apply to hundreds of similar areas in the lake states. Over a small ridge at the south end of this lake lie two good-sized pot-holes. The first one calls for a quarter-mile hike in; the second is about that much farther beyond the first. No names, of course. Just pot-hole lakes. In Maine they would call 'em ponds.

Both are naturals for mallards and ringnecks early in the season and for bluebills when the flight comes down from the north. Yet there are ardent hunters owning property on the shore of that lake who don't know those pot-holes are there! And if this helps 'em any, they're welcome to them. I'll find some new ones.

The technique of getting "back in there" unquestionably calls for a canoe or a portable boat of some kind. This is no place to discuss that at length, but the up-and-doing fisherman is handicapped without one. For example, river float trips offer one of the best ways of filling a creel. Still, in these days of hard-fished, easily accessible waters, float trips don't get the play they should, even here in Wisconsin, a state of many rivers.

Over in Madison the Wisconsin Conservation Department knows, from wardens' surveys, that this state has some 8,000 miles of known, charted trout streams. Of course, most of these are not float-trip waters, but over and above these streams there are many thousands more miles of other streams containing bass, northerns and walleyes, most of them navigable—and pretty much neglected by fishermen.

32: Inaccessibility may not always be a matter of distance. Nearby fishing waters in your own bailiwick may hold the answer

Running into the famous Wolf River at Gill's Landing, near Weyauwega, is the Waupaca River. You can make a 12-mile float trip down this smallmouth bass river from noon to a little after supper time. And you can nail some dandy smallmouths. The river hardly ever sees a float-tripper.

Fred Peters of Wolf River says, "Not enough fishermen make that trip to stick in your eye." Why? "Because they can get boats much easier on the Wolf." For that kind of inertia the complaining fisherman is deserving of little sympathy.

It isn't that these back-in-there places are not known. In Wisconsin they are pretty well mapped, and so they are in Michigan and Minnesota. The Wisconsin Land Economic Survey has detailed maps of six or eight fishing counties in the north. These show lakes, rivers and hunting cover in great detail. In addition, most of the fishing country has been aerially mapped, and map sections are available through the Wisconsin Highway Commission. Fishermen who declare there is no longer an angling frontier should have a look at some of these maps, showing waters with no roads to them.

Map-making can go the other way, however. Among my friends I count a certain county highway commissioner, a splendid fisherman and an extremely capable engineer. For years his office annually issued a revised highway map of the county. For some time he kept on including the old logging-day tote roads, most of which led to streams.

He told me once his county has more than three hundred miles of these old tote roads, many of them still traversable by autos! And then I got hold of one of his maps and saw that some of the old tote roads were omitted. Another map came along in due course, and it showed even fewer tote roads. By and by he had a road map showing only the United States, state, county trunk and town highways. Why?

"Well, sir," said he, "the fishermen nowadays go too fast in their cars to see where a tote road branches off; so why make more work for the draftsman?"

The truth is that an old and healthy concept of the camping-cruising game is slipping a bit. Not for lack of places to go. But at least partly for lack of people willing to do their own wilderness housekeeping for a few days while "back in there." Let us be completely honest about this.

As an ex-Boy Scout, I've had my share of canoe toting, browse bed making, camp cooking and dish washing. I will, at the drop of the hat, shove these jobs off on someone else and do something twice as laborious in return. Anything to get out of the routine.

I have no delusions about trying to mix comfortable cruising and enthusiastic fishing. They don't mix very well unless you are a work horse and a bear for punishment. When you should be out there with a fly rod, you are likely to be found staking down the tent. There is just one answer to the fellow who wants to skim the fishing cream—get a guide and pay him for doing the housekeeping.

A muskie enthusiast with whom we have often fished puts it this way. "When I go fishing, I want to fish. I don't want to bother with dishes and blankets and tents. I came to fish. By gosh, I will fish! That's why I always hire a guide. When I do that, I just double my fishing time in the woods."

He just doubles his time. That's worth considering.

Then I know another ardent "back-in- there" fisherman. This gentleman once dropped a live porcupine in my lap; so you may be sure I know him well. He goes annually for two weeks into far-off Canadian waters. And he goes to fish. No housekeeping for him. He just wallows in fishing. A few years ago he probably broke the world's record for a northern pike, but didn't know it.

That was in Fog Lake, Ontario. He worked on a northern for a half hour. When the fish was brought exhausted near the canoe, his guide measured it by laying a paddle parallel to it and marking the paddle. They had no tape measure. Three days later they came across two gold prospectors, borrowed a tape and learned that their northern was ten inches over the recognized world's record.

Inaccessibility may not be a matter of distance. Near-by waters in your own bailiwick may hold the answer. A shining example of tremendous sport-fishing resources, almost entirely unexploited, is the Mississippi River where it runs between Minnesota and Wisconsin. Why that is, heaven only knows. Ol' Miss' elbows down between these two states for a couple of hundred miles. It's like a long, narrow ocean washing their borders. And you've got to kick people in the pants to make them go fishing over that way.

It seems that fishermen just do not associate good fishing with a river carrying the commercial loads the Mississip' now carries, since the $500,000,000 navigation dams and locks went in. It's too bad. The natives over there just carry on a piscatorial pogrom all season through.

Up at Red Wing, in Minnesota, they call one great dam pool "the live-box." Farther downstream a bit, at Alma, Wisconsin, a fellow could live wholly on fish from rod-and-reel fishing if he wanted to do so.

Two splendid highways parallel the river, No. 61 on the Minnesota side and No. 35 on the Wisconsin side. Thousands of tourists come scorching up and down these north and south corridors looking for fishing, apparently oblivious of the fact that the Father of Waters, at their elbow, rich in cover, feed and spawning grounds,

184

seldom lets down a guest, be he a seeker after the succulent catfish or a fly-rod fanatic bent on smallmouths.

This is "back-in-there" water right on tap at the roadside. I've talked with Mississippi River folks about it by the hour. Fellows like Lyman Howe, the Prairie du Chien publisher; Ed Anderson, the sporting-goods man at Red Wing; Capt. C. F. Culler, chief of the U. S. Bureau of Fisheries, mid-West division, at La Crosse. Why don't these embattled fishermen have a go at those Mississippi bass—and walleyes and northerns and what-not? One and all, they answer: "You've got me."

One of the most indefatigable "back-in-there" fellows I know is a Milwaukee dentist, F. H. Coburn. The good doctor, who prefers his muskies on a fly rod, is always trying to find out what's over the next hill. As a result, he does pretty well at the fishing game. He fishes far and wide over the state, and when he hasn't the time to go too far he makes a 20-minute run in his car up the Milwaukee River and catches smallmouth bass!

That statement, of course, makes me out a liar to 10,000 Milwaukee fishermen. Not that they have given the old Milwaukee a try. Oh, no. They just know there's no use in trying. But Dr. Coburn, with no more skill than the average, but with considerable more initiative, has discovered that he can pick off some good smallmouths in water that the old guard quit fishing years ago. This is a "back-in-there" place simply out of mind. Not very good smallmouth fishing, of course. But in emergencies a smallmouth devotee will be satisfied with a brace, whereas in wilderness waters he might expect limits for the stringer and more to be put back. Anyway, there ought to be more Doc Coburns.

A fellow hates to think that the fishing clan has lost the knack of getting out on its own. You hate to think of fishermen trudging along the same old angling trail, year after year, with slight success. In all truth, the enthusiast should bend himself to the art of looking up the less hard-pressed spots. He will, if he is a man of consequence and self-reliance, do it on his own; and if he keeps his mouth tightly closed, who shall blame him?

Fish are like gold; they're where you find them. And it's getting harder and harder to find them in places where there are a great many people fishing, day after day, season after season.

Lest this reporter has seemed to preach, he begs the privilege of relating just one tale about the fellow he considers the champion of champions when it comes to getting off the beaten trail. This person is, of course, the honorable President of the Old Duck Hunters' Association, Inc. Mention a new spot to him, and his nostrils quiver like a beagle on the scent of a cottontail.

For years he and I went on week-ends to the Namakagon River, in Sawyer County, Wisconsin, to fish for brown trout. He got tired of it. He wanted new worlds to conquer. So one day when a garage attendant in Cable accidentally mentioned a stream called Cap's Creek, the President was all ears. He got all the dope, including a map scrawled on an envelope. Then he dropped me off at the Namakagon and sought out Cap's Creek. No, he wouldn't take me in with him. He had found the place, hadn't he? (You discern here the genuine "back-in-there" guy.)

I fished the old Namakagon, a splendid brown-trout stream, and did fairly well with browns on floating flies. But nothing to compare with what Hizzoner did. He came back at nightfall with a limit creel of big brook trout. All out of Cap's Creek, he said.

That went on for an entire season, with Mister President mum as anything about it all. Always he got the fish. Always he gave no inkling of the secret the man in the garage had imparted. It was the next year before I learned the truth. Another resident of Cable unveiled the truth of Cap's Creek to me. Asked about it, he replied: "Cap's Creek? Hell, man, it's a state fish refuge!"

So a man can make a mistake, but by and large he can't go wrong by getting "back in there."

The Milwaukee Journal *editors certainly must have known what a gem they had in MacQuarrie; otherwise how could you explain sending him off on a five-week tour of the Sunny South? Despite MacQuarrie's claim in this story that everyone was doing it, it's hard to believe very many working folk were able to go for that length of time.*

He did submit many articles back to his home paper. Several of these are included in the "Traveling Man" and "Conservationists" chapters in Dogs, Drink and Other Drivel.

While this article was printed in 1942, the actual tour took place in February, 1941, before Pearl Harbor and the U.S. entry into war.

Sportsman's Journey

Outdoors, February 1942

One morning last winter I locked the garage doors and headed south. Before returning to Milwaukee five weeks later I hunted quail in Alabama, fished on the Gulf coast, took in a couple of rousing bird dog trials, trolled in the Gulf stream, wandered in the astounding Okefenokee swamp and –

Wait a minute. This is getting pretty headlong. And anyway what I did is of no importance except as it reveals what others can do. Indeed, what others are doing by the tens of thousands. It was a sportsman's journey. Sightseeing was incidental. Biggest hurdle is just starting out. No longer are such trips the pleasures solely of the wealthy. No longer do Pa and Ma wait for that "ship to come in" before going. Pa and Ma have learned from other Pas and Mas that "everyone goes south now." The northern sportsman, contemplating snowy game fields, will learn all about that when he rolls south to see for himself.

He will see trailer camps with a thousand outfits parked. He will see a fleet of charter boats at one dock numbering upward of a hundred. He will see a country with an important industry built around the little bobwhite quail. He will see hotels and wayside cabins in use which hardly have the paint dry on their walls. And he will see license plates from a score or more states on the cars of brother sportsmen.

I remember that morning of departure. Beginnings and endings have a way of coming sharply into focus. Perhaps that is because of the American habit of liking to go and liking to come back. It was snowing a little. I checked over the bags and duffle, startled at the way they filled the car. But then, I reasoned, five weeks is a long time to be gone and I was waiting on the sweet time of no man's laundry.

The start-off is all a great part of it. It is a time of anticipation, of course, and in this case that was blessed with a certain smug certainty that things had been planned ahead as well as they could be. Beyond where the great smudge from Chicago oozed out over the countryside in the gentle northeast wind, the snowy straightness of U.S. highway 45 gave way to clear, fast concrete. Through the corn country towns of Illinois, each earmarked with identical grain elevators, then further south into southern Illinois, and by then it was raining.

Ha! Rain at Harrisburg, Ill., and last night snow in Wisconsin.

Here was a definite step in that transition of climate which the southward moving horde peers through car windows to see. No doubt about it, one of the thrills is the constant lookout for the little signs which say "You're getting there, Mister."

The first cotton field, brown and scraggy under the clouds of the second morning. But a cotton field! Then came Paducah, and the majestic flood of the Ohio, more winding roads through sleeping fields of corn and cotton and finally, shining green grass on the road shoulders. Gettin' south. fella!

And then, from the corner of an eye, whisking by a cross road of two muddy ruts comes a Black man on a mule, with a sack of flour over the saddle. There, exactly, was the place where the north left off and the south began.

The second afternoon I drew up in front of a hotel. On the steps, waiting, was a small, compact man in boots and khaki, scanning the passing traffic – Braxton Oswalt, of Ethelsville, Alabama, who'd been there only a half hour. Just so nicely can the sportsman-on-the-go stick to his schedule in these days of good cars and endless roads.

This was like coming back home for I had hunted here before. Later when I drove into the plantation yard and black, grinning Johnny and Albert Corder came into view, standing by a fire of chips, it seemed time had just stopped in the two-year interim, for they were doing precisely the same thing 24 months before when I bade them goodbye and pulled out for home. An Alabama Black man, on a frosty day, can build a fire of chips quicker than you can say "B-r-r-r!"

A frosty morning in Dixie, a couple good horses, a half dozen worthy shooting dogs, Johnny and Albert bringing up the rear in their customary high spirits – there you have a few assorted reasons why upland bird hunters dig up their shootin' boots and head south in January.

190

Let no one misunderstand. This native of Wisconsin does not propose to abandon the ruffed grouse and the sharp-tailed grouse and the gorgeous, clattery pheasant. Perish the thought! But there comes a time ....

There comes a time, gentlemen, when winter lays heavily upon the land, when patience is more a necessity than a virtue. And then the cure is a morning on quail when the bright sun eats up the Dixie frost and makes the needles of the longleaf pine glisten as if they had been varnished. Then the rich smells of warm, sedge-grown earth are like an old tonic suddenly remembered and taken in great gulps. Then the hunter man who but faintly remembers last autumn's pheasants may live again similar moments. And if we know our hunter men, they will be taut as fiddle strings as they drop out of the saddle and march up, guns ready, to the place where Doc and Judy are pointing.

Doc took our eye. A leggy pointer, close enough for the heavy cover and wide enough for the open reaches, he was one of the intense kind that drools a bit when the scent is there, and stands until ordered in to retrieve. The same Doc, urged into his kennel that evening, after being down four hours, ran whimpering back to the pick-up truck in which the dogs were carried to the hunt. It takes the firecracker bird dog to do that, especially when just inside the kennel gate are the feed pans and the warm taw beds.

Those Alabama bobwhites .... They say no man can eat 'em steadily for 30 successive days without tiring of them. Heaven grant that someday this worshipper at their shrine will get a chance to try it. This worshipper feels, as Johnny Corder put it, it might be like sending a rabbit to fetch a head of lettuce.

Sorry to say goodbye to Oswalt and his chicken dinner with hot corn sticks and pecan pie and afterwards the light-wood fire on the hearth and a bowl of home-grown peanuts close by and endless talk of dog and gun into the wee hours. Sorry to leave Doc and Johnny and Albert and the far, sunny reaches of Alabama's piney hills.

But this was a sportsman's journey. There was an itinerary. I knew a place ....

The bayous of the Gulf of Mexico, in the vicinity of Gulfport and Biloxi. There would be some speckled sea trout, some Spanish-moss-draped trees and a man could feel, waiting for April in the north, the sudden tremble of a casting rod fighting back at a fish.

I rented a boat for 50 cents, got more live shrimp than I needed for a similar sum, and put-putted out there. The sun was warmer than it had been in the quail country and the sea trout were perfectly willing to take either plugs or shrimp. I put them all back. On this one stretch of bayou perhaps two dozen boats were fishing that day, but the one I'll always remember was that containing the two retired school teachers.

Our boats drifted together and I had a strike and collected a two-pound trout. I offered it to them, and they accepted it only after I explained I just wanted to catch 'em. They were a bit sniffy at first when I said I had just the one.

"Humph!" said the big fat one in the back seat. "Look into this bag."

Those two old dears had enough sea trout there to last them for a week. They explained they were supplying fish for the whole neighborhood. No license, no bag limit. Just go out there and haul 'em in.

On the road again....

Shuqualak, Miss., for an afternoon of watching dogs run in the national quail championship, and the biggest horseback gallery I ever saw at a field trial. I counted 120 horses at one time. My, oh my, how these southern folk go for those field trials. They remind me of a crony who, in moments of stress, is wont to cock his heels on his desk, go wall-eyed staring out the window and declare: "A horse and a dog, that's it."

And so to Thomasville, Ga., center of a hunting preserve country that will make the northern sportsman's eyes bug out. Thousands of acres managed for quail, turkey and deer. The sort of thing, they keep on telling us, that is coming for the north as sure as the rising sun, what with posted lands and the difficulties which beset farmers and hunters in their relations with each other.

I went away from there convinced that the northern states must meet this problem with a two-edged sword – a broad program of public shooting grounds, by any practicable method, and a glad hand to the private sportsman who wants to spend his own good money on his own preserve.

I found Herbert L. Stoddard 12 miles out of Thomasville on cozy Sherwood plantation. Formerly a taxidermist and confrere of the late Carl Akeley of Africa fame, Stoddard is the man who has become the country's fountainhead of advice and information on the bobwhite quail. His book, "The Bobwhite Quail" has no equal.

To walk with him an hour or two over these piney quail lands is like being given a new pair of eyes. The sportsman of this day can hardly afford to pass up the information that men like Stoddard are providing. Students of wildlife, especially of upland game, go to him like the bee to the honey tree.   Sportsman's journey? Indeed the Stoddard visit was a part of such, although I never fired a gun for two days while with him – and what's more, never thought of it. Just that fascinating can be the philosophy and learning of such a wildlife expert. The sportsman of today is hearkening more and more to the Stoddards, just as farmers, 35 years ago, began to hearken to county agents who told them to plant alfalfa.

Albany, Ga., next stop. And here again was a touch of home. On hand were Larry Henning and Art Mueller, of Milwaukee, the former with his Spunky Creek Nina, put down with her daddy, Spunky Creek Coin, in the United States amateur quail championship. Coin won the stake, eventually, and Nina was injured by colliding (this is not a field trial pun) with a stake.

Let the man from the north know that, invariably, he can arrange his January-February schedule to include a taste of these trials. They are a fetching part of the picture, to anyone even faintly interested in bird dogs.

If Southern hospitality is just a phrase to the northern gunner, let him contemplate what happened to me. I had not been on the grounds of these trials for 10 minutes when an utter stranger, Siego Farkas, of Albany, walked over and offered me the loan of his horse. The northerner cannot help but remember such an incident, and the south is full of them. He will also remember, beyond all doubt, the lads in greasy coveralls at the filling stations who greet him with all the chivalry of a knight in shining armor. Things like that are good for us "damn" Yankees.

I drove east in Georgia to Waycross and found John M. Hopkins, superintendent of the great Okefenokee swamp, now a national refuge. U.S. highway No. 1 goes down one side of this vast area, which Hopkins declares is the largest swamp in the United States, excepting the Everglades, which he holds is not a swamp.

Mallards and black ducks by the thousand winter in Okefenokee. And a great congress of wading birds. And over all the vast swamp an air of profound isolation and mystery, heightened by the gray Spanish moss of the cypress trees. Uncle Sam is getting things ready here to entertain the public. He is building walks into the swamp, so convenient that even lady tourists in their fine clothes can trip in there, take one look, say "oh-h-h-h ..." and hustle back to their cars and the roaring sociability of U.S. highway No. 1.

For the present the Ok'fenok' as the natives call it, is still its old, gloomy, forbidding self, headwaters of the storied Suwannee river, home of bear, deer, turkeys and fish. No hunting is permitted but fishermen should bring along a bass rod and a box of tackle. Largemouths up to ten pounds are not uncommon. The day I fished it, in a cold downpour, only a few small jackfish were taken.

Fishermen should remember their best point of entry is on the Fargo, Ga., or west side. Go to Fargo and follow your nose, over soft but bottom-solid sand roads which lead into the fishing camps edged against the swamp. No fisherman will ever forget the place. Here, if anywhere, silence and the brooding mystery of all-outdoors, come home to roost.

But go and see it for yourself. I pushed on to St. Petersburg for a day of more speckled sea trout fishing in Boca Ciega bay. It was one of those half-hazy days when you get sunburned before you know it. The sea trout were doing famously. After that there was a thrust inland to a place I had long wanted to see –Lake Apopka, famous for its big bass. As luck would have it, the northwest wind brought cold, so much of it the citrus growers got out their smoke pots, and we got right out of there, bassless. But we're goin' back there some day.

All through this trip I continually had to repress an impulse to just roost some place for a week or two. But I had places to go.

Like Gordon's Pass, for instance, which is just a few miles out of Naples, Fla., and is a fisherman's hideaway deluxe. The Pass itself is a spot on the Gulf coast where the ocean comes rushing inland to the everglades through a 100-yard wide opening in a beach of white sand. Palms bend over this scene and there is fishing galore. Most of it is done back among the 10,000 islands of the everglades.

When I was there the place was filled with more than a hundred parked trailers, all housing those far-seeking, close-lipped gentry who have a knack for picking spots where there is sure to be something on the other end of a line.

Not the least of the fun at Gordon's Pass and also fishing up the nearby Palm river, was cleaning the fish at night, feeding the offal to bottomless pelicans, and even reaching down and patting a pelican's bobbing head after handing him a mouthful. A wonderful bird, indeed!

It was while in this sector, fishing with an old comrade of northern waters, Allan E. Bakewell (he swipes my rowboat in the summer) that I achieved what he says was a signal triumph. With a five-ounce fly rod and fiddler crab bait I caught two good-sized sheepshead and Brother Bakewell declares this is strictly against the rules, for the fly rod lacks the backbone to stick a hook into the toothy face of a sheepshead.

I had to admit, however, after netting this pair, that one had been snagged on its soft outer gill cover and in the case of the other the hook just lodged between two teeth. The fish never really closed on it. Also with Bakewell I ascended the Palm river in the Naples sector and had a go at snook with casting equipment. They were lurking beneath the mangrove roots close in shore. Any reasonably manipulated plug did the trick. Sir Snook is decidedly not a bum, for he comes thrashing along the surface to snatch bait, much like a hungry smallmouth bass after a bass bug.

Miami next stop. The sportsman arriving here of an afternoon can whet his appetite with a visit to pier Five along about 5:30 o'clock. Then the charter boat fleet will be in, captains and mates lounging about or cleaning the day's catch of dolphin, amberjack, kingfish, sailfish, or what have you? Out of that indigo blue Gulf stream almost anything is likely to pounce on a bait.

First of all the stranger to the Gulf stream looks to see if it's actually true that the green of the coastal waters is separated sharply from the indigo of the Gulf stream. Indeed the waters are so divided, but it does take some little while for the neophyte to get the idea that the Gulf stream is really a river in the ocean.

There was, that day, some business with a dazzling green and yellow dolphin and that was pretty snappy fishing, considering how dolphin like to jump. But it was nothing to the workout the husky man in the other seat beside me had with a 100-pound sand shark. No leaper, but stubborn, is Sir Shark. The husky man, in good trim, for he keeps that way for this purpose, worked on that shark for 34 minutes. It was like hitching an 18-pound test bass line to a turpentined dog.

Any fisherman worthy of the name learns to depend upon his exploratory instinct. None is more helpless than the questing angler who will not skirmish for himself at filling stations, barber shops, pharmacies – anywhere that it appears the fisherman's tartan is chewed to tatters. Which will be almost any place where more than three men foregather any time in Florida.

Vero Beach was the jumping off place in this case. Three interviews with filling station gallants in which the whole three casually mentioned the name of Bobbie Bragg. They mentioned others too, but all were on common ground with Bobbie Bragg – "see him first." This is one of the ways the fishing fraternity spots the signs and reads the portents. Such casual, repeated name-mentioning is as plain to a fisherman as a hobo's cryptic chalk signs on a water tank.

Bobbie Bragg was cleaning a reel. After he got through explaining that this particular make of reel corroded faster than other good ones in salt water he settled down to a little preliminary sparring. Part of the game. But I had my foot in the door. Fishermen can hardly be expected to leap at each other with information.

However, after the handshake has been given, the lodge ritual read and the coast looks clear, there will come a moment when the Man With the Dope will let drop a recipe. No Chamber of Commerce stuff, this. This is the real McCoy, the voice of the local oracle, the laying on of hands as it were between fishermen.

"Go down to the second bridge out of Winter Beach and get hold of Emmett Walker. Do it now. He may be carryin' someone out if you wait until morning."

It was that simple. A half hour after invading Vero Beach I had Emmett Walker hog-tied for the following morning. That next morning he was staking out his Jersey cow when I got there. Then he filled a pail with live shrimp bait and said "Now, where did I leave that other boat? Oh yes, drive up the road two miles ... "

From men like Emmett Walker the northern bait caster can learn plenty. This is natural, for the Emmett Walkers see few days

196

pass when they are not working a plug somewhere around tangled mangrove roots. There is an assurance about their style. They wield a plug rod with the air of men very familiar with same. Emmett Walker with his stubby four-foot rod, expensive multiplying reel and his slap-slap of the line on the surface as he retrieved his bait, jerkily, was a fine picture of a man going about a business about which he knew a great deal.

Here we caught speckled sea trout. One went over 5 pounds. "Good enough to mount," opined Mr. Walker. And here also we caught a dozen channel bass, astoundingly powerful for their size. The biggest we boated that day was 10 pounds. Laugh, dang ye! Yes, I know the world record is over 74 pounds. And I know too, that 10-pounder gave me a new concept of what that much fish muscle can do pitted against a 14-pound line and a light tubular steel casting rod.

In the high moment after the landing of this fish I made the inevitable comparison – was he as gimpy as a spring-run rainbow trout in the Wisconsin Brule? I think I thought he was, pound for pound, for maybe a couple of hours. Anyway my wrist ached, but when it stopped aching the channel bass went back to his proper notch of things gamey. No, he is not quite the equivalent of a spring-run Brule rainbow. The rainbow is close kin to a bolt of lightning.

A poor way to honor so gallant a fighter. I am ashamed for being so inept in trying to say how much I really respect that channel bass as a fish of action.

It was in this Indian river country, 10 minutes off roaring No. 1, that one of those little extra scenic dividends was collected. This consisted of rows and rows of Australian pines, alternating with royal palms on the back roads. Scenes like this can be duplicated in a hundred places in Florida.

The pace quickened after Florida. There were more quail in North Carolina, and a day on a Robinson Crusoe island, owned by Uncle Sam, two miles off the coast out of McClellanville, South Carolina. It is Bull's island, an inviolate game refuge, another of the spots which the government has grabbed and barred to hunting for all time to come.

Sportsman's journey? Without hunting?

You bet! Creep down through the palmetto of Bull's island with Superintendent Hills and see some of the wild turkeys they are keeping pure of strain. The finger will not itch for the trigger. Not until places like Bull's island breed thousands and thousands of turkeys and then maybe there will be enough to distribute around on the mainland for shooting ground stocking.

The fattest mallards and black ducks I ever saw lifted lazily from dammed ponds on Bull's island. Bought from Gayer Dominick, New York broker who operated it as a private shooting preserve, Bull's island has become a mecca for wildlife students and photographers. Lorene Squire, noted woman bird photographer has built her camera blinds around Bull's island ponds and Etcher Dick Bishop, of Philadelphia has made some of his fine slow motion waterfowl movies there.

Here again the off-the-trail sportsman learns something. In the former shooting lodge Uncle Sam will board a visitor for $2.50 per day. The room is included as a gift. It seems there is some department regulation against Uncle going into the hotel business but he can feed you! And give you a room!

Few go there because they don't know about it. The caretaker and his wife are lonely. Not five miles away as the crow flies thousands of motorists blast north and south with not the faintest idea Bull's island is open to them.

Someday, if everything goes well I hope to enjoy the luxury of a nervous breakdown. Assuredly, so important a step shall not be undertaken lightly. I aim to plan it carefully, for March or April, and then I shall go to Bull's island and hunt shells on the beach, sit in blinds with a camera and fish for mullet off the government dock.

The pace picked up again after leaving that country. No attempt is made here to write an itinerary of the whole trip. The idea is merely to record the high lights and if possible hold up a part of the bill of fare that awaits the winter-pent northern sportsman in the cold months. There was one last place I wouldn't have missed for anything – Waynesville, North Carolina. No man who has ever listened to the music of a hound should ever pass up a chance to drop in on the Plotts here and see them and their famous hounds.

These Plott hounds have been bred by the same human families for five generations, or since Jonathan Plott emigrated from Heidelberg, Germany, to the far-away colonies before the Revolutionary war. "Naow jest which Plott do ye mean, sir?" I was asked in Waynesville of a chilly afternoon when the shadows were lengthening in the Blue Ridge mountains.

"The one with the Plott hounds."   "Well sir, there's nine families of 'em in these parts an' ever' last one of 'em has Plott hounds."

We found enough Plott families and enough rugged Plott bear hounds to completely fill a dog man's day. Bear hounds pure and simple, bred to trail and close with the black bears of the mountain country, they are unlike any hound in the world. Brindled, burly and belligerent, the Plott hound that declines to close with a cornered bear "never comes down off'n the mountains," as Vaughn C. Plott put it. In this manner the fighting strain has been kept up.

Plott hounds have gone into the West and down into Mexico and over into the coastal swamps of South Carolina to hunt bear, lions and also the few true, wild boars that are still found in isolated mountain hideaways of the Blue Ridge. Many of them chained in Plott yards on the outskirts of Waynesville carry great healed wounds "where a bear fetched him a swipe."

It is startling to find hounds that fight. Hounds are dogs whose predominant trait is nose. But here are hounds with nose and the spunk of Airedales for the finish after the quarry has been trailed. Vaughn Plott had a word –

"Don't go tellin' folks these hounds has Airedale blood. They ain't nary a drop of it in 'em. They were German hounds originally, crossed with curs, and later other hound blood to keep the nose good. Not a bit of Airedale in 'em. Understand I say that knowin' that Airedales are the only breed I ever saw would go with them all the way in a fight with a bear. I'll say a good Airedale is as good as a good Plott hound, but they are not mixed."

Heroes of fiction, the Plott hounds have figured in hundreds of epic scraps with bears. Vaughn Plott remembers one disemboweled by a bear –

"We killed the bear and I picked up the dog and held his hide together. He was living. Passing the dead bear this dog writhed out of my arms and went at worrying the bear again. We sewed him up and he was in on the finish of many bears after that."

During the war years, MacQuarrie and all sportsmen felt the pinch of the rationing of tires, ammunition, gasoline and other needful items for going long distances in pursuit of sport. While Mac included the woodcock hunt that became "Old Deacon Woodcock" in The MacQuarrie Sporting Treasury, *most of his examples here took place in that precious square mile of the Thoroughfare at Middle Eau Claire Lake. The day that turned into "We Shall Gather at the Icehouse" is certainly contained here, as well as a deer-hunting story written in more detail for the* Milwaukee Journal *and reprinted in* Dogs, Drink and Other Drivel. *While that square mile was by no means close to Milwaukee, MacQuarrie often spent an extended time there when he was on vacation. Of course, he dropped in whenever his reporting route took him anywhere nearby.*

One quandary is that Mac never wrote up a story for a magazine or the Milwaukee Journal *of a duck hunt 1,000 miles coming and going, and you can bet that, if he had made such a trip, he would have told the story. Probably the hunt at Red Lake, Minnesota, found earlier in this compilation, was that story, just a wee exaggeration of the distance.*

The Prodigal's Return

Field and Stream, May 1944

It's always fun to dream of the far places, and even more fun to go there. But if we can't, let's not lose sight of the sport which is to be had in the familiar scenes near home.

Sure, I want to fish the feeders of the Upper Nile, where the homesick British have planted brown trout. I want to hunt the Kodiak bear in his rainy haunts. I want to drink a toddy over a lion within sight of Kilimanjaro's snows.

Passions like that burn in many an outdoorsman's breast. Let no man leer at them. They are the candles in the far windows that keep us a-going. Also—and much more to the point—they are the private hopes that keep us padding along the familiar trails.

Most of us will smack our lips over anticipation and feast upon realization. In the long run, we will settle for the back forty where the pheasants hide and for the not-too-far trout stream where a brace is triumph enough.

Waiting for the time of enough money is treacherous business. I was very close to one who tried that. He was a good man, tireless on the stream and a fine legger in the bush. There came a day when he confessed he was tired of tramping ten miles "for a couple of ruffed grouse." He said: "I've seen everything and done everything around here. Now I'm goin' to make a pile and head right straight for New Zealand. There's a river there called the Tongariro. Ten-pound rainbows are common . . ."

That's the way he talked. "The heck with hunting any more whitetails," he said. "I want to slay a sladang."

He was a normal, un-rich American with a family to educate and a business to worry over. For him the problems came annually, like dandelions—in the regular sequence of events. He had to buy a new car each spring to keep up with the neighbors. He had to think about his lovely young daughters and their future. He had to work like all hell just to make the mare go.

So he pinched. Being decent, he pinched as you would expect he would. He pinched himself. He quit the local hunting and fishing game cold.

I bought one of his fine split-bamboo trout rods. He sold out completely—waders, shotguns, decoys, boots and just about two hundred pounds of the finest wool and canvas outdoor clothing that money could buy. He was in a hurry to get the stuff out of his way, once his mind was made up; the reason was that it hurt him so. Thank heaven, I paid him a fair price for the fly rod.

The victim was true to his mortal delusions for a year. He missed the rainbow run. He saw no surging smallmouths smash his bass bugs. He watched autumn glide into winter without studying a sunrise from a duck blind. Deer season came and went without him there to mix the sourdough.

Occasionally I saw him on the street. He spoke of the great responsibilities upon him. Of the money he hoped to make. Of that "some day on the Tongariro." Of the future African hunt.

Then there was a long interim of winter when I did not see him. He was busy piling it up. It was not until spring, when the rainbows were running, that he came back into my life. He came by night to my front door—haunted, beaten and bewildered—and begged the loan of a rod and a pair of waders.

"Any old things would do," he said.

No haunted man was he when he went down my front steps an hour later, laden with the necessary gear. In his right hand he clutched his dear old split bamboo; some 9 ½ feet of weapon weighing well over 6 ounces—fit for combat with spring-run rainbows. Festooned and draped, hanging from the other arm, were all the other needful trappings a man must have to achieve Nirvana on a trout stream—in his own bailiwick or on the fabulous Tongariro.

Little by little he picked up where he had left off the previous year. By June he had repurchased his stiff bamboo muskalonge rod. By early August he had recovered a couple of bass rods. By autumn he had his shotguns back home. Come deer season, and he was once more a man with his fine, restocked .270.

It all cost him a pretty penny, as pennies are counted. But he got 'em back, and life became worthwhile again. Creaking through the snow with him one gray morning to our deer stands in the cutover, I asked him about Tongariro—wasn't he going there some day?

He took a deep breath of the clean air of north Wisconsin's deer woods and said, "To hell with the Tongariro!"

No mention of new dreams of conquest came from him. He reverted to his former status of a plain, happy man. He ran his business. He married off his daughters. He bought a new car almost every spring. In springs when he couldn't afford it he did what most of us do. No longer does he sacrifice today's sport for tomorrow's faint promise.

To me he taught a lesson, even though I am solidly riveted to native things and especially keen on the country I knew as a boy, which may be just my good luck. Often since then I've thought of him, especially since the era of travel rationing set in. He is still at his old trades as the seasons roll around for they are easily reached—right in his back yard. I am wondering if his hard-won lesson could help others now, when movement is restricted.

Will the local coverts satisfy that craving? Will the local streams turn up a fish or two? I think they will. Twenty miles from where I sit typing this in a very big city, I have found the best woodcock hunting I ever had. Ten miles in another direction from this spot, due east into Lake Michigan, I landed a 10-pound lake trout not long ago. Thirty miles from here, in almost any direction but east I have found the finest pheasant shooting there is—in a state of some 52,000 square miles.

Of course, not every page of the complete outdoorsman's diary may be filled with so little traveling. But I think the majority will agree with the idea, which is simply that there are rich veins of sport to be worked within striking distance of home. Every man will know for himself what lies close by, and in the learning perhaps he will hark back to native acres not too far away, accessible by train, or even afoot—where a man knows the country and the country knows the man.

Who shall deny that the automobile was a boon? It carried us to far places. Still, it must answer for some sins. Here is one.

Two hundred miles from Chicago, in Waushara and Waupaca Counties in Wisconsin, are some splendid trout streams: the Pine, the Willow, the White, the Mecan, to name a few. Time was when these central Wisconsin rivers bore the brunt of the state's trout fishing.

Emerson Hough, of "Covered Wagon" fame, loved this country and fished it hard. Local legend has it that he wrote most of *The Covered Wagon* in between trips to some of these trout waters. If it was good enough for Emerson Hough, you may imagine how good it was. What happened to it?

By the early 'twenties the ubiquitous Model T was a universal fact, pressing new, well-defined ruts just 52 inches apart in this sandy terrain. By the time of the fateful 'thirties the auto was everywhere, a magic carpet, and anything less than a paved road came to be known to engineers as "a temporary highway."

Men who had once trekked to the "central counties" for their trout fishing began roaring past their old stamping-grounds with their toes manipulating the whims of 100 horsepower. Another two hundred miles of driving was nothing.

The "central" trout streams fell off in popularity. Only in recent years have they been rediscovered, and it is noteworthy that the prodigals returned before this day of curtailed travel, brought on by the war. Can it be that the novelty of just going far for its own sake was wearing off before the tire shortage?

Once I traveled more than a thousand miles, coming and going, to get some superlative duck shooting. Having tasted it once, I do not yearn to return to it. Less than a week after that expedition I found myself sitting in a back-home blind and counting it a splendid day, although my bag, as I recall, totaled just four bluebills.

Sour grapes—sour grapes sweetened by a little homeopathic humility in view of current conditions? I think not. I think other outdoorsmen will back me up. I think they will tell, if prodded, of the surprising bass from the "fished-out" stream. I think they will say that it will be all right with them if they can get to know their own, close-in country "as well as Grandfather knew it." Or even as well as Dad knew it. I think the near-by areas are going to do the job, and I think the boys who have been tramping on the accelerator know it too.

It is quite amazing the way wildlife flourishes near large population centers. The biggest muskalonge on record was taken almost within sight of Detroit's large buildings. Here in Milwaukee County, a tiny county where 800,000 people live, is "the greatest concentration area for pheasants in the state," according to Wisconsin's game experts. They have begun trapping the birds to get them into hunting country, for no guns may be discharged in Milwaukee County.

A favorite place of mine is one of those boyhood spots, a square mile of hunting and fishing country which has been kind to me for more than thirty years. It is some distance off, but it will always be accessible. Its versatility is the thing that draws me back to it, season after season. Something would be missing from the year if I could not hunt it or fish it—just that tiny square mile of country.

There I have killed deer, partridge, woodcock, snowshoe hares, prairie chickens, many species of ducks, and in season I have taken bass, wall-eyed pike, northern pike, bluegills and other pan-fish beyond remembering. It is by no means exceptional. I know many other richer hunting and fishing grounds. The point is that it is country I know, and country that seems to know me when I go there. Aren't the thousands and thousands of patches like this one the areas that will get the workout in the ensuing months?

How well do we know these areas—we of the heavy foot on the pedal and the restless yen to go? Well, an ardent fisherman friend of mine gave me an answer a few years ago. He lived for years on the shore of a likely small-mouth bass lake. Yet one day in the duck season, when I asked him if he'd ever been "beyond the high hill" which rises from the shore of one of his fishing holes, he confessed that he had not. A 30-minute walk took us there.

We found that an arm of his lake penetrated back into a shallow wild-rice field, deep enough for fish only in certain open pockets. Later he took some nice smallmouths out of those pockets, and I built a useful blind on the edge of one of them. That made me wonder how many other sportsmen, restricted to small areas, did not know what lay beyond their "high hill," accessible via Shanks' mare.

Let me tell of another spot, in a lake country. The big lake is excellent when the bluebills are moving through, and fair fishing water too. It is a country of beckoning hills with long vistas down rugged, trough-like valleys where the second-growth is coming along to hide the jackstraw slash created fifty years ago. One bay of this big lake is overworked by duck hunters. I know; I have sometimes helped to overwork it. Beyond this bay, over a short portage, lies a pot-hole lake a generous quarter mile long and almost as wide. Another short hike from here brings one to another pothole, big enough to deserve the name of lake, for it has about twice the acreage of the first.

Both are excellent bluebill spots, with a mallard now and then to make things spicier. Yet I know people living not four miles from these pot-hole lakes—duck hunters—who do not know these waters are on the face of creation. I know one old-timer who, viewing airplane photos of these pot-hole lakes, expressed profound astonishment. A walk of less than two miles would have brought him to both places.

Surely, that is a punishment visited upon man by the easy-going automobile. Here in Wisconsin, my friend Ernest Swift, Deputy Director of Conservation, has a name for the addicts—"running-board fishermen." He has watched the transition as long as I have. He knows that, with autos, there is such a thing as use and abuse.

He saw the last great drives of cork pine go down the Chippewa, saw the Model T build the roads, saw those same roads get too good and in turn destroy the Model T. He saw a new generation forget the old ways of camp and trail, and he saw men of an earlier generation take it the easy way; and he thinks it sums up to that little matter of "use and abuse," in so far as autos are concerned.

"Somewhere along the road," he says, "we have lost the way."

One of the great nuisances with which he has to deal is fire lanes. Are those roads and trails fire lanes, or are they highways for people to drive on? Let Ernie Swift answer:

"We built those hundreds of miles of fire lanes to move fire-fighting equipment quickly and to provide fire-breaks. They are secondary roads, unfit for steady use. Only on state-owned land have we opened them for autos. We cannot legally open the many other miles of lanes because we do not own the land over which they run. All we have from the owners are easements which say we may use them to stop forest fires.

"What has been the result? To most people those trails are roads, something over which to drive a car. They see them and yearn to penetrate them with their cars. That would defeat the whole purpose of the lanes by increasing the fire hazard. But the habit of the auto is powerful. And we in the department are old meanies because we do not permit motorists to do something which the law, and our contract with owners, forbids us to do. Just that firmly has the auto taken hold of the sportsman."

Let me tell you about the hunting in my thoroughfare country, in that square mile area which I know, and which seems to know me. I want to show what it will produce in a day's going; and I contend that thousands of outdoorsmen could show the same, or better, if they would speak up.

It is a fine thing to feel on familiar terms with an ancient tree, or a familiar hummock, or a place where deer pass by. From the back door of my cabin I move south over deer trails, some of them beaten a foot into the soil. Snowshoe rabbits infest the oak and pine here. I should shoot them; they are eating my trees, and my neighbor's trees. But I do not shoot them. They seem gay, and I haven't the heart. So I pass them by, skirting the lake for a piece, and then plunging again into the bush, which is jack-pine, Norway pine, scrub-oak and many, many other species and varieties.

I cross the road where I once missed a running shot at a buck. It is a place I can never forget. The President of the Old Duck Hunters' Association, Inc., attended to that. I missed the buck in the last ten minutes of the last day of a deer season. He was loping easily, his great rack outlined darkly against the snow. I missed, and the President spoke unforgettable words.

I dive into the bush again beyond the road where I missed, staying on the deer trails, for the going is easier. Let's say it is partridge season, Within fifteen minutes from the cabin I have missed at least a pair, and decided to tighten up my reflexes. It is hard shooting, flash-shooting out and out, but glorious shooting in the pale yellow days of late October.

I come into a sizable grove of Norways. There I did not miss—once. But the President had said, "He was standing, wasn't he?" and that I admit, and even now remember the breadth of his rack and its symmetry. Other days come flashing back.

Perhaps I get a chance at partridge before I am out of the grove. Perhaps I pelt one successfully as he planes through ragged birch boughs. Perhaps I miss. What's the difference?

Then to the thoroughfare, which winds lazily through this little hunting ground. I comb one side of it, cross the rickety bridge which spans it, and stop to peer down into clear green water for a glimpse of a smallmouth or two. I go over the hollow-sounding bridge and again on to the sandy trail which answers to the name of road.

What's that? Mallards! Sure as sin. Mallards at the left bank of the river-like thoroughfare, in close. A man could stalk them. I do. I've often taken home a drake or two from this little patch. It's the ragweed there that draws them.

Away from the thoroughfare and through the bush. A big doe gets up lazily and skulks off. Here in a clearing where a farmer had failed, I once flushed fifty sharp-tailed prairie chickens. That is the sort of thing the home-country hunter remembers. Another time I asked Oscar, the trapper, about a peculiar track I'd seen in the snow. Otter, he said.

I go along. The day is bright and my bag is not heavy—it is just enough. The land is not my land. I don't know who owns it, but I feel that I own it.

Did last August's blow beat down those big, old popples on the far hill? Sure enough, half of them are gone, prone and rotting already, or maybe they were ripe when the wind hit them.

Has the far bay of the lake, to my left, caught the fancy of the migrating bluebills yet? Indeed, it has! There they sit like old friends, glinting in the sun.

The fat woodchuck that has the hole in the hill—is he still as suspicious as ever? He is—more than ever. All I see is a brown flash as he darts earthward.

A pair of partridge flushes. There's usually a pair not far from that woodchuck's mound of sand. They may be dusting in brer woodchuck's diggings, for all I know. Maybe I'll get one. . . .

Good hunting? Well, yes. Good to this extent—I've hunted my thoroughfare country, and it was like visiting an old friend. You can't beat the home country!

A day-by-day travelogue of this 1945 hunting trip filled the columns of The Milwaukee Journal *for a week in late October, 1945 and is included in* Dogs, Drink and Other Drivel. *MacQuarrie also used this hunt as a vivid example of his job in "The Life of an Outdoor Writer," found later in this present compilation.*

Holiday *is an upscale travel magazine, so MacQuarrie would have been introduced to many new readers who didn't subscribe to the outdoor magazines of the day.*

Pheasant Capital of the World

Holiday, October 1946

Feathered rainbows—millions of 'em—bring bird bonanza worth $20,000,000 a year to South Dakota

Before the leaves have fallen, thousands of spare rooms in South Dakota will be occupied by strange men with shotguns. So will every available hotel room in the state. For during the last days of September, the advance guard of the greatest posse of pheasant hunters in history will be walking purposefully through the South Dakota cornfields where pheasants swarm like a plague of locusts.

Scientists call the pheasant phenomenon an irruption. But hunting men call it the best pheasant hunting in the history of powder and shot. Practically everybody that ever peeped down a gun barrel or swung a shotgun up for a snap shot will tell you that the United States has seen no upland game shooting to rival South Dakota's "feathered rainbows" since the days of the passenger pigeon. Some twenty-five states offer pheasant hunting. None has ever boasted pheasant hunting on a par with South Dakota. Estimates of the State's pheasant population range from

33: Man, dog and gun make a perfect trio wherever game birds fly

12,000,000 to 55,000,0000, which only proves that you can't pour game birds through an adding machine.

The rise of South Dakota to its pinnacle as gun-barrel mecca of the U.S. began back in the twenties. Lloyd Blow, native farmer-gunner, said, "The birds began to increase so fast in the early twenties we were afraid they'd eat out the farms. In some of those lean years, we had to sack potatoes as soon as we got them out of the ground. If we didn't the birds got 'em."

We'd been walking down a corn row while Blow was talking. The sky was crystal blue and the air was Dakota crisp. As we neared the end of the eighty-acre field a flock rocketed into the air. When the guns stopped somebody yelled, "Must 'a' been a thousand birds in that flight." "Not more'n five hundred," grunted Blow. "Settle for seven hundred and fifty," said another hunter.

It's like that in these farm fields. Hunting parties report putting as many as 3000 pheasants in the air during the late season when the birds tend to flock together. This writer, who has hunted every upland game bird between Winnipeg and Florida, never saw anything like the 1945 season for numbers of birds taken or numbers of hunters who went absolutely daffy with glee. (This year's season, incidentally, begins September twenty-ninth and runs to January twenty-sixth.)

The eighteen gunners in our party, for instance, gathered around four parked cars, and each of us took eight cocks apiece from a 500- pound pile of prime game meat gathered in less than three hours.

You'll be walking down a corn row, minding your own business, squinting a little because the day is so bright and listening a little harder because the breeze is talking in the corn shocks, when—br-r-r-rup—up they go! Pheasants wobble in flight. One quarters, another slants away low, grazing the cornstalks, still another reverses and comes right overhead pushed by a tail wind. You choose fast and let go. You drop the one soaring—and, so help me, he looks as big as a wild turkey!

South Dakota's bird bonanza, which is worth, according to one enthusiastic estimate, a cool $20,000,000 or more annually, mushroomed from an original $20,000 expenditure by the state, according to Elmer Peterson, thoughtful director of the State Department of Game, Fish and Parks. "In the late nineties," Mr. Peterson recounted, "Dr. A. Zitlik of Sioux Falls planted some birds which did well. In 1914-15 South Dakota spent $20,000 to plant some 11,000 birds. That's all we ever spent. We never tried to propagate birds artificially and we discouraged feeding them in winter, because we wanted only the strong birds to survive."

God and the farmers did the rest to help the South Dakota pheasants multiply. The farmers set a nice table for the pheasant with the corn, wheat, milo and other grains they grow. Nature caters to the feathered rainbow with wild sunflower and pigeon's grass. Prairie grasses and other seed-producing wild plants grow rankly to the edges of cultivated fields.

The arrival of the mechanical corn picker in the thirties helped. It leaves a good many cobs lying on the ground, more meat for the birds. The farmers don't miss this wastage, because their hybrid corn produces so heavily that a lost cob here and there doesn't rob the crib.

There is no doubt that the pheasant has proved a greedy citizen and taken unfair advantage of the hospitality accorded him. Many farmers say that a pheasant can tell by sixth sense exactly where a grain of corn has been planted and will walk down a row and pluck out every seed kernel. When the corn comes to an inch or so high—"Then you have to stand there with a shotgun," says Peterson. By 1942, Peterson said, pheasants had multiplied to such an extent that conservation officials were concerned, not with what the pheasant crop would be but with getting sufficient hunters out to keep the bird population down to a practical level. Peterson's job is to see that enough pheasants are killed to keep the crop damage low and at the same time to maintain a sufficient stock of birds to keep the hunters happy.

Many farmers regret their hospitality to the birds imported from Asia and wish they could be rid of them. But scientists declare that extirpation of the species in South Dakota is well-nigh impossible even if hunting were permitted the year round. John Pheasant is a resourceful bird, the only game bird known which, artificially propagated, successfully returns to the wild when released. His secret of survival seems to be that, even though caged, fed and watered, he never becomes tame. There were birds in abundance, even after the 1944 estimated kill of 6,000,000, and the 7,500,000 kill of 1945.

The man with the shotgun is a welcome visitor in South Dakota. No Trespassing signs are few and far between. When a hunter is confronted with one he may be sure in most cases it was put there by a farmer who just wanted to have a look at the hunters moving down his corn rows. The invariable answer from the farmer is: "Why, go right ahead, long as you asked."

The birds were a farm problem long before the men with scatterguns came to help out the farmers. These happy hunting grounds were not discovered by the hunter in any rush. In 1937 South Dakota sold only 811 nonresident hunting licenses. After that the nonresident sales went like this:

1938 1,815
1939 2,841
1940 6,274
1941 11,072
1942 15,776
1943 17,488
1944 43,315
1945 86,996

The 1945 out-of-state hunters had as company 97,603 resident hunters and 17,325 servicemen. The 6,341 resident servicemen got licenses free, and the 10,984 nonresident paid a dollar each.

The 86,996 out-of-state pheasant posse of last year is a lot of hunters, in any state's language. Particularly is that true in a comparatively sparsely settled state and one not geared to the resort business. The story of how South Dakotans take care of this gigantic incursion is a fascinating one.

Once the South Dakotans made up their minds to invite out-of-state sportsmen they went all the way. When hotels were crammed and appealing for help, the townspeople and farmers revealed a Western hospitality to thousands of sportsmen. Homes everywhere were thrown open.

The situation in Huron is typical. Nevin Jamison, manager of the Marvin Hughitt Hotel, could have rented one room 25,000 times from August to mid-October—if he had the room to rent. Everything had been reserved months before. C. Irving Krumm, secretary of the Huron Chamber of Commerce, resigned his job and opened a lodge for hunters. John Chapman, returned serviceman, took over Krumm's job and sent out an SOS to the townspeople to take in visiting hunters.

Huron calls itself the Pheasant Capital, stages an annual baseball Pheastival, the last one of which attracted many of the members of the Tiger and Cub teams which met in the World Series. The ballplayers—Phil Cavarretta, Mickey Livingston, "Dizzy" Trout, Paul Derringer, Hy Vandenberg, Andy Pafko, et al.—staged an exhibition game and went hunting.

I landed in Huron late one night and called John Chapman for a hotel room. He'd been up since 6 A.M. He explained in a weary voice that he could not find a hotel room for anybody if his life depended on it. He fixed me up in the home of Jack Brandt, and when I got there, road-weary and dusty, a complete stranger to Jack Brandt, there was a snack on the table waiting for me. That's what I mean about South Dakota.

Another of South Dakota's hospitable gestures was made last October when, with the aid of the Izaak Walton League, the State Game, Fish and Parks Department provided a pheasant for every man on the battleship South Dakota.

The South Dakota, which saw heavy fighting when we were battling the Japanese in the South Pacific, was the ship that was always referred to in wartime dispatches as Battleship X.

In the Hughitt Hotel lobby, anyone not in hunting clothes looks out of place. Upstairs in the Elks' lodge were fifty cots accommodating hunters who could not find even private rooms in Huron. The private rooms are often treasured. As an instance, Chapman's assistant secretary, Mrs. Virginia Bullis, had to say "No," to Tom Girdler, steel magnate, when he came looking for a hotel room. She found him a private room and he has asked her to reserve the same one for him for the 1946 season. Huron is building a new eighty-two-room hotel. It will never handle the mobs as long as that pheasant population stays near its present level.

Mrs. Hazel Jones is another of Chapman's aides. She works the telephones, giving aid and comfort to sleepy, homeless hunters. Many a day she gets to work at nine and remains until after 1 A.M. "when the last bus comes in." In the first month of the four-month pheasant season she found private accommodations for 2297 hunters in private homes, got to bed at dawn and was back answering the telephone before noon next day.

Nick Cullop, manager of the Milwaukee Brewers baseball club, who played his first league ball for Madison, South Dakota, set forth from Milwaukee for Britton, South Dakota, in a big car. "Nothin' to getting a room in a hotel if you know the ropes," Nick explained. After being turned down a half dozen times, Nick and a party of six slept in a straw stack halfway across Minnesota. "Coldest dern sleep I ever had," Nick vouchsafes. "Tell your friends to stay home 'less they carry their own cot."

In Huron, Cliff Schlegel, city editor of the Huronite and Plainsman, says there is a persistent story around town that two New Yorkers, unable to find lodgings to their liking, bought a house for $3000, lived in it two weeks while they hunted, and sold it for $3500 before they departed. Asked how his community was benefiting financially by the hunter invasion, Schlegel explained: "Just say there is a guy by the name of Ole. Owns a farm near here. Made more money last two years renting rooms to hunters than he ever did farming."

34: Several million birds are taken each year - millions remain

It was John Chapman who got out a pencil and "made a guess," that the 1945 season brought $20,000,000 in outside money to South Dakota. He admits it is a mere guess. Since the season ended with 86,996 nonresident licenses sold at twenty dollars each that's $1,739,920 as one single item. Licenses are not by any means the only expense of the hunter.

The hunter is almost ubiquitous. Pierre, the state capital, as well as Mitchell, Aberdeen, Watertown, Woonsocket, Miller, Gettysburg, Lake Preston, all present the same picture—towns teeming with khaki-clad men.

216

Lake Preston is a typical smaller city of the South Dakota pheasant boom. Here Lyle Halverson, restaurant man, got four hours of sleep per day in the first five weeks of the season. He fed 250 hunters three times daily in this city of 812 population. H. Kopperud, the banker next door, figures Lake Preston will see something like $200,000 in strange money in the season. Out in front of his bank while we chatted stood a new civilian jeep, sent to Kopperud by an official of Willys-Overland to be kept in readiness for his arrival. If that jeep seemed broken in some when its owner got behind the wheel, he can blame Kopperud and me. Jeeps are handy for making surveys.

Do South Dakotans, living in a pheasant paradise, like to eat pheasant? Only two said, without prompting, that they did. Many seemed a bit cagey about it, as though it would be disloyal to South Dakota to dislike the multitudinous bird on the table. But it is obvious South Dakotans have eaten so many pheasants that they are now able to take them or leave them and would prefer in many cases to leave them.

And that gives point to the story of faithful old Shep, a black-and-white collie type of hunting dog I encountered in the country southwest of Miller. His owner had bobbed his tail as a puppy in the possible belief that he might turn out to be a springer spaniel. This burly farm dog watched our hunting party disembark from autos, put guns together and march through the corn. He got up off the farmhouse porch and followed us with a purposeful air.

We said, "Good ol' Shep."

When the first bird fell, good old Shep was on it like chain lightning and streaking home with it. We decided that was the last we'd see of Shep. Five minutes later he came again to seize another cock and dash home. Before we had hunted out that field, Shep had sneaked in to pick up and take home no less than five of the cocks we downed. When we got back into our cars there he was, lying on the farmhouse porch. It seemed to me he was sneering a bit and maybe thinking: *You city slickers coming out here to hunt my cornfield!*

I walked around to the summer kitchen on the back of the farmhouse, despite Shep's growls. The folks were not at home, Shep had nineteen pheasants, stacked on the kitchen floor.

What could have happened, though I'll never find out, is that when the farmer came home and saw what Shep had done he confused Shep no end by declaring, "Dern yore hide, dog, you bring another one of them pheasants in here and I'll cut off the rest of your tail!"

The business of plucking, cleaning, freezing and shipping birds by the millions can be strenuous. Last year many places in South Dakota ran out of dry ice and phoned desperately to Minneapolis and Sioux Falls for help. In Huron the chamber of commerce asked the railroad to spot refrigerator cars in the yards solely for the purpose of moving processed pheasants eastward. At Lake Preston, Mrs. Violet Nisheim earned $750 in the first month of the season plucking and cleaning birds. She is one of hundreds of Dakota housewives to whom the seasons have become a financial windfall.

How long will such hunting—and its concomitant prosperity—last? Will the hunters kill all the pheasants? R. S. Laskowski, United States meteorologist at Huron, noted for his long-range crop forecasts, says: "It would be impossible to exterminate them."

Director Peterson says: "We propose to manage the pheasants so they are kept under control."

Jim Dunn, who tills 1000 acres near Britton, asserts with a faint Irish accent; "The birds'll be here 'atin' up the corn long after us Dunns are dead and buried."

During the dozen years that Mac and Jim took their cottontail annual hunt the Wisconsin harvest ran from three quarters of a million to 1.3 million. In recent times, it's been about one tenth that number. Furthermore, the leading counties in those days were located in the southeastern part of the state, near the population centers of Milwaukee and Madison, while today the rabbit harvest is higher in the hilly western part of the state. Fencelines, stone piles and woodlots are rare on the fertile farmland, and if this farmer's woodlot still exists, it probably has a house nestled on it.

I wish I knew who Jim was. MacQuarrie must have met Jim and started this tradition soon after he moved to Milwaukee, but I don't remember reading an account in his columns over those years.

The Cottontail Annual

Outdoors, December 1948

"What's a better way to usher in the Christmas season than hunting rabbits with an old friend?" Each season just before Christmas when the hearts of men turn warmer and the cedars stand black against the snow, Jim phones me. He is a gentleman, a fine companion, a great friend. He announces:

"We'd better make the Annual tomorrow. Dogs are in hard shape. I haven't hunted the cranberry marsh for two weeks. Been saving it .... "

I've looked forward now for twelve years to Jim's pre-Yuletide summons to chivvy the cottontails of southern Wisconsin. And this time, though I had just returned from a big game hunt in Alaska, I looked forward to the day with Jim more than ever. There's something about going back to old, good places no matter how far afield the hunting and fishing trail takes you.

Going with Jim is no hasty, headlong affair. He plans well and deliberately. He is your philosopher's hunter. If we nail a few, well and good. If not, we've still maintained tradition and have gone to the winter woods to keep the annual rendezvous with Peter Rabbit & Co.

The cranberry bog is just out of town a piece. Well, thirty miles, if you insist. It is almost a half mile long, half as wide, includes a fair-to middlin' mallard hole and in winter is a desolate, tundra-like expanse surrounded by prosperous farms. Years ago someone made a noble and expensive attempt to turn this flat into a cranberry bog. But the plan didn't work and today the bog is cherished solely for its rabbit hunting.

Jim, a cottontail man of record, is one of several valiant beagle hound owners in southern Wisconsin who have access to the bog. "All I did was knock on his door and ask permission," explains Jim. "Now and then I leave a box of shells at the farmhouse." To explain Jim further, let it be added that he has never been denied permission to hunt by any farmer. Seems to depend on who you are and how you ask ....

In the car with us as we took out for the bog were Jim's three rabbit dogs, Molly and Joe, fifteen-inch beagles, and Sport, a beagle-foxhound cross. Many a rabbit hunter in Wisconsin favors the long legs of a good cross-bred hound for rabbits.

At the farmhouse overlooking the bog there was no haste. Jim had a box of candy for the farmer's wife. Then town and country chewed the rag about politics, the international situation and more germane matters, such as the superiority of red cedar for fence posts. As we headed for the bog the farmer called to Jim:

"You don't turn up anything down there, better you try the wood lot 'long-side the cornfield. They're fat as butter – on my corn!

A few inches of new snow lay over the bog and there had been a morning mist, remnants of which hung vaguely over the place. "I don't like the looks of it," Jim said. "Dunno why, but fog seems to kill scent. Maybe it'll blow off later on."

Jim was right. The three hounds, all proven rabbit dogs, had a time of it at first. No frantic bugle broke the bog's stillness and Molly, the ace of the pack, kept returning to Jim with an "Oh, the hell with it" air about her.

Still, it felt good down in there. The day was alternately sunny and cloudy. Up on the hilltops a little breeze moved through the high oaks but in the bog there was scarcely a breath of wind. It made for a comfortable day and it did not matter if the outlook was unpromising. There was good talk. There was the hope that scent would return. And there was always the wood lot 'longside the cornfield.

Fresh tracks were plentiful enough, but scent seemed elusive. Molly transmitted her disgust with the proceedings to the other dogs. The best they could do was insert noses into subterranean rabbit apartments and inhale and exhale with hankering snuffs.

"We'll do better after a bit," Jim predicted.

At noon we sat on a bog hummock, munched sandwiches and finished off a thermos of coffee. We also cultivated our immortal souls with palaver, which is the best way it should be with rabbit hunters, or any hunters.

The sun was high, almost warm, when we resumed the campaign and when the indifferent Molly finally tore loose with a full-throated "Stop thief! Stop thief!" Jim's eyes danced. Sport and Joe raised further testimony to Molly's allegations and the bog rang with fine melody. The find had been made so quickly that Jim and I did not have time to separate and take stands.

"That rabbit can feel Molly's hot breath on his neck," Jim grinned. "Listen to her give!"

The rabbit took the dogs to the far end of the bog. We thought then it might leave the precincts and duck out for higher country, but this was a rabbit determined not to be driven from its own home by yapping dogs. The rabbit could have holed in a score of places. Instead, it chose the gallant way and I suspected then as I have many times that some rabbits, sure of their fleetness, let the chase go on for the sheer fun of it. This one made a fatal mistake. Driving toward us, it broke into the open from a patch of brown bog grass, veered back into it, but too late. Jim bowled it over, pocketed it and waited for the dogs to finish the drive. One sniff at Jim's game pocket told Molly all she needed to know.

Now she was a different Molly, alert, interested, and her mood set the pattern for the other dogs. Gone now was the indifferent manner, the rolling, reproachful eye, the tail without enthusiasm. Little do we humans know of the world of scent in which a dog lives.

Jim, who properly field marshals the goings on in his cranberry bog, sent me across to the west side to make a stand on a promontory of solid land from which I could look down on the bog. He assigned himself the job of roving the marsh, taking up shooting stations as the cover and the work of the dogs indicated.

Five hundred yards from me there was further business, short and sweet. Molly, the nonpareil, opened first and from her ecstatic outburst it was plain that she was close to fur and fairly intoxicated with the fumes of redolent rabbit. The other two dogs had barely joined the chase when Jim's shotgun sounded.

The Annual was going well. But was Jim to get all of the shooting? For a long time I held my place and pondered rabbit hunting.

Most important game animal in the United States in point of number of persons involved . . . grand game animal . . . the most sport for the greatest number ... the farmer, the townsman, the brushwood boy, all have a go at Br'er Rabbit ... too bad no cheap, successful way has been found to rear rabbits artificially, like pheasants ... maybe they'll hit on it someday.

Still, here in Wisconsin some of the clubs are putting a good idea to work ... trapping cottontails in the cities and towns where they're a nuisance and releasing them in wild cover ... there's a suburb of 15,000 at the edge of Milwaukee (Whitefish Bay) ... the beagle fancy of the county claim it could produce the best rabbit hunting in the state but there's a county ordinance forbidding the discharge of firearms ... a pack of beagles would go crazy in Whitefish Bay ... and what those bunnies don't do to the gardens and shrubs!

Rabbits indeed ... no escaping 'em, and who wants to? Here I am fresh from Alaska where I picked out a big bull from a head of hundreds of caribou ... and this is just as much fun . . . never will forget the survey the hunting dog men made. They discovered to their astonishment that in southeastern Wisconsin there were more beagles than all the other hunting breeds together ....

My soliloquy was interrupted by the tireless Molly on the trail of something coming my way. As the rabbit bounded in range I missed slick and clean, but the second shot tumbled him and Molly was satisfied with a couple of sniffs. Jim called her. How she knows that voice with its "Heeyuh! Heeyuh!" It was apparent Jim had decided the rabbits were concentrated at his end of the bog.

Before Molly was half way back to Jim, Sport and Joe were at it again. Molly joined them joyously and the exuberant uproar echoed and re-echoed against the hills. Once again this candidate chose to leg it toward me and when it shot from cover I did not miss.

A few minutes later Jim joined me. "We've got enough. Let's not burn it out."

"Two more for the farmer?"

"Golly! I'd almost forgotten. We'll hit the wood lot."

It was getting on in the afternoon when we had our two for the farmer. The dogs were running down some, even Molly. We drove back to the big city through the little towns festooned with Christmas evergreens. The dogs drowsed and Molly whimpered and twitched.

"She'll run rabbits all night," said Jim.

In the big town the shoppers were out in force, harassed looking and tired, we agreed. They threaded their way in and out of traffic and the nervous horns of the automobiles blared for no good reasons.

224

How many of them, we wondered, knew that not far beyond the city limits there was clean white snow, timbered patches and solid country ground?

How many indeed? Jim always feels sorry for city people when we return from the Annual. He counts himself among the world's luckiest men and besides weekends, takes his full three weeks' vacation hunting rabbits. His word on a rabbit dog is sought after and respected by the rabbit hunters of southern Wisconsin. He has owned scores of dogs since boyhood, and his sudden transformation from quiet, easy-going Jim to veritable David Harum in a hound deal is something to witness.

Mrs. Jim met us at the door, and someday when there is plenty of elbow room I shall report the way Mrs. Jim prepares rabbits. Many's the time I have hornswoggled my daughter, who imagines she does not care for rabbit meat, to gorge herself on Mrs. J's recipe.

We parted at the door.

"Merry Christmas, Mac."

"Same to you, Jim, and Mrs. Jim and Karen."

Within two weeks I was heading south to hunt quail. And that is fine. But I know no nicer way to begin the season of Christmas than to go with Jim on the Annual.

We've done it for twelve years – always just before Christmas when the hearts of men turn warmer and the cedars stand black against the snow.

Then Jim phones.

Gordon MacQuarrie made many hunting and fishing trips on the Milwaukee Journal's *tab but none so grand as the Milwaukee Public Museum collection expedition to Alaska in 1947. It's a wonder how fast the world was changing in those post-war years. He had just published "The Ultimate Automobile" about a Model T in 1944, although the story had to be a few years old by then. Now here he was winging thousands of miles and reveling in the flight. And the flight crew was having just as much fun- the captain came back and chatted with him as they approached Anchorage.*

He wrote four magazine articles about this expedition, the two that follow, and two more about the Mackenzie River red husky, especially about Kenai, Bud Branham's lead dog.

Keith Crowley gave a good summary of this trip, with pictures, in his Story of an Old Duck Hunter, *and you can read the daily dispatches back to the* Milwaukee Journal *in* Dogs, Drink and Other Drivel.

Sourdough Geese

Field and Stream, January 1949

Alaskan bush pilots aren't the daredevils most people think. Bud Branham was a good example

This is about one of the world's oddest waterfowl—the emperor geese of Alaska—but it is also about four men, a memorable flight over the Alaska Peninsula and a certain stout little airplane.

You've heard about the Alaskan bush pilots. How they fly in all weather over some of the most hazardous routes on the continent. How they stick together like new flypaper and hop off at a moment's notice to rescue each other, or anyone. How they make old, outmoded planes do their bidding. How they land them on glaciers, mountainsides and the gravel bars of rivers.

And perhaps you have thought of these pilots as reckless, feckless gentry, as takers of needless risks, and as pilots of beat-up crates which have never seen the inside of a repair shop. That picture is wrong. Very often, because they cannot afford to do otherwise, they do fly ancient aircraft. But if you check the hangars at Merrill Field, Anchorage, you will find those boys nursing their airplanes with all the care a loving mother bestows on her first-born. In that way they live to fly another day.

I know many of them, and one of them I know very well indeed. Generally they are of the same pattern—warm, friendly guys, not much on the talk. It must be that the men who look often upon the bright face of danger learn to be humble and generous. The one I know so well is Bud Branham, who is also the laird of Ptarmigan Valley, an area which holds a lion's share of record moose and caribou heads.

One Sunday morning in late October, Bud stood beside his two-motor amphibian studying scribbled weather notes. The flying weather was not good. Not bad. Just the same old thing for the peninsula, or "the chain," as Alaskans refer to the long peninsula and the Aleutian Islands. This cradle of storms has produced winds exceeding 100 miles per hour, and the right-hand bower of the wind is the treacherous, sudden fogs.

Bud munched an apple from a peck-sized bag held under an arm. He was thoughtful for a moment over the weather report, then announced: "Well, gentlemen, let's have a look at it. Who wants an apple?"

The three passengers—Lester, Owen and myself—munched away as Bud took the amphibian out over Cook Inlet. Our destination was Port Heiden. We wanted seven typical, preferably big, emperor goose specimens for the Milwaukee Public Museum. Seven—no more, no less. The museum group was already planned. We had collected moose and caribou, ptarmigan and redpolls, hawk owls and other native Alaskan species. Now for the little-known emperors.

Things went smoothly before we got to the mouth of Clark Lake Pass. Off to our left smokey Iliamna volcano reared up 10,000 feet or so and not far from it stood formidable Mt. Redoubt. The changing hues of the Alaskan mountains caught the fancy of us three chechakos. In the course of a sunny day they glow with all the colors of the spectrum. Ask any conscientious artist who has tried to capture those subtly changing hues.

Clouds and fog lay over Clark Lake Pass. Bud bit into an apple, laid it beside him and, munching, spiraled down 4,000 feet to get beneath the curtain. Thereafter that day we flew beneath the overcast.

Once well into the pass, it was like flying in a gigantic trough, with mountains to right and left. Over long, narrow Clark Lake the green glacial water of the lake reflected an eerie green hue on our underwings.

Iliamna Lake spread out mysteriously beneath the low-hanging fog. This lake is as large as Huron. We crossed it in ten minutes, fifty to one hundred feet above its luminous green surface. Beyond spread the tundra. Trees grew smaller and smaller, then disappeared, and below us was the crazy pattern of yellow-brown tundra and thousands of tundra lakes of all shapes and sizes. They looked like broken dinner plates, with here and there an unbroken one, perfectly round.

The ceiling came lower and the plane knifed between it and the monotonous tundra. At times we were no more than fifty feet above the ground. The sensation might be likened to riding a very swift motorcycle just a few feet off the ground. When Bud detected a squirminess in the back seat where Owen and I sat, he produced his big sack. "Anybody want an apple?" Then he added, reassuringly: "I've flown this about two hundred times."

Nearing Naknek Field, once a busy Army airport, now held down by the CAA, Bud looked eastward, frowning a little. Then he caught a weather report from Naknek. It was getting late in the afternoon.

"Gentlemen, we sleep here tonight."

One of the CAA officials had spent that Sunday on a near-by trout stream. Two of his rainbows weighed about 14 pounds each. This season the Naknek fishing crowd is resolved to prove it has the largest rainbows on the continent.

"We've broken world records here and never knew it," one explained.

In the night a Bering Sea snow squall brought all hands to the plane to sweep off snow, and when the snow stopped falling we got into sleeping bags. The last thing I remember before falling asleep was Bud tossing an apple core into the air, hearing it drop with a small thud, and then Bud rolling over in his down bag.

Next morning the overcast was a little worse, if anything. Nevertheless Bud said, "Gentlemen, we'll have a look at it."

The fog over the tundra was indeed worse than the day before, but we were out of the pass, the area was flat as a platter, and Bud found that out a bit over the surly Bering Sea he had a ceiling of perhaps one hundred feet. The race beneath the fog continued, with the Bering Sea beach and cliffs at our left, the sinister sea beneath us and disappearing in the smother to our right.

Two other flyers that day also found the narrow open corridor through the fog just off the beach. We knew they were coming our way, thanks to the Port Heiden radio. They burst out of the fog not one hundred yards to our right. Our ship veered in toward the cliffs and the two small ships "scattered like a covey of quail," according to Owen's description. They were the small-plane round-the-world fliers, Truman and Evans, high-tailing it for Anchorage in the soup.

Port Heiden is a collection of empty Army barracks, some of them still wearing war-time camouflage. Here again the omnipresent

CAA holds down the fort. Without the CAA, safe flying in Alaska would be next to impossible. It is such men as the crew at lonely Port Heiden who maintain the radio ranges, watch the weather and also, though it is not their job, give aid and comfort to visiting airmen.

As we were tying down the amphibian a boisterous jeep with a hand-made plywood top rolled down the runway, and out of it climbed a huge man. The ceremony of introductions was over in a minute. Our friend was big Sam Langford, weight 270. An old Navy chief in submarine service, Sam, now with the CAA and once of Memphis, inquired: "Y'all gonna hunt emperors? I reckon there's a million of 'em round here."

Sam is a hunter of parts. We understood each other from the first. And when Sam learned that Lieut.-Com. Bud Branham had been in Navy sea-air rescue work during the war. . . . Ah, well, suffice it that before an hour had passed they had agreed that an ensign in the Navy is the equivalent of a general in the Army.

It was Sam's day off next day; so he came along with us to the tide flats after emperors. Lester, Owen and Bud became intrigued with a sprawling marsh, partly cut off from the sea by a ridged beach. Sam and I chose an old gun emplacement on the beach, and I must say it made a splendid blind. It was five or six feet deep, earthed up on the sides, with a good-sized, timbered and earth-covered cave-like rear into which we could retire when the wind got at fingers and toes.

There was no thought of decoys. They'd just be a nuisance in that concentration of the regal emperors. Geese, all emperors, traded back and forth between sea and land. Beyond us in the gray surge of the Bering Sea lay islands and barrier reefs which the high tides alternately conceal and reveal. At low tide field-glasses showed thousands of geese using on the tide flats and reefs. Comfortable as the old gun pit was, we saw that the trading geese were coming in to a long, narrow arm of the sea some distance away.

This arm, so straight that it looked like a man-made canal, paralleled the beach, and on its land side were stacked thousands of empty fuel drums, mementos of Uncle Sam's prodigious job of fortifying Alaska. We took up positions behind a pile of drums that overlooked the canal. Emperors were flying in from the sea to feed in the sheltered canal.

The old fuel dump made an acceptable blind. Geese coming in from the sea swept over us and on both sides of us. Did you ever try to judge good waterfowl specimens on the wing? There's just no doing it, and we were determined to take no more than the seven the museum needed. It would have been simple to sit there and rake them down. Hunters have described this goose hunting as the best in the world. I have no reason to doubt it.

Emperors looking as big as Canadas came within range. But we held our fire. We had a plan. From time to time in the canal-like ditch geese slid in to feed. We figured when big ones came along to collect them. It was extremely simple. Three lit on a mud-bar at the edge of the ditch, and just when I had made up my mind that they were as typical and large of any we would see Sam whispered, "That big 'un in the center is as big as two geese."

As we stood up the three took off. Sam's pump and my ancient automatic dropped them in the ditch.

That was all we took. There were the others to think of. They were entitled to a shot or two. It might be thought this was poor sport. I assure you it was not. We made a comfortable windbreak out of empty drums, squatted in the center and enjoyed ringside seats at one of the grandest wildfowl shows it has been my pleasure to behold.

How they flew that day! Thousands and thousands of them. Squads and flocks and winged armadas numbering in the hundreds. We made a game of it. As geese came in range we pulled up on them with empty guns. Sam was like a big kid playing hooky, pulling down imaginary emperors and keeping up a running commentary spiced with the accent of the South and the jargon of salt water.

The early gloom settled over the sullen sea. The longest barrier reef, two miles out, disappeared in a rush of white-topped tide and Sam grinned: "Could have killed a hundred. Three's just as good. But if you write this down, who you gonna to get to believe you, man?"

The others had not fired a gun. But they had found their place—the center of the big sea marsh, accessible on foot at low tide. That night Owen and Lester, skilled taxidermists, were up late preparing the skins of the three geese.

Never go hunting with museum collectors unless you are prepared to help them with the onerous work on specimens. After the poor fellows bag their creatures the real work begins. None of us will soon forget the hide, horns, head, hoofs and every last bone of a 1,500-pound bull moose we toted five miles. But that's another story.

Alaska's emperor geese are the real sourdoughs of the territory. There are only scattered records of this goose being found in the United States, and how those few vagrants got so far away from their ancestral home has not been explained. The emperor lives and dies in Alaska, breeding among the tundra lakes and on the islands and barrier reefs of the Aleutian chain. As winter's cold presses against the ocean from the interior the emperors seek the misty, moisty reaches of the peninsula and its islands for their winter home.

We weighed our biggest goose that night and to our astonishment learned it went a scant six pounds, though it had the proportions and heavy down of a much larger bird. Incidentally, our taxidermists unblushingly announced somewhere around midnight that our big "gander" was actually a lady goose. But it was all right. The other two were gentlemen.

Some have called the emperors the handsomest of American wild geese. Me, I'll take the impressive regimentals of a good big North Dakota prairie honker, though, admittedly, the emperor carries more color. All of the head and the back of the short neck of the emperor is white, the breast dark brown to black and speckled. There is blue on the back and wings and slate in their flying feathers. The story goes that they are mediocre table birds. We found it otherwise, and met no emperor-goose hunter in Alaska but who agreed with us. They were as fine on the table as a Canada.

Next morning we leaned into a Bering Sea half-gale on a two-mile hike to the big marsh. The geese were moving in again. Watching them, you wonder if they ever stop flying, and where do they find elbow-room out there on the sea islands and reefs. Bud and I lay on a ridge of black Bering Sea sand and watched Owen and Lester hide themselves in the rank grasses. Geese hovered all about them, and we read their thoughts: "How in the world does a man decide which are good specimens in the air?" Within an hour they resolved their doubts and picked out, from hundreds, four busters that completely satisfied even their taxidermal zeal.

That afternoon they finished all seven goose skins, packing them carefully for the long trip back to the states. By nine our little expedition was in the hay. Bud shot a final apple core into a trash box and switched out the light. All of a sudden it was morning and there was Bud, first man up, once more reading scribbled weather notes. He munched a pre-breakfast apple and made up his mind: "Well, gentlemen, we'll have a look at it."

We hated the going. Quick friendships are made among the men of rod and gun. Sam Langford made us promise to return in the spring. "There's a big brown bear loafin' round here that's got a track like a snowshoe." All of the kindly, helpful CAA employees crowded round for a warm handshake.

One of those boys who wished us bon voyage was frozen to death last New Year's Day in a sudden blizzard riding a 60-mile wind and carrying a temperature of 8 below. He died within a mile of the CAA mess hall, and when Sam wrote me of it he surmised the boy may even have seen the mess-hall lights between gusts of snow. Gentlemen, if you ever fly in Alaska, save a cheer for those CAA boys. They're your guardians.

Climbing out of Port Heiden, we went above milling flocks of emperors. They flew in skeins and clouds over the tundra lakes. The weather was fine at first. We passed over Naknek, which Bud dotes on calling "Knickknack," left the treeless land and saw the spruces gradually grow bigger and more numerous. We crossed Lake Iliamna, and there beyond lay the beginning of Clark Lake Pass—socked in.

"Gentlemen, we land."

An alternative route which would have fetched us over Alaska's valley of ten thousand smokes was also plugged with fog. But we were glad for the chance to see Lake Iliamna from the ground. It is about the color of Lake Superior—steely, like a tempered knife. The mountains rise around it. You look at it and speculate.

One of these days this will become one of the great fishing-recreation resorts of the continent. Alaskans with vision look to the time when recreation becomes the territory major industry. For the present Lake Ilianma is your wilderness.

Two Indian women in a roadhouse on the edge of the tossing lake served us an excellent meal. Bud studied more weather reports and we headed for the pass. Larry Rost, a skilled Anchorage charter flyer, got off a few minutes before us. It was rough over Clark Lake and over the huddle of buildings and the sawdust pile that is Carnelian Point. In the narrow pass the air smoothed out—and the fog settled down.

Then began as brilliant a bit of seat-of-the-pants flying as I shall likely ever see. In one of the few places in the narrow pass where the two-motor ship could be turned for safe descent, Bud put it down until once more he was beneath the smother. We were seemingly only a few feet above the rocky bottom of the pass where glaciers wound into it and across it from the high mountains at either side.

Did I say the plane got beneath the fog? That is not quite true. At no time in the three hours we were in the pass were we completely out of fog. Looking forward through the windshield, I could see nothing. But each way we looked to the sides could be seen the contrasting streaks of white snow and glaciers against the steep, dark mountains. Bud Branham read his way through that tortuous path by studying the mountains at either side. He knew every inch of the features of those mountains, and when Owen, who sat beside me, plucked my sleeve and pointed to ice on the wings Bud produced the inevitable sack. "Been through it two hundred times. Who wants an apple?"

To us it was nip and tuck. Bud chewed apples even after the radio receiving apparatus stopped functioning. He kept on reporting his position to Anchorage. Where was Larry Rost in his small, single-motor plane?

Watch for him," said Bud. "His flying time is about up—gas. Hope he made it to the beach at Tyonek."

After that the air-speed indicator iced up and Bud speeded up the motors to make sure he was getting maximum speed out of the icing plane. Ice formed and blew off and formed anew a dozen times on the metal wings. Then we were out of the pass, and as we burst through the fog above the village of Tyonek there was Rost's plane, being drawn out of reach of the Cook inlet tide by villagers and Rost waving fifty feet below us to signal that he was O.K. He had landed on the beach.

Fifteen minutes out of Anchorage, over Cook Inlet, the radio receiver functioned. The Anchorage dispatcher had heard Bud all the

234

way. He thanked him for reporting Rost safe. It was a laconic conversation, a matter of routine, until Bud finally chuckled, "We had some fun back there." Formality fell away from the dispatcher's voice. He permitted himself a small laugh which was really a salute to a fine aviator and said: "Thank you, Mr. Branham. I've been watching your progress all afternoon with great interest."

The Alaskan railway tracks showed up beneath us, and Bud dove at Merrill Field with all the power on, like a homing pigeon near the cote. On the ground two grinning mechanics took over the plane. Owen, Lester and I knocked off quarter-inch strips of ice from the wings and Bud produced the inevitable sack. "That's a mighty fine little airship. Who wants an apple?"

In the heavily loaded jeep heading the last few miles to the Westward Hotel in Anchorage came the anti-climax. The jeep skidded on the icy road in the path of a heavy truck, but was steered into the ditch, out of it and back onto the road. From where I was, stretched out on duffel in the jeep's rear, I saw the five-ton truck bearing down. When we were out of danger, Bud shook his head and announced, "I just don't feel safe in automobiles anymore."

This is one of four magazine articles MacQuarrie wrote for the American Legion Magazine *from 1947-1951. With the return of WWII veterans, the American Legion tripled its pre-war membership to 3.3 million. Certainly some of these would have read MacQuarrie before, but he would have gained a new following with these young veterans ready to resume normalcy in their civilian lives.*

MacQuarrie was proud of pulling off the coup of getting an exclusive with America's favorite son, General Eisenhower. The Milwaukee Journal *column for this story is also found in* Dogs, Drink and Other Drivel.

The Life of an Outdoor Writer

American Legion Magazine, February 1949

Meet the culprit who hunts and fishes on company time and earns his dough telling you about it

"Gentlemen," said the speaker, "I give you the man with the easiest job in Wisconsin — Gordon MacQuarrie, outdoor editor of the Milwaukee Journal. In the summer he spends his time fishing in the north woods. In the winter he goes quail hunting in the south. His topic tonight is Alaska where he and four others have just spent $15,000 of the company's hard-earned dough on a big game expedition."

It used to annoy me to know that the public regarded an outdoor writer as a non-contributing member of society. But long ago I learned the thing to do was plead guilty to getting away with murder because that's the way John Public has us outdoor scriveners pegged. No use spitting into that kind of wind.

In more than 12 years of newspaper work devoted largely to writing daily about hunting and fishing I have met thousands of men who would "trade jobs with you anytime MacQuarrie, you lucky dog." While I suspect that this is one of the penalties suffered by all who live by the typewriter, I submit that outdoor writers are the most envied of the lot.

I'm guilty. I get to the best fishing grounds. I am there, on salary, with a cute little shotgun in the bright frosty mornings in Dixie when a nice pointer has a covey of quail pinned down. I am wading (with full pay) some fetching trout stream like Wisconsin's Brule when my fellow Americans are toiling away in the towns. I know where the good duck blinds are and how to get into 'em — with expenses.

Guilty your honor! I throw myself upon the mercy of the court.

Yessir, judge, it is true. They paid me to work on a 36-pound muskie in the north fork of the Flambeau River when the members of the jury were living in town by the sweat of their brows.

Yamph — I mean yessir your honor, that's right. It was me who had holt of a six-pound brown trout the night Truman was nominated.

Yessir, guilty by the book I am. Yup — I mean yessir — when all Alaska was worried about proximity to Russia last fall I was shooting emperor geese on the Bering sea.

Guilty? I'll say I'm guilty. Oh boy, I mean your honor, am I guilty! Howzzat again? Two years in the salt mines . . .? Just what I deserve. Thank you. Yes, I have one last request — may I make a final statement?

Understand this. The outdoor man on a newspaper must be all things to all men. He must be able to answer a thousand and one questions about how the fishing will be at Walligazoo lake tomorrow, not today, mind you! He must know where there's a good place to hunt moose in Ontario. He must know how the channel bass are hitting in Florida's Indian River. He must be able to tell a subscriber over a telephone how to tie a Turle knot in a nylon leader that won't slip. He must keep the peace among the brethren and settle multitudes of bets. Naturally part of his paid job is to do considerable — er — ah — research. Is it my fault if this turns out to mean a lot of hunting and fishing trips? Gotta know the answers, after all.

All the great outdoors is grist for the mill of the outdoor editor, even if he hasn't much to edit but has got to get out and create his own news, then edit it himself. Inevitably we of the cult find ourselves just "covering" our own activities, and most of the breed dislike the first person singular so we resort to evasive action such as "this reporter" or "this observer." It's a hell of a way to write but the outdoor reading public doesn't like too much "I" in its copy.

Come along with me on a typical trip, to South Dakota in the pheasant season. It'll take about 10 days but after you're on the road three or four days you lose track of time's passage.

I leave Milwaukee on a nice morning in October. The leaves are turning. Later in the day the haze of autumn will hang over the horizon. First stop is Jefferson, Wis., 45 miles from Milwaukee. Story there. The local Rod and Gun Club has worked out a new, though expensive way of rearing pheasants in pens. By afternoon I have picked up the story, plus pictures and have mailed film and copy back to the office in a mailing bag just the right size.

The story — straight news — is written in the seat of my car which has an extra powerful dome light for night scribbling. More than half my stuff is written on a typewriter resting in my lap. I also knock out a daily column from accumulated notes. By seven o'clock that first evening I am the visiting speaker at a rod and gun group in Edgerton, Wis. By midnight I'm asleep in the home of a friend, and off early next morning for Evansville, Wis., to see how Bob Antes is coming along with the Wisconsin Raccoon and Foxhound Association.

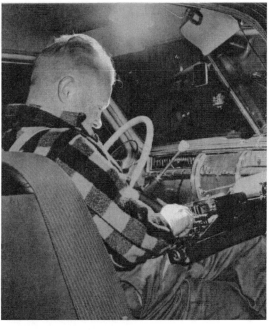

35: MacQuarrie's office afield is his station wagon equipped with special lights for typing the day's doings at night

Bob is coming along just fine. Evansville is the hound dawg capital of Wisconsin and each September the scene of the important Tri-State field trial. I write another story in the car, straight news about the latest hot shot hounds in the Evansville area. Then I write another daily column. The column is telegraphed to the newspaper and the hound story mailed in with photographs.

As I go along I stay on the public hunting and fishing grounds because that's where the people go, and people are news. Resort owners can be a problem to outdoor writers. They like nothing better than a visit from an outdoor writer — for the advertising their area may get. Consequently many a time the outdoor fellow gets himself invited into hunting or fishing clover, and it can be embarrassing. I long ago learned to avoid resorts. Here and there is a resort keeper who understands the situation and treats his scribbling fisherman just as he does any other customer. No newspaper of repute permits its outdoor man to travel on the cuff, any more than it permits its baseball men to travel at the expense of the ball clubs.

The second night I enjoy the luxury of a Madison, Wisconsin, hotel room and the next morning visit state conservation department officials. A couple good yarns develop and I remain in the hotel another night to write them up for our Sunday outdoor page, the columns of which yawn interminably.

Fourth day. Still quite a way from South Dakota. Have patience. We'll get there.

Over at Mount Horeb there's a man with an elegant collection of sporting guns including some precious jobs stocked by the late, great Alvin Linden, of Bryant, Wisconsin. It's noon before I finish with that story. I mail in the yarn with a roll of film from the Dodgeville, Wisconsin, post office and head for Mineral Point, one of Wisconsin's colorful towns, and one of its oldest. The old Cornish lead miners' homes there have always intrigued me. It's a little bit out of my line but I always look around for something good. Might be a daily column at the Point.

There is! A husky man in overalls is up on top of an old stone building ripping out stones and sending them crashing to earth. I yell at him to cease and desist. He calls down: "What'd yuh want?" I explain I just want to climb up his ladder while no stones are sliding down. "Come on up," he says.

"I hate to tear down this building. Got to. Building a new garage. Look at that stone work. Hundred years old, hardly any mortar holding it together. They knew how, those old boys. You won't find men today can put stone together like this. I mortally hate to wreck 'er. . . . Right over there in that old building U. S. Grant used to stop overnight. This place is lousy with history. Here I am tearing part of it down. . . ."

I write a daily column in my car about the man who unwillingly destroys history, hand it to Western Union at Mineral Point and head for the Mississippi River. There's a riverman and guide there I want to chat with a bit — Bill Koch, Lynxville, Wisconsin. I find Bill mending his commercial fish nets. He gives me the lowdown on the duck flight to date down the big river which was once the world's greatest waterfowl flyway.

240

"Punk. We got to do something about our ducks." I write it as a straight news story, wire it to the office and shove off across Minnesota. Halfway across the Gopher State I stop for the night in a small town. Hotels are jammed but I find a room in a private home. The pheasant hunting army is on the march. In the morning I'm off again, arriving before noon in Lake Preston, South Dakota, almost in Minnesota.

The South Dakota pheasant hunting story is building up. I spend the afternoon and evening in Lake Preston interviewing the banker, the restaurant people, the hotel owners and many others, including a dozen thrifty housewives who are cleaning up nice pin money shucking the feathers off thousands of pheasants. The town is teeming with hunters.

I'm on the edge of the big story of the trip. Can feel it in my bones. Bird hunters in such concentrations as this were never before seen in the United States.

That evening in a restaurant I dine at a counter with seventeen hunters from Dixon, Illinois. They're heading out next morning for a place they heard about south and west of Miller. Do I want to take a chance and go 'long? Sure Mike! By six o'clock in the morning our four cars are burning up the road to Miller. In two hours' time eighteen of us collect seven pheasant cocks each. At one moment when our cornfield drive ended we had 500 to 1,000 pheasants in the air. The world's greatest pheasant hunting. A hundred thousand non-residents.

At noon I say goodbye to my Dixon friends and take out for Huron, another of the pheasant hunting hot spots. Huron is bursting with hunters. Hotels full, everything reserved for months. The Chamber of Commerce has listed 200 private homes where hunters are being accommodated in true western style. I prowl about Huron, talking with the local publisher, the game wardens, the hunters. Three concerns are operating night and day rubbing feathers off pheasants with revolving brushes. The town has run out of dry ice.

The Chamber of Commerce assigns me to a dandy room in the home of a barber. I talk long distance for fifteen minutes with Elmer Peterson, South Dakota conservation director, and have all I need to round out the story. I write until 3 a.m., some 5,000 words, and send it off next morning to Milwaukee. I know it's a solid, objective news story. So does the office. They run it for a solid page, with pictures.

Now I can go look up my own gang. They're up north a piece at Britton, near the North Dakota boundary. I arrive in the evening. They ask me where in hell have I been. Russ Lynch, *Journal* sport editor; Wally Lomoe, *Journal* managing editor; Nick Cullop, manager of the Milwaukee Brewers baseball team; Uncle Pinky Gebhardt, and John Irving Cronin. Oh boy, it's good to get with your own gang! They've had a whale of a time on pheasants. They play cards while I drop asleep on Nick Cullop's bed.

In the morning we hunt. Same thing . . .pheasants everywhere. Big Nick with his 16-gauge shows us all how to shoot, wipes my eye, and I resolve to try to get in more practice at the traps. I stay overnight and hit the back trail in the morning.

Up in northern Minnesota there's a man who's raising beaver successfully under artificial conditions — concrete houses. Feeds the beaver popple logs. The beaver eat the bark. The logs are burned as stove wood. Good yarn. I write it sitting in the back of my car, along with a couple of daily columns and shoot it to the office.

Next day I'm nearing Brainerd, Minnesota and run into a sudden, early season snowstorm. It comes so quickly I have to park on the shoulder and wait it out. In fifteen minutes it's over and I go on.

Duluth, Minnesota. Well, let's see. . . .Could hole up here, but there's an old log cabin sixty miles away in Bayfield County, Wisconsin. Better keep a-going. By 2 a.m. I am opening up the cabin. The wind is howling. Might be some bluebills. Before daylight I spread two dozen cork decoys off a point of land reaching into an arm of the Middle Eau Claire Lake.

The bluebills are in all right! Hundreds of them. I quit at noon, close up the place and head for the north fork of the Flambeau River, 120 miles away. Louis Johnson, guide, riverman, and the finest muskellunge fisherman I have ever seen greets me. His wife Eedie feeds me a grand supper. Next day Louie and I get holt of a dozen muskies—we save one going around 18 pounds. Beautiful Indian Summer day. Red hot muskie fishing.

Here the trip ends. Following day I drive back to Milwaukee and for the next three days catch up on accumulated notes and correspondence.

There's the typical trip. I've traveled some 2,000 miles, hit the high spots of the northwest's hunting and fishing country, about all an outdoor editor can do.

Now that I'm back in the office I have to answer the telephone. This job can get pretty hectic at times. Just before the opening of a major fishing season I've answered more than 200 phone calls in a day. Your outdoors fan is a chummy bird who likes to make with the palaver. And he is also a faithful subscriber who is given every assistance.

Sometimes there is no helping the inquiring customer, like the lady with sail boating in mind who wanted to know which direction the wind was blowing on distant Lake Winnebago — "and can I depend on it to stay in that quarter all day?"

Women make about half the calls to *The Journal*'s outdoor editor. I don't know how it is with the rest of the boys but the men of Milwaukee seem to have powerful influence over their womenfolk. The ladies are given every consideration, of course, though sometimes their questions run into a five-minute tete-a-tete.

Often the lady of the house puts her questions into the mouthpiece while the voice of her ever-loving husband can be heard prompting in the background. I picture the prompters as gentlemen spread out on the davenport with newspapers strewn on the floor and tobacco ashes floating here and there.

And from the relieved "thank you" from the inquiring housewife who has just got the answer she needs, I'm convinced the ladies make these calls to get the old man out from under their feet.

Drunks in taverns find the outdoor editor a shining mark. They are forever getting into arguments over the size of the world record muskie, the depth of Lake Geneva, or when the deer season opened in 1936. The conversations all come to the same pattern.

A wager has been made. First one drunk calls with his query. If the answer wins him his bet I hear him turn from the phone and say: "See? What'd I tell yuh?" If he's obviously wrong he wants to pick an argument. After the first call there'll be about two minutes of silence. Then the phone rings again. This will be Bettor No. 2, the loser, checking up.

If you tell him he loses, more than likely he vows he is going to cancel his subscription. They never do. But I've learned that 40 years is the average length of time in which drunks have been "subscribing to your lousy newspaper."

Sometimes when I'm stuck in the office the paper makes me earn my pay. Office assignments come the way of the outdoor editor, just as they do to any general news reporter exploring a beat.

In times of stress a desperate city editor will send the elevator man on a story if he has to. I've chased disaster pictures for our paper and returned to the office late Saturday night to finish up the Sunday outdoor page. When I groused about "all this hard work I got to do" the c.e. reminded me that the pictures of disaster I had recently chased "got you outdoors, didn't they?"

The outdoors is a large place.

One disaster I covered has never really got the name of disaster. Yet it was the worst hunting disaster in the history of this country. It just so happened that a lot of other news was busting at the time and the press associations never really found out what went on.

I am talking about the Armistice day storm in the Mississippi valley in 1940.

When the wind started to blow from the west the duck hunting clan from Minneapolis to Dubuque got out on the river bottoms with shotguns. They had every reason to hope the wind would send ducks down the big river. The season had been mediocre. By evening the wind was hitting 'er up to sixty miles an hour. Before morning it was six below zero.

Winona, Minnesota, was the focal spot of the hunting deaths. I got there in jig time. Gordon Closway, of the Winona *Republican-Herald* and I were up all night covering that story. When we hit the hay in the morning we had thirty-one dead duck hunters from Red Wing to Dubuque. Bodies were found after we quit the story. Funny thing about the whole business was that newspaper readers outside of Winona and Milwaukee never learned that this was a catastrophe. Nice thing I remember: The *Republican-Herald* each Armistice Day reprints the 2,000 words Closway and I wrote of that story—just to remind people to be careful.

The outdoor writer goes to interesting places and meets interesting people. One of the nicest guys I ever met was Ike Eisenhower, on his first visit to Wisconsin in August, 1946 to fish Big Lake in Oneida county with his brothers. Harry Butcher, the General's wartime Naval Aide, has said that Ike swore he was going to drop everything and devote his life to nice, peaceful fishing when the war was over. He went fishing, all right, but I'm afraid we newshawks didn't give him too much peace. It was all supposed to be a secret. The news leaked a little bit. The night before Ike got there Bob Boyd, *Journal* photographer, and myself were skulking on the outskirts of Minocqua. Ike was due on the morning train.

Strangely, no other daily newspaper found out about it. So Bob and I had Ike to ourselves for the entire next day. When the train pulled in Ike got off. Amateur photographers swarmed by the score.

Boyd slung an arm around Ike's shoulder and said:

"Look, Ike, I'm a newspaper man. We've got to get some stuff quick to wire into Milwaukee, so do as I say for the next three minutes."

Ike turned on that famous grin.

"You're not supposed to be here."

"I know. I'm here, though."

Ike helped line up his brothers while Boyd shot pictures.

We wire-photoed them into the office and beat it for Big Lake where Ike — oh, what a man! — had promised us he wouldn't go out on the lake until we got there for more pictures. Ike was pacing the dock in old khaki. He had a European type spinning rod in his hand and was obviously anxious to try it out. Boyd shot picture after picture of him. After a half hour Ike demanded:

"When you guys gonna finish?"

"Relax . . . relax . . ." Boyd told him. Ike sprawled into a beach chair alongside of Homer Bell, chief of Wisconsin State Police and chortled:

"I know how to relax in all the languages known to man."

Finally the relentless Boyd said he had enough pictures.

Hunting and fishing are recreation. Like Ike, most people approach it in a recreational frame of mind. I'm continually surprised at the ladies. Not only are they in it in a big way themselves but plenty of them, come Christmas, shoot the bank account on a little something for Joe. They may fret and fume at Joe's absence from home and fireside but they keep encouraging him with appropriate gifts. It can't be anything but love.

Last Christmas one wife whose voice had a gleam in its eye, phoned in a dither. She wanted a thoroughly trained black Labrador retriever for her husband. The dog had to be of good blood lines and with ancestors who were field trial winners. I told her that kind of package would cost her anywhere from $300 to $1,000.

"There's nothing too good for my husband," said she. So I gave her the addresses of all the professional trainers and breeders in the middle west. She thanked me and said she was sending along a bottle of Scotch. I never got the Scotch but I ran into one of the trainers at a field trial and learned she had got her dog—for $700.

I don't know how many women I've helped make Christmas a happy day for Papa. It's part of the job. Without a little guidance the ever-loving gal will march into a store and buy an expensive fly rod reel for a man who is a bait caster. One wife with a husband who hunted nothing but birds, with shotgun, asked me if she ought to buy her old man a Mauser. A Mauser for bird shooting. ... A bird would sure know he was hit with one!

Wisconsin has been a fishing hangout for presidents since the time of Grover Cleveland. Cleveland, Hoover and Coolidge all came to the fabulous Brule River.

The most maligned fisherman of the three was Silent Cal. The newspapers depicted him as a lowly worm fisherman. The fact is that Coolidge became a very skillful wet and dry fly fisherman under the tutelage of John LaRock, guide, and the late George A. Babb.

Cal learned fast. In addition to learning fly fishing he became a pretty fair shot with a shotgun while he was on the Brule in 1928. Colonel Starling rigged up a little trap layout, and showed Cal how to swing ahead of the clay pigeon.

One day Cal was busting clay birds in the presence of 30 newspapermen. After each shot Colonel Starling, head of the White House secret service detail, would take the shotgun away from Cal, open up the action, look through the barrel, then re-load the gun and hand it back to Cal.

Cal got very tired of the routine. After Starling had looked through the barrel about seven times Cal grinned and said:

"There's a hole in it, Colonel."

Starling let him hold the gun after that.

We outdoor writers get around, all right. My dad, who is 86 years old and a cabinet maker by trade thinks his son is working some kind of outlandish racket by "running around the country in one of them damn station wagons—and all he's doing is typewriting." I guess I give my dad a bad time. He thought sure I'd learn to be a better cabinet maker than he.

My dad and I meet now and then at my shack in northern Wisconsin where he holds forth. Most every morning the same ritual takes place. I'm writing a little something for the *Journal* before breakfast and my dad walks in and says: "Dammit Gordon, are you going to work today, or are you going to typewrite?"

After a bit my dad hums a tune or two, sometimes breaks into a powerful baritone in Gaelic, grabs his tools and goes to work while I sit there in front of a typewriter.

There have been times when my dad came rushing up the hill from the lake — "Gordon, the wall-eyes are hitting to beat hell. I'm catching 'em right off the end of the dock. I had holt of one must've gone six pounds." And then I reply:

"Pa, save out about four for supper. I'll filet 'em."

"They'll go good," my dad says, and then he adds:

"Still typewriting, eh?"

From late May through early June 1947, the province of Ontario sponsored this showcase of its fishing waters for Midwestern outdoor writers. MacQuarrie and Dave Roberts were two of the eight who participated. Of course, Mac sent dispatches to the Milwaukee Journal. *A couple of them were included in* Dogs, Drink and Other Drivel, *including an abbreviated telling of this present story.*

Nothing to Write Home About

Outdoor Life, April 1949

No sockdolagers, no leviathans—but those brookies were battlers, and there were thousands of them! They put pep into jaded anglers, and climaxed a great trip

The train rolled east along the Lake Superior shore from Nipigon. After Heron Bay the sun rose brightly and lit the wilderness beyond the tracks of the Canadian Pacific Railway. It was late May and most of the Ontario lakes were wide open, though winter lingered in some iced-up bays. Swollen creeks, island-studded lakes, and lonely little way stations of the Big Bush flashed by. In the seat opposite me was Dave Roberts, well-traveled fisherman from Cincinnati, Ohio.

The trainman came along. Dave asked him how much farther it was to Chapleau.

"Not far," he explained cheerfully and vaguely. "Going fishing?"

"Yup," said Dave, and added, "Not that I care much right now. Feel like I don't need any fishing for a long time."

The trainman looked at Dave. "If you don't want fishing," his glance seemed to say, "why are you on this train? And what's the idea of all the gear you're carrying?"

What the trainman did not know was that we had traveled about 3,000 miles in Ontario, skimming the cream of some supreme fishing. Now, with fish up to here, we were looking forward to the end of the trip and home. Yes indeed, even enthusiastic fishermen can get that way.

In that big sweep through the sprawling province we bad certainly caught fish. We had poked into good corners of big Lake Nipissing for some wall-eye pike fishing of the kind late-summer visitors seldom see. We had flown into lake-trout and brook-trout waters. We had harassed the northern pike and the wall-eyes in the Sioux Lookout and Kenora country. We had even hunted bears in the

Ontario spring season—with no luck. But the following day a whirl at the Nipigon River made up for that dismal failure.

Now, more than a little weary after a long, action-packed journey, we were heading for Chapleau and then on to Toronto, our starting point.

The little places where towns huddled against a wild backdrop of spruce and Laurentian rock flashed by: White River . . . Amyot . . . Franz . . . Lochalsh . . . Dalton . . . Nicholson . . .

"Chapleau next station!" the trainman cried.

A few minutes later, as we stood on the station platform checking duffel and rods a youngish-looking candidate for anybody's basketball team bore down on us. Dave whispered: "Is that one man or two coming our way?" Indeed the Chapleau welcoming committee of one was enough man to make a small group. He introduced himself, Vincent Crichton, provincial wildlife specialist, all six feet six inches of him.

"There's any amount of fishing around here," he explained. "But I thought you boys might go for a little whirl at brook trout."

Dave stiffened like a pointer and his eyes gleamed. Yet only four days before he had taken a fine string of brook trout in another Canadian wilderness. "Lead on," he said.

There was no tarrying in Chapleau. Vince had a boat ready and also a fourth for the party, Pete Esling, of Toronto. Like ourselves, he had simply thrown himself upon the mercies of Vince Crichton without knowing what lay ahead.

Within half an hour we were putt-putting up the—hang onto your hats!—Kapusqueshishing River. (I doubt if I could spell it again.) The day was bright, the wind very sharp, and the temperature in the low 30's. In wide stretches of the you-know-what river flying spray came in over bow and sides and right there our new acquaintance, Pete, proved the manner of man he is.

Wearing a sheepskin coat that enveloped him like a tent, he took over the bow seat and gallantly soaked up most of the spray. He was not only an excellent windbreak but a great entertainer. He had spent a year of the second World War billeted with eighteen pipers of the Seaforth Highlanders and when the wind and spray did its worst he met it with wild highland songs.

He gave us "MacGregor's Gathering," and "The March of the Cameron Men," and "The Road to the Isles." It is not every man who can be a happy minstrel in a spray-soaked sheepskin.

We made a portage over a water retention dam, embarked, and went on. About an hour of daylight remained when we pulled up in a small cove of the river, hiked over another short portage, and found ourselves on the shore of a little lake of maybe 200 or 300 acres.

"This is it," said Vince.

"What's its name?"

"Well, sir, I can't tell you. Some call it Green and some call it Banana."

So that's the way it was! They hadn't got around to agreeing on a name for it yet. A splendid omen.

"All I know," Vince continued, "is that it's red-hot because I came in here the other day and left another canoe."

Up to that moment be hadn't mentioned our destination. A laconic man, Crichton, the kind who doesn't announce what he's going to do but just goes ahead and does it.

He put up a nice little green wall tent in jig time. He started a cooking fire and burned wet wood immediately by some magic I do not understand. He spread air mattresses and sleeping bags. He pointed out fresh moose tracks, and finally broke out a cooking kit and looked up significantly.

Dave took the hint and headed for the canoe. It was full dark when he returned—in a matter of twenty minutes or so—with a dozen bright Ontario natives about a foot long. "Holy smokes!" he exclaimed, "they'll hit anything and there's millions of 'em."

Once again Vince performed his abracadabra at the fire and we ate perfectly cooked brook trout (Vince is a deep-fat man), fresh homemade bread, and potatoes that hadn't been boiled to pieces. Such a man, that Crichton. . .

He did two or three things at once. He'd make a pass at the fire and rig up a drying rack for spray-drenched clothing. He'd open a can of condensed milk, and with the other hand lay a fresh stick on the fire in the spot where it did the most good. And he made excellent coffee in an aluminum pail.

"Anybody else been here this season?" Dave asked.

"No. Too many other spots closer to town."

The snow was a bit deep back there in the bush. And it was a chilly evening, right smart chilly. Everyone except Vince got into sleeping bags early. We watched a big moon roll over the pointed spruces. Beyond the open tent fly Vince sat for a while by himself, which is the way of many thoughtful veterans of the Big Bush. I think they just like to be alone.

The sleeping bags warmed up. The moon shone coldly. I saw Vince reach up and adjust a steaming garment on the tall drying rack without getting up from his log. . .

And then it was morning. There was thin new snow on the ground but the sky was clear and Vince was conducting certain rites at the fire as though he had never been to bed at all.

After breakfast, Dave got that bird-dog look I had come to associate with him in 3,000 miles of varied and superb fishing. He headed for the lake. Vince gave the fire a pat on the back and yelled to him: "Hold on. I'll paddle you around a bit." Esling and I took over the other boat and went at it.

At first they didn't come easy. There's such a thing as getting acquainted with a spot, even virgin waters. It was a morning for numb fingers and that eternal hope of all anglers that Dave's promise of the night before would come true by day. In twenty minutes or so Pete nailed one with a deep fly in fairly deep water some fifty yards offshore.

Was depth the answer? It sure was. We began to take trout regularly and they were all of the amateur stripe like the willing kids in the Golden Gloves tournaments. Maybe wilderness trout never learn to be cagey.

It didn't seem to make much difference what fly was used. Get it four feet down. Or maybe six feet. Troll it, retrieve it in little jerks, or just let it dangle there motionless and pretty soon one of the king's subjects from that cold green water had bold of it and was boring down. There must be thousands of brookies in that lake. Vince said it contained only trout.

Nothing to write home about. No sockdolager. No leviathan. No memorable scrap with the champ. Most of them were between ten and fourteen inches—although Dave took one with a dark back and golden belly that went about sixteen inches. They were fat and deep through the middle. And there were lots of them.

We passed Dave and Vince as they made a turn around a small island.

"How many, sir?" Vince asked.

"I dunno. Must've put back four or five dozen. Maybe more."

For the record I tried several floaters. No dice. Though there was a nice little ripple on the water those trout would have none of the surface stuff. They wanted their breakfast brought right downstairs to them and you may be assured, Pete and I waited on them hand and foot.

As we got the hang of it—a slow fly, down in there—we caught trout just about everywhere in that little puddle. We caught them off log tangles projecting from shore. We took them in middling-deep water of six to eight feet and we took them smack-dab from the middle of the lake. Vince guessed that they were dispersed everywhere because the lake was "turning over." Or, in other words, its oxygen content was uniform everywhere.

Also I tried small spinners and tiny metal wobblers and suchlike. The result was the same. The brookies would grab anything in the line of No. 10 flies from a gaudy Parmachene Belle to a demure Brown Hackle. They took tiny plugs that are imitations of larger ones used by bait casters, and one accepted a bass-size hair mouse. It would have been the perfect spot for a spinning rod.

Sure, that kind of fishing is too easy. But this dues-paying member of the Old Duck Hunters and Drop on the End of the Nose Association dearly loves to wallow in it now and then. We saved enough fish for a second breakfast and a few to take home and this time when Vince cooked he talked. Evidently he had found us properly appreciative of his lake.

"You Yanks don't have to believe it," he began, "but the Chapleau area is the largest game preserve in the world—6, 700 square miles, set up in 1925 as a reservoir for fur animals like martens and fishers. Also moose and lynx. It's against the law to fire a gun in the Chapleau, but we run up against some poachers. I've pinched lots of them.

"I've found some odd things in here. We've got one big beaver dam in the preserve made only of stone. You needn't believe that either. No one else did until we took photos of it. Later I wrote a full report on it for the provincial government. Each stone was placed in the hollow or cup of the stone below it. Silt from the river made it tighter than a wood, mud, stone dam like you usually see.

"The Chapleau is hardly touched. A lot of people simply never heard of it. One reason is there is no way to get into it by automobile. You've got to come by rail. Even if you own an automobile in Chapleau—and it's a town of more than 2,000—you can drive the car only forty miles. Then the road ends and you have to turn back. One of these days they'll hook up that road with the main highway—"

"And then what?" Dave put in.

Vince swept his trout-turning fork in an arc and told it all in one expressive word: "Whoosh!"

After a moment of silence, he continued: "There's one river I'd like to show you. It's the Gooseberry. Remember that name and plan to come back. I've caught trout there up to five pounds—and I'm no trout fisherman.

After another cup of coffee we went back at it again. It was a bit warmer but still no day for trout to surface. How I would love to have a crack at that little gem some soft June evening when the rising trout make the surface look as though it's being rained on.

Even so, fishing such as we had that day is too good for mortal man, and altogether too much of a good thing for a steady diet. If it were all like that there'd be fewer anglers, for fishing without a challenge is not really fishing. Plenty of times I've returned from back-in-there trips where I've had similar experiences, and been more than happy to work hard for a mess of bluegills on a near-by lake.

That day we simply got tired of it. The gleam faded from Dave's eyes and we began thinking of home again. Vince, with train time in mind, called a halt at 3 p.m. and had the gear packed and the portage made in half an hour. I don't know how he does it. He seems to putter; he never moves swiftly. But things get done.

Returning down the river (the name of which I refuse to decipher again) we found that the wind had shifted so that we were facing it. But that noble man, Pete Esling, took over the wet corner in the bow and sang.

During the three-hour run, Pete gave out with some of the quaint repertoire the Seaforth pipers had taught him. I repeat, it isn't every man who can sit in a water-soaked sheepskin and sing, "I'm Owre Young to Marry Yet."

By the time we made the second portage Pete had the rest of us knowing enough words to go along away with him on the refrains.

Finally we slid into the dock at Chapleau and said our good-byes to Vince and Pete. Shaking Dave's hand, Vince remarked: "We've got just as good trout fishing six miles from town but I wanted you boys to get a taste of the country."

Dave gave him an odd look. But I know he was satisfied.

36: Photograph from the Milwaukee Journal June 8, 1947

Old Indian Chief Dead, But His Lesson Lives

The Milwaukee Journal April 12, 1953

Vince Crichton, 6 foot 5 inch ranger for Ontario's 6,700 acre (*actually 6,700 square miles*) Chapleau game preserve, wrote me the other day to say that Simon Cheesewahwininnie had died and that the department of Indian affairs of the dominion is looking after his estate. The letter from Vince, superb woodsman and good friend, sent my thoughts back six years to a day in mid-May. It was the day I did not get The Story. It was the day that I missed the boat by a country mile and all because (or so I have consoled myself) of a noisy outboard motor and high wind. Vince was hurrying me back to catch the eastbound Canadian Pacific train at Chapleau. It was nip and tuck because we had remained as long as we could at a tiny brook trout lake some 30 miles down the Kebasquasheshing river over a short portage. That country, hard to get to by car, is alive with lakes teeming with brookies. Well. There was Vince in the stern of his 18 foot canoe getting all the speed he could out of his ancient eggbeater. The motor was making a lot of noise and we were going straight into a strong wind. About seven miles out of Chapleau we saw an aged Indian in a canoe near the stream bank. He was tending muskrat traps, paddling in and out from the shore among overhanging trees. He was alone and as we passed him, rather swiftly, he turned from his work and smiled at us and waved. I was close enough to note that he had a serene, happy face. He fairly beamed at us. His eyes were very bright.

I wanted then to ask Vince about him because he was so old, and so far from Chapleau, nearest settlement but it was a chore to climb back over the duffle in a tossing canoe and what with the motor roaring and the wind tearing at my ears I just sat there for another hour and waited until we got to Chapleau.

Then Vince told me about the Indian. He was Simon Cheesewahwininnie, chief of the Ojibway band at Chapleau, almost 80, and a highly respected man among his own people and the white residents. He had gone to a missionary school and a teacher, Canon Prewer, an Englishman, had helped him invest his little savings from his trapline wisely so that he was a man of some substance in the community.

Vince said that because of his age, Simon had asked the band to relieve him of the duties of chief and a new man was soon to take over- Jacob Chambett. But now, old but still agile and able to fend for himself in the Ontario bush, Simon still went long distances from Champleau to inspect his traplines, either afoot over forest trails or by canoe. I speculated to Vince that it was a pretty risky business for such an elderly gentleman and I'll never forget Vince Crichton's reply.

I'll never stop kicking myself for not halting and interviewing that great Indian, for Vince said to me, just before I caught the train:

"Oh, the chief doesn't mind being alone in the bush. He's used to it. He's been blind for years."

Somewhere in Ptarmigan Valley

Outdoor Life, May 1951

They got their caribou after a journey by dog sled over Alaska's bleak tundra. And on the way back—believe it or not—Bud was gored by the dead bull!

At the first light of dawn Bud Branham twisted out of his sleeping bag, lit spruce shavings in a Yukon stove, and parted the tent flaps.

It was a good day. Clear sky. Shining stars. Puntilla Lake frozen. And nameless peaks of the Alaska Range snowy and spooky in the stingy November light from the southeastern sky.

Bud yelled at the log cabin where I was supposed to be sleeping: "Get up, you cheechako! We might see a caribou today."

"Been dressed for an hour," I said.

"Brush your teeth?"

"Yamph . . . put on a pair of your socks, too. The Siwash socks you bought in Anchorage."

"You wolverine! Come to breakfast!"

So began a fine day in Ptarmigan Valley, not far from Rainy Pass in the Alaska Mountains 100 air miles northwest of Anchorage.
. . .

After breakfast the sun got out of bed, too, and went right to work painting a drib of pink here and a dab of purple there until the mountains were smeared with magic colors. Artists do poorly trying to follow the changing hues in Alaska. Some have gained partial victories. Usually they wind up just like writing men: "If you don't believe it, go see for yourself."

In the long morning shadows Bud stretched the dog harness on the snow and summoned Kenai, his lead dog, a Mackenzie River husky. Kenai wiggled his nose through the collar. He was that eager to get going. There was frost on his red coat—but no frost in his heart.

One by one Bud called up the six other members of his varsity team: Kusko, Sockeye, Kobuck, Flop, Yukon, Tip.

"Straighten 'em up, Kenai!" he shouted. The lead dog leaned into his collar and pulled the harness taut.

"Mush!"

Something like 600 pounds of dog almost jerked the light sledge off the ground. Bud had to lay on the brake going *uphill* through spruce and willow. That first mile went pretty fast as the team blew off steam. Our objective was any place in Ptarmigan Valley where caribou might be found.

The valley is a 100-mile-long stretch of tundra five to twenty miles wide. From the mountains around it the valley looks flat as a floor. Actually it is hilly, rough, laced with streams, and almost treeless. A large percentage of the record caribou heads taken on the continent are the Stone's caribou taken in Ptarmigan Valley.

We used the dog team that day for two reasons. First, because it permitted us to range far in search of the vagrant caribou. Second, if we found a nice bull the team would save us a back-breaking job of packing.

There was barely enough snow for good sledding—two to ten inches of it. Sometimes the dogs had to pull the sled over dry tundra. However, the Branham varsity team was in hard condition and didn't have to extend itself. Whether good snow or solid tundra, it was a lark for the huskies.

Bud put the team across Indian Creek on a spruce-pole bridge improvised a few days previously. As they say in Alaska, the creek had "glaciered up" under the bridge. In other words, some parts of it had frozen so that the slight bridge held well.

It was a fine morning, indeed. We traveled up a long, gentle rise from Indian Creek to the floor of the Ptarmigan Valley and set sail down the middle of the tundra. The sun was still painting the mountains locally known as Cathedral Peaks. The sledge runners slipped along almost silently. Where the going was good both of us rode, one in the sledge, one on the runners.

Following a team of Mackenzie River huskies by hanging onto the rear of the sledge is fine sport. And the dogs were enjoying it as much as we were. Whenever I put my inexperienced hands over the handlebars every dog in the team looked back and laughed at me.

It was an unusual day for Ptarmigan Valley. The wind likes to blow there—hard. But now there was hardly a breath of air. Old Kenai felt so good that when he hit one of the little tundra lakes he pulled out the throttle and dragged his team over the slick at top speed.

Stops were made to glass the tundra because distance is a fooler in that country and binoculars are a must. Five miles up the valley, and no caribou yet. Just empty, rolling tundra spotted with snow of a thickness greater than the eye, at a distance, would guess.

Caribou had been sighted in the valley a few days previously. Where would they be now? Bud Branham figured we might have to go clear up the valley before we located them. Our hope was that the wandering bands had moved in close enough to give us a one-day selection for an elegant bull.

There's an old saying: The time to get your caribou is when you see it. And it's true enough because they are easy to kill but hard to hunt. As Branham says, "They're here today and gone tomorrow. They'll travel fifty miles in twenty-four hours."

We found the caribou two miles beyond where they had been previously sighted. Two hundred or more were grazing beyond a tundra knoll that rose about 100 feet from the general level of the valley. Although that knoll was hardly more than a wart on the valley floor, it provided enough cover to begin a stalk. The field glasses revealed several shallow draws we could use to get behind the knoll.   However, it remained to be seen how near we'd get without being detected.

Half a mile from the knoll Bud tied the sledge to scrub willows. Long before that Kenai's ears had gone up. I'm convinced the smart lead dog could either scent or sight caribou. My guess is that he scented them. In any case, by the time the sledge was secured all seven dogs in the team were sharp as tacks. Tipped off by Kenai, of course. Or do you want to argue? All I can say is the team knew what was going on.

I unsheathed a .30/06 turned out by the late Alvin Linden, of Bryant, Wis. I hoped fervently I would be half as good shooting that cannon as Linden had been putting it together.

The stalk took no more than twenty minutes, I suppose, but it seemed like hours. Sometimes we went on all fours, sometimes flat on our bellies. And sometimes we snaked across elevations on the tundra in full view of the herd. In places where the snow was crusted I wallowed through it like an otter, following Bud's wake so as not to break snow crust twice. It's noisy.

When we got behind the knoll, with the herd still not spooked, I stood up and worked the kinks out of my back. Bud said, "If you'd lose ten pounds you'd be a good man again."

"For a typewriter athlete I'm doing all right," I said.

"Well, we'll see about that," Bud retorted. "Let's go."

We inched up the knoll and peeped over the rim. Below, 100 to 150 yards away, was the main part of the herd. I had estimated 200. Bud, working with the glasses, said 400. He also said: "You're the darndest newspaperman I have ever met up with. You underestimate."

Fair bulls were within easy gun range. There was a big one off to the left. We liked him through the glasses. Maybe he'd move in closer. He did.

It was quite a show. The big bull moved toward the knoll, now and then lunging at small-fry bulls just to let them know who was boss. And whether the young ones liked it or not, they respected him. Once he lay down. Then he stood and strolled toward us.

Bud said: "We could kill forty caribou from this knoll. But one in a lifetime is enough for any man."

A solid man, Branham.

It looked as if the old patriarch with the snowy cape, dark underbody, and light back was going to be ours. I waited to let him drift away from the herd. Then I inched up a bit higher on the rim of the knoll. The big bull caught my movement. The herd saw him break into a trot and there was a lot of milling movement 100 feet below us, 150 yards away.

Maybe I'd waited too long or moved too soon . . .

The patriarch headed toward the herd. If he reached it I'd never squeeze off the trigger. Just then he trotted into the clear and I fired. I heard the whap of 180 grains on flesh. Fur flew like dust low down and in front. The big one collapsed.

After the shot there was panic in the herd. Calves bawled. Cows grunted. The herd milled aimlessly. When Bud and I walked down the knoll the whole band took off. Their ankle joints clicked like a noisy clock. Those animals are trotters. They remind me of Tennessee plantation walking horses. Their backbones are that straight and steady.

I would not care to kill another caribou unless for good reason—such as the near starvation of a party of men which prompted Stefansson, the arctic explorer, to stretch caribou on the ground by the dozens. This bull was collected for the Milwaukee Public Museum. His coat was immaculate; his black hoofs polished; his antlers the color of weather-beaten mahogany.

The Stone's caribou in Ptarmigan Valley are like pictures on a Christmas card. Of deer, I think the white-tail is most graceful. The Alaska moose is the heaviest. The caribou is the most handsome. In Alaska veteran hunters like Branham do not like to hear people from the "outside" mention caribou and reindeer in the same breath. They hold that the reindeer is a small cariboulike mammal, domesticated.

We dressed out the bull, then Bud went back for the dog team. Old Kenai had his ears down. He knew what had happened and I'll bet he'd have given a two-day supply of dried salmon to have joined in the hunt.

Just hoisting the bull onto the low sledge gave Branham and me a bad time. Finally Bud got a good grip on him and heaved him up. He estimated the caribou's weight at 500 pounds. I said 400. Bud repeated: "You're the darndest newspaperman I ever met. You underestimate."

The trip back to camp brought the laugh of the day. The caribou's weight shifted so that the antlers were dragging against tundra, and Bud had to reload. As he grappled with the carcass it shifted once more and the left antler whipped around and skewered Bud neatly in the seat of the pants.

It looked serious for a moment. There was Bud sprawled over the caribou with rope in his hands. And there was that antler extending through his pants. I was worried until I noticed the horn hadn't touched Bud's skin. At the same time he began to laugh. "Gored by a dead caribou! I'll never live it down."

The day's mishap occurred when one runner of Bud's light sledge struck frozen tundra. The runner bent like a willow limb—except that it didn't spring back into shape. Unfortunately, Alaska has no hardwood such as is required for sledge runners. So Bud wasn't trifling with his pocketbook when he murmured: "I'd give $500 for a piece of hickory or white oak."

We pushed the heavy carcass off the sledge and left it lying on the ice of a narrow tundra lake with Bud's jacket hung on the horns to ward off wolves. Then we went back to camp for Bud's heavy sledge.

The sun was busy again painting the mountains purple when we made the return trip, reloaded the bull, and finally hauled it to the camp on Puntilla Lake. Could be both of us staggered, especially me, as we hung up our trophy.

After supper Branham said: "We got to head for civilization tomorrow. Dry my socks out, son."

Mac was now in his 50s, what we commonly call middle-aged. Little did he know that death awaited only a few years away. Yet, from this sentimental telling of his love of the northwest sand country, one can feel a summarizing of a sportsman's life.

My Favorite Spot - The Jack-Pine Barrens of Northwest Wisconsin

Field and Stream, August 1953

Whether you travel the old logging grades or modern concrete highways, there is always good fishing ahead

A favorite place for me is one that offers a lot of everything. I have been looking for the best places for a good many years, pursuing a line of duty that has taken me as far north as Alaska and south to Key West. But I always return to northwest Wisconsin, knowing that at any season there will be something going on outdoors. And I have the feeling, when I hit the northwest counties, that I am home again, and that's a nice feeling, don't you think?

I am like the mailman who takes a walk on his day off. When vacation time rolls round, which can happen in any of the twelve months, I am likely to be found of an early morning lying on my back in bed contemplating the 16-inch log beams of a large room and wondering how in time I am going to get to all the places I want to get to.

This headquarters shack is on the west shore of the middle lake of the Eau Claire chain in Bayfield County. A glance at your map will reveal it as the hub of a wheel, as it were, from which I can, within a few hours' run by car at the most, touch some of the best fishing and hunting country on this continent. I can even fish the Eau Claire chain and save some traveling, but it has been some five years since I wet a line in these appealing waters. The road is forever beckoning. The little people in the trees fly down and whisper in my ear.

"Now the Four-way Lodge is opened—now the Smokes of Council rise—

Pleasant smokes ere yet 'twixt trail and trail they choose—"

The roads over which I travel can be anything from the slickest ribbons of concrete to the little-known and far more interesting county trunks, town roads unnumbered and unnamed, on down to the humblest and the best of them all, the old tote roads and logging grades, relics of other times. The latter survive disuse nobly. Knowing how swiftly and jealously the wild reclaims an abandoned farm, I am mystified that so many of the old logging roads remain navigable by car. Maybe the trickle of travel over them by Model T's, Model A's and occasional jeeps is just enough to keep them open.

You can drive for hundreds of miles on these quite unknown and unmapped roads, and many of those miles, especially in the jack-pine barren lands, are on ground almost as hard as concrete. A few years back the Bayfield County highway commissioner totted up the old logging grades and found that a single county had more than four hundred miles of such roads.

In looking at a map of the northwest corner, imagine that there extends from about Ashland south and west a widening triangle of sand, almost to the twin cities of Minnesota. This, roughly, marks the jack-pine barrens of the northwest. An hour after a cloudburst you can drive a car anywhere. Just getting lost out on the barrens is a lot of fun. You always come out somewhere, and you might find a new lake or an unknown jump-across trout stream.

But I was lying on my back staring at the ceiling. Within one hour's time I have been known to consume a breakfast of steel-cut oatmeal, two dishes of prunes, eggs, bacon and coffee and be sixteen miles away, fly rod and gear at ready, prepared to step into an 18-foot cedar-plank canoe at Stone's Bridge on the upper Brule River.

The 45-mile-long Brule is easily Wisconsin's most famous trout stream. At times it is Wisconsin's best trout stream. The fact that Presidents of the United States have chosen it for vacations has nothing to do with its character, and that's what it has—character. Fishermen from coast to coast come to try it. Magazine-cover illustrators take one look and set up an easel. I know three Brule devotees who are in the throes of writing books about the river. Suffice it that all is well with the Brule, and likely always will be, through careful guardianship of private land on its banks and through the state's ownership of 7,750 acres of the important, so-called Brule bog, which is the forest sponge that forestalls floods and erosion.

On some mornings, staring at those log beams in the shack, I have been inspired to head west from twenty to seventy miles, depending on whim, and find myself fishing for smallmouth bass in the upper St. Croix River. A road map will show you where it rises in Lake St. Croix in Douglas County and—here's odd one—runs into another Lake St. Croix, above Prescott, before it reaches the Mississippi.

The praises of the surging St. Croix have been well sung. The late Irvin S. Cobb, who entered the Anglers' Hall of Fame by explaining that the difference between a fisherman and a golfer is that a fisherman smells worse, came back to the St. Croix many times. Will S. Dilg, spark plug in the founding of the Izaak Walton League of America, was another St. Croix fan. If there is anyone around who remembers Bill Vogt, Minnesota's ace with fly and bait rod, he may recall that Bill was addicted to taking muskies on a fly rod from this river. It is now little known as muskie water.

It's smallmouth water de luxe. The upper reaches, above where it slides beneath the State Highway 35 bridge in Burnett County, offer some "pretty hot water," as the guides put it. They mean rugged rapids. The fly rod is the standard implement if you want fun and lots of it, and yellow feather minnows are standard lures. If I must name the one man living who knows the most about the St. Croix and its satellite, the Namakagon, which feeds the St. Croix, he would be Ed Nutt, the state forest ranger at Webster.

There have been times on that upper St. Croix when, in a day of fishing with dry trout flies, as big as No. 4's and 6's, I have caught and released—Oh, what's the use? No one will believe it, except possibly people like Jack Lynch of Gordon, who has done it himself.

Float trips are the thing on the St. Croix. Minnesota anglers seem to fish this river in greater numbers than Wisconsin anglers. That could be from the proximity of Minneapolis and St. Paul; and anyway, half the river belongs to the Gopher State, as it forms the state boundary from about Riverside to Prescott. There are enough smallmouths for everyone.

On some mornings when I am seeking inspiration by studying the ax marks on those ceiling beams, I am taken with the impulse to shoot the works, all or nothing, and go for a muskie. This is like catching undulant fever. You think you're cured, and it backs up on you. The odd muskie, you may be sure, is taken from the Eau Claire chain at my very door, but there are better places for this kind of fishing. The muskie fever can move a man profoundly, as the previously quoted Kipling wrote:

". . . for the Young Men's feet are turning
To the camps of proved desire and known delight!"

On such mornings I am indeed in a quandary. Sawyer County, less than an hour away from me, down what is now known as State Highway 27. My, how time does fly! Remember back there in post-War I days when it was a nightmare of mudholes with stretches of corduroy? Sawyer is one of the counties in the United States that boast some of the world's finest muskie waters. Hayward is the county seat, and no visit there is complete without a pause at the office of Julien Gingras, publisher of the weekly newspaper. Surely, everyone knows by now that Hayward would hardly be in existence if it were not for the muskies.

A few doors from Ging's office is the business place of John Moreland, a state conservation commissioner and a man ever ready to lend a sympathetic to a questing fisherman. Then there's Oscar Johnson and Tony Burmek and Walter Risberg and others—all with their keen ears attuned to the muskie grapevine.

You find out from these helpful fellows what the box score is. Maybe they're hitting on Lac Court Oreilles. How about Peterson's bar in the Chippewa Flowage? The old hands call that flowage the "Big Chip" from its size—18,000 acres. Maybe Flambeau Louie Johnson has been in town from Snoose Boulevard, off "Highway sempty," with tidings of muskie deportment on the Flambeau River's north fork or on Round, Blaisdell, Butternut, or fifty other lakes.

As I said, muskie news up there travels by its own grapevine. If Scully Gustafson of Park Falls or such of his comrades as Bill Smart or Dan Vicker have blooded a good muskie, the fact is sure to be known before long all up and down State Highway 70 from Minocqua to Spooner. To keep the record straight, I can reach these places from my lair on the Eau Claire chain, and get back home after fishing, in one day. Sometimes I even fetch back a muskie.

Many times on a thrust south into the muskie country with its "name" waters I've given up and settled for a batch of crappies on, let's say, Big Chetac Lake, out of Birchwood in southwestern Sawyer County. It was this eight-mile-long, 2,177-acre body where Wisconsin fisheries biologists first discovered that brother crappie can get too dang numerous, to the disadvantage of other species in the same waters.

Since then the state has compiled a list of some three hundred lakes where the crappies are dominant and where they want lots of pressure put on crappies by the hook-and-line fisherman. The folks who fish Big Chetac are certainly giving the crappies tarpaper. On our last visit to the lake there were more than eight hundred boats for rent!

The big-fish fever in that northwest corner can also be abated in an hour's run by car up to Bayfield on the Chequamagon Peninsula that juts into Lake Superior and tapers off in the twenty-three lovely islands of the Apostle group. In more reckless days I was given to trolling for lake trout on this big water, using a canoe equipped with sponsons.

I quit abruptly one day when my companion, possibly even crazier than I, suggested in all earnestness that we load up gasoline for the five-horse kicker and take her all the way across Lake Superior to the mouth of the Nipigon. For a minute or two I actually considered the idea. But I realized I must be cracking up, for in one minute's time a sudden blow on Lake Superior could end all my fishing forever.

Nowadays, any one of the twenty or so charter boats that troll among the islands suits me just fine. My favorite fishing ground is a rocky underwater shoal called "the hump" off Devil's Island, farthest north of the group. If a diver ever goes down there, I want it known here and now that at least two dozen of the spoons that are wedged into the rocks belong to me. And I'll bring witnesses to testify, including Joe O'Malley, the civic conscience of Bayfield, and Ben Waskow, game warden.

Time was when the National Park Service took a long look at the Apostle Islands. They were never included in the national park system because the reports of field men said too much of the virgin timber had been taken off. Well, sir, in twenty-five years the island forests have done a pretty good job of growing; for that matter, there are still tremendous virgin stands of hemlock and hardwood on a few of the islands. A couple of days of trolling in the air-conditioned Apostles can do a summer heat victim a power of good.

I long ago learned not to cherish the oversize lake trout. In the Bayfield country, they call those lunker lakers "siscowets."

They're blunt-headed, fat, deep-going rascals, mighty handsome and reasonably game. I once brought home a 28-pounder. We baked it, and you could smell it about the house for the next two weeks. Lakers under 10 pounds are far better, but, no matter what size, they are nice to see down through twenty feet of gin-clear water, twisting and turning as they roll themselves up in your line.

I should interpolate here that in my goings and comings to the haunts of fish and fowl in the northwest I am constantly crossing trout or bass streams or coming close to them. I can't possibly list them all here. But three trout streams are dear to me: the Sioux, out of Washburn in Bayfield County; the Marengo, about fourteen miles south of Ashland in the county of that name, and the upper Namakagon, in the Cable or Seeley areas, in southern Bayfield and northern Sawyer Counties.

If I live to be a hundred, I'll not forget the first time I waded the Namakagon which, I should explain, is a trout stream in its beginnings and a prime smallmouth stream farther down. My first shot at it was in the early twenties, a whoop and half a holler out of Cable at a place called Squaw Bend. On about the third cast of a single wet fly, a Red Ant or a Black Gnat, I can't recall which, a two-pound brown seized it and was creeled. I thought I was a helluva guy.

This was going to be too easy. Gentlemen, I fished that river for the next half dozen weekends without so much as seeing a trout. Then, one memorable Sunday, wading upstream, came one of the finest dry-fly boys I have known. He was John Ziegler of Superior, Wisconsin, and he showed me how. Not many ever get to be as good as he was. He tied his own floater for the Namakagon, a nameless item far as I know, hardly more than a dry Brown Hackle, tied sparsely. After that illuminating afternoon I began to take Namakagon browns.

If you're beginning to think I do not stay in my shack very long at one time, you're right. But there are days when I'm content to bide there and do nothing more exciting than search for trailing arbutus or pick a duck or listen to partridge drum or hang an ax handle, depending on the season and the powers that animate me. In the autumn on winy, frosty mornings I have little time for contemplating the log beams of the big room. It is at this season that the North reaches its breath-taking climax. It's a great pity that most of the fishermen and sojourners do not see it then, when it is at its very best.

Not every autumn presents those prolonged weeks of superb leaf coloring. Rain and wind can make short shrift of a promising landscape. But about every third year there'll be a windless, rainless spell of maybe three weeks when the leaves remain on the trees. Walt Disney in his most flamboyant moments never dreamed up anything like it. The maples are fire-red, often beginning in mid-August. The oaks turn russet. The poppies throw in seasonings of lighter yellows. The secret of all this splash is the dark background of pine.

In recent autumns in that blazing setting, the ruffed grouse have been at cyclic peaks. They'll decline again soon, as they always have, and they will come back again, as they always have. The prairie chickens of that country are definitely in a critical condition, as they are almost everywhere. But two excellent research biologists, Fred and Fran Hamerstrom, of Plainfield, Wisconsin, have come up with what a lot of people believe to be the prescription to save them, and something is being done about it by the State Conservation Department.

I can walk down my own road, which is long and twisty, and expect a shot at a partridge. But it's nicer to go away for a bit. I like to drive about twenty-five miles north and east, perhaps stop at Drummond and make talk with Art Lee and the others, and then get lost on the tote roads and partridge country of Chequamegon National Forest. Just aim the car north out of Drummond, park it, and start hoofing it along the roads and trails.

If I have the time during deer season to be at the shack, I like to wander among the hills and woods, sometimes quite aimlessly. I find this more satisfactory than holding down the below-zero end of a two-foot log, waiting for a buck to come along and give himself up. There have been deer seasons when I went fishing, and at least one deer season when I hunted ducks.

Believe me, I have no word of complaint against the comrades of the deer woods. They are a hearty clan. They look fine in their gray wool hunting pants stagged off above the ankle and their red hunting jackets. A lot of them are very cozy fellows to have in camp, men capable of whipping up a mulligan fit for the angels.

At the opening of a deer season I do not cavil when the camp chief yells, "Ro-o-l-l-l out! It's daylight in the swamp!" In the first days of the hunt I go, as commanded, to my stand or to do my stint on the drive. But before the season is half-way along you will find me, the sly one, pretending to be busy at innumerable non-existent chores about camp. I never can tell when I'll be swept by a mood which demands that I split a stack of firewood or fix up a bait of pancake batter. Sometimes I just sit before the fireplace with a contemplative pipe and meditate.

It's in the duck season that I become most completely alive. While I do not make it up there every duck season, I have landed at some classic moments, such as when it seemed that all the bluebills from Canada were piling through. It is then that I like to arrive at the shack, perhaps late of a chill evening replete with snow flurries. I like to stop by Charlie Warner's place and ask him what he's seen. If he allows as how he climbed the Smoky Hill fire-tower and saw big strings of 'bills moving south, the outlook is bright, for Charlie is a tower man in the forest protection service and a fine hand at putting his finger on the days when a flight reaches its peak.

Whatever Charlie reports, I shall take off in the morning. I may motor down to the end of my own lake and set up housekeeping in Pat's blind. I may drop a skiff into Mud Lake to look and see—and possibly to shoot. I may drive in the early dark a few miles south to Mulligan Lake, where the wild rice is so thick that the mallards use skiffs to get through it.

On occasions when I depart for the northwest corner, I say farewell to a man of authentic Scandinavian ancestry who has retained a sure memory of the sound and use of the Norske dialect as she is spoken, despite his exalted eminence in the field of daily journalism. So when I tell him I am taking off for the land where he used to trap skunks and get sent home from school for stinking so horribly, he raises an imaginary glass and relapsing happily to the days of thirty years ago, offers this toast, to which I add a heartfelt response: "Skol to the nort'vest."

Fish and wildlife biology were young sciences that came into their own during the time MacQuarrie was writing. He had, of course, corresponded with and written stories about Aldo Leopold almost as soon as he got to the Milwaukee Journal. *But it took state and federal agencies some time to develop and staff these new programs. Through the 1930s and early 40s, Mac often sought out the wardens for stories and updates. In the deer wars of 1943, that changed a bit, as he learned from Leopold and especially from deer researcher Bill Feeney and wrote extensively about the unpopular concept of managing deer to match their habitat instead of for maximum numbers.*

In the summer of 1955 it appears Mac found a treasure trove of new sources of fish and wildlife biologists and wrote several columns a week about the new developments going on in the state. It's quite likely that this may also have been the period when he began working on this present article.

The version included is found in the Wisconsin Academy of Arts Transactions *in Fall 1959. The same title was printed for a national audience in* Outdoor America in *1960.*

Here Come the Biologists

The Wisconsin Academy of Arts Transactions, Fall 1959

Now that the airplane is here to stay and no one objects to vaccination against smallpox, it is remembered that yesterday's fishing and hunting man got his information about coming seasons from a whiskered old guide who lived a quaint and smoky life back in the cutover.

This oracle of the gurgling pipe was an eminent figure of his time. He tested the thickness of muskrat houses and peeled onions in the dark of the moon to forecast weather. In the off seasons when he wasn't guiding, he had a lot of time to think, and he could show you how a hair from a horse's tail would turn into a snake if you put it into a rain barrel.

A few of them are still around, but not too many, and those that persist are often synthetic self-made characters upholding an old tradition for the sake of local color, and usually sadly in need of dry cleaning.

The genus began disappearing as long as 20 years ago when bright young men with book l'arnin' began getting interested in game and fish. In the hey-day of those uncombed fakers, if a hunter wanted a prognosis about an impending duck season, the old fraud would provide him with a prediction based on the bluewing teal nests he encountered in casual rambles between his still and his salt lick.

Today there is no guessing on continental duck production. The game managers, the game biologists, the conservation wardens, of all the states and the prairie provinces of Canada just pile up a factual picture of the duck population by going out in the field and counting them. That count and attendant forecasts of plenty or scarcity has been reliable for more than 15 years, and gets more accurate with each passing year.

They will tell you, will these bright young men from the universities, what the average size of the duck clutch was in Manitoba, how the birds made out in the critical drought periods, and during moulting, and when the wildfowl got off for the south, it is these trained men of science who forecast with remarkable accuracy what the duck hunter may expect along the flyways of America.

So it goes in a world of change and progress. The old giveth 'way before the new. The prophet with the whiskers and the gurgling corncob did give something to the world, but not much, except humor, on this order:

At a wordy public battle in Wisconsin, this reporter listened to the whiskered pundits of the north woods. They declaimed in the presence of several qualified and patient biologists, plus William J. P. Aberg, who was then chairman of the state conservation commission.

Pains were taken to set the old geezers aright. Toward the end of the day, Bill Aberg, waving the olive branch, asked one particularly rock-headed bush rat what he really thought about the proposed deer management plans. The gaffer then did asseverate:

"I haven't made up my mind. But when I do I'm going to be damn bitter about it."

The changing scene of conservation and wildlife requires trained eyes to prescribe for it. Twenty years ago the word "biologist" was just becoming known in the picture of natural resources conservation, as the public saw it. It was in the 20's and 30's that the era of transition set in, when "biologist" came into the picture, and when the prophetic old timers who quoted their grampaws began to assume less importance in what is a very scientific and complicated business.

Today no state in the union is without its corps of fish and game biologists, game managers, foresters, forest entomologists, pathologists, and their like. Some state departments are now that the bright young men they hire hold doctor's degrees, no less.

If this revolution of management of fish and game—this whole new attitude toward the soil, its landscape and its creatures— must be attributed to one person, it would have to be the great Aldo Leopold, who honored the University of Wisconsin with his civilized mind in the last 20 years of his life. There is not a man in this field who will deny that the modest Leopold, with the brain of a scientist and the heart of a poet, was the fountainhead, the inventor, the pioneer genius. He is fast becoming legend.

All over the United States today, and in Canada, and some foreign lands, you will find Leopold's boys- men who took degrees under him while he was director of Wisconsin's department of wildlife research. Author of hundreds of scientific papers, Leopold was also the author of the more tender and possibly immortal "A Sand County Almanac," in which he set down the foundations of his thinking. Leopold originated the concept of "the land ethic." He said a great many things now quoted widely today, but let it not be forgotten that in his day he was upbraided- even reviled- by those ignorami whose knowledge of wildlife ended with what grampaw told them. Leopold said:

"We abuse land because we regard it as a commodity belonging to us. When we see land as a commodity to which we belong, we begin to use it with love and respect. There is no other way for land to survive the impact of civilized man, nor for us to reap from it the esthetic harvest it is capable, under science, of contributing to culture."

Leopold owned a little shack on 160 acres of land on the Wisconsin river near Portage. There he liked to putter around with bird banding and wildlife habitat improvements, and if you got up early enough in the morning, he would supply you with sourdough pancakes baked on his open hearth.

Returning from his shack to Madison, one day, with his son Starker, the latter halted the car in a little town for a pack of cigarets. From the store came the blare of a radio, broadcasting a critical football game between the Chicago Bears and the Green Bay Packers. This puzzled Leopold. When Starker returned he was asked, in complete seriousness:

"Starker, who are the Packers?"

It took just about one year for this newspaper reporter to convince Aldo Leopold that he was really interested in the things stirring in the Leopold department at the university. Once he made up his mind that I would not brutalize the facts of this tender, beginning science, he became the greatest news tipster of my experience. He was alive with ideas and it should be added that he knew news when he saw it, and knew what to do with it.

I sat beside him one day in 1938 at a conservation meeting of some kind, I forget what. Leopold leaned over and tapped me on the knee- "Get in touch with David Thompson and the others in the

Illinois Natural History survey. They know something new about fish management."

The story that came out of that tip was of the Illinois scientists almost completely upsetting old theories of fish management. They put the fish hatchery in its place, a subordinate place. They stressed management of habitat. They urged more hook and line pressure on public waters, less restrictions on sports angling. That basic concept has spread to almost all of the states.

Leopold's influence is greater today than when he lived. His own sons and hundreds of others are going at the business of producing fish and game by methods undreamed of two decades ago. And yet, they often fail. But they expect that, as doctors expect to lose patients. Then again, they often succeed, often gloriously.

Wisconsin's deepest lake, Big Green, provides lake trout fishing for sportsmen, although, since the 90's, when lake trout were introduced in it, that fish has not been able to reproduce itself in Big Green. The youngsters in fisheries biology in the Wisconsin conservation department figured out what was wrong and solved the problem.

By skin diving they found out that the lake bottom was muddy, with no rocks. Lake trout eggs fell to the smooth bottom and were being gulped by thousands of mud puppies. So, these bright young men persuaded the Green Lake county board to dump thousands of tons of big rocks and little rocks into 80 feet of water. Thereafter, the lake trout eggs fell between the rock crevices where the mud puppies could not get at them. Big Green is now producing lake trout; there is no further need to plant it with fish brought expensively from a distance.

Those same young fishery biologists think ahead, too. Since the sea lamprey, invader from the Atlantic, has practically exterminated the lake trout of Lake Michigan, they guess, now, that some day, when the lamprey hordes are controlled- if ever- they will have to go back to Big Green for lake trout and lake trout eggs for re-planting Lake Michigan. It is important to them that the lakers in Big Green are Lake Michigan lake trout, a strain well suited to that lake- and possibly for biological reasons not now known.

They go out of their way, do these young biologists and game managers, to provide good hunting and fishing for sportsmen, and often the wonder if they are being appreciated. Like as not they are not appreciated much; in fact they are not even well understood, and it is a fact that they are their own worst public relations agents.

A trained biologist testifying before a state legislature's committee is a sitting duck. They are not trained in debate. They know nothing of the parliamentary tricks. Any apple knocking assemblyman with an axe to grind can take these youngsters apart without reaching too deeply into his mental resources.

There's a big, shallow duck lake by the name of Mud, in Columbia county, Wis. All of its shoreline was privately owned and the owners contended that the lake was not navigable, and so, charged the public hunters who used their shoreline for duck blinds.

Fred Zimmerman, waterfowl biologist, put a stop to that nonsense. He did it by the simple process of dropping a boat in the lake and rowing around in it to prove it was navigable. He made quite a fuss about it, and, in the fullness of time got to the Wisconsin public service commission, which controls all water levels in the state.

The commission ruled that Zimmerman had proved Mud to be a navigable body. That softened up the shoreline owners so that they listened to reason and leased 500 acres of Mud lake's shore to the state, for public access. It is doubtful, today, if a dozen hunters remember that it was young Zimmerman who proved Mud lake's non-navigability a myth.

No contests in which these biologists have been engaged have been more bitter, or more fraught with sloppy emotion, than the problem of managing deer in this country, especially the white-tailed deer. Pennsylvania, New York, Michigan, Colorado, Minnesota, to name a few, have gone through the battle to reduce deer herds to the point where the animals can be sustained by their natural food, without dying of malnutrition in bad winters.

Not all of the states have won that battle. This is because they permit, for political reasons, the untrained and the emotional to have a hand in the management of this critter.

The biologists are not guessing about deer; they don't care a fig about what grampaw said about them or how he made the popple trees bend and sway with the ba-r-o-o-o-m of his .45-90. The biologists have pitted their conclusions, drawn from long study, against the empirical opinions of the whiskered, gurgly pipe school- and in many states have won, at least for the present. But the barber shop biologist, lineal descendant of the "old guide" is a tough and resourceful fellow, and he will be around for some time to come, albeit in a diminishing role as the years pass by.

When these young scientists first pressed into the conservation picture there was some resentment from some game wardens. It was natural, and it was expected. The game wardens saw these youngsters becoming important men in local communities, asked to speak before the luncheon clubs, too! Mostly that human difficulty seems to have been resolved and the wardens are on the team- some of them more vehement that the trained biologists in sticking up for science against guesswork.

I think I saw the perfect example of that cooperation at one of those white hot state hearings on deer management in a northern town. A particularly vocal local expert was opposing the biologists on everything, and repeatedly breaking into deliberation without permission from the chair. This bird had a system. He would stand up and yell: "I can take you out there and show you just what is going on in the woods."

He was getting to be very tedious. A husky game warden with a booming voice saw his chance. The nuisance jumped to his feet and began, "I can take you out there---." Whatever else he said was drowned in the roaring voice of the game warden. "Take HIM out there right now!" Three hundred or so people in the crowded room laughed as one and before the hearing was finished the biologists had their way- thanks to an assist from a big brother warden.

The nature fakers, who have not been effectively squelched in this country since Teddy Roosevelt's classic blasts at them from the White House, get short shrift from the young men of game biology.

At a meeting of trappers I heard one of the barber shop experts tell a conservation commissioner that a beaver can think. George Knudsen, Wisconsin's beaver study leader put an end to that beaver foolishness by explaining, with many examples and photographs, that beaver are actually given too much credit. Among other things, he showed how they fell trees so that they cannot possibly be used for food, or dam building.

It took the biologists of the country to teach the muskrat trappers to take the rat crop as it came along, and not permit them to increase beyond the carrying capacity of their habitat, with resultant disease. The biologist get out out in the marshes and wade, lifting the tops off muskrat houses in the spring to see how many young are being produced. They can forecast heavy or light rat production from such spring surveys.

The biologists re-make trout streams. Hundreds of them have been brought back to good trout production. Wisconsin's' one-time famous Prairie river of Marathon county, is as good an example as any. A young fishery manager, Ralph Jones, with a crew, worked on the Prairie for five years.

He found a river of shallow, gravely rapids, with few holes and too warm summer temperatures. Stream structures were put in to create holes. Cattle were fenced out, but crossings and watering places were left for them by intricate fencing which prevented them from trampling down banks. Trees that halt soil erosion were planted by the tens of the thousands. The Prairie has come back.

Quite often the stream biologists deflate fishermen by proving that streams alleged to be "fished out" actually carry big populations of highly desirable trout. A classic example of this came off in California under the direction of Paul R. Needham, a fisheries man so good that California stole him from New York.

Needham counted the trout in a California stream where "nobody was catching any fish." In ten sections of the stream he counted more than 24,000 brown trout of catchable size- and he never said a word about fish being smarter than fishermen.

The biologists and managers are putting lands to use so that they fulfill their best potential. Wisconsin's 30,000-acre Horicon marsh is one of scores. Both federal and state men have had a hand in these jobs. Horicon had a long history of abuse, via expensive attempts to drain it and grow crops.

It didn't work. Everybody lost money. But, gradually the state and federal governments acquired the 13-mile long marsh. They re-established water levels, for water is a chief and simple tool of the managers. In an average autumn nowadays days, 50,000-thousand Canada geese call Horicon home in spring and autumn.

The managers are good at little, patchwork jobs, too. A typical such is French creek, 1200 acres in central Wisconsin. The biologists and managers took a look. Nobody wanted it. The state bought it, cheap. In one day, the managers, with one bulldozer, pushed up the earthen wings of a little dam. The next day they finished the dam with poured concrete and plank flash boards, and that put the French creek flat under control with that all important tool, water.

The result: unwanted wire grass was killed. In its place came plants valuable to wildlife- cattails bulrushes, round stem and smartweed, the latter a prime mallard food. That worked so well, by attracting waterfowl, that the state went a step further. It leased 3000 acres around French creek marsh for a public hunting ground. The once useless flat has been put to work at what it can do best.

Despite the public scorn they have been subjected to, these new scientists are quiet and orderly fellows. They just keep on plugging away. They like their jobs because they feel like they are being useful. It is not so much a business with them as a way of life.

There's a plant, leatherleaf, that likes shallow water and damp ground. It is a plant created by nature as a machine for turning water into solid ground. It is worthless for game, except for cover. The northern states are full of it. In places in the north it as great a curse as the floating hyacinth of Florida. It crowds out useful plants, like wild rice. Up north on Rice Creek flowage in Wisconsin, Larry Jahn, Wisconsin waterfowl research leader went to work on a thousand acres of leatherleaf with chemicals. The cost was slight. When it was killed back he spent $50 of the state's money on wild rice, purchased from a Menomonie Indian. The rice now dominates that marsh and it is a favored duck hunting place.

The little jobs they do are so often overlooked, or forgotten. Up in northwest Wisconsin, George Curran, a game manager, found Totogatic lake, headwaters of a good sized river, plugged with an illegal dam, put there by real estate interests to raise the lake's level and provide better swimming.

Curran brought that case to the public service commission. The commission directed Curran to knock out the dam and restore Totogatic to its natural level. Curran did it the next day, with two boxes of dynamite. Totogatic's level dropped a couple of feet and within two years the drowned wild rice within it completely covered the lake. Back came the ducks and back came the Indians of the nearby Odanah reservation to harvest wild rice there for the first time in 10 years.

Always the managers and biologists are working uphill, against pre-fixed public notions of how game and fish should be managed. No one goes to a barber shop to have his appendix out, but when it comes to calling the shots on fishing and hunting, everyone is an expert.

The young men know, as they go along, that education is their best ally. They peg away hard at this, with literature, movies and lectures. It is a fact that very often, after the public has been thoroughly briefed, it strings along with the bright young men with the college degrees.

It takes a trained biologist to say "I don't know." The rest of us have all sorts of glib answers for nature's mysteries. James W. Kimball, was a game biologist in Nebraska and South Dakota before he became director of Minnesota's fish and game research.

He was in South Dakota during the biggest irruption of ringneck pheasants known, in the world. Flocks of a thousand or more were quite common. They declined in numbers, and Kimball, who undoubtedly knew more about the birds than anyone in South Dakota, said, when asked why they declined:

"I don't know the cause."

He speculated. He discussed his endless investigation. But he finally said what only brave men say, "I don't know."

A lot of battles have been won and a great many more remain to be fought. The public is learning. And it is hard, hard work for the young men of scientific fish and game management. They remind me of the story of the boy who acquired a stepfather after his mother's divorce. His own father was permitted to visit the boy at intervals.

Once, visiting his offspring, the father asked how things were going.

"Pretty good, dad."

"You get enough to eat, son?"

"Yes, plenty to eat."

"You get some spending money now and then?"

"How about recreation?"

"Well, my step father takes me for a rowboat ride every morning. No dad, I don't mind the rowing. And I don't mind my step father throwing me overboard every morning. It's fighting my way out of that sack that gets me down."